The Sword and the Cipher

By

Riley O'Connor

ZMOK
BOOKS

The Sword and the Cypher by Riley O'Connor
Cover image by Tommaso Dall'Osto @tdosto on instagram
This edition published in 2024

Winged Hussar Publishing is an imprint of

Winged Hussar Publishing, LLC
1525 Hulse Rd, Unit 1
Point Pleasant, NJ 08742

Copyright © Winged Hussar Publishing
ISBN PB 978-1-945430-71-8
ISBN EB 978-1-958872-51-2

Bibliographical References and Index
1. Science Fiction 2. Space Opera 3. Adventure

Winged Hussar Publishing, LLC All rights reserved
For more information
visit us at www.whpsupplyroom.com

Twitter: WingHusPubLLC
Facebook: Winged Hussar Publishing LLC

The Sword and the Cipher

By

Riley O'Connor

Prologue

The junior lieutenant had followed the admiral back to the bridge of the *Exemplar* with some difficulty, despite the admiral's small stature. She paused several paces up the final staircase when she no longer heard his labored pacing. Admiral Sorkitani turned to look at the lieutenant expectantly, the way a butcher might wait for a slab of meat to weigh up on a scale. The lieutenant was bent over, appearing to rest his legs, feet, lungs... no doubt by the time the admiral enumerated his complete list of ailments he would be ready to proceed. Admiral Sorkitani swept some imaginary dust off her sage green uniform, admiring the pearl stripes of command while trying not to show the condemnation she felt. The lieutenant straightened then, pulling at his own rumpled uniform.

"I apologize, Admiral," the lieutenant gulped. "My studies have kept me from my physical training routines lately."

Admiral Sorkitani allowed her officers plenty of free time, but took care in knowing how they spent it. The lieutenant's excuse would be a reasonable one, if he included time spent studying the bottom of an empty mug. But Sorkitani knew the mugs at the officer's lounge were not empty for long.

"See to it that you focus on the fundamentals of your routine, rather than... indulging... in one particular area," Sorkitani lectured as patiently as she could. She put her well-polished boot on the next stair. "Then your priorities should fall into place."

"Why did we go to the barracks, anyway? We could have broadcast our communication, or sent a courier, and never had to leave the bridge," the lieutenant said, managing it all in a single ragged breath.

"Knowing when to delegate is an important aspect of leadership. This was not one of those times. Our lance troopers have performed incredible exploits today. Actions they may never be called on to do again. They deserved to be commended in person," Sorkitani explained. She resumed her quick pace up the stairs. The lieutenant swung himself up and followed.

Though Admiral Sorkitani's first instinct was to kick the junior lieutenant a few rungs down the ladder of command, or indeed all the way to the floor, the Counsel had reminded her in her latest consultation that negative reinforcement could only go so far. Besides, the man had shown remarkable aptitude for both fleet tactics and diplomacy. He merely needed the proper motivation to get him back on track. Or so the distributed artificial intelligence of the Counsel had assured. Though the final decision was ultimately hers by way of command in the field, only a fool would repeatedly go against the guidance of the collective will of the innumerable neural networks of the Union Precept.

"There are many within the Union Precept that disagreed with our actions today. The events in the coming weeks will vindicate us, however." Sorkitani knew what was waiting for her on the bridge. Like her lieutenant, she dreaded the top of those stairs, albeit for vastly different reasons. She had detected the suppressed fear in her bridge crew's wavering voices when they had asked her back to the command platform as soon as possible.

"We were right to do so," the lieutenant wheezed. "The Starkin were warned many times about possession of the hostile weapon so close to our inner quickspace lanes. When we acted on the Counsel's foresight, we were avoiding the need for further bloodshed. If we can follow up on our victory and ensure the remaining—"

"Yes, I am aware of the nuances of our own plan," Sorkitani snapped. She immediately regretted losing her patience, but it had been a long couple of days since she last slept. She slowed her pace slightly and glanced back at the lieutenant. Bringing him along had been the Counsel's idea, after all. "If you could save every Union Precept citizen on one of our worlds, would you do it?"

"Well of course, but..." the lieutenant began, but quickly trailed off.

"There is no right or wrong answer, Lieutenant. This is all off the record."

"Ah, well then, I suppose it depends on what it would cost. We would need to know how many people live on the world, the disposition of forces in the area, supply chains..."

"A logical progression and reasonable inquiry. Very commendable."

"Could you narrow the parameters at all?" he asked.

"Sometimes all we have is what little we are given, and the resolution to see it through," Admiral Sorkitani said, her gaze focused far beyond the walls of the bridge.

The lieutenant opened his mouth to reply but thought better of it. He grunted in affirmation and used the breath saved to propel him to the top of the stairs just a few paces behind his superior.

Admiral Sorkitani emerged onto the rear command platform overlooking the bridge, her boots tapping on the floor tiles currently projecting a pristine marble façade. The sprawling room reminded her of one of the old orchestra halls. The personnel modules for weapons, communications, and navigation systems were laid out beneath her in tiered rows, all facing the front of the *Exemplar's* bridge. All had their part to play in her symphony, which she conducted from above on her command platform. Her bridge crew paced among the consoles here, busily expanding and collapsing holographic displays, passing along new information, updating ship movements, all the while giving their admiral a healthy amount of space without appearing to be doing so.

The wall projections gave Admiral Sorkitani an equally clear and terrible view of this system's shattered defenses. A massive rail gun wandered into the magnified view of the bow cameras as an orbital platform drifted close by, just a few hundred miles in front of the *Exemplar*. The weapon maintained the elliptical path of its orbit, despite its bent and ruptured frame.

The junior lieutenant approached the command platform railing and gripped it with white knuckles. "It appears that the remaining Starscum are not all interested in peaceful resolution, as we would have hoped," he said.

"It is our duty to make them interested, and please refrain from such vulgarities on my bridge. Starkin is acceptable if pressed, but Stevari is the preferred term. This clan in particular should be delineated as House Drovina, to avoid indirect condemnation of the other houses." Sorkitani brought up logistics of the Ulastai system and began sorting through the damage. "Some retaliation was to be expected. This was one of their larger worldships, and a fast blockade runner at that. Likely the ship that witnessed the destruction of their capital ship at Carnizad."

"It is a shame that they bore witness to our attack and escaped," the lieutenant noted, at last able to breathe evenly.

"On the contrary... now they have evidence of the consequences that result when they willfully disobey our requests. Remember, this was no smuggling run or dodging of tariffs. Drovina possessed a deadly virus acquired through trade with exiled colonies," Sorkitani explained. *Or so the Counsel claims.*

The lieutenant looked down at his boots. "I understand, Admiral. *All* trade with the colonies is unauthorized. We could not allow such a weapon in anyone's hands, even our former allies."

A sudden motion pulled Sorkitani's attention from the screen. The admiral scanned the bridge and discovered a small rodent scurrying along the far wall. Its gray fur was difficult to spot among the rows of equipment.

"Lieutenant, what is that vermin doing on my bridge?" she asked sharply.

"What? Oh, the, I see..." the lieutenant stammered. "Nothing to worry about, Admiral. Rats do occasionally get on board during port stays. Most are relegated to the storage holds and exterminated, but some manage to sneak about."

"I am not interested in excuses, but results," Sorkitani turned to provide a suitable display of annoyance to her subordinate. "I have already flagged it for removal by the sanitation drones."

Sorkitani glanced back at the trespasser but saw it had already vanished. She returned her attention to the forward display.

"Now, what were you saying?" the admiral drawled.

"Oh, sure. So one time I saw a rat that, no joke, was bigger than your—"

"About the Stevari's trading habits."

"Oh. Of course," the lieutenant stammered. "We could not trust any such weapon in their hands."

"I believe you said former allies."

"Correct, Admiral."

"Our alliance with House Drovina is far from shattered," Admiral Sorkitani said, "the targeted destruction of a worldship and its auxiliaries was necessary, given the risk involved of the unknown entity. The Stevari of House Drovina will all understand the actions we have taken soon enough." She turned her scrutiny to her forward screen and panned out until she could see a handful of the many hundreds of systems that made up the Union Precept. Its vastness was all the more impressive by its unity of purpose: expansion, advancement, and prosperity. It was a triumph of the human spirit and machine efficiency. "I shudder to think how many systems the latent virus passed through before we tracked it down, that dagger poised at the very heart of civilization. Fortunately, it is out of the hands of the conniving Stevari."

The lieutenant gazed out into the projection of Ulastai and its lone red star.

"Is it true that they reproduce through..."

"Traditional means? Yes, exclusively," Sorkitani replied. "Their women even carry their children to term within their own bodies."

"That's... not even legal anywhere in the Union Precept," the lieutenant noted.

"Indeed. The process propagates nature's cruel chance of heredity on a helpless individual, and sets that burden on society," Sorkitani said. "You know, many find my short stature odd for an admiral."

"Not at all, ma'am," the lieutenant replied, a little too quickly.

"Yes, well, it is no abnormality. My family had a generational contract with the Precept Navy. Our shorter height gives us a natural advantage as pilots, as well as overall improved metabolic efficiency and survival rates. Being the first in my family to achieve my current rank, I have since ended the contract. My progeny, if indeed I decide to create any, will be given the best hereditary suites available to forge their own path.

"I'm sure they'll decide to follow in your footsteps," the lieutenant said with a smile.

Sorkitani ignored the sycophantic remark and tried to imagine what enhancements had led to her subordinate's current state. The Union Precept covered the cost of basic genetic editing free of charge upon artificial inception, as an investment in an individual's health and future contributions to the Unity. But there would always be some who squandered or neglected their gifts.

"Well, that remains to be seen," the admiral said with an air of indifference. "The Stevari on the other hand, preserve the human genome entirely unaltered. At least as much as they can, inherited as it is from our shared ancestors."

The lieutenant turned away from the destruction on the screen to gaze in wonder at the admiral.

"So, they would not switch off a single gene to save a man from blindness, or mental disability? What about saving a woman from a terrible disease?" he asked with a singularly fixed gaze.

"The Stevari augment their natural deficiencies with technology, and corrective surgery when necessary. But your analysis is correct, the biology they are born with must remain untainted in their eyes. Whereas heredity is simply another tool for us, they maintain ancient history as a biological imperative."

The forward display zoomed out in response to a directed thought, and the mercurial network of quickspace passages that connected every system appeared. The lights undulated and squirmed, a can of worms the size of galaxies and probably larger. The only reason every planet was anything other than impossible to travel to due to the restrictions imposed by the sheer scale of the universe, was due to these quickspace lanes. Somehow, humanity had long ago linked many of their solar systems through these passages, all tied together at a blue star of unknown origin and location. All that was known now was that they worked. The center of all these locations, the mystical object that made it all possible, was the blue star known as Alpha One. The first and last place in any journey. A ship traveling through a quickspace lane across Alpha One could make a journey of a thousand years in mere days, assuming it was not lost to the depths of the star.

Following the myriad paths of her fleets around the Starkin vessels, Sorkitani allowed herself a slight smile. Friendly ships were highlighted in a light blue: forward mobile fleets, reserve fleets, supply caravans, all locked together in dizzying harmony around the few red dots representing the ships of the Starkin. Their frigates and cruisers posed little threat to the Union Precept now. Even the oversized, so-called worldships of the Starkin were no real danger when surrounded with sufficient firepower. The destruction wrought here at Ulastai would not need to be repeated, and soon, Admiral Sorkitani would complete her task. The worlds that were her duty to protect would be safe from the virus, just as the Counsel had assured her... and her alone.

The Sword and the Cipher

Chapter 1

Safe upon the soil below
Teeming masses live and die
Come with me, to thee I'll show
Our soaring cities in the sky

But if we tread not careful
And linger long around
Those who far beneath us dwell
Will bring us to the ground

–Stevari Children's Song

Thick flakes of ash drifted lazily through a haze of dust as Nacen reached blindly for a handhold. Every piece of equipment on the ship had neglected his attempts to interact with them remotely, and this hatchway proved no exception. Granted, some functionality was bound to be lost when a ship is systematically boarded, disabled, and subsequently crashed into a planet's surface. At last, Nacen grasped at a handle, which gave way after more than a modest supply of force. He gave a grunt, swung the great door open, and stepped into what could no longer in any honesty be called the great hall of the *Asura*. He could recall the illustrious chamber filled with no shortage of food, dance, and good cheer. Few of the carefully arranged pillars and tables remained intact, let alone in their proper place. Fissures ran along the walls in a macabre renovation of the former décor's florid patterns and elegant filigree.

Nacen's cropped, auburn hair lay damp beneath the hood of a tightly bound crimson cloak. His pan-atmo mask echoed with a faint whisper of his muffled breathing but more importantly filtered out any harmful particles in the air. Most of it was dust kicked up when the worldship crashed onto the planet known as Carnizad, but there was ash from organics like trees and other vegetation onboard as well. Nacen exhaled sharply through the mask. At least, he hoped it was only from the plant life.

Though it now felt like an expedition that stretched over days, Nacen had been methodically making his way through the ruins of the *Asura* for just over four hours. He and his crew had started at the stern which, although it had been less damaged by the crash as it was the last section to hit the ground, appeared to be the first that the enemy had targeted. They proceeded slowly, not only to thoroughly search for survivors but also to make sure they were not crushed by falling debris. It was to the bow that the ship's beacon lay transmitting its covert signal, or at least should be. Like everything else in the ship, it remained eerily silent.

The silencing of this signal, unique to the Stevari's own vessels, had been what drew Nacen back to the homefleet's station on Carnizad in the first place. When functioning properly, the beacon transmitted a clandestine signature even across quickspace. This allowed various far-flung Stevari to locate their house's worldships at any given time. This was critical for emergency meetings and, as Nacen knew well, avoiding certain family reunions. The beacons were designed to mimic an aggregate of solar output, hydrogen spin-flips, and radio-wavelength background noises that occurred naturally in the universe. The beacon was a technological marvel: magic to most Stevari within the homefleet, and a sheer mystery to those without.

The mask's dark lenses filtered out the harsh light now streaming through breaches in the ceiling, making the room resemble a charred painting. The captain's two druvani, his personal bodyguards, crouched in the gloom no more than thirty paces away. Their own crimson robes were wrapped tightly around lightweight, serrated brown armor plating. As Nacen approached, the closest rose to meet him. Something glittered in his right hand.

"The room is clear, Nace." Camlo turned the object nervously in the nimble fingers of his artificial right hand. The limb was tungsteel all the way to the shoulder. Nacen saw the object was a fragment of something, glass maybe, or the remains of the clear panels that made up the shattered solar canopy above.

"Just like every other room we've been in. Even the emergency bunkers." Nacen squinted his eyes at the shadowed corners of the room, as if willing someone, anyone, to appear there and explain what had happened.

Camlo made up half of his druvani contingent. A baroni or colonial governor could have up to three full squads in their garrison. As the captain to a small trade frigate, however, Nacen considered himself lucky to have any of the elite bodyguards at all. His younger cousin by a third his own age, Camlo's eagerness to learn seemed to be matched only by his penchant to forget.

Beskin stood at attention, his rebreather concealing his hawkish features as he scanned the room. Light periodically glinted off his lenses, streaming in from one of many wide gashes in the ceiling. The man had been Nacen's first druvani and continued to serve not only as a bodyguard, but as a trusted advisor.

"Relax, Beskin," Nacen said, "I know it's unsettling, but we performed a thorough resonance scan from the *Carmine Canotila*. If there was anyone still here, we would have found them. Let's proceed."

"It's not the living I'm worried about, Captain. The Unies took off in a hurry, but who's to say they didn't leave any parting gifts for us?"

"We'll proceed carefully then." Nacen resumed his pace, no faster or slower than before. The twisted corridors and buckled frame of the great worldship *Asura* laid themselves out before his mind as though he were looking at an old picture recording. "Let's keep moving to the bridge. Or what's left of it."

Nacen scanned his surroundings. Though completely still, anything could be hiding in the debris strewn all around him. With each hushed step, his eyes darted to another remote corner of the room as the trio made their way to the doors across the hall.

"Not seeing any hidden explosives, Nace," Camlo chirped.

"Of course. That would defeat the purpose of them being hidden," Nacen replied. He knew what Camlo had meant, but someone had to start holding his cousin responsible for some of the things he said.

Nacen reached the door and beckoned Camlo forward. He hesitated. His face was a shade paler than normal, apparent even in the dim light of the hollow ship.

"You're going to let Beskin's worrying get the better of you?" Nacen forced himself to crack a smile. "I know you haven't been druvani long, but I figured you had more sense."

"Thousands... thousands of Stevari lived on the capital ship. Our brothers, our sisters, how could they all have perished?" Camlo let the shard of glass fall. It clattered on tile but did not break. Nacen didn't realize the druvani had still been carrying it. "Even if most died in the boarding action, or the crash, a few must have survived."

"I don't know, Cam. Maybe my father was able to evacuate those still aboard. Maybe a bold baron was able to make landfall and get them before the Unity dusted the planet, or they got taken prisoner. I don't know," Nacen said again, "but I intend to find out."

"The galley gardens were two floors below this one. There's nothing left but..." Camlo turned away. "Where do the old heroes of Drovina lay when their resting place has been taken away? *Kaha,* even this gathering hall could have inspired a thousand poets for a thousand years. Now look at it."

"I don't know, I'd be pretty inspired if I owned a repair dock," Beskin said glibly. "We had better keep moving."

Camlo pivoted and set off down the corridor. Beskin followed, his head swiveling at shadows. After half a backward glance, Nacen closed the gap. They continued in darkness for a long while. Nearing the next junction, Nacen parted his lips to speak. Instead of speech, an aching creak of warping metal echoed through the corridor. The maddening groan was followed by a clatter and metallic ringing. During the split second of clamor, Camlo and Beskin moved up to the T-junction and held the barrels of their plasma carbines down the right side of the corridor to the source of the offending noise.

Nacen opened his encrypted communication channel with a double-click of his tongue. In an instant, he was connected to the pilot of the *Carmine Canotila.*

"Lina, we need a targeted scan in the ship," he hissed. His heart pounded now, and the tension of not knowing what could be out there made the order seem blunt and fearful. He withdrew his sidearm, loaded it with a compact plasma core, and knelt behind a pile of rubble to cover the corridor.

"Sure thing, Captain," Lina snapped crisply back. "By your tone, I'd say you were requesting an airstrike."

"No time for games, Lina. We need a resonance scan in... section fifty-seven. Tighten it down to fifty meters. Send the high-res readout to my pad if you can."

"Good, because we don't have any missiles. This is a shuttle after all." Lina hummed to fill the intervening silence.

Nacen allowed himself to close his eyes. He felt his shoulders relax at her makeshift melody. He hadn't realized how heavy his eyelids felt before now. Fifty meters. This was practically a hair's breadth for a quickspace trader like himself, but here in the ruins of the *Asura,* it held his whole life, and possibly his...

He considered how familiar Lina would be with the metric system, being a former citizen of the Union Precept. Though it was practically ancient, it was still generally used as the galactic standard in most places outside of the Union Precept. The U.P., on the other hand, had its own relatively newer standards that made little sense outside of human anatomy and astrophysics. Nacen snapped back to reality. Had something moved down the passage? He peered down the dark corridor, willing something to emerge into the pistol's sights.

"Okay, Captain, I'm reading nothing outside the massive battle damage to the hull and interior. I suspect you've seen plenty of that down there already. Jumping at ghosts?"

"Some ruined parts of the ship must still be settling." Nacen loosened his grip on the plasma pistol slightly.

"Most likely. This planet isn't exactly what you would call stable after the Unity's bombardment."

"Agreed. We're going to keep moving to the bridge to recover the beacon. Set the scans to automatically update every few seconds and extend the range to seventy-five meters. I think that's twenty-four parslats back in the Unity."

"Learning your old measurements was not the hardest part about flying for the Stevari, Nace. Maybe I will even throw in the silly prefixes when it's convenient," Linasette chided gently.

"What *was* the hardest part then?" Nacen asked as he kept pace with his bodyguards.

"That would be learning the dulcinet. If you count how I played as learning, anyway," the pilot noted. "I still do not know why they require each crew member to know a musical instrument."

"It's part of the well-rounded education and general enrichment that makes our way of life so enviable," Nacen replied smoothly as he stepped over a fallen pillar.

"Right..." Linasette said with exaggerated dubiousness. "Well, I will let you know if I detect anything. You let me know if you need a nice serenade. I hope your trip stays nice and boring."

"Thank you, Lina. Stay in touch." Nacen set his pistol in its magnetic holster and withdrew his digital pad from its pouch on his thigh. He navigated to the stored scans of the ship with a few deft strokes. Lina was right, there was no activity outside their own, plus the two household troops covering the lower levels. He placed the pad back in its protective sheath at his hip.

Camlo and Beskin lowered their carbines as Nacen turned to face them. "Alright, let's move on up to the bridge. We're getting close." He set off at a cautious pace straight down the junction.

The druvani alternated who entered each room first. Scan, breach, secure, and repeat.

Camlo ducked into a dark room and brought his weapon about until giving it the all-clear. Beskin strode in, crouched low to the ground, scouring the darkness for potential threats. Nacen followed them patiently, never questioning, simply leaving them to their methodical work. He kept his focus to the side passages and the corridors they left behind, always ready to hear back from Linasette in case she discovered something from her resonance scans as the *Carmine Canotila's* perched safely outside the ravaged hull of the worldship.

Scan, breach, secure, and repeat. Minutes passed as the trio cleared every individual room, each one barren except for debris from the ship's destruction at the hands of the Union Precept navy, and finally its last defeat by the invisible hand of gravity itself. The rooms felt alien to Nacen, despite having walked them for much of his life. As they approached a wide, circular frame that once held a set of double doors, Nacen felt his pulse quicken. His hands trembled, and he did not try to stop them.

"It looks like the doors were blown open by an explosive," Camlo said from behind, "a plasma charge, if the scorch marks are any indication."

"Hard to tell," Beskin replied, "could have even been a fractal discharge, considering the state of the bridge."

His bodyguards' speculation barely registered in Nacen's mind. He strode onto the bridge of the former capital ship. The grand chamber had been reduced to a collapsed ruin. The floor was fractured in three areas. The room now resembled a cavern of glittering tungsteel and smashed displays. Nacen stepped cautiously over the floor, which lay at a twenty-degree angle in relation to most of the walls. The floor was solid as he slowly eased his weight onto his front foot. He moved to the center with growing confidence, being careful not to trip over the uneven ledges of the former gantry. Nacen gave a slight intake of breath. If he had been in command, perhaps this unmerciful disaster need not have happened at all. Silently he cursed his father's whims to put him at the helm of his old, ungainly trade ship *Lusterhawk* and its sister shuttle the *Carmine Canotila*, rather than in command of a proper cruiser of the homefleet.

"I'd always wanted command of this ship one day." Nacen's voice thickened.

Beskin advanced carefully behind him. "I won't fight you for it."

"If I were here, maybe I could have helped swing the battle. Or even avoided it." Nacen clenched his fists as he felt a bubbling anger rise in him, one that he had suppressed out of necessity since arriving at Carnizad. His ire was not directed at the perpetrators of the destruction, but at the man who had set him to the side, where he could do nothing to avert this disaster.

"No need to worry about it, Nace," Camlo said, "there's nothing we could have done."

"Exactly!" Nacen shouted and kicked a stone into an already cracked screen. "If I had a cruiser of my own, maybe we could have actually done something. Instead, I get stuck with this tiny, pitiful..."

"I assume you're not talking about the *Carmine Canotila*, right?" Linasette transmitted over the encrypted channel.

"Lina! No, I just... we're on the bridge. What's going on?" Nacen asked. He had forgotten she would keep the channel open in order to report faster, and to detect any disturbances in communications.

"Resonance scans are picking up movement around the bottom of the ship. Are you guys okay?"

"No contact with anything so far. More tremors?"

"Seems likely. Still, keep an eye out. I'll be here ready to evacuate you in my tiny, pitiful, decrepit—"

He winced.

"Of course. Thank you, Lina." Nacen beckoned with a gauntleted finger across the room. "Spread out. Look for any trace of the beacon."

"If it's here, we'll find it, Nace," Camlo said, already sifting through a chunk of twisted metal and dead screens that was once a control panel.

"Which is precisely why we won't find it," Beskin said. He kept at attention, always shifting his piercing gaze, as if daring something to come out of the shadows. "If we are not detecting it, then it was likely either taken by the Unity or destroyed by Yoska to prevent the former. Your father would never have given up the beacon, or his ship for that matter, while there was still breath in his body. Not while the *Asura* was his charge. Not even when he flew the *Lusterhawk*. He was a man I was proud to follow."

"Do you ever miss it? Being under his command, I mean?" Nacen asked.

Beskin gave a knowing smile. "I still am. Yoska's last order was to protect you as I had him for all those years."

Nacen found himself smiling, despite himself. He turned and resumed his search of the bridge. They had to be thorough.

Jeta and Shukernak, the last of his skeleton crew of household troops, had investigated the bunkers. Perhaps the trufalci had been fortunate enough to find something, or someone, useful. If not, Nacen figured his next goal would be to regroup with any Stevari outside of Union Precept space. Regroup and salvage what was left of House Drovina. He had to believe there were survivors out there, somewhere. He shook himself out of his reverie and clicked open a general communication link to his trufalci.

"Jeta, how is the search coming?"

"Not very successful. Nothing here but dust and memories," Jeta said, a small sliver of hope in her voice. "But we still have a few living quarters to check before we rendezvous with you on the bridge."

"She means we haven't found anything," Shukernak interjected, "and we're not gonna find anything in this blasted heap. I say we get out of here before the ceiling comes down on the people that we know are still alive."

"Better keep your chin up then. Perform your sweep of the living quarters, then meet us on the bridge. I'll have Lina come get us in the *Carmine Canotila* soon and we'll be back on the frigate before you know it. Understood?"

"Without wood, the fire dies," Jeta declared.

"Where the houses go, wealth shall rise," Nacen said, returning the oath.

He turned his focus back to the bridge. Camlo was sifting through another pile of debris as Beskin approached the gantry where Nacen was surveying the area.

"Soft-wave gamma fingers and low-frequency combs are all coming up zero," Beskin said in his cold, calculating way. Nacen would have sworn his druvani was rebuking him for wasting his time, were it not for Beskin's stoic demeanor. "It looks like the Unies took the beacon, or destroyed it. Every trace of the *Asura's* network has been erased as well."

Nacen sighed. "In any case, let's go ahea—"

From beneath the deck came a deafening groan of metal and rumbling earth. Nacen steadied himself in case a larger quake followed. "It looks like the ship isn't as stable as we thought. Better get moving."

"More sounds of a dying ship?" Camlo asked to no one in particular.

Nacen's mind conjured images of Union Precept commandos lying in ambush, pirates salvaging the wreck, and deepsun raiders scrounging for fuel and slaves. There were many scavengers that picked at the carrion of quick-space.

"Your guess is as good as mine," Nacen said.

"Maybe the ship is haunted," Camlo said earnestly, his voice raising half an octave.

"Okay, maybe not quite as good as mine. Let's keep moving."

Beskin nodded his agreement. Camlo glanced about, his stance still braced wide from the tremor. "Uh... good idea, Nace."

Nacen led the way out of the bridge with a brisk pace and clicked open his communication link to his ship. "Lina, can we get a complete scan of the ground three kilometers in and around the *Asura*? It seems like the tremors on Carnizad are getting worse. Run me an updated analysis on the atmospheric content, too. My mask is reading a slight increase in sulfur and heavy metals."

There was silence on the channel and nothing more.

"Linasette Derada, this is your captain. Please confirm orders." Nacen opened up his comm link to the trufalci. He made three low taps of his tongue against the back of his teeth, wordlessly indicating that an immediate likewise response was requested.

The silence of his comm channel was punctuated by another rumble that emanated from the decking beneath Nacen's feet from far below. The high-pitched cry of a firearm echoed off a distant corridor.

"Sounded like a flux driver. One of ours?" Nacen asked. He was not sure whether he spoke to his druvani, his silent crew, or to himself. He hoped the trufalci were on their way to the bridge.

"Definitely gunshots. Solid projectile. Hard to gauge the distance from inside the ship," Beskin snapped.

Another burst of flux fire echoed down the corridor. The walls all around shuddered with rapid, booming vibrations as though hundreds of people were pounding on them, desperate to escape. Nacen broke into a sprint toward the source of the gunshots with his druvani following just behind, all weapons at the ready.

Scavengers picking at the carrion of quickspace, he thought again.

***

They ran, the walls around them ringing like a gong.

"How did our sweeps not pick up any of this until they were right on top of us?" Camlo shouted back from the front of the trio.

"Whoever they are, they must have some serious stealth tech. Could they have hacked our comms?" Nacen made a quick glance to either end of the current junction before continuing.

"They could have been waiting here the whole time," Beskin countered.

A loud hum preceded the next set of poundings.

"Okay, are we getting closer to them, or are they moving closer to us?" Camlo darted into the room and held his organic hand to his ear.

"I don't know, Cam. Just keep moving and check your corners. We need to get to our trufalci and get off this ship."

Sweep, breach, clear, and repeat. The druvani advanced quicker than before, but not sacrificing their thoroughness for haste. They wound their way to the trufalci's last known location in the sprawling living quarters. The humming fired up from behind this time, and Nacen whirled around to face it. With a crash, the wall panel a dozen paces back clattered to the floor. It had crumpled as though it were paper. He did not stay to watch what, if anything, came out.

"Keep moving!" Nacen jerked forward to resume his run. "We can't afford to stop or get bogged down. Whoever they are, they're coming in from all around us!"

"Good, now we can shoot the *chodras* from every direction!" Beskin called out.

They rushed into the room where the trufalci's last signal had been before their connection was lost. The large, oval room was large enough to fit dozens of Stevari comfortably, with places for their possessions and other amenities. On the floor of the quarters lay a pile of tiles surrounded by up-turned earth. In the center was a hole, nearly Nacen's own height across, that had been bored through the ship from the ground below. He could not see far into the opening, but it must have been deep indeed. He thought he heard shuffling below. Maybe it was just falling rocks? He found himself questioning all of his senses.

"Where'd Jeta and 'Nak go? They were just here!" Camlo said, pacing across the room.

Nacen ignored Camlo and investigated the scene. Dents from flux rounds marked the surrounding floor and some of the walls around the room. The standard flux driver was essentially a portable rail gun that a soldier could wield as easily as a conventional rifle. A magnetic field would be induced along a series of rails to hurl a metal projectile at fantastic speeds at the target, albeit much smaller and slower than a proper ship-mounted rail gun. The weapon could be fired in nearly any conditions, even the vacuum of space, as long as the internal parts of the flux driver were intact.

The floor tiles were crumpled, much like the wall panel had been. Though the thickness of the panels could not compare to the nanite-reinforced outer hull of the *Asura*, they should have held up better than the discarded tissue paper of bent plating that lay before him. Nacen's mind raced to think of an explanation.

"Camlo, cover the door on the opposite end. Beskin, watch the door nearest us and plot an escape route."

They could leave and abandon their trufalci, but that would leave woefully few Stevari left in his crew. After this slaughter, the homefleet could ill afford such losses.

Camlo lit up the hall outside the door frame with plasma fire from his carbine.

"Don't shoot to kill if you can help it, either of you!" Granted, the interlopers' intentions were likely not good, but at least Nacen had not been fired on yet. They had plenty of opportunities to engage, but they appeared to be encircling him. The fallen panel could easily have landed on Nacen himself. Or he simply could have been killed instantly by an explosive sent through the wall. Something was off about this attack.

Nacen considered the warped panel again. The panels must have been warped by some sort of portable compression technology, perhaps a mass condenser. The compression fields could be used for anything from exerting small forces at a distance to tunneling through solid rock and, apparently, reinforced steel. The attackers could be Armads, possibly survivors of the Unity's attack. There had to be some sort of a guild presence on Carnizad: a mine, refinery, or manufacturing facility.

"*Kaha!* Cease fire, they're not Unies!" Nacen shouted over the disciplined bursts of plasma.

Camlo lowered his carbine and looked at Nacen with incredulity. "Well then, what do you expect us to—"

The druvani was suddenly flung back by some invisible force. His limp form crashed onto an antique chest and slid against the floor in a heap. Beskin ran over and began laying down suppressing fire on the door that Camlo had most recently been watching.

"Beskin, get out of here and back to the ship! I will try to deal with—"

Before Nacen realized what was happening, several huge figures stormed into the room from the far door. One crouched over Camlo, who was making a grab for his plasma carbine. The hulking figure slapped a black, ring-shaped object around his head, and the druvani slumped down to the floor.

Nacen tried to raise his hands in surrender. He knew these were not Union Precept troops and therefore likely not his enemy. His armor grew tight around his arms and legs. His extremities became numb. Raising his hands was a supreme effort, but ever so slowly they crept toward the ceiling. He managed to release his pistol, which clattered to the floor. Nacen barely got his hands waist high before his entire body was lifted off the floor.

The rough leather soles of heavy boots around heavier feet echoed across the floor. A large form rose in his dimming vision. The man had the rough skin and ample frame of an Armad, men equally adapted to the vacuum of space as to the deep inner mantle of a terrestrial planet. He was massive, even compared to his fellow Armads. Like his companions, he wore gray plating festooned with yellow stripes and other shapes over his chest and extremities. These areas were presumably more vulnerable, though Nacen wouldn't know it looking at his stony skin.

Nacen now realized with mounting terror that he could not breathe. His vision narrowed to a tunnel. He could feel his heart thumping against his recast armor plating. Against projectile weapons, his armor would harden and sharpen itself against at the point of impact to divert a shot. Against plasma weaponry, it would change its surface properties to absorb high levels of heat. But against his heart, the recast armor held fast, unaware of how it constricted its wearer.

An intense quiet washed over him. He noticed Beskin's plasma fire had ceased, and two bodies lay still on the floor that were not his own men.

At last, the Armad spoke. His voice was a deep rumble.

"Yep, definitely one of these Starkin traders. Soldiers by the looks of them. You lucked out friend, my compatriot here wanted to blast a hole straight through you."

"It's not too late, Chalce," a gritty voice behind him said, "all we have to do is tell the boss that some Conglomerate troopers ambushed us, and we just started shooting."

"Ambushed us in our own tunnels? Well... you're so dense, the boss might actually believe it." The hulk of a man grunted and turned his slate face back to Nacen. He grasped Nacen's pan-atmo mask in his huge grip and tore it from his face with ease. "This little vulture is more useful to us alive."

Vulture? This was *his* ship. Well, in a way it was. The accusation was outrageous. Nacen had shown them a modicum of restraint, and they treated him with disdain? He opened his mouth to chastise them, but his objections came out as nothing more than a gasp for air.

"Alright. You've got a choice, Starscrap. I can tune down my condenser and we can have a nice, relaxing walk down to see the boss, or you can take a knuckle-induced nap with your friend and hitch a ride on my shoulders. I only had one sleeper ring. Don't worry, I won't be bothered by the weight."

Nacen felt some of the pressure let off his spine and chest. He gasped for air, this time succeeding in sucking down some oxygen. A sensation of pins and needles filled his arms. He resisted the urge to call the big man a murderous brute, though it was by far the tamest of the outbursts his shocked mind had conjured.

"I'll go quietly," Nacen croaked.

The Armad called Chalce gave a sloppy half-grin. "Well look at that. He's smart for a Starkin, too." The Armad gave another signal, and Nacen was free. The captain was not prepared to bear the weight of his own armor as he rose, his blood just now rushing back to his extremities. He fell forward and just barely caught himself on his palms. He gritted his teeth and, as he shook with rage and exhaustion, all his cultivated diplomacy melted away.

"When people talk about somebody being as dumb as a rock," Nacen wheezed, "you're the rock. What in quickspace are you doing mucking around in the ruins of an *actual* civilization? Even the tattered remains of our shattered halls are greater than you could conceive of in one hundred lifetimes. You should have kept digging in the other direction until you hit the core so you could throw yourselves into it."

"Hmm." The Armad shrugged his wide shoulders. "I've made worse first impressions."

Chapter 2

Dust clung to Nacen's skin and lined his mouth and nose. He had been unsuccessful in contacting his crew through the squad's encrypted communications link, and his hands were shackled in front. Aside from blinking the perspiration away and scraping his lips with a dry tongue, he had no reprieve from the heat as the group plunged downward into the tunnels.

The ground sloped down at a steep angle. It was all Nacen could do to not slip on the compacted earth that formed the walls of the tunnel. Though the tunnel was quite narrow for the lead Armad, Nacen had plenty of room to maneuver laterally to avoid the worst patches.

At first, Nacen's mind filled with plots of escape. In the close confines of the tunnel, he might be able to use the Armads' size against them. If he could remove the petrifying halo device around Camlo's eyes and take on the Armads one at a time, he and the single druvani may be able to overpower them. But he had no idea how many more Armads the tunnels contained and how quickly they would be able to react. Camlo's state upon coming out of his induced sleep would be of dubious use, as well.

Deciding his time was better spent in a diplomatic capacity, Nacen ceased his thoughts of slapping Camlo into combat readiness and began planning potential negotiations with the Armads' leader. He would obviously need to be more circumspect than his initial meeting in the *Asura*. Espousing their common plight, the shared losses at the hands of the Unity, would make a good foundation. From there, he could gauge the Armads' reactions and respond with appeals to logic or emotion.

"Captain, come in." Nacen perked up. It was Beskin. His encrypted communication channel wasn't lost after all.

Nacen responded with three clicks of his tongue.

"Good, you can hear me. I am assuming you are able to respond but choose not to."

One click for yes.

"Okay. I was able to locate Jeta and Shukernak and get back to the ship before more Armads could find us. What is your status?"

"Good work, Beskin," Nacen whispered as softly as he could. He turned his head, counting on the Armads' loud ambulating to drown out his soft whisper. They had not heard him. "I'm fine. The Armads have Camlo in some sort of mind interference restraint, but I suspect he will be alright or they would have simply knocked him unconscious. Where are you?"

"We're in the *Carmine Canotila*. We have not moved from our initial landing in case you were able to escape and find us."

That made sense. Nacen could not reach out much more than half a kilometer with his own implants, and probably far less in these tunnels. But with the help of the sensor relays on the ship, Beskin could establish communications at much farther ranges.

"Okay, you need to get to higher ground. Somewhere the Armads can't dig up around you."

"Sure. Linasette will get us repositioned. Now, where are they taking you?" Beskin asked smoothly.

"Not sure, exactly. Some sort of subterranean base if looks are to be believed. We're quite a ways below the surface and still going." Nacen attempted to peer around the lead Armad known as Chalce but couldn't see past his enormous frame.

"Should we mount a rescue operation?"

"That's going to be tricky in these tight tunnels." Nacen risked a quick glance backward. There were four Armads, all armed. "We don't know how many there are in total, and we'd be fighting on their home turf. Let me try to talk my way out of this."

"Okay. Good luck, Captain. We'll be on standby to recover you."

"I appreciate the sentiment, but I don't want to lose any more Stevari today."

Beskin paused briefly. "Understood."

Nacen ended the transmission. Had Beskin truly understood that this meant abandoning himself and Camlo if they were not successful? Nacen was not sure Beskin would obey such an order. He hoped he would not have to find out.

After another ten to fifteen minutes of miserable, grim marching down into the network of tunnels, the group came to a set of metal doors that had been constructed directly into the rock. The lead captor, Chalce, approached the doors and groped a device suspended by cable near the entrance. The Armad jabbed at it a few times with a stubby index finger, and the door reluctantly crept open. Nacen memorized the pattern as two vertical sections separated slowly, like the hungry jaws of some subterranean beast. The Armad craned his head back toward the group.

"Home sweet home."

Nacen clicked the squad's comm link to provide Beskin the passcode in, but he was greeted by nothing but silence. Somehow, between the distance and intervening earth or jamming, the Armads were blocking his signal.

A rough shove got Nacen walking again. The chamber beyond looked to have been put together haphazardly. The ruddy brown cavern walls rose to meet a high ceiling. Rather than being festooned with stalactites like a natural formation, the top of the chamber was smooth as though it had been carved out by machinery. A wall of rubble had been piled high against the right wall, and support columns jutted out at odd angles. Dust hung in the air, and Nacen could make out the thick, acrid scent of motor oil. The floor was piled with primitive machinery, stacks of weapons, and scrap metal. Nacen recognized much of the scrap from the *Asura's* structure and weapon systems.

Three more iron jaw doors stood in the rock of the wall to the far left. Nacen eyed the huge drill of a tractor maul leaning on the chamber wall near the middle door.

"Try to go for anything, and I'll be polishing my armor with your guts," Chalce warned.

"I wouldn't dream of it," Nacen replied. He pondered going for the weapon for another instant anyway, before wondering how effective his intestinal tract could possibly be as a cleaning agent. "When will you take us to your boss?"

The Armad huffed. "It's on my list."

Nacen decided patience would prove better than inquisitiveness and allowed himself to be led to the door on the left, which groaned open to reveal a makeshift prison of metal bars on either side of a narrow path. They removed Camlo's halo device from around his temple, and the druvani immediately began to stir, blinking rapidly and rubbing feeling back into his limbs. Nacen was relieved to see that his cousin appeared to have recovered from the experience with no more damage than a long nap on a boulder would have rendered, though they would have to check his vitals when they got back to the ship to be sure. *If* they got back.

The Armad swung some sort of pendant over a heavy lock on the third door to the right, and it clattered to the side.

"C'mon, get in. I don't have all day." The Armad waved an apathetic hand to the interior.

Nacen did as he was told, fuming from their refusal to answer for their deeds.

"Yes, this will do nicely," Nacen said brusquely. "When will you be taking our orders for dinner?"

The cell door slammed shut. Nacen watched his captors' backs as they shuffled out of the room. He grabbed his crimson cloak. It was covered in mud and dust. He struck the center of the cloak hard, and the fabric stiffened to absorb the blow as it was designed. It had the added effect of knocking most of the muck off the cloak, to Nacen's satisfaction.

"*Kaha*, that was rough. I feel like I just performed a combat drop without a chute," Camlo said, leaning against the cell wall for comfort. The moment he made contact with the bars, he jolted away. "Agh! The bastards electrified the bars. Talk about overkill. Why not just keep us knocked out?"

"It is a bit excessive, but it does give me an idea." Nacen inspected the bars a bit closer. "If we're stuck here longer than expected, or the Armads decide to keep us locked up indefinitely, we—"

"Or use us as slaves, torture us..."

"Okay, granted, there are a lot of unpleasant possibilities," Nacen agreed. Camlo scoffed aloud. "We may be able to adapt the power along the bars to send a release signal to the lock. Armad tech is rugged, but our Stevari tech is adaptable."

Camlo raised his eyebrows in mild incredulity. "I'm listening."

"The coil regulator in either of our plasma rifles could probably handle it, we'd just have to rig it up between the bars and the lock."

"...and get our weapons back," Camlo added. "The Armads might have an issue with that. Even if we got out of the cell, we'd need to escape the tunnels."

"We just need to get to the point where Linasette can swing in and drop trufalci off to retrieve us. I identified a few tunnels on the way here that looked promising, should the main passage be inaccessible."

"Oh. Nice one, Nace."

"But if I can just have a few minutes with their leader, I'm sure I can convince them to let us go." Nacen knelt down to inspect the heavy lock on the door. The small box was plain and completely enclosed. He tapped it gently. It did not appear to be connected to the powerful circuit like the rest of the cage. That could be a problem.

"They're not the most loquacious types," Camlo said, "you'd get more out of their mouths by performing dental work on them with one of their tractor mauls."

The doors to the room opened with a clank. Chalce entered with two more Armads in tow, huge mass condensers swaying on thick straps at their sides. Nacen saw three more guards just outside the door in the main chamber. Not wanting to look suspicious by pulling away suddenly, Nacen tapped out an idle rhythm on the metal lock and gazed off at nothing in particular.

"You can see the boss now." Chalce's eyes narrowed. "Step away from the door. Both of you. Unless you want to take another nap." He tapped at one of several a black halos now secured to his waist.

Nacen and Camlo nodded and stepped back in unison as the Armad approached. The cage rattled open at Chalce's outstretched hand. Nacen spread his arms in an outward flourish, as far as they would go without touching the electrified cage.

"Lead the way."

***

Chalce shoved Nacen and Camlo toward the door to the far right of the main path. It cranked open to reveal a domed chamber roughly ten meters across. Several slate-colored pipes broke through the walls and wound their way up through the ceiling. A leak somewhere had filled the chamber with a haze of steam and made the room more humid than the rest of the caverns. A fan whirred away somewhere to negligible effect. The perimeter of the cavern was nearly barren but was scattered with some debris and machine parts. Five Armads dominated the room, gathered around a large slab in the middle. The flattened boulder was situated at waist height and well-suited for a command table. Nacen got the feeling the Armads were working with what they had and that they didn't want to be here anymore than he did. That, or they were just a lot more desperate.

Nacen entered during a hushed silence. Most of the attention was directed at an Armad at one end of the table, his arms held akimbo. He was not the largest, but his darker hide made him stand out from the rest of the group. A deep scar cut across the man's left eye and down his cheek, and another ran from the right of his jaw and beneath his chin. Several other Armads turned to see the new arrivals, but his scarred visage only contemplated the holographic images projected onto the table. More time passed. Nacen grew bored of observing the dull surroundings. Eventually the scarred man spoke.

"We've searched for survivors long enough. It is time we consolidate our position now. The guild needs to expand upward and reconstruct the agricultural den and hydroponics. All we've rebuilt will be useless if we cannot feed ourselves."

The Armads around the table gave stern nods, packed up their gear, and exited the room. Two of them glared at Nacen and Camlo on their way out.

"Chalce, welcome. It seems you brought back more than instructed." The scarred Armad beckoned the group in and placed his large palms on the slab table.

"We found more interlopers, Basaul." Chalce approached the table and stepped to one side to allow room for Nacen at the table. "These two are part of the group rummaging through the wrecked Starkin carrier we've been salvaging."

The lead Armad seemed reasonable enough. No need to resort to groveling, not yet at least. Nacen figured with a diplomatic attitude, he could negotiate his way out.

"Greetings. I am Nacen Buhari, son of Yoska Buhari who serves the homefleet as steya, guide and keeper of the house. You do me a great honor to allow me into your guild hall." Nacen placed his left hand behind his back and gave the slightest of bows. "Please, remind me of the name of this guild and its prestigious leader with which my family has done business on Carnizad?"

"We are the Extrata guild, and you may keep your formalities. Our guild hall was destroyed in the Conglomerate's bombardment of the planet, along with the Starkin ships grounded here on Carnizad." The Armad gave a dismissive wave. "This is merely the section of a mine we've been able to restore. My name is Basaul Torrs. I am the acting overseer of this den. Enough of my business, what is *your* business here? Your soldier, the one that got away, killed one of my men."

"A simple hello would have sufficed," Camlo said. Nacen shot him an icy look that he hoped would ensure his cousin's silence for the remainder of the talks.

"I take full responsibility for what happened, but your men assaulted us completely unannounced," Nacen explained, "I told my troops to stand down, but they are trained to defend me at all costs."

"We can't risk losing more men to Conglomerate forces. Chalce's orders were to shoot on sight."

Nacen bit back the insult he had ready to go. There was that word again. Conglomerate. It must be their jargon for the Union Precept. They had encountered Unies on this planet?

"*You* can't afford to lose more men?!" Camlo balked. So much for silence.

"Apologies," Nacen said before his cousin could utter another word. "We merely sought to return to the homefleet to resupply and turn in our profits. When we saw the... destruction..." Nacen did not have to fake the lump growing in his throat. "We searched for anyone signaling for help and, not finding any, proceeded immediately to our capital ship to look for survivors. If there weren't any, we figured we could at least recover the ship's beacon so that other Starkin ships could come to us in the future."

Basaul nodded and shifted his weight forward on the table. "Just who is *we*? There is at least one other Starkin running around here."

Nacen hesitated. He could give the truth or lie and say only he and his two druvani were here. Perhaps a bluff would serve his aims better. Perhaps there could be a great many ships in the system. The Armads obviously wouldn't respond well to threats, but they wouldn't be able to do much against any significant military force. But even if a bluff were to work, he might have to agree to a ransom demand. Or worse, follow up on the threat with his scant crew. True, the frigate *Lusterhawk* was in orbit with more trufalci. But these were not the military types even in ideal conditions, and invading enemy sub-terranean vaults on a collapsing planet was far from the best of conditions. To boot, Folbix Rinkesi might just decide he liked Nacen better on Carnizad. The master of the *Lusterhawk* would take no active steps to see Nacen undone, but some nagging feeling in the back of Nacen's mind told him that Folbix would have little problem in simply leaving the system if Nacen missed his deadline. Yes, the truth was still his best way out.

"I am the captain of a lone, Cutlass-class trade frigate, the *Lusterhawk*. Aside from my druvani here, I have one other bodyguard and only three house-hold troops planetside. We arrived on Carnizad via our light scouter, the *Carmine Canotila*."

"Not much for a recovery team." Basaul shared a grim smile with Chalce. "Not that there's much to recover. As we speak, half of my men are going back to the capital ship. We've located your shuttle and should be within range to tie it down shortly with our compressor fields. You can be much more helpful in rebuilding the guild."

Nacen's back stiffened. "We're not here to help you pick up the piec-es of your guild on this dying world. We are here to recover House Drovina's beacon and leave."

"I don't give a dram who you are or where you came from. You're here now, on my rock. You'll do as I say."

Nacen had become more aware of the steam clouding the room. His skin was becoming sticky and moist. The Armads seemed to be immune to the humidity or at least gave no sign that it bothered them.

"Surely we can work out some contract other than enslavement. I say again, I am Nacen Buhari. My father has been the elected steya for several cycles now. We merged with all the families of the house that day, not to rule but to guide."

"It seems to me that your family has merged with what's left of my king-dom now, here in the rubble and the earth." Basaul beckoned at the chamber around him, littered with the salvage of the capital ship.

"What are you doing here? Surely the Extrata guild's presence was much more significant than a few tunnels," Nacen asked, trying to keep the moral high ground.

Basaul puffed up a bit at this. "Our guild hall, despite being fortified and far below the surface, was struck in the bombardment that destroyed most of your Starkin ships while they were still at harbor."

"How did you manage to survive the Unity's attack?" Nacen asked. The empire was generally known by whatever acronym was fancied in the part of quickspace you found yourself in, though their democratic sensibilities balked at the notion of empire. Federation of Worlds, Union of Planets and Planetoids, Dominion of Unified Mankind and Beyond... each acronym was dumber than the last. Nacen tended to call them by the name adopted by most planets convinced to join their fold: the Union Precept, or U.P. for short. Often he and other traders simply called them the Unity, or Unies, though generally not to their faces.

"You mean the Conglomerate? We got lucky," Basaul stated. "We were surveying one of our deeper mines, far away from the direct bombardment that split open the crust and destroyed much of your grounded fleet."

There it was again, the qualification of a fraction of the whole fleet. How much of the house had been destroyed here? It was difficult to tell accurately from an orbital scan. Much of the destruction had been from Unity wreckage as well. Now would be a good time to satiate his curiosity.

"A tragedy for both of our families, to be sure. The eminent guild hall of Extrata brought low. Our entire fleet, destroyed. There are undoubtedly other cargo ships that survived, but with the loss of the homefleet... they'll eventually need to consolidate into other houses, if they're lucky enough to be given the chance. It seems far more likely that the Union Precept, or Conglomerate as you call them, will pick us off," Nacen said sternly.

Basaul tilted his head to the side and frowned. "Your homefleet isn't destroyed. Your father's carrier... what do you call them? Worldships? One of those, and no more than one hundred smaller craft. But plenty escaped through the star tunnel. Why do you think the Gloms did such a poor job cleaning up here? Their navy left in a big hurry, as soon as they were sure of the complete destruction of your capital ship. They made planetfall, cleared it out, and took off."

It was Nacen's turn to look puzzled. "They left? How'd they manage that?" Nacen's heart fluttered and his mind buzzed with questions. Some of the family *still lived*. "Who led them, where did they—"

Basaul raised a heavy hand. "We may be living under a rock, but we've been busy. I will show you what we discovered, but only because knowledge will not liberate you. Soon your friends will be our captives as well. We will need your Starkin nanite technology to help us rebuild some of the more intricate infrastructure of our world."

"My last orders to them were to hold their position and only move to evade capture. We are willing to help you to some extent, but we cannot stay long. The news of some of the homefleet's survival is a tremendous relief to us." Nacen shared a look with Camlo, and in his cousin's eyes he saw the joy he knew was in his own. "Please, tell us, how many Stevari managed to escape?"

Basaul glanced at Camlo, then back to Nacen and gave a grunt. "The Gloms ambushed three worldships here at Carnizad, along with a large flotilla of trade craft and supporting strike craft. Many managed to escape through the system's quickspace tunnel."

"This is... astounding. Thank you for sharing this with us," Nacen said enthusiastically. If they could get back to the *Lusterhawk*, they could search for the other beacons. The fact that they had not detected any was not encouraging, however. "But why was the Unity, the Gloms, gunning for the *Asura*? It is larger and more populous than many of our major worldships, but it doesn't explain why the Precept navy attacked us with such unrestrained vehemence."

"I know only what our few remaining orbital relays showed us," Basaul said. "Best to perish such thoughts from your minds. What's done is done. Now we rebuild."

Nacen shook his head and felt a few beads of sweat from the steamy room shake free. "Forgive me for saying so, but your priorities are all off. This world is dying. Atmospheric content contains a high amount of sulfur, which is rising by the hour. Magma flows have covered a substantial portion of the surface, and don't tell me you haven't been detecting the massive tremors."

"This world isn't dying," Basaul scoffed. "The increased volcanic activity has merely given us access to more resources. The environment is changing, sure. But we were made for extreme environments. We will rebuild Extrata, and one day again the guild here will thrive."

"You're right, it's not dying. It's already dead, and you will be too if you don't get out of here." Nacen extended a finger toward the chamber beyond. Nacen had not seen any female Armads, which was a very bad sign for them, as they generally ran the show. A show of his own knowledge could be what he needed to intimidate the Armads. "From what I've seen, you don't have the necessary manpower..."

Nacen's onslaught was halted by the Armad's fist pounding on the table. "You think yourself better off? If the Conglomerate wished, your homefleet could be dust! Do not speak of *my* fate, for it is at least in my hands."

"How many men do you have? I've seen nearly no more than a dozen," Nacen countered. "How long do you expect to survive here on your own? You seek to lose yourself in daily tasks of rebuilding. Don't you see your world has already crumbled? It's time to move on."

"He has a point," Chalce spoke up beside Nacen, putting an end to his reticence. "We could rebuild our ships and get out of the system with the help of these Starkin. Establish our guild on another world, or perhaps merge—"

"Do not listen to the honeyed tongue of this pirate," Basaul rumbled. "He and his band were here to steal what's now rightfully Extrata property."

"Property of your guild?" It was all Nacen could do to not laugh aloud. He managed to allow only a slight puffing up of his sternum. "How successful would your guild be without our trade?"

"Enough. Your words are nothing more than the dust that clouds our passage."

Nacen took a step forward and clenched his fists. Any thoughts of restraining his anger fled along with his hopes of negotiation. "My troops will make gravel of your men if you try to hold us down."

"That's enough," Basaul said firmly. His brooding eyes were locked onto the table, though the projections were currently off. "Chalce, take them back to their cell. Inform me when we have the Starkin scout ship and the remaining crew in custody."

He felt a powerful grip around his forearms from behind. The negotiations wrapped up with more than a few protests by Nacen and Camlo, which were duly countered by aggressive prods and pushes by their Armad captors and their mustard yellow flux drivers. Though the Armad design of the portable rail gun appeared much cruder, Nacen was sure that the core principle of speeding up projectiles with a power magnetic accelerator was identical and would kill him just the same. The Armad gun itself might even function well as a club. Soon, the pair of Stevari found themselves back inside their small cage within the prison chamber of the Armads' warren. Nacen tried one last attempt as the door rattled shut.

"Wait, surely you see reason here. You said it yourself!" Nacen gasped, exasperated. "You can get off this planet and find a more prosperous world!"

"It's not for me to decide. It was not my place to have said anything." Chalce turned to exit the room with two other Armad guards.

"But—"

Nacen's only answer was the slam of the vertical slats of the chamber door.

"Kaha!" Nacen swore as he kicked the door of the cell. A jolt traveled up his leg and gave him a painful and surprising shock. He suppressed any further profanity. "Enough wasting time, we're getting out of here."

"Are Beskin, Jeta, and 'Nak going to come rescue us?" Camlo asked.

"We're not waiting for the crew. You heard Basaul. Half their men are tunneling around trying to entrap the *Canotila*. Even if our crew could overpower them and rescue us at tremendous risk, they've already done us one better. They've pulled away some of the Armads down here."

"There weren't many to begin with." Camlo nodded slowly.

"I know the unlock pattern for the main gate, maybe they use the same one for all their doors here. Let's get this cell open. We may not need the regulators from the plasma carbines. There are some adaptive control systems in your artificial right arm that could do the job if we hook them up to the lock."

"Uh, sure, whatever I can do to help." Despite his assurance, Camlo hesitated a moment. "Just… try to minimize the shocking."

"Don't worry, we should be able to remove them first. Just have a seat." Nacen laughed. He bent over Camlo's right arm of tungsteel rods and silichrome plating all the way from the shoulder to the hand. They lacked the technology on the small trade ship to regenerate it, so his cousin had to make do with the replica arm that their engineers on the *Lusterhawk* had put together. Nacen had never asked Camlo exactly what had happened in the firefight on the asteroid trade port in which he lost the arm, mostly due to guilt from having him posted there alone to begin with. He may not even remember the experience, having been passed out with nearly a third of his blood missing when Nacen and the crew had found him.

"Sometimes I miss the original." Camlo flexed the fingers of his ersatz hand. "The sensations this one provides don't match up right with my left arm. All the best soft feelings: grass, silk, skin… they all feel dull… like chalk."

"I'm sorry to hear that." Nacen said, tinkering with the plates on Camlo's hand. "But you helped save people."

"Yeah, but not good enough. A lot of people still died."

"That's not your fault. Rogue Unity soldiers killed those people. Sometimes your best has to be enough. There, got it." Nacen pulled out a white chip from behind Camlo's metal tricep analogue. The fingers on the metal hand went limp.

"Camlo looked at his hand and gave it a few shakes. "Same to you, Nace."

"What?"

"What happened here isn't your fault." Camlo looked up from his list-less limb. "If we *were* here with your father, then we'd probably have gone down with the *Asura*, too. Don't beat yourself up about it. We'll set things right."

Nacen smiled despite himself. Nacen offered Camlo a hand to help him up. Camlo went for it, but his fingers dangled uselessly. Camlo chuckled.

"Right." He gave Nacen his left hand and the captain hoisted him up. As Camlo rose, the ground trembled slightly. Nacen waited until it ceased, then placed the white chip next to the door lock. Not being able to connect to his ship's network, Nacen was limited in his capacity to alter the chip. He carefully keyed in the sequence for test mode, and the chip began reacting to the cage's circuit. Nacen frowned. The Stevari technology was flexible, but it had its limits. He desperately wished he had access to a terminal from the *Carmine Canotila*, or his digital pad to interface with. But the Armads had taken the tool along with their plasma carbines.

"There's something I've been curious about," Camlo wondered aloud. "How come we haven't been able to pick up the other beacons? We should be detecting them, especially across a couple of quickspace passages."

"Maybe the Unity found a way to jam or alter the signal. Or maybe, even worse, they managed to figure out how to track it. That would explain why they were able to corner the *Asura* here at Carnizad."

Camlo kicked the ground. "How are we going to find out where the homefleet is?"

"We'll figure it out. They're not likely to go into Union Precept space, so that only leaves a couple of options from here. I'm sure we could find some clues. Maybe hack into those observation relays the Armads have."

Another tremor, significantly more powerful, reverberated across the chamber. Several rocks and a few puffs of dust were knocked loose.

"Woah." Camlo glanced at the door. "Do you think Beskin and the crew are trying to rescue us after all?"

"I gave them strict orders not to."

"So, that's a maybe?" Camlo asked hopefully.

Nacen regained his balance and strode to the door. "It must be a quake or tectonic shifting or something as a result of all the damage to the planet."

Behind him, Nacen could hear Camlo pacing. He allowed a test current to pass through the chip and made a few adjustments.

"What, you don't trust me?" Nacen turned back around and grinned, expecting the door to slide open as he did so. When he heard nothing, he whirled around and examined the arm's chip again. He tapped in the sequence to change from test mode to power mode. The command signal to open was still off.

"Well, sure, but sometimes—"

The door slid open with a crash, and Nacen pumped a fist in triumph.

"I'll never question you again," Camlo said. "Now let's get out of here."

"Certainly." Nacen grabbed the chip and strolled out of the cell toward the iron door, his druvani close behind. He felt another slight tremor. "Now, don't feel the need to agree with me *all* the time. I do value dissenting opinion as well. In fact, it's often crucial when—"

Nacen nearly jumped out of his armor when he heard the turning of the gears of the big door in front of them that heralded its opening. He placed the chip on the nearest cell door's enclosed lock, and it popped open as the cage's powerful currents were channeled through the chip to provide the necessary command. Thankfully, it had been the same as the last lock's. The iron jaws of the main door were beginning to open.

"Quick, get in!"

"What are you—"

Nacen grabbed Camlo by his recast armor's collar and dragged him into the cell, following him closely behind. He snatched up the control chip and palmed it as the doors opened. Nacen, his heart racing, was surprised to see the charcoal skinned Basaul enter, with the huge Armad known as Chalce beside him. Slowly and deliberately, Basaul approached the cell. Chalce shot confused looks between Nacen's current place of captivity and the cell further down the row. He opened his mouth, but it was the overseer who spoke first.

"As much as it pains me to say it, Starkin... you are right." The Armad's scarred face did not betray any emotion, but nevertheless, his words carried sincerity. "We cannot stay here. Carnizad's deteriorating state aside, we have far too few men to rebuild the guild's infrastructure here. Forget iron alloys and microchips... we'll be out of food soon."

"These are difficult things to admit, surely. It takes a big man to admit when he is wrong." Chalce crossed his arms and Nacen fumbled at his choice of words. "...erm, what will your next course of action be?"

"We shall take our best ship and fly further into the Prominar Rim. Extrata has allies. We will make do."

Despite his newfound direction, the Armad still seemed crestfallen. Nacen wondered if it had to do with the loss of his guild here. Would it be difficult to rebuild on another planet?

"So, you will let us go?" Nacen asked.

"Indeed," Basaul said. "We have no quarrel with House Drovina."

Nacen gave a look of surprise. His words clearly must have had some effect on the Armad leader. Or perhaps he was simply the first to state the concerns, bringing voice to the issues that Basaul and his underlings had stubbornly refused to acknowledge.

"We wish you only the best. Will you tell us through which quickspace passage the homefleet retreated?

"Of course," Basaul began, "to ensure cooperation, we will give you the information you seek once we have departed this world."

The Stevari captain frowned. This was not exactly a step in the right direction. But then, Nacen couldn't blame the man for being overly cautious. The sentiment seemed to come from a desire to prevent future conflict. Nacen would play along.

"Very well," Nacen said plainly. Then, an idea struck. Further cooperation was a long shot, but it couldn't hurt to ask. At least, he hoped it wouldn't.

"I suppose this is where we part ways." Basaul said, unlocking the cage.

"Wait," Nacen began earnestly, "come with us."

"While I appreciate your Stevari sense of humor, our place is not among the stars."

"Our fleet has survived a long time."

"Even the assumption that they're still alive may be forlorn."

"Consider it, at least," Nacen asked sternly.

"I already have." Basaul turned to exit the chamber.

The Starkin were taken through the middle door in the main chamber, hitherto unexplored by the pair. Here, a handful of Armads were laboring around a huge bulk of a mustard yellow vehicle that could have been declared a geographical landmark in its own right. Round nodules emerged from it more like ledges and crevasses than storage compartments and drone docks. The vehicle was nearly ten meters long and twice the height of a man, if the man was a genetically enhanced super soldier. Big silichrome crates and bulging bags were being loaded into side compartments. What appeared to be six huge buckets were slung on each side of the contraption. They would do no good as wheels, so Nacen assumed they were some type of suspensor technology to counteract gravity. They would need about one hundred times as many of whatever they were to propel the monstrosity by traditional rocket propulsion.

Jutting prominently from the vehicle's front were two mandibles featuring an array of dark lenses. Nacen glanced at the dusty yellow edifice from the front to find yet more lenses, giving him the impression of a massive insect. He was sure if he had been more familiar with the technology he would find it elegant in its own right. As he still maintained both his senses of vision and style, he found the vehicle repulsive. Still, judging from the smooth walls of the cavern and the tunnel leading out one end, it seemed his only way out. Should this insectile monstrosity lead them out of the underworld, he would grow immensely more fond of it. He found Chalce, who had joined in the hubbub of loading up the beast.

"I take it this is the way out?" Nacen asked.

"Nothing gets past you," Chalce said, patting the captain's ruddy brown recast armor hard with his palm. Basaul walked to the other side of the vehicle and began issuing orders to unseen technicians.

"This seems like a crude way to reach the surface," Camlo noted.

"Crude?" Chalce scoffed. "This hauler is outfitted with a top-notch suspensor system, built-in thrusters, and a fully adjustable anti-matter field on the bow. If that sounds crude to you, you're free to grab a shovel and dig up."

Nacen was not shocked at the tech level involved but was still a little surprised. He supposed he had expected a big drill or something. He figured Camlo was silent because he was seriously considering the shovel option.

"Are we all going to fit in there with all your gear?" Nacen glanced around at the Armads still laboring around them.

"You two won't take up much space, go ahead and take a seat. Don't worry, we already loaded up your carbines and other tools." Chalce clambered up into the crew compartment from a hatch on the top. "Then again, we could shove you in with some of the crates just to be sure."

"Chalce does like his elbow room," a passing Armad added with a smile.

Nacen and Camlo picked two seats by the rear, hoping to avoid being sandwiched between two Armads. This, as it turned out, was not an issue as the transport appeared to have been made with more Armads in mind than the thirteen total remaining. After they finished loading the vehicle, the remaining crew piled in and they got underway. The hull of the vehicle shuddered intensely as the suspensor field kicked on. They felt thruster ports kick in and the whole edifice lurch forward. It lumbered through dirt and rock as if they weren't even there which, after it hit the forward anti-matter field, they effectively weren't. The speed with which it maneuvered up the dusky tunnels belied both its bulk and Nacen's grasp of physics, and soon, the group was churning their way to the surface.

Nacen tried to relax, but the hum of the suspensor buckets and annihilation of matter made this difficult. He *was* matter, after all, and both his mind and stomach took offense at what was happening out there. Compounding this anxiety was the fact that Basaul and Chalce seemed to be deeply locked in debate in the front cabin as they drove. Twice, Chalce had given a quick glance back at Nacen before turning and continuing his argument with the overseer.

Camlo leaned into Nacen's ear and spoke loudly, though he could barely hear his young cousin over the hauler's ascent. "He looks like he wants to throw us in front of this thing!"

It likely wasn't anything to be worried about. Chalce seemed one of those people who could always find something to be ornery about.

"At least it would be over quickly," Nacen said glibly. Then he sat back and closed his eyes, letting himself be buffeted around, the sound of the vehicle the only overwhelming noise.

Nacen was lurched from his meditations as the hauler burst from the ground. For a split second, he felt himself go weightless in his seat before he was slammed down. Around him, the Armads whooped and cheered their exhilaration. Nacen gave Camlo a nervous glance, but his cousin was too busy massaging his neck to pay his captain any mind. Blinding light streamed through the window slits in the driver compartment.

"What's the matter, Starscraps?" the Armad to his immediate left jeered. "Not your first ground pound, is it?!"

"Normally when we do a combat drop, we come from above, not below." Nacen shouted over the ringing in his ears, indicating a downward motion with an index finger. "And when there's an actual need to hit the surface, we use a suspensor chute and a field dampener to lessen the impact. That way we're in peak condition for combat."

"Sounds like more Starkin trinkets and more chances to fail," an Armad to their right commented. "Just give me a steel bar to grip and another to swing at the enemy!" Another round of whoops reinforced this as the pervading sentiment among the Armads.

"Gladly," Camlo grumbled into his comms so only Nacen could hear. "Let's see how that works out when we accelerate through quickspace."

As Nacen smiled, another voice spoke over the link.

"Camlo is that you?" Beskin's voice came in loud and clear in Nacen's concealed earpiece. "I've finally managed to reconnect. What are you guys doing in the middle of a crater almost four kilometers from the *Carmine Canotila*?"

"Beskin, can you hear me?" Nacen asked as soon as he was sure no Armads were looking directly at him. He spoke with minimal movements of his lips. The puppeteering skill was required of all Stevari combat troops, though

Nacen had mastered in his youth with actual puppetry, of all things. The perks of a well-rounded education.

"Yes, we're transmitting from the *Canotila*. So you successfully escaped from the Armads?"

"You could say that..." Nacen started to explain.

"More like we escaped with them," Camlo interjected.

"With them?" Beskin's puzzlement was plain.

"We convinced them that leaving Carnizad was the only rational choice left," Nacen said. "Or at least gave them the push they needed. They're taking us to the ship, then they're taking off themselves."

"In their own ship?"

Nacen shared a quick glance with Camlo.

"Presumably, yes."

"You don't know?" Beskin stammered. "Do you have your weapons at least?"

"They wouldn't do us much good, surrounded in close quarters with Armads."

"I hate to point out the obvious, Captain, but..."

Then it hit Nacen like the butt of a flux driver. Basaul's sudden change of heart, the ride up to the *Canotila*... it all seemed too easy. Beskin's intuition was right. Nacen had been so caught up in negotiating their escape that he didn't consider the fact that the Armads could renege on their promise and take their ship by deception. It was even possible they'd wanted off the planet all along, but simply didn't have the means to until the *Carmine Canotila* showed up.

"There's a possibility..." Nacen began to spell out the logical steps. "They could use us as hostages to gain access to the ship. If they simply tried to overwhelm us by force you could just fly away. Or scuttle the ship if worst came to worst."

"*Kaha*," Camlo cursed, just now catching up. "How do we get out of this?"

Nacen's mind flicked through possible solutions. Most ended up with Nacen and Camlo dead in a canyon and his ship fleeing the system, clueless as to where House Drovina had fled.

"Okay," Nacen paused to let the plan sink in. "If the Armads decide to take us as hostages and get onboard the ship, we need to play along. Don't tell anyone on the ship what's going on, we need their reactions to be genuine. Pick a new place to meet up, and set up an ambush. Give 'Nak the plasma support gun and a nice view. Have Linasette make the deal, with Jeta and yourself waiting with the storm bikes. That will put our heaviest weapons against their greater numbers."

"We left the storm bikes on the *Lusterhawk*."

Nacen cursed. "Fine, on foot."

"Okay... how many are we talking about here?" Beskin asked.

"Thirteen," Camlo replied. Nacen could hear Beskin grit his teeth even in the transmission.

"That is... far from ideal. But we can handle this."

Nacen was preparing to give a reply when he saw Chalce rise from the driver compartment and meander purposefully to the back where Nacen and Camlo were strapped in. The big man grabbed onto a safety bar and knelt down to Nacen's level.

"Alright!" Chalce shouted over the hum of the hauler. "We're en route to your ship's last known location. Tell 'em to expect us."

"Already done," Nacen said with a smirk. This was technically true, after all.

"Good." Chalce gave a quick jerk with his head. "Boss wants to see you in the front. Now."

"Of course. I'd be more than happy to oblige." Nacen unfastened his restraints, ignoring a concerned look from Camlo and a dropping sensation in his gut.

Chapter 3

The hauler, now more brown with dust than yellow, skimmed along as though Carnizad's hills and boulders were no more than sand sifting through outstretched hands. Nacen's tall frame wobbled unsteadily for a brief moment before he steadied himself on the resonating floor. Chalce led Nacen to the front of the vehicle and plopped down in the copilot seat with a mighty thud. He beckoned Nacen to stand between himself and the overseer. Chalce contented himself with looking out the side of the window, whose blast shield had retracted to reveal the now barren wasteland of Carnizad.

Basaul kept his gaze forward and his hands on the hauler's thick, rubberized steering wheel. The blasted landscape rolled past, though very little was visible past the few hundred meters directly in front of them. Though no intruding boulders nor craters were any obstacle, every few seconds Nacen had to brace himself as the craft was buffeted about by high winds. A large, yellow sun shone through the dull gray sky, its bright light diffused through choking dust.

"Down in the tunnels, we have to close the blast shields on the front windows. They would soon degrade under the high-energy stream of the solids we destroy through the anti-matter field. We go off of radar mostly, using elastic waves traveling through the ground as we dig through it. Below ground, sensors give a good approximation of our surroundings. Up here though," Basaul gestured at the front window, "we can put up the blast shields. Get a clear sense of our surroundings."

Nacen nodded, unsure of the old Armad's intent.

"I need to be sure I can trust you, Captain," Basaul said. Nacen blinked. It was the first time the Armad had referred to him by his title. "I need to know that your household troops, your... trufalci, aren't going to attack us when we get to your ship."

"Why would they?" Nacen asked.

"We've not gotten off to a good start. I apologize for that. The situation has been... tense, to put it mildly."

"Well, rightfully so," Nacen admitted. "The U.P.'s plans for annihilation very nearly came to fruition."

"Regardless, I know it is suspicious that we are taking you to your ship. I will level with you, we're in a bit of an awkward place. Our guild's hangar bays were destroyed in the bombardment. I suppose the bigger surprise would be that there was anything left of Extrata to salvage at all. We need a ship to get off the planet."

"You'll not succeed in taking mine," Nacen said defiantly. It was time to stand his ground. He crossed his arms, but was forced to grasp Chalce's seat as the hauler lurched to the left from a stiff flurry of wind.

Basaul took his eyes off the route ahead for a moment and looked at Nacen with wide eyes. The Armad's deep scars resembled dark canyons on the Armad's suddenly sunlit face. "You... you thought we were planning on taking your ship by force?!" He unleashed a raucous laugh. "You Starkin are too much entirely..."

"Well, we figured if you took us as hostages, you would force my crew to give up the ship," Nacen ventured.

"Now there's an idea," Basaul mused, feigning a mock interest by stroking his chin. "No. No doubt even if such a plan were to succeed, you Starkin would have a host of traps and surprises waiting for us around and within your ship. There has been enough bloodshed of our kind these last few days to last until the blue sun dies. We need to—"

A bright beam of light flashed across the front window.

"What was that?" Chalce leaned forward, trying to get a better view of the surrounding landscape.

Nacen ducked and braced himself in the tight doorway. There were only a few things that could have been, none of them good.

"Solar flare?" Basaul offered.

The hull of the vehicle rang with a metallic crack, and the hauler skidded to the right. Basaul strained against the wheel as it bucked and spun in his iron grip. He managed to regain control just as another blow collided with the hauler. The vehicle swerved, and Basaul briefly lost control of the wheel. By the time he wrested it back, Nacen felt his stomach turn. The outside landscape swirled and the darkening sky flew away, turning to flat earth as the hauler careened. Nacen fell to the floor, wrapping his arms protectively around his head. In a moment, it was over. The cabin lay still.

Nacen breathed. He was alive. That was always a good start. The ringing of the hull meant whatever struck them had to be a solid projectile. Given the effect it had on the Armad hauler, it had to be big. Perhaps a heavy flux cannon, or some other slug or rail gun weaponry. The flux cannon operated on the same principle as the flux driver, but used a larger and faster projectile.

"We're under fire! Everyone out, now!" Basaul roared to the cabin. Then he turned, flabbergasted, to Nacen. "This isn't you, is it?"

Nacen stood, shaking his head, and stepped to the side just before Chalce plowed through and clambered up the ladder in the rear.

"Everyone up and over!" Chalce bellowed. "Take up arms and establish a perimeter!"

"It's not my ship or crew. We have nothing groundside that could do this." Nacen's face was white as he tapped at his earpiece. He couldn't connect to any of the *Carmine Canotila's* communication channels. The best case was that they were being jammed. The worst case was he no longer had a ship to connect *to*.

"Go work with Chalce to defend the hauler," Basaul said. "I'll stay inside to run diagnostics and repairs. I'll let everyone know when to pile back in."

"Do I get any say as captain?"

"Captain of what? A ship that can't help us? My rock, my rules."

Another beam lashed out against the cliff the vehicle had collided with, and earth sprinkled onto the roof.

"There are those who would contend that."

"Well, go change their minds." Basaul turned back to his controls.

Swallowing his bitterness, Nacen returned to the crew cabin. He had had quite enough of the Armads giving him orders, though he contented himself that he would act the same regardless. He withdrew his pan-atmo mask, thankfully undamaged from Chalce ripping it prior, from its pouch on his belt and strapped it over his face. The synth-leather sealed itself with the press of a button on the rear strap. His hand subconsciously grazed his digital pad and was also thankful it had been returned intact.

He found the hauler empty now, save for Camlo poised eagerly on the ladder. The captain nodded and followed up behind his druvani. He gripped the ladder, all too aware of his lack of a firearm. He saw Camlo disappear over the top and moved up. He paused, not wanting to jump out until whatever gun had taken out the hauler fired again, which appeared to be fairly slow.

Slowing his breathing and looking up at the red sky through the hatch, Nacen waited. After a few seconds, an explosion sent a smattering of dirt over the hauler, some sprinkling down into the hatch. Nacen hefted himself up and ran across the top of the hauler, staying low. He hopped deftly down to the cracked earth where a half dozen Armads were clustered around the vehicle. The ravine was perhaps the height of three men at its deepest. The scar in the earth ran from the large gap the hauler was stuck in now to beyond Nacen's obscured sight. He hoped there was some way out of the ravine, or else all of their efforts to repair the hauler would be in vain. Suspensor fields could perform miracles but could not carry the hauler up a sheer cliff face.

"Get the rest of the guns out and get in position!" Chalce shouted, towering over the others.

"The compartment won't open," one of the Armads moaned.

"It must have been jammed in the crash," another added.

"Excuses won't save your useless hides." Chalce raised his compressor gun, and the Armads ducked to either side. With a loud hum, the compartment crumpled and flew five meters from the hauler.

As the Armads snatched up their hefty flux drivers and mass condensers, clearing the area one after another, Nacen saw that one of the big suspensor buckets had taken a direct hit. It was quick thinking that Basaul had managed to get the vehicle into the ravine and away from enemy fire. That or luck.

Nacen's attention snapped to the ridge to the east, where an explosive shell collided with the edge and showered the bottom of the ravine in fragments of hot clay. That was no rail gun. The trajectory from the sky could only mean mortars. If they stayed here, they were doomed. An Armad shoved a hefty flux driver in Nacen's face. He eyed the ugly, drab block of a firearm with reluctance.

"The only way I'm going to hit anything with this is swinging it like a club. You must have my plasma rifle in there somewhere. Keeping looking." Behind him, Chalce was placing the Armads into position around the bottom of the ravine, perfectly aligned to be taken out by a single mortar round. "Fine, that'll do," Nacen said. He grabbed the weapon and reached down to his boot, retrieving a thin vibro-knife from the sole.

"Hey, I don't remember giving you any knife," the Armad protested.

"Well, I don't remember you taking it away from me, so I guess we're even," Nacen grinned as Camlo snatched another flux driver from the man, and the two ran to the edge of the ravine. The Armad scratched his head before joining his two crewmates in extracting the mangled suspensor from the vehicle.

"Don't be too pleased with yourself over a knife, Captain," Camlo chided.

"Why's that, Cam?" Nacen asked quizzically. Rarely did the younger druvani criticize his actions.

A wan smile grew from Camlo's solemn expression. He gave a furtive glance down to his hip, where he revealed a string of the plasma grenades under his cloak.

"Where'd you hide those?" Nacen asked, impressed.

"Starkin, glad you could join us," Chalce thundered at the approaching pair. "Get to the far end of the canyon before the enemy arrives. With luck though, we'll have the hauler mobile before that happens."

"Lady Luck and I aren't on speaking terms right now." Nacen shook his head. "Even if we got the hauler up and running, we could be more easily dispatched coming out of the ravine than the first time. We need to defend the hauler from without, and take out whatever heavy weapon did that to us in the first place."

"No, we stay and defend. We can't just abandon it."

Another mortar round struck farther down the ravine.

"Hear that?" Nacen pointed to the offending blast. "That's mortar fire. If any one of those lands here, or even a couple of grenades when the enemy closes in, we're as good as dead. Fish in a barrel can at least swim around."

"So what do you propose?" Chalce asked.

"An ambush for an ambush."

Chalce glanced up and down the ravine, pondering this.

"Fine. We'll send out gun drones to deploy a smokescreen and spread out, five meters between each man."

"Make it ten,"

"Don't push me, Starkin." Chalce pushed a finger to his right ear. "Change in plans. We're going up and over."

Nacen tried out his encrypted channel and found the jamming could not block his short-range bursts. He set his comm link to scan and jumped onto the Armads' frequency. There was a host of grumbling. Nacen and Camlo ran to the south side of the small ravine where no Armads had been stationed. They found a path suitable for a short, easy climb, shouldered their weapons with thick straps, and waited. The Unity, if indeed this was the Unity, had to be getting close by now. Were they too late? No, now was not the time to question. They had a plan, they would stick to it.

The gun drones soared overhead, barely visible and completely silent in the blowing dust. A moment after they cleared the ridge, white streaks filled the dusty sky and blossomed out into a thick curtain of smoke.

"Up and over!" Chalce bellowed. Nacen winced, and his ear drums throbbed in pain. The comm link had not been necessary.

The flux drivers swayed heavily on their straps as Nacen and Camlo made their way up, threatening to throw off the duo's balance, but they glided smoothly. One handhold to the next, without breaking pace. Sweat matted

Nacen's forehead and clung to his robes, both from the exertion of scaling the ridge and the sweltering heat.

Nacen had crested the lip of the canyon. The ground shook. This was not enemy mortar fire, but another quake. Nacen heard a cry from behind and turned to see Camlo lose his balance as he swung over the ridge. Nacen darted to the lip of the ravine and thrust out his hand, not caring if he would tumble down himself. Camlo's metallic hand fastened around Nacen's hand of flesh and bone. Straining, his hand feeling as though it were being crushed in a vice, Nacen helped his cousin clamber over the ridge.

"Thanks, Nace," he breathed out between short breaths. "Here I thought I was supposed to be *your* bodyguard."

"Don't forget to repay the favor, then." Nacen staggered to his feet.

The pair ran through the obscuring haze, careful not to trip over any rock or crack in the ground. Boulders emerged through the smoke. Nacen darted behind a ridge, and Camlo went left. They stayed still. Dust mingled with smoke and settled on their cloaks. Nacen scoured the landscape to the left and then the right. A dark figure moved through the smoke, keeping low and silent.

The figure drifted through the haze like a pale ghost, its armor covered in ash. As it neared, Nacen noted the slit of a front visor running across the front of the round helm, above a recessed lower face guard. With that helmet, it could have emerged here in this blasted canyon from epochs-old pages of history, had it not also been carrying a plasma rifle in chalky, ashen gauntlets. These were indeed Union Precept forces: lance troops, by the look of their kit. They must have been sent here to ensure there were no survivors among the wreckage.

Hefting his heavy firearm, Nacen leaned fully out from the protection of the ridge. The trooper's head swiveled, and darted toward cover. Nacen's flux driver barked as he snapped off four rounds, ensuring the trooper never reached it. He collapsed, cloak still fluttering in the smoke. The sharp snaps of magnetic discharges echoed down the line, followed by bellowed orders. The smokescreen lit up a shimmering blue as lances of plasma cut through in reply.

Distant figures revealed themselves by their rapid discharge of plasma. Nacen picked the closest one, fired off a few shots, and moved on to the next as his target faded into the smoke. Whether they were alive or dead, he could not be certain. He knew only to keep firing. This was where they needed to be, Nacen thought: close to the Unity's troops. The lance troopers could not unleash their mortars here without risk of hitting their own men.

Nacen's next shot, aimed at a ghostly figure attempting to outflank to the west, sent out crackling bolts of energy as it failed to connect with its target. His next volley, perfectly sent to hit the trooper's chest, likewise fizzled against the invisible wall. The Unies must have deployed shield drones. The small white robots would be practically invisible in these conditions.

A plasma beam struck the rock in front of Nacen, and his vision flashed white. His pan-atmo mask's lenses dimmed to prevent him from being blinded, but he felt a searing pain across his face and pulled back behind what little cover that the rook formation provided. Nacen held there a moment, waiting for his vision to recover, when a scream from the other side of the rock stirred him to action. Nacen whirled back around, fully expecting to take a plasma shot, but saw the trooper who had closed the distance drop his weapon. His armor was dented, with more dents popping into existence with every second. The trooper's limbs convulsed in agony, bending and snapping at obscene angles. Finally, the chest armor was crushed past recognition, and the screams were silenced as the twisted form tumbled into the dust.

An Armad strolled into Nacen's vision, swinging his mass condenser as he strode forward. He surveyed the trooper's body and frowned. The Armad brought the huge rim of the barrel down on the trooper's helmet, shattering the visor. After inspecting the trooper further, he smiled to himself and looked up at Nacen.

"No need to worry, they're falling back all along the ridge," the Armad assured him. "Chalce is ordering us back to the hauler."

Nacen's stupor from what he had just witnessed wore off. "Oh, *kaha*."

"What? We won!"

"No, they're just making space so they can clear us out with their mortars. We have to follow them."

"Well, I'm following orders," the Armad replied.

"Camlo, on me," Nacen said.

"The Armads are falling back, Nacen," Camlo said from behind.

"Right, and we're going forward." Nacen clenched his jaw in irritation. Camlo started to turn away but stopped when he noticed Nacen was serious. Shrugging at the Armad, Camlo followed after the captain wordlessly. They cleared the smokescreen, and Nacen glanced at what he thought was an enemy but was merely the lifeless hull of one of the Armads' gun drones.

"Chalce, listen to me," Nacen spoke over the short-range comms link, "I believe the Unies are falling back to make use of artillery. We need to stick close so they don't have the opportunity to use it, at least until the hauler is fixed. I'm maintaining comms silence for now. Buhari out."

"How'd you get on this channel, Starscum?" Chalce grumbled in Nacen's ear.

Nacen turned back to Camlo and flashed the hand signals to indicate they go silent until contact with the enemy is made. They climbed over steep ledges and around great pillars, keeping low to the ground.

"Maybe you misheard. I'll talk slowly for ya. Now, how'd you—" Chalce's demand was cut off as Nacen severed his link to the Armad channel.

Behind them the ground shook, and Nacen heard an enormous blast. Chips of rock showered down around him. This was no quake, but an artillery barrage. Three more explosions rang out, even further back. They had to keep moving, Armads or no.

Nacen and his druvani continued their laborious slog across the uneven ground. He stared into the whipping dust storm down the sights of his flux driver, keeping alert for movement. In his fear, his mind dared them to emerge and end the eerie silence dominating all but the howling wind. Eventually, the thunder of howitzers became louder than the barrage behind them. Nacen steadied himself on a ledge he had just scaled and peered over. He could just make out the end of a howitzer's massive barrel over a nearby rock formation. A second later, the ground shook and Nacen saw the air blur with a discharge of heat. Another howitzer sounded in the distance, very close to the first. Nacen counted fifteen lance troopers milling around the guns. They were outnumbered, that was certain, and that was only counting the troopers Nacen could see.

He turned back to Camlo, who looked up at him through his pan-atmo mask with eager eyes. Nacen gestured that two heavy weapons and over fifteen hostiles lay over the ridge. Camlo's only gesture was to ready his flux driver. Nacen grinned behind his mask.

Nacen returned to his surveying of the battlefield. Then, a subtle movement caught his attention, far to his right, barely within the confines of his sight. It was large, some sort of heavy weapon platform. The barrel was too low to the ground and too long to be another howitzer. Could this be what had disabled the hauler?

Turning back to Camlo, Nacen signaled with his hands that he had spotted another enemy to the right and wanted to investigate. Camlo returned his intent to follow. All they needed now was some sort of distraction. They could be easily spotted as soon as they moved over the ledge sheltering them.

Prime plasma grenades, over that formation to our right, Nacen signed. Camlo began turning the grenades at his waist, but he stopped and gripped his gun when they heard weapon discharges over the ridge. It was the snap of flux projectiles, followed by the hiss of plasma discharge. Nacen smiled. The Armads had followed. All they had needed was hard evidence that Nacen's hypothesis had been correct. Hard, sharp evidence. Hopefully next time they would be more eager to follow. Nacen swung over the ridge and jumped behind the nearest boulder. He stole a glance and saw nearly two dozen troopers running to oppose the Armads' attack. Hopefully there would *be* a next time.

He ignored the opportunities he had for several clean kills and kept advancing to the rise on his right. There was now no indication that the enemy had set up on the hill, but he knew what he had seen. And if he was wrong, he could always use the location as a crow's nest to fire on the lance troopers below.

The howitzers had stopped pounding now, their crews having picked up small arms to defend their weapon platforms. Nacen had a hard time spotting the Armads in the dust and rock, but he did see the crushed figures of dead lance troopers. He had to admit, he was impressed. The Armads' mass condensers were proving extraordinarily effective at close range.

The ground quaked, and several rocks tumbled free from the incline. Some of the large ones, bigger than Nacen's head, smashed on the ground below. It would be quite a fall if he lost his grip or slipped on the treacherous slope. He confirmed Camlo was close behind and turned back to focus on the task at hand. He maneuvered his way around the hill, and his view of the battlefield disappeared, as well as his fears of being shot in the back.

Though Nacen could no longer witness them, the constant background of shouts and gunshots still permeated the ash-choked valley below. With one precarious handhold at a time, they ascended the rise, until they peered over the crest. The top was a twisted mass of rocks which had created several winding gullies across the hill. At the far end lay another rise. A massive flux cannon rested behind the hill's crest, its crew of five troopers tending to the weapon and adjusting its aim with tedious care. It was pointed up and over Nacen's head. He guessed it was aimed at the ravine where the hauler was undergoing repairs, no doubt waiting for it to emerge. These men and women fought on, the watchmen left behind to ensure none escaped the graveyard that Carnizad had become. Nacen swore to make sure that they wouldn't either.

"Okay, Camlo, listen up." Nacen knelt down by his cousin. "You're going to flank to the right. Be sure to stay out of sight of the crew. I'll flank left. We're far enough away from the main battle, and the Armads are on the opposite side of the howitzers anyway, so with any luck we won't be spotted. When you give the signal, we'll both storm over that last rise and take out the platform's crew."

"What's my signal?" Camlo asked. Nacen tapped at the string of five grenades at Camlo's hip. Camlo raised his eyebrows. "Oh. Got it."

"See you on the other side," Nacen nodded and stepped down, ensuring he was completely out of sight of the big rail gun's crew. A glance back confirmed Camlo had disappeared around the other side. He made his way around the hill more slowly than he wanted, being careful not to slip. Navigating laterally along the steep slope proved just as difficult as scaling up.

As he made his way along, he considered the state of things to avoid the recurring thoughts about being shot in the back. Assuming Camlo and he could destroy the cannon, they could rally with the Armads and fall back to the hauler. By then, they could board and be moving too quickly for the howitzers to reliably target them, then escape Carnizad. This was assuming the Armads were still alive when Camlo and he destroyed the weapon platform.

Nacen reached the top of the hill and laid against the ridge where he knew the weapon platform was deployed just mere steps on the other side. He could even make out voices and footsteps. The hurried voices reminded Nacen of his own allies in the valley below. He switched on his earpiece, already tuned in on the Armad's channel.

"...everyone back in the hauler, it's as fixed as it's ever going to get," a voice boomed over the comm link. This had to be Basaul.

For a moment, the voices increased in volume, and Nacen thought he had been found out, but he reassured himself they would not have heard the small speaker in his ear.

"We've got a long run back, Basaul," Chalce replied, "and the Gloms are still packing some major artillery. It's gonna be costly. The Starscum are definitely dead, too."

Nacen opened his mouth to protest over the channel but realized the weapons crew might hear him, close as he was. It would have to wait. Where was Camlo, so they could take this weapon out? He began to anticipate the grenades, so that every moment was charged with a disappointing anxiety.

"Damn, too bad. That'll be hard to explain to his crew," Basaul said. "Any other casualties?"

"Yeah, Gabro got nailed by a howitzer round. Kimber took a plasma beam to the chest. We have five more wounded, but you know us... still fighting."

"Damn," Basaul cursed, significantly more vigor palpable in his tone than when he had learned about Nacen and Camlo. "Hold on, I'm coming to get you."

"Copy. We'll ease off on the Gloms and play safe 'til you get here."

In the distance, Nacen heard a thunderous roar. This was no natural denizen of the wastes of Carnizad, but the now-active suspensor buckets and anti-matter field of the Armad hauler. Nacen pictured it hovering ponderously over the side of the ravine.

Over the ravine. Into sight of the flux cannon, assuming the dust could not completely obscure it. Even so, they could triangulate its position based on the sounds it emitted, surely. He couldn't wait much longer. With or without Camlo he was going over the ridge. A lance trooper shouted, and Nacen heard the cannon groan as it was eased into a new position.

Kaha. He had to move. Now.

With slow and deliberate movements, he slid the barrel of his flux driver over the rock he lay against and brought his head up. Five lance troopers manned the cannon. Their sleek, white armor transformed them into simple playthings of war. These were not men and women, but toys to be filled with hatred and bullets. He took aim at the nearest crewman, but his finger hesitated on the trigger. Something had landed at the foot of the trooper. The woman did not notice, captivated by something on her screen. Nacen's eyes widened and he ducked back behind the crest of the hill.

"Fire!" he heard the woman shout. But it was not the end of the rail gun's barrel that erupted.

A chain of explosions split the air and turned the hilltop into a blaze of brilliant light. The temperature of the air around him, already stifling hot, briefly became that of a stellar core. Bits of rock wedged themselves in Nacen's armor and tore through his cloak. After he convinced himself he still had all of his limbs, Nacen swept over the crest.

Three figures lay in the rocks, now mostly scorched to black. They stirred, and Nacen put a flux round through the helmet of the nearest. The second was crawling toward the weapon platform, and Nacen put the trooper down. The third was now leveling a plasma pistol straight at Nacen. He turned to put the trooper in his sights, but the trooper's faceplate exploded as a flux round exited their head from behind. Camlo rose from the opposite edge and fired two shots into something or someone Nacen couldn't see.

"Yes! Take that!" Camlo shouted.

Nacen did not share in Camlo's revelry. The only satisfaction he would take today was getting off this planet. Anything else was just an obstacle for him to destroy or, better yet, evade.

"Do not revel in the removal of pawns from the board, Cam. They merely do their duty. Rather, keep your mind on the game." Nacen crouched to inspect the cannon. Bits of rock continued to rain down across the hilltop.

"Yeah, you're welcome." Camlo sighed and kicked the body of the nearest trooper who still grasped the pistol. "The plasma grenades didn't harm these guys too much."

Nacen decided not to belabor the point now.

"They did superficial damage to the cannon, as well. I suppose we'll be okay as long as there's no one left to man it," Nacen said.

"Well, then I've got bad news," Camlo said with unease.

"What?" Nacen turned to see Camlo looking over the crest of the hill.

Plasma beams stabbing up from below was the only answer Nacen needed. Lance troopers were coming to wrest back control of their weapon.

"Tell me you still have a grenade we can plant inside the end of that rail gun."

"Uh... I still have a—"

"Shut it, I know you don't," Nacen bit his lip. "Use that arm of yours and see what you can do to disable it. Get creative if you have to. I'll hold them off."

"But Nace..." Camlo begin.

"That's an order." Nacen dropped to his stomach and crawled to the edge of the hill while Camlo took his spot. He keyed his earpiece, confident that making any more noise on this hilltop could not possibly worsen the situation.

"Basaul, listen up. We've secured the flux cannon. It's what disabled the hauler. You're safe to proceed."

"We're nearly there anyway, but thanks," Basaul replied over the channel. "Wait... Nacen?"

"In the flesh," Nacen peered over the edge and fired at a lance trooper nearly halfway up the slope. He ducked back as plasma beams collided with the ridge. "For now, at least."

"What's your position?" Basaul grunted and shouted something unintelligible.

"I'll tell you... he's on top of that hill," Chalce said. "That explosion was you? What in the name of the great quake are you doing up there?"

"Silencing their big gun so it doesn't put another hole in that junker of yours," Nacen said as he inched toward the ridge again. He peaked over and fired as many indiscriminate shots as he could down the slope before the plasma beams answered.

"Well, hold on as long as you can," Basaul ordered.

Nacen wasn't quite sure what to make of that. So the Armads could drive off and leave them to the Unies? Would his crew believe the sob story Basaul would surely feed them about his heroic sacrifice?

Camlo shouted at Nacen and fired his flux driver, sending a trooper to Nacen's right toppling down the hill.

Nacen backed off the ridge, falling back to Camlo and crouching behind a singed boulder.

"Nacen, I'm sorry, but I cannot disable that gun with just my hands." Camlo waved the palm of his right hand in exasperation, and Nacen could see the metal had been scuffed badly in several places.

"Well we need to do something. The U.P. are gaining ground, and we need to disable the gun before we can leave, or they'll just shoot us in the rear."

Nacen jumped at a movement and put suppressive fire over the lip of the hill. He started at the hum of the hauler's suspensor field, much louder this time. He took an instinctive step back as the flickering lenses of the hauler's front appeared above the hill, and then the rest of the enormous vehicle. Dust and rock flowed out beneath its distorted bow as the hauler heaved itself over the crest. It continued forward, driving straight into the enemy flux cannon. Its anti-matter field disintegrated the weapon platform, turning its steel alloys to vapor as easily as it did rock. The air itself shrieked. After two thirds of the weapon had been shaved off into the atmosphere, the anti-matter field flickered off and the lenses darkened.

The hatch opened, and an Armad popped up, resting a big forearm on the cupola.

"What are you waiting for? The end of the world?!" he shouted.

Nacen glanced around him. Every horizon continued to thicken with black smog as Carnizad's crust continued to split deeper by the hour.

"Doesn't look like it's too far off." He beckoned to Camlo and the two ran. At some point earlier, Nacen realized, he had dropped his gun. He did not bother to recover it. He scrambled up the side and ducked quickly into the hatch, not knowing when the Union Precept troopers would summit the hill. He and Camlo made it into the crew cabin, finding themselves surrounded by a similar site as outdoors. The Armads were covered in ash, dust, and dirt. Many carried severe burns from plasma and bleeding wounds from shrapnel. Nacen tore off his pan-atmo mask. The crowded cabin reeked far worse than the world outside, but at this point, he welcomed it.

"I never thought I'd be glad to be stuck in here with you all again!" Nacen grinned and raised his stiff arms in jubilation. Several of the Armads gave throaty cheers and stood to slap him on the back or briefly shake his hand. Most stayed in their seats, glowering at him or simply ignoring him.

The hauler lurched, and Nacen braced himself against the ladder. As Camlo belted himself back into his seat, Nacen nodded at him in satisfaction and made his way carefully to the front.

"Nacen!" Basaul greeted him with a hearty slap on his shoulder. "I hear you're more than a little responsible for us making it out back there."

"Well, my druvani and I couldn't have triumphed had your men not followed up and kept the Union Precept busy," Nacen said honestly.

"The Gloms?" Chalce scoffed, but kept his focus on the path of the hauler. "We did a lot more than keep those them busy."

"To be sure. You stood your ground and more. Much of that company won't be leaving the valley." Nacen gazed out of the window, thinking back to the twisted bodies he had seen. He never thought of facing the U.P. across a battlefield. The worst he'd experienced before now was losing a client.

"Is there any danger of them chasing us now?" Basaul asked seriously.

"Possibly," Nacen said, still gazing out into the blasted landscape. The sky was still darkening by the hour. "But if they had the capabilities to pursue us in a ship, I think they would have done so by now. Even if they had a ship, it may not be adequately armed for ground combat, or we depleted their numbers enough to the point where they do not wish to try it. In any case, we'll have to keep a sharp eye out. But I think we're in the clear for now."

"Regardless..." Basaul waved his right hand indifferently. "We made a decent team back there. What say you to making our cooperation more official?"

"What are you proposing?" Nacen wrinkled his eyebrows.

"I would pledge to continue Extrata's service to your house, but in a more militaristic capacity. I would like my engineers and techs to join your crew, Captain Buhari."

"You can't be serious." Chalce whipped around to face his boss. "This isn't what we discussed."

"Silence, Chalce. I have given this due consideration. It is our only reasonable way forward. Our fate is not on some dusty moon or begging at the feet of some lesser guild."

"They killed one of our own," Chalce pounded the dash of the vehicle, leaving a noticeable dent. "Besides, *all* our lives may be forfeit after today if we join up with their house."

Basaul shook his head slowly. "All of our lives were made forfeit with the destruction of our guild hall. How do you expect to make more Armads? Surely you see some value in assisting this Starkin in saving what's left of his house?"

"Of course," Chalce snarled. "You question my loyalty?"

"Never. But our loyalties have shifted. For now, we must follow a different path." Basaul turned in his seat to address Nacen once again. "I will listen to you and take your orders under consideration. But my men are still under my command. Are these conditions suitable to you?"

The terms were reasonable, even generous. The Armad had not asked for payment, but Nacen was sure that would come up at some point. There were a few points to clear up before any formal deal could be struck.

"Ask any of my crew, and they'll tell you I will take any idea into account in order to find the most prudent course of action. But on my ship, my word is law," Nacen said flatly. "To question my orders in battle could prove disastrous."

"Fine, fine. Now please, put aside your suspicions. Know that since we last shook hands my actions have not betrayed my word. I shall see you to your ship." Basaul extended his right hand while keeping his left firmly in control of the steering column. "Now, let's shake again on our newfound alliance."

Nacen clasped the Armad's hand, much more confident in his own grip this time. "A man's word must be like a good tree. The roots are fastened deep with a strong foundation, and the branches extend upward into the sky, into the future. My word is good."

"That's what I like to hear," Basaul said. "We'll make the announcement when we arrive at your ship. In the meantime, it might be a good idea to think about what you might want to say to your own people."

Nacen nodded and returned to his seat in a daze.

Camlo mouthed something at him that Nacen didn't catch. He keyed his earpiece surreptitiously instead of shouting back at his druvani, and spoke softly.

"I was wrong, the Armads are definitely on our side. You can stand down."

"Sounds like something you might say with a flux pistol pointed at the back of your head," Beskin suggested. Nacen couldn't tell if he was joking or not over the encrypted channel.

"You know we have signal words for that contingency. In any case, maintain your position and stand down. Greet them with smile and cheer, not bile and jeer. That goes double for 'Nak."

"Of course. Oh, and Nace. Brace yourself when you see the *Canotila*."

"Why do you say that?" Nacen asked.

There was no response.

After catching Camlo up on the situation, Nacen considered the joining of his own forces with the Armads. They would give him a measure of brute strength and numbers the Stevari crew of the *Carmine Canotila* dramatically lacked. Shadowing even this was the fact that Basaul alone held the knowledge to find the fleeing survivors. Nacen's thoughts drifted to the countless Stevari of the homefleet. Had anyone else been attacked? Were they coming to help, or were they fleeing Union Precept space even now? He had no way of knowing. He had six sisters and four brothers. At his last reunion, half of them were serving on the homefleet. His eldest brother, Zura, was certainly still at the helm of one of the great worldships. It was not Zura's temperament to cut and run but, at the behest of his father, he would do what was best for the house.

The mammoth vehicle slowed to a halt at the foot of a short cliff. The rear hatch was flung open, and the Armads piled out. Aside from the overseer, Nacen was the last to exit. He dropped down the short lip and took stock of his surroundings. They had halted at the base of a range of broad mountains. The only way up the ridge appeared to be through two narrow paths. Linasette had selected an excellent spot for an ambush, had it come to that. Nacen fell in behind the Armads and made his way up the path. The sky was still a luminous red gray, but now black billows formed in the distance. Soot or ash from volcanic activity, no doubt.

Basaul walked up and shrugged in Chalce's direction. "Chalce is my second in command. He was a very capable squad leader in the guild. I was grooming him to be overseer one day. His temper makes it difficult, but he has fire in him. He'll prove himself a fine leader yet. He shall address the crew."

Chalce stood on a small ridge overlooking the hauler. White particles of ash hung in the air around him.

"There's been a change in plans, brothers," Chalce said over the din.

"We're just dropping the Starscu... Starkin off. Ain't that right, Overseer?" one man interrupted, turning to Basaul and Nacen.

"Yeah, it's a lot easier fitting them in here than us hitching a ride with them to the hangar bay," another added.

"The hangar bay was destroyed in the bombardment, too," Chalce answered crisply. A hush fell over the Armads, which didn't last more than a couple of seconds. This was apparently news to them.

"So, what, they're dropping us off in another system?" a man guessed.

"No. We are accompanying them to find and assist the people of their fleet." His appeal was drowned by vociferous outcries. "This isn't the way I wanted it. This isn't the way the boss wants it, either. But it is the way it is, and the only way we can stay alive right now." Chalce gave Basaul more than a slight frown as he stepped off his dusty rostrum. "They'll do what you want. For now."

Basaul shifted his concern to Nacen. "That's one issue dealt with. Chalce does better when he has some semblance of control, even if he didn't make the decision." Nacen returned a shrug, unsure of how to respond to the Armad's candor. "I need to know that your trufalci aren't planning an ambush."

"My word has proven good so far, hasn't it?"

"For the most part." Basaul heaved a pack over his shoulder. "I know about your little escape attempt back at the cell block. We may favor brute force for its simple efficacy, but this does not mean we do not understand more subtle approaches."

"Oh." Nacen's eyes drifted to the ground. "To be fair, I thought you were going to enslave us."

"Our negotiations had not gone well." Basaul nodded to Nacen and the pair began marching up the path. "This is mostly my fault. I was blind to the reality of the situation."

"I admit, our presence may have been a bit suspicious," Nacen replied.

The prow of the ship could be seen as the group concluded their jaunt up the steep path. Nacen hurried over the ridge and was rewarded with a full view of the *Carmine Canotila*, his ship for better or for worse. The sleek edges of the crimson craft rose above the rock. Its curved exterior resembled the ancient waterborne order of cetaceans on long-abandoned Earth, a design with an eye toward aesthetics over function. After all, water provided infinitely more resistance than the vacuum of space.

The ship dwarfed the Armads' excavation vehicle but was moderately sized for stellar standards. The trade ship could easily hold a full squad of trufalci, a captain, his druvani, pilot, and support crew. Embedded in the compact design were cargo holds, barracks, armory, the small flight deck, even a meditation room. A rail gun was tucked away under each of the two main wings, and a rapid-fire rail gun lay beneath the rear hatch. Nacen now saw that deep plasma wounds lay in the *Canotila's* flank. Huge holes marred its surface. Even his scout ship had not escaped the final resting place of the *Asura* unscarred.

Gathered around the stern was Nacen's remaining crew. His pilot, Linasette, wore what he assumed was her formal fleet attire. It was a crisp uniform of deep, red velvet, very unlike the folded robes of the house troops. He had honestly never seen her wear it before. Her flat blonde hair lay perfectly straight beneath a red cap, just grazing her shoulders. She was pretty, beautiful even, lacking the artificially sculpted look of most Union Precept citizens. All of the standard genetic alterations from being born in the Unity were present if you knew what to look for. She had a perfect set of pearly white teeth; the small, unnaturally round ears; and eyes that became reflective in the dark. Her face, as always, was an unreadable mask of discipline.

Nacen's crew doffed their pan-atmo masks as Nacen and the Armads approached.

"Excellent placement of the ship, Lina, though we are a bit close to the volcanic activity for my liking."

"I didn't have a whole lot of options, Captain," she replied flatly. "We took many direct hits from unseen ground forces."

"We should get out of here as soon as possible. These earthquakes are escalating."

"Agreed, but repairs need to be made first," Linasette insisted.

Nacen wanted to argue, to point to the horizon beyond and tell her a Union Precept force could be rallying for another attack. But Linasette knew the ship, and he knew she would be right.

Standing at attention to the pilot's right was Beskin, his plasma rifle tucked away at his side. On the left, the trufalci Jeta gave a polite smile. She wore her brown locks plaited down her lower back. Her devotion lay more in the machines within the *Canotila* than the crew or captain, but Nacen accepted this as a perk.

Shukernak stood behind Jeta, a full two heads taller and nearly the size of the Armads themselves. Nacen had long ago stopped bothering to force 'Nak to keep his robes compliant with trufalci standards. Sleeves had a tendency to be stretched or torn off. Even a well-fitted jumpsuit and robe would soon find itself torn on the corner of an engine or caught under an ammunition drum. His brow was knitted in a perpetual look of concern. Though Nacen had known they'd escaped, it still warmed his heart to see them in the flesh. He nodded to them both.

Nacen placed himself between the groups, knowing it was his place as captain and negotiator. Much had happened between himself and each individual group, and now was the time to clear the air. He cleared his dusty throat and coughed. As much as it could be.

"Friends," he said to his crew, "it warms me greatly to see you all alive. But it is neither our wit nor strategy that sees us reunited." Now he brought his attention to the Armads. "It is by the hands of Basaul, chief leader of Extrata, and the stout men who serve him in these dark hours. It is here in these ruins of a ruined world that we must strike a new path, to save what remains of the house before all is lost. We may lack the means to deliver the justice which the Union Precept deserves, but in each of our hearts we carry the will to preserve what our ancestors before us have built. We will find what remains of the homefleet and deliver them to safety in whatever way we can."

The Stevari side broke into cheering while the Armads gave a few obligatory nods and claps. He noticed more than a few sideways glances and faces ill at ease, even amongst his own crew. To break the tension, Nacen came forward and grasped Basaul's forearm. "Without wood, the fire dies."

"From the houses, wealth shall rise," his crew finished.

"I do not know about your Stevari poetry, but we will move forward together," Basaul said.

The two sides moved together and shook hands, like two streams converging to form the humble beginnings of a mighty river. But Nacen noticed among friendly smiles were more than a few grimaces. Out of the corner of his eye, a few Armads shoved past Beskin in the general cheer. This new alliance would need to be guided along with care and tact.

Nacen led Basaul and Chalce through the tight corridors of the ship, pointing out each location. "The rear ramp isn't the only way into the cargo hold, we also have two transporter mats for beaming down personnel and supplies." Behind them trailed the Stevari crew and Armads, heaving their personal effects and weapons inside.

Next he showed them the armory, filled with neat rows of flux pistols, rifles, repeaters, as well as a half dozen plasma carbines. One crate contained a few marksman flux drivers, and other smaller crates held compressed ammunition and grenades. There were components for mortars and several drones as well. A heavy plasma repeater and ex-cal levitated serenely in anti-grav suspension. Short for explosive microcaliber railgun, the ex-cal was a Stevari variant of the traditional flux driver which fired smaller, explosive rounds at an astonishing rate of fire. It was typically used by a pair of trufalci as a squad support weapon.

"We will store your weapons in here. The armory will be kept a neutral zone, with only myself and Beskin having access."

Shukernak and Chalce groaned loudly in protest.

"Relax. It's a short ride back to the *Lusterhawk*," Nacen reasoned. "If you want to polish your cannons in the meantime, just come get permission."

Shukernak grumbled something barely audible.

"Here is our meditation room." Nacen beckoned to the comparatively small room after passing the barracks and flight deck. "We use this for sparring, drills, any number of training exercises. You can offload your supplies in here."

"Excellent. And where shall we be *staying*?" Basaul glanced around impatiently.

"Umm…" Nacen stumbled over his next words. "Also in here. The good news is holographic imaging means you can change everything in the room to suit your needs as well: lighting, walls... If you want the night sky above, we can program whatever planet's view you want. We have over two million celestial spheres in the House Drovina logs. Or maybe some dim cavern light would suit—"

"It is not aesthetics, but reasonable space that concerns me, Captain." Basaul grumbled. "What about the armory? Surely we can place the weapons in compression to save space?"

"I'm afraid that goes against our maintenance protocols. Besides, there is more space here. I'll tell you what. With our crew being a little light we have some room in the barracks," Nacen conceded. "I'll give that up for Chalce and yourself, and reside with my crew."

"That will suffice."

"Good. Get your crew settled in then meet me in the bridge in ten minutes. We have a flight plan to arrange."

Chapter 4

Nacen entered the bridge of the *Carmine Canotila* and exhaled with delight as he took in the spacious cockpit. Linasette was already at the helm, back in her gray flight suit.

"Already out of your formal wear? I thought the look suited you."

"I'm not one for formal occasions." She continued to expand displays to include nearby star systems, and statistics spilled over the screens.

"You'd prefer we got into a firefight with them?" Nacen asked.

"That may have been less awkward."

"Well, it could have gone a lot worse," Nacen crossed his arms and leaned back against the sloped wall.

"We're not out of the woods yet."

"What woods? This is a barren planet."

The pilot, now content with the displays, turned to give him a hard glance. "Just an old Precept saying."

"Ah." Nacen paused to consider his next words carefully, studying the star charts as he did so. He did not want to reopen old wounds, but he needed to know who he could trust in the days to come. True, Linasette had been pilot of the ship since his father was captain, but she flew fighter craft for the Precept navy in another age. She had lived and breathed as the distributed artificial intelligence of the Counsel willed.

"The U.P. did a lot of damage," he said finally. "To us and the Armads."

"Yes. Analysis of the debris finished recently. The *Canotila* estimates nearly two hundred vessels destroyed. Not all scout ships like the *Canotila* or fighters, either. Five cruisers and twenty-seven frigates were eliminated."

"They brought a lot of firepower against us. This was planned aggression."

"That seems undeniable at this point," Linasette noted.

"I wonder what their motive was to attack us like this. They see our trade with other civilizations and what amounts to free movement within quickspace as a threat, no doubt, but before they limited their reactions to trade embargos or quickspace blockades. None of which amounted more than an inconvenient detour for us, of course... but nothing so bold as an outright attack... an outright massacre."

"If it makes you feel any better, Captain, the homefleet took them for a lot. Nearly half the total debris out there is from Precept vessels."

"No, Lina. I've had enough of this loss of life. The thought of any more... just makes me feel ill."

"You don't have to tiptoe around me, Captain. Say what you want to say."

Nacen sighed. "You were raised in the U.P., Lina. You flew fighters with them for years. Longer than you flew for my father."

The pilot was silent for a moment. Her face did not betray her inner thoughts.

"So, you want to know if I'm going to turn on you, or what?" she asked stiffly.

"Nothing so drastic. Do you have any sympathy for the people you left behind?"

Linasette drew a steady breath and exhaled.

"I grew up on a sprawl world. I had it better than most. My father joined the Precept navy at a young age, and he worked his way up the ranks fast. Fast enough to get the attention of some serious brass. At first, he would come back once a year for months at a time. He would take me fishing at a wildlife reserve near our home a lot. As soon as he was gone, I was already counting down the days until our next trip. Later on, he made admiral. He disappeared for years, but he provided for us well. Not that there wasn't anyone on Fomalhaut that wasn't taken care of, with the generous Counsel seeing to every detail of our welfare. Eventually, I grew of age and enrolled in flight school. I didn't care to be an officer, at least back then. On the night before I left, my mother disabled my alarm and I overslept. I woke up late in a panic, not realizing what she'd done or why. I dressed into my school uniform and rushed downstairs, apologizing on my way. I stopped, dead in my tracks, when I saw my mother's smile. She was cooking, a hobby she rarely explored, and had done up her hair in soft, black curls. She explained that I wasn't allowed to start my lessons that day, or the next. Dad was coming back. Vice-Admiral Derada was returning from his latest campaign."

Nacen nodded for her to continue.

"When he came back, I didn't actually recognize him. It had been years since I'd seen him, and I was only a child. I only had a vague memory of what he looked like. The decorated admiral's uniform and well-worn features to match covered this vague image I had from childhood. Anyway, I went to a wildlife reserve with this stranger. The same one, actually. Hiking, fishing, camping, everything we used to do together. I warmed up to him eventually. We swapped some stories, laughed. You know, our typical outing. Then his demeanor changed. He started talking about his campaign, recent events, the strange culture of the warrior colony worlds he had battled against. Apparently the war had been costly, but we'd been victorious with good terms. Part of these terms required the surrender of some of the conflict's commanders. A hostage exchange in good faith. The Counsel, with its composed intelligence, found the exchange for one human in return for the recruiting and mining rights that came with integration into the Union Precept irresistible. He would go as a diplomat, a liaison between cultures. My father, never one to neglect his duty, left the next day."

Linasette paused again. Her next breath was not so steady.

"We never saw him again. My mother received some of his effects, after all, he was no longer military. We got his uniform, badges, awards, and his service knife... this ornamental dagger with a not so ornamental history, according to some of his stories. Sometime after I had shipped off to flight school, my mother took that knife, and..." Lina stopped, as though she could not find or face the words that came next. "Look, the Counsel may be perfect, or close enough to make no difference, but people aren't. Some slip through the cracks. You can call the adaptive algorithms of the Counsel omnipotent, adaptable, benevolent... and to some extent it's all true... but to me it was a thief. It may not make all of the decisions, but it serves as a guide for everyone and everything. Nothing should have that much power. No one should have that over their heads."

Nacen let the silence hang there out of respect.

"Thank you, Lina." Nacen finally said. "I'm sorry I doubted you."

"Good, because I hope to never tell that story again," the pilot said, turning toward the forward displays. "So, what's our next course of action?"

"To find out what happened here. Ideally we meet up with whatever Stevari vessel came in, rescued the lifeboats, and made it out. But we have no beacons to go off of. Failing that, we need to find any part of the homefleet still out there and warn them about what happened here."

"Good idea," Linasette noted. "The most likely place I figure we can find someone is Pulcara. The system is not far from here, and it's a relatively short quickspace trip into Xandran space. There's no way the U.P. would risk straying too far into the Colonies of Xandra. Then again, the homefleet survivors could have made a clean break and crossed into Mangost and simply outrun the Precept navy. Any possibilities stick out to you?"

"Both of those plans seem equally likely to bear fruit, though Pulcara is certainly less risky. My gut is telling me Mangost. Some of our captains are not ones to cut and run when things get interesting. If my oldest brother Zura had the helm, he'd go to Mangost for sure. He wouldn't trust the Xandra Colonies nor the Union Precept if he could help it. If it's my father or one of the baroni, I could see them leaning on the Xandra for assistance. But I don't know if my father is even alive, or where the others are without the presence of the beacons. So many uncertainties..."

Nacen felt hot anger rise in him again and wanted to send his fist into the holograms dancing in front of him... mocking him. He raised it, balled his hand into a tight fist, then took a breath and managed to calm himself. Linasette continued his conjecture.

"The nearest quickspace lanes in Union Precept space are Ulastai and Casimir, though I find it difficult to believe anyone in the homefleet would go there now. Possibly we could catch someone leaving U.P. space if we are still on good terms. The Urias tunnel is quite a bit further off, and House Orizon has a stranglehold over that part of the Prominar Rim, but we cannot dismiss it as a possibility. A worldship's shields should be able to hold out that long over Alpha One."

"Yes, traveling across the great blue sun is dangerous business," Nacen said, "We'll see what Folbix thinks of our travel options when we get back to the *Lusterhawk*."

"Another question is whether or not we can trust the Armads," Linasette noted.

"I'm not sure about all of them, but I do trust Basaul. It's the way his second in command, Chalce, disagrees with him that bothers me."

"I've always heard being able to disagree with one's commander is a sign of good leadership."

"That explains why I keep you around." Nacen smirked.

Linasette's reply was cut off by a whir of the doors behind giving way. The heavy footfall of wide boots filled the small chamber as Basaul and Chalce entered.

"This is your command post?" Basaul asked. If Nacen didn't know better, he could have sworn the Armad was raising one craggy eyebrow.

"Yes." Nacen nodded. "This is where the pilot maneuvers the ship and controls functions like our inertial dampeners, artificial gravity, homeostasis programs, course plotting…"

"Very good, very good. Speaking of which, I am sure you are more than ready to receive the information we have on your fleet."

"Yes, of course." Nacen rose from the chair over which he had been leaning.

"We do not know exactly where the Starkin worldship went after it picked up survivors during the battle. But we know its shields were severely depleted during the battle. Based on our calculations and some assumptions on Starkin propulsion, we believe the only choice they had was to go to the Ulastai system."

"What?" Nacen floundered. He didn't know where to begin unraveling the knotted ball of sheer absurdity. "That's ridiculous. How did you come by this information?"

"Sub-orbital drones picked it up on visual. They're quite reliable. Would you like to see some of the data?" Basaul asked and extended a small cartridge to Nacen, who froze. If the Armads caught some of the battle, then they could identify the mystery worldship that had attempted to save the day. He snatched the cartridge from Basaul before he could realize this was a terribly rude thing to do and tossed it to Linasette.

"Lina," Nacen began, "run this footage through our filters and make sure it's authentic."

"Aye, Captain."

"I would have thought they would retreat through more neutral territory, toward the Colonies of Xandra for safe harbor. The enemy of my enemy and all that. Not into the space of the people who turned Carnizad into *that*." Nacen gestured to the back of the cabin, assuming the Armads would get the picture.

"I don't speculate, Captain. I'm just telling you what happened," Basaul said.

"Well, what one sees doesn't always reflect the truth. I've learned that the hard way. Throw the video on screen, Lina." Nacen waited for the displays to shift off of ship logistics. He imagined what would unfold on them, daring fleet actions and bold maneuvers. None of what his imagination conjured would be reality, he knew, for he had seen the aftermath already. He had walked through it. Felt it. "Lina, any troubles interfacing with the Armads' data storage?"

"No, sir," the pilot replied after a short wait. But these things take time. "Here you are."

The forward displays blended into display, on which a terrible spectacle of flashing lights from weapon discharges and igniting munitions played out. Eight Precept battleships, five worldships, dozens of cruisers, and a veritable swarm of well over one hundred smaller frigates were visible on-screen, mostly as mere pinpoints of light, hurling everything they had at the Stevari homefleet only partially visible on the drone's display. The cruisers spanned the gamut from flat behemoths that disgorged bombers to bulking battleships sporting colossal rail guns. The screen glowed with beam weapons, missiles, and flak. As the Precept navy moved in, even more vessels made themselves visible from elsewhere in the system, drawing to close the noose. But the Stevari line was far from static. The vast, maroon ship that could only be the *Asura* was turning to bear on the Precept fleet. It dwarfed even the largest dreadnought-class battleships of the Precept navy, and the countless smaller ships were flies buzzing around its mighty prow. The *Asura* gave off sparks as life-supported portions of the ship were blown apart and sent into space. Others collapsed and were isolated to maintain the integrity of the worldship. But still it fired into the encircling Precept fleet, destroying large and small craft alike. The rest of the Stevari fleet was more concerned with maneuvering around the *Asura* than in fighting back. Even so, they appeared to be suffering horrendous casualties. Other, smaller craft were visible traveling from the Stevari capital ship to the worldships and other survivors in the center of the homefleet. Lifeboats, perhaps.

Eventually, House Drovina's strategy snapped into focus. The *Asura* was sacrificing itself so the remaining worldships could escape, along with many of the lifeboats. From the unseen shift into quickspace beyond it, another ship emerged, visible only due to the light emitted by its rail guns and plasma beams as it tore into the nearest U.P. battleship. Nacen recognized this craft in its long, serpentine form with undulating curves. It was a carefully outfitted blockade runner called the *Burning Stag*. Its captain had traded size and armor for faster acceleration and more firepower. The tradeoff had paid off massively in its missions running blockades and smashing fortifications the blue sun over, turning Nacen's eldest brother Zura into something of a celebrity amongst the Stevari fleets.

Nacen watched as the *Burning Stag* slowed its descent in perfect time to turn and pick up several lifeboats, raking the two nearest cruisers with its broadside. Then it was making a beeline straight for entrance to the quickspace passage. The Precept naval forces seemed of two minds. Half their ships redoubled their efforts on the static ships and facilities on Carnizad as the *Asura* fell toward the planet in its death throes. The other half, perhaps because they were in a better position to do so, pursued the *Burning* Stag. The hopes of many Stevari ships were extinguished before they could reach quickspace. The perspective changed as the Armads' orbital satellites were presumably destroyed. Then again. Then the screen went black.

The fascination of his older brother's tactics wore off, and Nacen became cognizant of how tense he had been. He tried to relax, bit back against the bile rising in his throat. Whatever ignorance or hatred or foolishness that drove the Union Precept to attack and split the family apart... he would make them pay, somehow.

"Nacen, I'm sorry..." Linasette began.

"What's to be sorry about? There's nothing about that battle that we didn't already know. My father died saving as many people as he could. Let's not make his sacrifice be in vain. What's our next move?" he asked no one in particular.

"Your father could have made it out on one of those lifeboats," Basaul remarked with pity.

"Yoska would never take a place on an escape vessel when one of his people stood waiting. That goes for double when his ship is under attack," Nacen insisted. "Now... back to the matter at hand. Pursuing the fleet is out of the question, of course."

"First we need to repair the damage the ground forces did to the *Canotila*," Linasette said. "All of this intelligence and planning does nothing if we're swallowed up here, or finished off by the lance trooper force."

"What if we scuttle our hauler?" Basaul suggested.

"I fail to see how that helps our current situation," Nacen said, "though it would be rather cathartic for me, personally."

"No, no, no. I see what the boss is saying." Chalce nodded. "We can dismantle the hauler and graft the plating onto this scout ship."

"I cannot imagine our technology will be compatible," Linasette huffed.

"It doesn't have to be pretty, just good enough to get us to our frigate, *Lusterhawk*. Folbix can set us up with proper repairs then," Nacen said, "but what then? We still don't know where the fleet is. Even if we go to Ulastai after Zura, he could go to a few different systems, assuming his shields regenerate. After that jump, the possibilities increase exponentially."

"Look," Basaul gestured with his hands as he explained, "you could try for a direct pursuit, but it would be difficult to catch him with such a head start judging from those kitted-out engines."

"So what do you propose?" Nacen asked.

"Find a way to cut around and meet them."

"Far less suicidal said than done. How do you propose that?"

"It's possible, *if* we knew the positions of the Conglomerate fleet," Basaul replied. "To get that information, we'd need access to a Glommy network with a connection to their artificial intelligence. Which means a military base or a planet."

"You're failing to convince me this isn't tantamount to suicide," Nacen said.

"Look, Extrata has a license to deliver ore to Daedalus Station. It's a big trade station orbiting a planet in the Tantalos system, just a few tunnels away. We could get into the station, find a node with access to their Counsel, and get out before anyone knows what we're really there for."

"Why not simply go to the Urias system and pledge ourselves to the guild there?" Chalce suggested in a manner of demanding it. "The Starkin could ask House Orizon to take them in. I'm sure they would accept, if only to have Drovinian royalty as their bootlick."

"We will do no such thing!" Basaul roared suddenly. "This is a matter of honor now. We will not slink away into the shadows."

Chalce lowered his head. "I am sorry. You are right, boss. I am sorry for entertaining the idea."

The Armad certainly did not sound apologetic, but then Basaul's outburst had been rude... and a little terrifying. Nacen tacitly agreed that Chalce's plan was out of the question. Though at the moment, Nacen felt some suspicion toward the pair. It occurred to him that this drama could all be a show, maybe to push him toward the Armads' preferred course of action.

"We're taking you on your word for a lot of this information. Maybe there is a nice bounty on our heads. What's to prevent you from turning us in?"

Nacen asked with a sly tilt of his head.

"You don't have a lot of options, and as you have pointed out, we've had easier opportunities to capture you before this." Basaul crossed his arms with a mighty scrape. "Believe me, I don't like the idea of staying inside a Starkin vessel for a prolonged amount of time."

"Alright. Let's proceed with the initial plan. You'll perform field repairs on this ship with the assistance of our trufalci, and when we get to the *Lusterhawk,* we can see about checking out this Daedalon place."

"Very good," Basaul rumbled. "We'll get rid of that Starkin flair... put in some sensible atmospheric heat shields..."

"But we don't have a need for physical shielding," Linasette protested. "Our ship's reactor creates phase shielding more than capable of deflecting heavy arms fire, let alone some simple re-entry or launch heat."

"Right, but say a Glom's plasma weapon weakens your shield as we exit?"

"Point taken."

Basaul and Chalce left, discussing the finer points of thermal expansion and mass-to-thrust ratios.

"What are they planning on doing to our ship?" Linasette asked with mild trepidation.

"Just minimal modifications to get us off this rock." Nacen replied. Linasette sat there in silence. "Surely that's better than being fragged by lancer forces."

"Hold on, I'm still trying to decide," Linasette replied.

"Well, while you're figuring that out, I'll be meditating in the barracks." Nacen patted the back of his pilot's seat. "Put a virtual bar on the entrance to make sure I'm not disturbed."

Chapter 5

The barracks was mercifully empty. After carefully removing his earpiece, Nacen no longer heard the taps and chimes of transmissions across all channels of communication. He breathed in and let his eyelids close. He planted himself in coiled serpent pose, his attachment to the dying world around him fading. After his third deep breath, he no longer felt the trappings of his own body and allowed his mind to wander.

He allowed each thought to take its place on the stage and play its part before dismissing itself. Confusion and resentment fled like sheep before a lion. Anger was a reckless giant, but it was nonetheless felt, examined, and released... at least for now. He sat and breathed like this for a long time. How long he could not be sure, as he no longer gave any heed to the number of breaths he took, or the passage of air in and out of his lungs. But there were thoughts he could not conquer through willpower alone, and as his ire left him, it was replaced by a deep sorrow. He could not indifferently dismiss the deaths of so many of his own people. So many journeys cut short before they had truly begun. The thoughts of more Stevari out there to find, and those that now counted on him to lead, were all that let him blink himself back into the makeshift meditation room with dry eyes.

Nacen nestled his communications earpiece carefully back into place and found a host of messages awaiting him. He powered up his pad to find three connection requests. Two room entry requests followed. Then more connection requests. What was happening out there? Nacen cleared the messages with a few practiced taps, donned his recast armor and crimson cloak, and exited. He wound his way through the tight corridors of the ship to the cargo hold.

He passed the actual meditation room where the Armads were setting up their gear for the short ride to the *Lusterhawk*, where they could then make more permanent arrangements. As he listened to his messages to make sure no Union Precept forces were nearby, he stumbled upon Basaul and Chalce arguing. After spending the better part of a day with them, this was no strange sight. Between the two of them sat a large, steel lockbox atop a crate. Their voices barked in a language he did not understand. Their conversation was low and harsh, like the familiar quakes of the planet, but as expressive as a chorus of Stevari vocalists. Nacen shot them a puzzled look. Basaul turned, closing the box with a quick flick of his wrist as he did so.

"Pardon us, Captain Buhari," Basaul said, "we are simply having a difficult time settling in."

Nacen made to speak but was cut off.

"Worry not. We shall make do until we reach your frigate."

"I appreciate your flexibility," Nacen replied in a tone that implied he would personally kick them right back into the valley he had found them in if his druvani found anything suspicious. He eyed the box and departed for the cargo hold. As part of his druvani's standard procedure, Beskin and Camlo would have checked all the stores the Armads brought aboard. Nothing suspicious had been reported. If you count flux weapons, mass condensers, and a few dozen grenades as banal traveling sundries, that is.

The light from the transporter section of the cargo hold shifted from a sky blue to a bright orange as Nacen approached it. The ship would prevent the mass transfer if Nacen were to cross into the light, he noted, as Jeta materialized just a few inches in front of his face.

Being reassembled just outside the ship was effectively zero-risk, and had been a safe and convenient way to move around ships for centuries. Transmitting matter, and oneself, was especially convenient in high traffic areas and in low gravity where locomotion could be difficult or slow. Nacen's own surprise by the arrival was not mirrored by the trufalci. She tore her pan-atmo mask up and over a damp ponytail, and sweat splattered the cargo hold.

"Nacen," she said, omitting his rank, "where have you been? Haven't you gotten any of my messages?"

"I was—"

"Never mind, it doesn't matter," she said brusquely. "The Armad engineers have gone too far. They're trying to scrap our engine to put in this big fusion monstrosity from their hauler. I don't care how inefficient they think our reactors are, I am not tearing out perfect good parts to satiate their egos."

"Okay,   what   do   you   recommend?"

"Stick to additional armor plating and shield generators only. I can work around damage to internal systems until we get back to the *Lusterhawk*. I need you to make them understand, because my expertise apparently isn't enough for them."

"Okay, I will relay your orders along. Anything else?" Nacen said to the panting trufalci.

"Only," she breathed, "do it fast."

"Why, are they getting impatient?" Nacen asked, securing the final portion of his crimson cloak to his shoulder armor.

"You'll see." Jeta shook her head.

Nacen donned his own pan-atmo mask and stepped on the transmat. In the blink of an eye, he was standing on the dry, cracked soil of Carnizad. The sky outside was even darker now. Swirling black clouds roiled over the horizon. The air was notably hotter, though not humid. Thunder cracked in the thin atmosphere. Half a dozen Armads were gathered around their hauler, now a tangled skeleton of its former self. They assailed it with magnetic rams to undo huge rivets, and cut off huge swathes with plasma torches. Several other Armads were clustered around the *Carmine Canotila*, pointing and arguing in their guttural tongue.

Shukernak was crouched on top of their vehicle, using a small but powerful plasma torch to free one side of the vehicle from its roof. The big trufalci's hood was up despite the heat. Nacen could make out his own reflection in the thick goggles. As Nacen approached, he squinted and put a hand up to block the harsh blue flare of the torch.

"Catch me up to speed, 'Nak. What's going on?"

"That's going on," Shukernak said, pointing to one section of the all-encompassing blackening horizon. "The whole damn continent is coming apart. Lina says we've got no more than two hours to get this job finished before we're up to our eyeballs in molten metal. We could fly to higher ground, but we can't relocate the Armad's hauler, which we're still in the process of salvaging."

"Work as long as you can, then. Focus on sealing off critical compartments. Anything else is unnecessary."

"But—"

"Save the serious repairs for the *Lusterhawk*," Nacen said. "Surely performing them on our own frigate beats doing them underneath molten rock."

"I don't know, that's probably a nice, relaxing bath for the Armads," Shukernak said, severing the next segment with a flash from his torch.

Nacen caught the Armad team up to speed with the plan for minimal repairs. Unused parts, no longer having a purpose in the expedited repairs, were left on the ground. Nacen felt a little guilty about leaving it all strewn about. After all, this planet did house one of his family's trading outposts. But the roiling blackness in the sky was only intensifying. The stars had long ago been snuffed out by acrid smoke, and the reverberations in the earth only grew deeper, as if some great beast had finally made up its mind to awaken from slumber. He supposed the trading outpost wasn't long for this world.

***

The engines beneath the wings of the *Carmine Canotila* unfolded and the craft took off with a mighty kick, blowing up a torrent of soil that settled in thick sheets on the scraps of the derelict Armad hauler. The powerful engines carried the Stevari shuttle through the atmosphere and into an expanse of stars. All the ruins of Carnizad and the ships that once carried Nacen's people through the stars soon lay in the *Carmine Canotila*'s wake. On the bridge, Nacen stared at the star charts and wondered where the homefleet had fled. It pained him not to have the beacon signaling to their ship, the hushed voice that had always sung them home.

"The Armads have returned to the meditation room to unpack and rest and rest a bit. They did good getting us out of there in one piece." Linasette said from her pilot's chair.

"I'm just glad we don't have a mutiny on our hands," Nacen said.

"I know they're none too fond of me after I dispatched one of them on the *Asura*," Beskin noted. "Have the Armads shown any concerning behavior?"

"No, I meant Jeta. You should have seen her when they suggested we replace our engine with an Armad make." Nacen tapped his index finger on his gauntlet as he crossed his arms. "But the Armads aren't much happier. I get the sense most of them would rather throw their lot in with some guild than follow us. Only Basaul and a couple others seem to be intent on helping us find survivors, and their motivation seems to come mostly from revenge. We can only work that angle for so long."

"We should welcome them. Make them feel at home." Beskin suggested.

"How do you reckon we do that?" Camlo asked.

"Traditionally, we would welcome strangers to our great house with a feast." Beskin frowned. "Let's use some of our deluxe rations and give them just that. The *Lusterhawk's* current stores will last for at least a few months, right? And that's with a full crew. We've been at under half strength for a while now."

Nacen nodded. "We could spare that, I think. Besides, we can resupply when we reach the homefleet."

"What if we don't? Reach the homefleet I mean?" Camlo interjected.

"Then we won't have to worry about rations," Nacen countered. "I am going to finish up ship modifications with the crew. Beskin, Camlo, start preparations for the feast. We can set up in the *Lusterhawk's* banquet hall when we arrive."

"Oh, I would like to prepare one more surprise for the Armads," Beskin said.

"Oh?" Nacen raised an eyebrow.

"You will need your dulcinet. Are you still familiar with the melody from the Black Dog of the Forest?"

"Yes..." Nacen pondered a moment, seeing what Beskin was getting at. "But that piece may not hold their attention. What about the Suitor and the Serpent?"

"Ah." Beskin grinned. "You always did prefer the older ballads."

***

Nacen had done a few rounds to make sure the ship was holding up as it should, or at least the best it could under the circumstances. Jeta had been mollified as the Stevari systems had been mostly unscathed by the Armads' meddling, though there were still holes and tears from the more aggressive modifications by Unity firearms. Regardless, the patched up shuttle was fast approaching the sole remaining intact frigate in the orbit of Carnizad. Nacen shoved his way past Camlo, who hurried by with an armful of precooked ration packages, and three Armads muttering some kind of disapproval at another's welding. Nacen tried to ignore the implications and continued to the bridge. The doors whisked open as he approached.

"Our estimated time of arrival at the *Lusterhawk* is seven minutes, thirty seconds," Linasette announced, answering the question on his mind.

"Very good, Lina," Nacen said with satisfaction. "Now please get Folbix on bridge comms. I would imagine he is quite eager to hear how our little sojourn has gone."

Linasette mouthed some words in Nacen's general direction that he only put together a moment after she finished.

"Contrary to your notions, *Captain* Buhari, running a frigate is a full-time job. Rest assured, my trufalci and I have been staying busy in your absence." The voice of Master Folbix Rinkesi put an unpleasant emphasis on Nacen's rank, as though placing it so close to his name dishonored the honorific.

"Master Rinkesi, I appreciate your taking the initiative in establishing communications," Nacen said. He was often shocked at how often leadership involved saying the exact opposite of what one was feeling at the time. And to think, his mother said his passion for acting would never pay off. He threw in a smile for good measure, just in case Folbix had video secretly enabled as well.

"Yes, well I was rather justifiably concerned when I had not received an update from you in nearly three hours on the sundial." Folbix said. He referred to time being marked by the reference frame of the great blue sun, the ancient humans' keeper of quickspace.

"Carnizad's fluctuating magnetic fields can wreak havoc on a signal." Nacen offered.

"Quite right. Were you able to locate the beacon or find any survivors on the *Asura*?" Nacen could practically hear the pretentious beard-stroking.

"No. By all indications, the beacon has been captured or destroyed. We were likewise not able to locate any Stevari."

"So you found absolutely nothing on that planet? I told you coming here was a waste of time."

"Confirming the beacon has been destroyed is certainly not nothing. And we did find a few others. Union Precepts, for starters."

"Precept forces? All my surveys of the planet showed it to be free of hostiles," Folbix replied, taking near personal offense at the claim.

Nacen knew he could have explained the situation more clearly. But if Folbix wanted details, he could read their after action reports. There would be plenty of time to do so
while traveling across the great blue sun. Besides, Nacen had a few minutes free and could use some cheering up.

"They preferred to be the ones doing the finding," Nacen assured the master of the *Lusterhawk*.

"Did they give you much trouble?"

"There is quite a bit of damage to the *Canotila* that will need to be tended to, and of course there's our delay in returning. You can coordinate repairs through Jeta. There will be many field repairs that will have to be removed before full repairs can be serviced."

"I am sure my trufalci can handle it," Folbix said.

"Undoubtedly. We also discovered a small but capable force dwelling underground. Or rather, they discovered us."

"Another U.P. ambush?"

"No, an Armad work crew. Tractor mauls, mass condenser, a heavy-duty hauler... the whole parslat."

"You lead quite an exciting life, Buhari," Folbix admitted. Nacen was glad to hear some cheer in the man's voice, even if it likely came from Nacen's own peril. "I assume you were able to fashion yourself some sort of victory, given that we are speaking now. Please regale me with the rest of your erm... deeds."

"Excellent intuition," Nacen began. "My druvani and I were captured, actually. We only escaped through shrewd negotiation. We fought our way back to the ship, just in time to patch up before the planet went to crap. Well, more-so anyway."

"Indeed. Well, next time I propose we outline a few more contingency plans to avoid such high-risk actions in the future. Did you lose any personnel?"

"No Stevari, fortunately. The Armads lost a few men."

"I shall shed as many tears for them as I did the Unity," Folbix said caustically.

"Don't speak so soon. Or loudly," Nacen added. He could hear rumbling voices on the other side of the bridge door. "We're going to have some guests. I would like you to designate some of our unused crew quarters for a dozen rather large people."

"I thought you said you found no survivors on the *Asura*?"

"They were not on the *Asura*, and they're not Stevari. They're the Armads, and they're our new allies."

The communication channel captured an outtake of breath that sounded uncannily like one of the volcanos that had blown on Carnizad.

"You do tax my patience sometimes, Captain Buhari. Now listen, this frigate runs flawlessly because of my efforts as master and my trufalcis' obedience to organization and standard protocol..."

"They're *our* trufalci, Folbix, and don't forget that in the event of a combat situation, they're under my sole command," Nacen chided, his façade cracking. "Besides, I always thought the *Lusterhawk* more or less looked after itself. It's not as if it's ever seen a battle before. Sure, the *Canotila* has been in a couple of scrapes, but that's neither here nor there. Don't pretend like all of that business about keeping trufalci busy isn't anything but theater to keep up discipline. It's not like we've had much to do on my father's old trade routes."

"One does not maintain order and discipline for wont of something to do. One maintains order and discipline to be prepared to confront the enemy, in whatever form that may take," Folbix added. "Now. Do you have anything else to report before your arrival? The trufalci shall see to your repairs and dormitory requirements. I shall see to the necessary security and ship restrictions for our guests."

"Allies," Nacen clarified.

"I will judge the situation for myself."

"Oh, and we will be throwing a feast before we leave the system. Prepare the hall for our arrival."

There was a brief silence and the shuffling of something soft.

"Very well," Folbix announced.

"Excellent," Nacen said, "I have the utmost faith in the trufalci's order and discipline to prepare for this scenario."

Silence followed as the communications link ended. Linasette turned in her seat.

"You realize that making an enemy of Rinkesi isn't helping your chances of promotion," she said.

"Please. I know Folbix would rather have continued serving with my father and mastering a worldship. He's just as keen on moving up as I am. We have a mutually beneficial relationship, in our own way."

"Okay..." Linasette started. "Let me rephrase that. You realize that making an enemy of Rinkesi is going to get us all killed one of these days. You should make an effort to work with him more."

"That's better. I appreciate your honesty, Lina. But I have worked out a good system here. Our back-and-forth is just a little friendly competition amongst equals." Nacen eased into the shuttle's copilot seat. There on the forward holoscreens, the increasingly large outline of the black frigate loomed.

Nacen looked on the *Lusterhawk* the same way he might a dilapidated pair of boots. It was just something he was going to have to put up with if he expected to get anywhere for the time being. It was more an obstacle than a path to greatness in House Drovina. His thoughts generally orbited between resentment and disgust, which was not saying much, because he generally thought about his command on the frigate as little as possible. The armored flank opened up as the *Carmine Canotila* approached, and the shuttle was swallowed up.

***

Nacen had never quite found himself comfortably at home in the *Lusterhawk*. Its hangar bay, just large enough for one fighter squadron and a single shuttle, lacked the space of the worldships. Its hall couldn't match the grandeur of their larger cousins, and despite compression technology, the closets were too small. It was all a matter of use, he reckoned. The worldships were large enough to accommodate all facets of Stevari life. It was on these that the traders were born, practiced their crafts, sung, danced, played, drunk, and died. Frigates, on the other hand, had to be small enough to keep their crew to a manageable level and big enough to make them profitable. Their job was to deliver goods to more difficult or more distant trade zones. They were the delivery service that no one wanted to do but everyone needed.

He rounded a corner and entered the last service hallway until he reached the bridge of the *Lusterhawk*. Light panels on either side flickered with a false flame. It annoyed Nacen on principle because a regular, more diffuse glow would be more suitable to the ship's lights and easier on the eyes.

"The last person we need to get on board with our plan to infiltrate Daedalon Station is the Master of the *Lusterhawk*, Folbix Rinkesi." Nacen looked back to make sure his entourage was still following. Basaul and Chalce likewise seemed to be annoyed, but more because the *Lusterhawk's* hallway did not support their full height. Basaul walked with his head cocked to one side. Chalce had to bend awkwardly. Beskin and Camlo brought up the rear.

"I thought you were the master. You're in charge, right? I did not bargain with you thinking you were a subordinate," Basaul said.

"As captain, I am in charge. The ship is my command and I have direct control of our household troops, the druvani and trufalci. However, Folbix oversees wellbeing, maintenance, and operations of the *Lusterhawk*. He is also in command when I am away."

"Ah," Basaul said, nodding sideways to avoid the ceiling. "He has been on this frigate a long time then and knows it well."

"Actually, we both transferred at the same time during the last cycle. That was about two years ago, by the sundial. He was my father's pilot back when he flew cruisers. But he knows the ship well, and the crew is very loyal to him."

"Shouldn't they be more loyal to their captain?" Chalce asked in what sounded more like an accusation.

"They're just as—" Nacen let out a quiet sigh. "Look... let's just stay oriented on the goal for now."

"Understood," Basaul grunted.

"Okay, you're the captain," Chalce said. His tone reminded Nacen of the unflattering way Folbix used the rank.

Nacen turned outside the proximity of the door sensors for the bridge, outstretched his hands, and practiced his best smile.

"Very good. Let me do most of the talking, and we'll be dining on our way to Tantalos before you can say—" The doors behind Nacen whisked open. Had he approached too close to the sensor? He turned around and clasped his hands together. "Master Rinkesi, it is good to see you again!"

The bridge lay at the heart of the *Lusterhawk*, with no direct visuals to the outside. Trufalci sat or stood at well-lit control panels around the perimeter. All took heed of the newcomers to their sanctum, all but those in the center of the great round room. Folbix Rinkesi was preoccupied studying a number of star charts projected around his central command hub. At their center blazed one image brighter than all others: a projection of the Prominar Rim, the local neighborhood of quickspace passages above the surface of the great blue sun. Nacen walked onto the bridge, crossed his arms, and leaned against a support column. No need to be so rigidly formal on his own ship, right? The Armads and druvani filtered onto the bridge behind him. They stood there, taking in the bright surroundings and making uneasy eye contract with the trufalci of the bridge.

"Nacen, it is good of you to join us," Folbix said at last, collapsing his charts. Master Rinkesi's short, squat figure suited his role as the master of the *Lusterhawk*. He could amble about its corridors easily enough but was most efficient planted at the heart of activity. He wore a deep red flight uniform, festooned with beige folds, stylized pockets, and honest-to-goodness gold epaulets. Nacen thought the décor would be terribly gaudy, had it not been hopelessly outdated. The master stroked a short but scruffy black beard, already flecked with gray despite him only being a few years older than Nacen. "We are mere hours from the quickspace passage. I have planned out our next few moves, I only need your approval and we can prepare the pre-crossover checklist."

"In good time." Nacen uncrossed one arm to gesture at the Armads. "This is Basaul Torrs, leader of the remaining Armads on Carnizad."

"Thank you for allowing us onboard your ship. It is a fine vessel from what I have seen," Basaul said, approaching Folbix.

"The *Lusterhawk* is outdated in many respects compared to newer Drovina frigates, but she has many surprises." Another stroking of the beard.

"And this is his second in command: Chalce," Nacen said with a jerk of his head.

Chalce took a reluctant step forward and nodded.

"I understood you held our good captain captive for a short while down there," Folbix noted.

"Yes, we threw him in our makeshift prison after he resisted my men." Basaul frowned and scratched at his collar.

Folbix forced a single, loud laugh. "I may have to call upon your services again, if the situation calls for it. Captain Buhari can be very strong-willed."

Basaul brightened. "Your brig had better be up to the challenge then. I don't think we'd have been able to hold him for long!"

Nacen stared at the floor and shook his head. Well, at least they were getting along.

"So, what were you doing on Carnizad? How were you able to survive after the Precept bombardment?" Folbix asked.

Basaul nodded.

"The Extrata guild headquarters was very close to the Starkin port. Nothing from that region made it through in one piece. Prior to this attack, we were stationed on Carnizad for five years to perform extraction of precious metals on the planet. My team and I were doing some exploratory excavation far from the bombardment zone. When it happened, we rushed back and investigated to find all installations destroyed. It's shocking what one can do from orbit. Surprisingly enough, the *Asura* was the most intact piece of hardware left on the planet."

"I'm sure it must have been difficult." Folbix nodded solemnly. "How long has it been since the attack? Since you've been on your own?"

"Nine days on Carnizad, so just under fourteen standard days." Basaul shared a look with Chalce, who nodded in agreement. "By the sundial, as you say."

"Yes, that is consistent with our analyses of the *Asura* remains." Folbix stroked his beard. "And you saw no signs of life until encountering the captain?"

"Correct," Basaul said. "We tried extensively to locate surviving personnel. The *Asura* was empty. All of her crew and passengers appear to have had ample time to get to the lifeboats. Whether they actually survived after that is anyone's guess. There were no survivors of the bombardment of the planetary facilities, however."

"Thank you. I know this must be difficult. I just have a few more questions. When did you find out there was some Union Precept presence on Carnizad?"

"The Gloms? We found out when Nacen did—when they shot us into a gulley. They were lying low until then."

"I thank you for returning him to me in one piece, along with the *Carmine Canotila*. I'm sure it couldn't have been easy. I look forward to reading a detailed report." Folbix chuckled. "That is, whenever Nacen puts down his dulcinet to write it out."

Nacen pushed off the pillar he was leaning against and stepped forward to reassert himself in the loose cluster. This nonsense was going too far. Before he could speak, Chalce stepped forward.

"Yeah, not only did we lose men to the Gloms, but your captain and his cronies took out one of our best." Chalce jabbed a finger at Basaul. "If you aren't going to mention it, I am."

Basaul gritted his teeth. "It will be in the official rep—"

"Your damned report might as well be buried in the rubble at Carnizad for all the good it will do, where the people of our guild now lay." Chalce now leveled his accusing finger at Folbix. "We need justice for our fallen, not hollow words with the people who caused this in the first place."

Nacen had an urge to step forward and put the Armad in his place. But he had spoken with both Basaul and Chalce and thought he had come to an understanding. He would let Basaul or Master Rinkesi settle this dispute. Folbix waited patiently, hands held behind his back. After a calm glance at each Armad, he stepped off his central platform.

"It seems I have given you praise in all the wrong places. Dealing with Captain Buhari can be difficult... trust me, I know. But there appears to be more at stake here than one trading outpost and a worldship. I am with you, believe me. I served as chief pilot under the man who held command of that fallen ship. Yoska Buhari was my first captain. I knew many Stevari on the *Asura*, and I dearly hope I can see at least some of them again. What we need now are answers. Justice must wait until later, and be informed by those answers."

Before this, Nacen had been vaguely aware of a background hum of activity in the bridge. There had been hushed voices, shuffling feet, and the soft clicks and whirs of personnel active at their stations. Now an oppressive stillness held sway over the room. No one seemed willing, or even capable, of breaking the silence. If Folbix was expecting an apology they would all be waiting a long time. But the master of the frigate had keyed him up nicely. Nacen decided now was the time to get involved.

"After all we've been through today, I am proud to say I can safely count you all as friends," Nacen announced to the quiet room, making up for his uncertainty with volume. He sauntered between Folbix and Basaul, trying hard to appear casual. "Let's save the vengeance for whoever deserves it. So. What do we need first?"

"Answers." Chalce conceded, his anger fading.

"No. Anyone else?" Nacen said lightly. He wheeled slowly around in place, gesturing at the personnel lining the perimeter of the bridge, at last facing Folbix. "First... well aside from a good stiff drink, we need a destination. "

"Very good, Captain, back to the crux of the matter." Folbix's hand flew back up to his beard and he strode back to his circular hub. Holographic screens unfurled around him. "With typical deceleration, we will reach this system's quickspace passage in just under an hour. As long as we determine a course of action before then, we will not be losing any time." Folbix waited. Nacen opened his mouth to speak but was interrupted as Folbix had only paused for dramatic effect. "The way I see it, we have two viable options. The closest system we can hope to meet up with Stevari vessels is Ulastai. It is in Union Precept space, and there's the rub. If the Unity is openly hostile to all Stevari, we are walking straight into the path of a loaded gun."

"I don't like how the worldship beacons have all gone silent," Nacen said. "It means that the Precept navy have destroyed them, or have figured out how to jam them. Either way, it makes me want to steer clear of Unity space."

"Is it not possible that they figured out how to track this beacon signal of yours?" Basaul suggested. "Maybe they did, and your pals switched theirs off."

Nacen raised a finger in objection, but paused. That actually made a lot of sense. "That's... a distinct possibility. Good thinking."

"We Armads pride ourselves on keeping a level head under pressure."

Nacen nodded gratefully, only avoiding staring at the flat top of Basaul's head with a concerted effort.

"Very well." Folbix tapped with his left hand and a screen disappeared. "With Ulastai out, that leaves us with Urias. It's quite a bit further out, but there is some distance between it and the Unity."

"In its weakened state, I doubt the fleeing worldships could have made it that far traveling through the tunnels." Basaul said, referring to the quickspace passages that linked many systems together.

"Right," Nacen added eagerly. "Basaul was able to calculate which tunnels the homefleet survivors would be able to reach with the *Burning Stag's* shields depleted. Urias was not on the list, not by a long shot."

"It is less certain we will meet up with Drovina ships there, but there will be someone to assist us. House Orizon has been cooperative in the past," Folbix suggested hopefully. "We need to keep our options open, and that means choosing a system where we have options, not just chasing after relatives on a hunch."

"Agreed," Nacen said. He approached the central hub, eyeing the screens behind Folbix.

"So you agree on Urias as our best option," Master Rinkesi affirmed.

"No." Nacen walked past Folbix and waved his hand around until he had priority control over the screens by proximity.

"But that only leaves Ulastai, and we already decided... hey! What are you doing?" Folbix protested. He squared up against Nacen but did not move to restrain the captain.

"You narrowed the list well, but you left out a key candidate," Nace began searching through Folbix's quickspace chart of the Prominar Rim. The huge prominence that gave the small portion of the great blue sun its name played across the background, a huge arc of stellar matter that had persisted for thousands of years, and likely would continue relatively unchanged for thousands more.

"With the failure of the beacons, we should go to the most likely meeting place for House Drovina ships while considering the safety of our own vessel. Ulastai makes the most sense."

"The Armads can give us more than just guns and muscle," Nacen said, ignoring Folbix's disapproving frown. Chersenus, Buluki, Tanzu... no, no, no... yes! Nacen increased the size of one of the tunnel projections on his current screen. He took a step back. "They have provided opportunity as well."

Folbix's frown remained fixed as he studied Nacen's choice. "Tantalos."

"Yes," Nacen replied.

"Forgive me for questioning well-established fact, Captain Buhari, but are you a complete imbecile?"

"Listen..." Basaul interjected before Nacen could craft a suitable invective. "As I explained to Captain Buhari earlier, we have a material delivery contract with Daedalon Station in Tantalos. We should be able to get into a node with Counsel access and work out where the ships of the homefleet are located, or at least where they've been. From there, we are well positioned to navigate within the Union Precept, or make our escape."

"Tantalos..." Folbix went back to running his fingers through his beard. "If you provide me with what you have on the station, Basaul, I shall plot a preliminary course. Tantalos, eh... I did say it myself—we need answers. Who better to get them from than the Union Precept's Counsel itself?"

Basaul and Chalce gave a detailed description of the station and some of their former contacts, and promised to retrieve more information from their guild logs back in their quarters. Nacen exited the bridge after they had finished, leaving Master Rinkesi to his calculations. He wondered if he had effectively forged a bond between Folbix's *Lusterhawk* crew and the Armads, or rather if the Armads had helped mend his bond with Folbix. Possibly it was a bit of both. Nacen had a paranoid feeling it was neither, and everyone was just using each other to stay alive. Most likely, he reflected as he stretched and blinked heavy eyelids, he just needed some sleep.

Chapter 6

"The ship will be fine here in the bay. There's no hostile activity anywhere near here at all." Nacen's voice was thick with reassurance as he leaned over the command console, doing his best to obscure a few charts from his pilot.

"Right now, sure," Lina said, taking her eyes off the live stream of data from Carnizad for a moment. "But just wait until you see the activity around here after people have had a few drinks. Secured doors sometimes have a funny way of opening up." Her gaze returned to her reports after a holograph drifted out from Nacen's backside.

He sighed. The crew had returned to the *Lusterhawk* hours ago and still Linasette refused to leave her shuttle, even after the initial repairs were complete.

"Well you can lock yourself up, even sleep on the bridge, if you want. But Folbix is keeping a watch, too. Set a proximity alarm if you're that worried. Just don't make me give you a direct order to come have a good time," Nacen teased. He would push his rank only so far. "Surely you can spare one hour? You'll be more alert when you come back after some light festivities. Besides, it's Stevari tradition to treat new arrivals to a feast."

"I'm not Stevari, remember?" the pilot replied.

"You say that even after all this time?"

Linasette stared at the video of Carnizad as it shrank imperceptibly slowly away. Lava flows the size of continents roiled over the surface.

"One hour," she said at last.

The sounds of merriment from the banquet hall could be heard as soon as the pair exited through the rear cargo hatch and strolled into the *Lusterhawk's* starboard hangar. By the time they had made their way along the central access corridor and up one level, Nacen could have sworn he was walking the bustling streets of a sprawl world again. The doors to the hall opened to allow them ingress, at least insofar as packed bodies and haphazardly placed furnishings would let them squeeze. Nearly fifty figures, Armads and Stevari alike, were engaged in eating, drinking, and yelling over one another.

Beskin and Camlo had made good use of the space. When tables had run out, ammo drums and weapon crates had been emptied out and lined up. Small compressor crates formed makeshift stools or else were stacked in the corners. The banquet hall had not been used for its intended purpose in quite some time. Nacen gave a nervous shudder when he noticed the lighted space left vacant at the head of the room, and he shifted the weight of the pack on his shoulders in anticipation.

An Armad with a faint blue tint to his craggy skin turned to face Nacen as he moved past.

"Hey, Captain! Good to see you made it!" the Armad extended a hand but noticed it held a mug. He drained it of its remaining contents, slammed it down on the table, and thrust his palm back at Nacen. "The name's Perido. Glad to finally introduce myself. I swear I watched you die twice back on Carnizad."

"A pleasure, Perido. It was a close call for a lot of us." Nacen grabbed the man's hand and allowed himself to be shaken vigorously for several seconds.

"Yeah, well... thanks for taking us in, and that goes extra for all this grub!" Perido said, beckoning at the crates topped with hot food. Nacen saw that his crew had prepared as lavish a feast as could have been hoped for. Grilled fish and chicken were piled on platters of steaming rice and vegetables. Mushrooms, meatballs, and greens floated in steaming bowls of thick, brown stew. Nacen even spotted a couple of platters of sweetcakes being passed around. The scent was intoxicatingly inviting, even as it contended with the stink of the battle-tested crew packed into one room. Not all had the chance to clean up since the offloading.

"A stranger should not sleep on a Stevari ship without first becoming a friend, and a soldier should not go into battle unfeasted!" Nacen cried over the din.

"Here, here!" an Armad at a far crate called back. A roar went up in agreement.

"I do have one question," Perido said, recklessly brandishing a chicken leg now. "When can we get our weapons back? Your trufalci stuck them in a secure hold somewhere."

"They were following my orders, just basic security precautions," Nacen answered.

"So... we're your prisoners, then?" Perido frowned at his chicken.

"What goes around, comes around," Camlo muttered quietly beside him.

Nacen managed to turn his wry grin into an understanding smile. "Not at all. We will return them whenever you exit the ship. In the meantime, you are free to check out designated firearms in our firing range. Most forms of plasma are acceptable, as well as smaller calibers of solid slug flux weaponry."

"But Shukernak—"

"Shukernak won't be happy until he can fire the ship's point defense cannons at asteroids. He has to follow the rules like everyone else."

Perido grunted in acknowledgement and diverted his attention back to his meal.

"I hate to be the sole voice of reason, but should we not conserve our rations with the increase in crew?" Linasette asked as she sat down between Jeta and Chalce.

"We'll have enough rations to get us back to the homefleet, assuming they're somewhere in the Prominar Rim. If we don't make it, then we likely won't have any use for them anyway," Nacen said.

"Can't argue with that," Chalce muttered nearby, though his tone suggested the opposite. Before he could follow up, his dissent was drowned out by another uproar from across the room where a trufalci of the *Lusterhawk* had apparently balanced an empty sweetcake platter on her head and was proceeding to juggle the tray's former contents.

Nacen settled down at a long crate next to Basaul, nestling his pack carefully behind him. He caught Camlo walking past with the last of the sweet-cakes still bound to their tray and grabbed one for himself before they disappeared or became airborne.

"Well done, Cam," Nacen said before stuffing a piece of the cake in his mouth. He pulled over a cup and topped it off with wine as he savored the moist dessert.

Camlo leaned over the captain's shoulder and picked up a large, gray tankard with noticeable difficulty.

"Hey, Beskin, we need more... uh, whatever was in these mugs. I didn't know we had mugs," he wondered aloud.

Basaul leaned over and swept the tankard from his hand.

"We brought more than just guns and harsh language, boy!" Basaul snatched up a massive, opaque bottle and emptied its amber contents into the tankard. "This is Ambrophyta, better known as nightcap. It's fermented from a moss that can grow in lightless, underground areas. We lost a lot of supplies in the bombardment, but I can tell you one thing—we won't be running out of this!" He hoisted the bottle in the air, and every adjacent Armad gave a shout.

A little while later, after the food had been cleared from the plates, and the plates mostly cleared off tables, Beskin gave a nod to Nacen, Camlo, and Jeta as they sat nursing their beverages and palavering with their neighbors. One by one, they excused themselves and made their way to the front of the room. Nacen untied his pack and brought forth the object he valued most on the entire ship: a hand-crafted, spruce dulcinet. Six flaxen strings were stretched over an ebony neck, longer than that of a traditional dulcinet, affording him a much larger range of notes.

A warning light flicked on over Beskin, bathing him in dull red. This and the amber glow over the front of the room that made up their stage was the only lighting that could be managed on short notice. Beskin's left hand was extended slightly toward the audience, and his right lay behind his back. Nacen sat in the corner opposite, on top of a crate of flux driver ammunition. He cradled the old dulcinet in his arms and, after quickly ensuring it was well-tuned in the warm hall, began plucking out a sweet melody. The room hushed as the music grew more energetic. Beskin began to sing, his confidence never wavering. At the front, Jeta and Camlo acted out the parts of the song as the druvani's expressive voice, so contrary to his usual cool demeanor, filled the room.

> "As children of the stars our journey is never truly done,
> but cast to keep our spirits free across the great blue sun.
> To call a single place one's home invites complacency,
> fostering reliance and followed soon by greed.
>
> Once upon a verdant planet, two homefleets did converge.
> From this lush world each one to the other tried to purge.
> But in the ashes of defeat, a new young fire burned.
> A child of each house found that in their heart the other churned.
>
> The joining of two lovers would cease eternal strife

and the warring of two houses could give way to joyous life.
When son of one wed daughter of the other,
he became the newest heir, an honor promised to another.

The forsaken prince swore he'd get his way, seized from the arms of lovers,
and with speed and cunning his fortune he'd recover.
Hand grasped hand, and every clan declared the other enemies no more,
but none could not see the enemy within that fate had yet in store."

The young and old, the grave and gay,
did rejoice and celebrate in levity.
Whilst in the atmosphere a ship of singular intent
crashed upon waves of gravity that foretold of its descent.

With men of arms and hearts of steel the prince set upon on the feast,
the curved vessel swept in fast and low, like some serpentine beast.
So taken was the party by treacherous surprise,
that not a single blade was raised to stop the stealing of the bride.

Before the prince had fled the sun he let the final ransom known,
he would return their daughter only if her suitor yields the throne.
Among bickering guests, the suitor could only glower.
He'd never bow to such a desperate grasp at power.

To this day he cleaves his way through the sinew of the stars,
counting days without his love not in seconds but in scars.
To find his bride and drag the scorned prince through the mud,
he tallies time not in years but in the serpent's blood."

Whispers filled the room as Beskin's final note faded. A brief applause sounded, rose quickly, and died. Conversation quickly resumed. Nacen was pleased to see at least a few Armads speaking with Starkin trufalci. The captain turned to see Beskin standing beside him, wearing a rare smile.

"That was one for the ages, despite the lackluster applause," Nacen said. "One of our better renditions, I think."

"We've made good progress today. But still, it is just one day." Beskin noted, back to his cold, calculating self.

"I get the feeling you're talking about the Armads, not my fingering technique," Nacen mused.

Beskin nodded, then moved closer to Nacen.

"I still don't like this, Captain," Beskin said softly into his ear, "the Armads went from keeping you locked up to joining up with us far too quickly."

"I know it's not easy, Beskin, but we do need them. They give us better odds in finding our family. Surely that's worth some risk. And if it comes down to it, we don't have the manpower to take on the Precept navy by ourselves."

"Better chances can still mean dreadfully low. Taking risks is one thing, but letting former captors into the places we sleep is entirely something else."

"Look... no one is authorized to pilot the *Carmine Canotila* except Linasette and myself, and even I have trouble getting onto the bridge of the *Lusterhawk* when Folbix is feeling protective. Even if a mutiny erupts with a dozen Armads against what... forty-two Stevari counting us... were successful, they'd be stranded in the vacuum of space and at the mercy of the next U.P. ship that happened across them. Life is full of mist that cloaks friends and foes, and obscures the future and the past. When we don't know which way is forward, it's important to keep moving and discern for ourselves."

Nacen packed up his dulcinet and made his way back to the table, making sure to speak with different Stevari and Armads. The wine kept coming as he made his way around the room. At one point, he was fairly certain he had one of the tankards of the Armads' Ambrophyta. The rest of the evening on the *Lusterhawk* passed with a blur as he listened to battlefield exploits, travels to distant planets, and again and again recounted his brief time on Carnizad.

***

Nacen could not remember when the festivities had broken up. His time in the great hall had been a blur in retrospect. He had made a point to connect with every person, and to his vague recollection, he had done so. He blinked in the harsh light of the frigate's bridge as an orderly crowd stood at attention. Most of the active shift was present, and Basaul and Chalce were allowed on. Nacen stood near the back between Linasette and one of the frigate's trufalci. He had a passion for painting beautiful landscapes, Nacen recalled. Or was it starscapes?

Master Folbix Rinkesi stood in the center of the bridge, his central command circle projecting one huge image. It was almost entirely black, save for hundreds of faint pinpoints of light. The *Lusterhawk* appeared to be headed into the tenebrous void between the stars, but in fact their destination should be incredibly close by now. Nacen always felt that Folbix was rather lazy in most respects, like shirking basic physical standards to spend more time idle on the bridge. Nacen was left to keep the trufalci in fighting condition, one of his few duties he took very seriously. Then again, Folbix claimed he only appeared idle to Nacen because he made all the hard work of managing the *Lusterhawk* look easy. Regardless, this was Folbix's show. Nacen would let him run it.

"I never liked quickspace travel." Linasette said quietly to Nacen, separating him from his musings.

"You don't care for the melody of the passages? The mercurial tides of the great blue sun?" Nacen said, legitimately surprised.

"I pronounce it malady."

"Travel through quickspace is probably one of the safer things we do with this ship. I've seen missiles fired across the bow of the *Canotila* and you not even blink."

"I've seen plenty of that sort of thing," she explained, managing to do so without boasting.

"So, enlighten me," Nacen goaded. Rarely had he found the pilot so loquacious. Maybe the festivities had managed to get her loosened up a bit. If nothing else, getting her to open up would help pass the time. The crew had been waiting for nearly an hour as the passage's exact position was tracked down. When preparing to enter the elusive and fleeting quickspace lanes, it was worth a second look before you leapt.

"The difference is that I know the purpose behind the missiles and the lasers," Linasette began after a moment. "I know they were made by people, and they're trying to kill me. Quickspace... well, who knows who set it up. We still don't even know how the lanes function, not really. We take it on faith that they'll work."

"Yet we fly audaciously through quickspace anyway. We take a lot on faith, you know." Nacen looked around the room as idle chatter rose and fell. "It's not necessarily bad. Quickspace has yet to fail me. Sometimes, faith is enough."

"And if it did fail, you wouldn't even know it." Linasette's subsequent shrug felt somehow intimidating.

Nacen pursed his lips. "Was that supposed to be comforting or threatening?"

"Just take it in good faith," Lina said plainly.

He knew plenty of stories of ships descending into the great blue sun that never made it back up again, or emerged from new realms of quickspace far from their destination. He stared at the central display, waiting for the passage to render itself visible and trying not to think about disappearing forever into that darkness or burning up beneath the waves of the great blue sun.

After staring out for a long while, Nacen's eyes began to grow tired and drifted. Many times he thought he saw the passage materialize, but each time he was disappointed. He stood at attention, refusing to go back to his quarters and get even a moment's rest while they neared so critical a threshold.

Finally, he saw what first resembled a comet. The distant light arced across the sky, barely even visible. After a few seconds, he saw another. Then another. The chatter on the bridge faded. On the holoimage, more and more lights clustered around a central zone in the blackness. These were the telltale signs of gravitational lensing, where the invisible passage revealed itself by bending space around it. This made the stars behind the quickspace passage stretch and mirror in astonishing patterns. As the *Lusterhawk* neared to the gate, the increasing number of stars that joined the swirling ring slowly traced out a perfect circle hundreds of kilometers wide.

"Continue present course, slow speed by ten percent," Folbix announced to the personnel around the perimeter of the bridge. "Hester, it appears your calculations were spot on. Well done. Lavinia, drop our bow by two degrees toward the hub. I don't want to risk clipping the rim."

The personnel labored away at the minute alterations as fervently as they had when speeding away from Carnizad. Excited conversation rose for a moment, but Folbix hushed it with a raised hand. Then the ship passed into the invisible surface, and distant Carnizad vanished completely. Nacen knew from experience that radiation levels would be spiking, with the ship's shielding increasing in magnitude to compensate. A glance at the nearest terminal appeared to support this. The shields would last for more than enough time for the jaunt through quickspace, but longer journeys would inevitably cause strain. If left alone for more than a couple of weeks, the immense heat and radiation of the star could eventually overpower the ship's shielding, fry critical portions of the *Lusterhawk,* and potentially leave them stranded.

"Alright, Nacen, I'm going to go check on the *Carmine Canotila*." Linasette twisted her arms forward and gave them a long stretch. "We should be removing the rest of the Armads' modifications soon."

"Very good, Lina," Nacen replied. "Try to forget about the fact we're inside a star right now."

"Thanks for that," Linasette gave him a blank stare before exiting alongside several trufalci.

For hours, the *Lusterhawk* roamed across the surface of the blue giant, its trajectories determined by the long-departed humans who created it. The view from the front display was that of a deep tunnel. The center was pure black, but branches grew from its rim, sprouting and dancing in a spectrum of lights far exceeding the capabilities of the human eye. The rich display of shifting lights was visible only due to the frigate's best interpretations of the high-energy particles that danced a deadly waltz with its deflective shielding. Nacen preferred to think of the display purely as art. He fancied himself an astute admirer of the great works created by the sentient beings scattered across both space and time. Not to mention that art was, on the whole at least, a bit less likely to kill him.

On the periphery of the screen, Nacen could make out the magnificent solar prominence of the great blue sun that gave this sector its name: the Prominar Rim. The massive plasma stream of hydrogen and helium arched through the star's corona due to the imperfect and fleeting structure of its magnetic field. Most ordinary solar prominences disappeared after a few days or months, but then the great blue sun was no ordinary star. This prominence had lasted thousands of years, with no signs of fading anytime soon. Nacen stared into the display and allowed his mind to wander. This was almost a form of meditation in and of itself. He wondered if any elements of the homefleet were traveling through a nearby tunnel. Perhaps one of his brothers or sisters was looking at those same wisps of solar radiation.

Suddenly, an alarm wailed. The display flared up as more particles joined in their tango. Nacen forced his way forward into Folbix's command circle to assess the situation. No sooner than he had reached it, silence resumed. Two trufalci in the center looked on at Nacen in amusement. Folbix turned to observe the disturbance and grinned.

"Nothing to worry about, Captain." Folbix grinned as though the alert had only signaled dessert. "Only a routine high-energy bombardment."

"Very good." Nacen swallowed. He could imagine the look on his face. "Do you have an estimate for our arrival at Ulastai?"

"We'll have plenty of time to plan our next moves, don't worry."

"I like to look at all the angles. The monsters are in the minutiae," Nacen added.

"Fine, but it really is just a best guess at this point," Folbix said unapologetically as he glanced at a nearby image. "No sooner than eight days, sundial macrocosmic standard. It could be as many as ten."

The nearest trufalci glanced up at this. "Pardon me, sir, but taking into account the increased—"

"Fair point. As many as eleven," Folbix corrected impatiently.

"Thank you." Nacen eyed the displays again. They were definitely more active, but the bridge crew appeared to have everything well in hand. "I will leave you to it then."

Nacen bade farewell to Folbix and the trufalci, and exited the bridge. His eyes were grateful for the dimmer light of the corridor outside now. Eight to eleven days starside... that gave him plenty of time to plan out an incursion with the Armads. But first he would have to catch up on some sleep. Between the sweep of the Asura, the capture by Armads, and the feast to top it all, off the last thirty hours had left him drained of nearly every faculty except the awareness of his aches and pains. A routine to normalcy, even for just a few days, would do him good.

***

"All of our drone strike craft are fully operational and fueled?" Nacen tapped at his digital pad as he consulted his checklist. It was nearly complete for the morning. The flurry of activity that had been cleaning, reordering, updating, and other maintenance by groups of trufalci had moved on to other sectors of the *Lusterhawk* for now, leaving just he and Jeta in the starboard launch bay. The bright lights shone over a small fleet of drones of all kinds.

"Yes, Captain," Jeta said, standing dutifully by as though she had just personally charged their fuel cells. As far as Nacen knew, she had.

"Weapon loadouts?" Nacen set his stylus tapping on the nearest fighter's flux repeater.

"Eight set to interception duty, including this one, and the other eight for bombing runs," she replied.

"How soon for a loadout change if we need it?"

"Five minutes if fully autonomous, four minutes fifteen seconds with minimal trufalci assistance."

Nacen checked a few boxes.

"Excellent. Starboard hangar is all up to protocol. How are repairs to the *Carmine Canotila* coming?"

"She took a few direct hits when we relocated to higher ground, but we have replaced most of the parts that had been simply patched up before. The ship will be... almost as good as new within two days."

"It just keeps getting better, eh? Nice work." Nacen lifted his right hand up to his ear and looked hard at Jeta. "Do you hear that sound?"

Jeta glanced around.

"One of the drones, maybe?"

Nacen shook his head. "Sounds like lunch to me!"

"Yeah, I suppose I could go for a quick bite." Jeta frowned. She looked back to the strike drone. "You didn't hear anything? I swear there's a humming in there now."

"Sorry, just a bad joke," Nacen admitted.

"Hmm... okay." Jeta smiled and turned to go, but Nacen caught her eyeing the drone.

They walked out into the main aisle and passed between well-ordered rows of handling equipment and spare parts. Their paired footsteps echoed on the metal lattice. Nacen admired the bay as they made their way along. Only Jeta could keep such a busy and cramped area so consistently orderly. Nacen cocked his head his head at a sound. It may have been distant footsteps, but they were moving much too fast.

"Do you hear something?" he asked.

Jeta halted and hit Nacen with a stare bereft of any amusement. "What is it, the salad bar this time? I'm not falling for that again."

"No, no, no." Nacen stopped and waved a hand before bringing it up to his ear.

"Hmm... okay..." Jeta nodded and pursed her lips. "Yep, that's definitely 'Nak. By the sound of it, he wants something."

"He's supposed to be in physical training right now. Besides, how could you possibly know that?"

"Experience," she replied just as Shukernak rounded a service drone, nearly toppling to the floor. Nacen gave a grunt of appreciation.

"Shukernak!" he called out. "Have you completed your cardiovascular regimen for the day?"

"No, sir!" Shukernak shouted as he closed the distance. "I needed to—"

"I recall seeing you in the mess hall not fifteen minutes ago, so if you have, then you've set performance records for several different species."

"Sure, of course..." Shukernak panted as he slowed to a stop. "I was just—"

"Running around the ship does not count and is, in fact, a minor hazard."

"I know, Nacen, I wouldn't unless it was—"

"Well then why are you here?" Nacen said impatiently. It had been a long morning, and his stomach was currently guessing what was on the menu today via rumbling.

A loud metal bang reverberated through the bay, ringing from some far off place in the *Lusterhawk*. The bright white light of the bay dropped off into an amber glow. A strobe in the corner began to blink in time to a wail over the ship's audio system.

"*That* is what I'm trying to tell you!" Shukernak shouted, launching several bullets of sweat at Nacen. "The Armads sealed off part of the training room... the exercise track I think. Normally I wouldn't be upset, but—"

"Why..." Nacen frowned. It was his turn to be interrupted, it seemed. Folbix's voice boomed all around.

"All forces mobilize and report to your rally sector to await orders. Use of heavy weapons is not sanctioned. Use plasma when available. Flux driver and flux pistol solid munitions are permitted only under five millimeters. All forces..." The message began to repeat.

Nacen turned to Shukernak, now a reservoir of sweat. "Do you think this is related?"

"It's... it's gotta be. Too unlikely to be a coincidence."

Nacen nodded. This was no time for second-guessing.

"Jeta, you head to your rally point to get further orders. Shukernak, you're with me." Nacen set down his data pad and made sure he had both of his pistols secured to his belt.

"Why do you think the Armads waited until now to try something?" Jeta said in defiance of the urgency of Nacen's order.

"After three days, and still roughly a week from our destination? You've got me," Nacen said, as insightful as he was patient.

"Maybe we're about to duck into a tunnel they'd rather use, rather than our intended one?" Shukernak suggested.

"That's... possible," Nacen acknowledged. "Jeta, get to your rally point on the double and get in touch with Folbix. Find out what quickspace passages are nearby and for *chodra's* sake, lock down that bridge."

"We could be under attack. You should get to the bridge," Jeta protested.

"Highly unlikely. Now go. 'Nak, you're still with me."

"But as the heavy weapons specialist, my rally point is—"

"It is where I say it is. Now come on." Nacen took off at as brisk a run as he dared in the closed confines of the bay. Shukernak followed after Jeta bid him farewell with a shrug. Nacen slowed around each corner before picking up speed again. It would do no good to be laid out cold by an armored druvani.

"My weapons are... at the rally point," Shukernak said between gasps of air as he caught up to Nacen.

"No time for that. We're going to intercept before the situation escalates into a full-scale battle for the *Lusterhawk*." Nacen slowed at an intersection and let three trufalci run past heading in the direction of the bridge. Flickering strobes lit up stern faces. Nacen turned back. "Do you prefer flux or plasma?"

"As in pistols?" Shukernak glanced down to his captain's waist. "What part of *heavy weapons specialist* do you not understand?"

"Flux it is." Nacen withdrew his flux pistol. He turned to the trufalci and hesitated a moment. His mind flashed back to a file he had read, one of the many inheritances that came with the *Carmine Canotila*. Shukernak's colorful personnel records included one notable firefight, an erratic and confusing affair that led to friendly fire causing the deaths of several Stevari. Nacen did not know how this was resolved, only from a single line from his father stating that it had been.

"Well?" Shukernak asked.

Nacen blinked and thrust it into the trufalci's hands. "Safety's on."

They resumed their brisk pace, but soon Nacen stopped short at the next hallway. A druvani was running in his direction, in the opposite direction of the trufalci that had just passed. He recognized the distinct auburn hair, an identical shade to his own.

"Camlo, where's Beskin?" Nacen asked. The two bodyguards were always together in a combat situation.

"On the bridge, where you're supposed to be," Camlo stopped quickly and snapped off a hasty Drovinian salute.

"Then why are you here?" Nacen imitated the salute with his plasma pistol.

"Guarding your body where I thought it might actually be," Camlo said seriously.

"Well fall in," Nacen turned and resumed his brisk pace. He didn't have time to catch everyone up to speed that he ran into. "Be prepared to move in on my mark, and if you identify a threat, act with your best judgment."

With a quick glance in either direction, Nacen dashed past the next junction, plasma pistol at the ready. He wasn't sure what he would encounter in the training area, or what he would do, but he would be ready. The small caliber of a flux pistol would present no threat in penetrating the ship, where even a small puncture while navigating the great blue sun could prove disastrous. The worst the plasma pistol could do is turn the interior of the hull to slag.

A shot rang out in the distance.

The *Lusterhawk* was not a huge ship by any means, and soon Nacen slowed as they neared the training area and Armads' quarters. He passed over the threshold of an enormous bulkhead door. The amber light in the training room gave even the most mundane objects a menacing quality, as though an enemy could be waiting behind a crate or a drone in any alcove. True to Shukernak's word, the entrance to the exercise track had been barricaded.

"Safety off," Shukernak whispered from behind.

Nacen took the opportunity to deactivate the safety latch that kept the plasma coil from charging. The weapon hummed softly in his hands as he approached, crouching low. Behind him, Camlo readied his plasma carbine.

Another shot rang out, followed immediately by a metal ringing. This time, the clamor was no distant impact, but delivered mere meters away. Nacen's eardrums throbbed, then rang. He gestured behind him, indicating he would attack on next shot. He did not have to wait long. A colossal hammer blow struck the ship on the other side of the wall, and Nacen spun around the corner, already searching his plasma pistol's sights for a target.

Five Armads stood clustered at the opposite end of the long, sparse room. One held a flux cannon propped up on a carbon-fiber exercise ball. Two other Armads held weapons Nacen did not recognize, though they were not raised or pointed in any particular direction.

"Woah, woah, woah! Personnel down range! Hold your fire!" the far right Armad hollered. Nacen recognized him as Loke. The Armads lowered their weapons. The long barrel of the flux cannon drifted slowly to the floor.

"Is that the captain?!" called a second.

"Hey, Captain! Barrels down goes for both sides! What's the trouble?" another shouted.

Nacen swore and lowered his pistol but maintained a hard grip. He glanced back and nodded for Camlo and Shukernak to do the same. Sweat coated Camlo's brow as he did so. He looked as though it was the ghost of his own grandmother they had stumbled upon. Shukernak gritted his teeth and lowered his weapon only as far as to limit the Armads' future footwear options.

"You cannot discharge weapons outside of the firing range." Nacen stated with as much authority as he could muster.

"Do you know how hard it is to get time on it?" Loke shot back. "Be-

The Sword and the Cipher

sides, we can hardly use any of our arsenal there. Even our smallest flux drivers don't meet the caliber restrictions."

"So you *did* read the firing range instructions?" Nacen shouted back.

"Well, Perido did," Loke said with a brackish certainty.

"What about the basic ship safety primer?" Nacen shot back.

"I think it's pretty clear at this point we didn't."

"Well, I'll enlighten you. There are to be no heavy caliber weapons discharged on the *Lusterhawk* under any circumstances, even live combat. If anything were to pierce the outer hull, the resulting vacuum could put us all in jeopardy."

At this point, the Armads must have realized Nacen and his team were not getting any closer. They began to amble down the track, leaving their heavy weapons behind them. Loke led the way.

"But Captain, we weren't shooting at the outer hull. We only shot at the interior, reinforced with extra material from the hauler of course. You know... the one we used to patch up your shuttle so we could get off that rock."

That gave Nacen pause, but his heart pounded on, combat adrenaline propelled by sheer anger.

"We could have shot you," Nacen scolded, steering clear of more rules and regulations for now.

"No offense, but I don't think *we* were the ones in danger here," Loke said.

"Yeah, we weren't the ones who walked onto a firing range," another, shorter Armad added. Traver was his name.

"It's supposed to be an exercise track, not a firing range! You were in danger because Folbix was ready to have all his trufalci ready to storm this place." Nacen concentrated and paved over his anger with grim resolve. "Or, less costly to him, he could have simply isolated this section and flushed you all into the photosphere of the great blue sun."

"Wouldn't that be the chromosphere we would burn up in?" Loke asked. Nacen was still too frustrated to tell whether he was genuinely curious or just being sarcastic. It all sounded asinine at the moment.

A few rooms behind them, back the way Nacen had come, a tremendous clash of metal on metal resounded. For a moment, Nacen thought the other Armads had set up another firing range. Then his anger faded slightly and realization filled its place. It was a bulkhead door.

"It depends how far up we were, and our relative speed on release. Without protective suits, we would be much more vulnerable," Traver noted.

"Sure, but we wouldn't burn up in the photosphere," Loke countered. "We could die from exposure, granted, but we wouldn't actually burn until we reached an actual gaseous layer."

Shukernak thrust his pistol downward and kicked at the nearest wall. "What are you even talking about? Do you realize how close you came to getting killed?"

The Armads all began talking more or less at once. Nacen licked his lips, hoping he was wrong about that bulkhead. His tongue was very dry all of a sudden.

"Do any of you have a connection to ship comms?" he asked.

"What?" Loke said with narrowed eyes.

"I said," Nacen began again, "do any of you have a connection to the *Lusterhawk's* communications? A mobile headset, or an earpiece, or anything?"

Shukernak shook his head. "I was on my way to physical training, I got nothing."

Nacen whipped around to his right. Camlo's sweat was rolling down his thin features now. His auburn curls straightened where they clung to his damp flesh.

"I… I wouldn't have… couldn't… not again…" Camlo stammered. His gaze had not strayed from whatever he was looking at ahead.

"Druvani, listen to me." Nacen stepped toward his cousin and got within inches of his face. He was shaking. What was going on with him? "Look at me. Look at me, please. Do you have any comms equipment we could use?"

Camlo looked into Nacen's eyes. His eyes shook too. Did his cousin realize what was about to happen? Or was he caught up with something else?

"What's the big deal? This was just a little misunderstanding." Loke shrugged. "Right?"

Nacen whirled around. "Showing up to a dinner party in battle armor is a little misunderstanding. The *deal* is that all of the air is about to be flushed out the side of the ship. I need everyone to spread out and look for a communications terminal, a headset, a digital pad someone left lying around… anything."

The Armads scattered, apparently having heard all they needed. Nacen went back to the door and fiddled with the controls, kicking himself for leaving his pad behind in the starboard bay in favor of his sidearms. The door and its controls may as well have been made of stone. He glanced around the room, which was lined with various equipment to help the crew maintain combat physique with or without artificial gravity. Among the rows of adjustable seating, cables, pullies, and weights, there were no communications devices. He turned back to the door controls and tried a few more combinations. Surely this had some means of communication with the rest of the ship. Whether that could be exploited was another matter.

"Sir," said a voice from behind.

Nacen turned. Shukernak stood behind him bathed in the amber emergency lights.

"What is it, 'Nak?" the captain asked, still trying new combinations with the door.

"Have you had any success?"

Nacen gave the trufalci an incredulous look. "No. No I have not. Thank you for checking."

Shukernak's wide features were suddenly bathed in red light. It flashed in syncopated rhythm to a much louder alarm now.

"I was asking because…" Now Shukernak had to shout over the intermittent alarm. His cadence came in awkward pauses between siren wails. "I may have found something you could talk through!"

Nacen ceased his useless tapping at the controls. "Lead the way!"

Shukernak nodded and set off out of the exercise room and down the Armads' makeshift gun range on the track. They hung a right and emerged in a utility room which appeared to be being used as temporary storage. Shukernak shoving a transmat crate away from the wall and revealed the black mirror of a powered down screen.

"Might just be on a closed loop, or not connected at all, but I figured it was worth a shot!"

Nacen nodded and opened a dusty control panel next to the screen. He keyed it on, and miraculously the screen turned on. It was a blank command prompt. Whatever this unit had been used for, it had not been updated in some time. He entered in basic commands to navigate around the unit's options. At some point, this appeared to be used to update shipping manifests and cargo logs. He scrolled down outdated menus until his heart nearly jumped into his throat at the sight of BRIDGE COMMUNICATIONS.

"I'm in! I'll have a word with Folbix and clear all this up!" Nacen yelled at Shukernak. "But get everyone as far from the exterior of the ship as you can and find something to hold onto, just in case!"

Shukernak gave a curt nod before disappearing around the corner. Nacen proceeded and entered in his command credentials. His fingers flew across the keys, not thinking of the horrible fate that awaited them if he did not contact Folbix in time.

He entered his code to initiate communications, typing it out deliberately and carefully. Nothing. His mind raced to think of what could be stopping him. It had to be Folbix. Finally, the helmsman had seized on an opportunity to eliminate Nacen and gain full command of the *Lusterhawk*. In a few moments, both Folbix's chief officer and obstacle would be floating in orbit around the great blue sun, with his frigate speeding away to some new, safer venture.

Nacen swore and struck the screen with his fist, with the only effect being a pain in his wrist. He became aware of a whistling in the air. No, that *was* the air... being sucked out through a multitude of starboard bays and vents. Anyone that wasn't jettisoned would likely asphyxiate within minutes. Nacen was surprised to feel a calm spreading over himself, like dipping into a pool of cool water on a scorching day. Giving up on the verification, he saw only his reflection in the black screen. He looked on with a sense of detachment. He never thought it would end like this. After a bad twist of fate on the battlefield? Certainly. Vaporized in an instant as his ship was destroyed by overwhelming firepower? Often a risk.

"I never thought I would go out this way," he muttered into the wind.

"What? You thought starboard would be more likely? What did Folbix say?" Shukernak shouted. How long had he been standing there? Nacen just stared back, unblinking. "What did Folbix say?!"

"I couldn't get a connection to the bridge," Nacen stated.

"So what's the plan? Everyone is secure in the interior, but I don't need to tell you we're losing oxygen fast." Shukernak said.

"I could say a few words," mused Nacen.

"What? You always have a plan. Are there any emergency O2 tanks nearby?" The trufalci gestured wildly as though he might conjure a few up. "Could we weld the vents shut?"

"No oxygen tanks in here that I saw. Welding every open door and vent shut, if we could find the materials to do so, would take too long."

"So there really isn't a plan," Shukernak restated.

Nacen gave a solemn nod, and Shukernak slumped back against the wall. A wave of auburn hair popped in through the door, heralding Camlo's puzzled face.

"Okay, so everyone is—"

"Secured in the interior, Camlo, I know. Thank you," Nacen said.

"Communication troubles?" his druvani asked.

"Folbix locked us out. He's taking this as an opportunity to get rid of us permanently." Nacen stepped back from the screen and crossed his arms. His head rushed and he felt momentarily disconnected from his body from movement. They were definitely running low on oxygen.

"What, he changed the passcodes again?" Camlo looked on, incredulous.

"Yes..." Nacen cocked his head. His cousin seemed to be caught on the wrong part of the statement.

Camlo stepped up to the screen and tapped a few keys on the board below it.

"Well as part of his new security protocols, since the Armads have joined on, he stepped up the passcode resets to once every three days. You should have received them in a message... yesterday I think? Could have been the day before. It all sort of runs together when you're crawling through the quickspace..."

Nacen stood there, shocked, his feet rooted to the floor by what felt like his own stupidity. "I left my data pad back in the starboard launch bay."

Could Folbix's entire plot have been explained away by Nacen missing a few minor updates in security? As Camlo typed away in front of him, a part of Nacen hoped it was that simple. Another part, quiet but demanding, hoped they would not survive to suffer the indignity of the comedy of errors that transpired. There would be many, many new trainings and protocols put in place to make sure this sort of thing would never happen again. He would see to that, alive or dead.

"That's okay, I think I remember it." Camlo was being remarkably cool under pressure, especially considering he had been outright paralyzed when they had first confronted the Armads here. "I have a pretty good... yes, there we go."

Folbix's control center was now illuminated on the screen.

"Well done, Cam!" Nacen exclaimed. He had to take a deep breath before continuing. He felt light-headed all of a sudden. "Now, how do we get audio on this relic?"

"Does he not see us?" Shukernak stood up and, after steadying himself, waved his hands about behind them. Folbix appeared to be intensely interested in a display off to the left. Nacen was no longer so hasty to abandon his treachery hypothesis.

"If this was all a test, Nacen, I've got to say, you might want to try stepping it up a bit," Camlo said as he fiddled with the terminal's settings.

"I'd laugh if I wasn't concerned about oxygen," Nacen shot back. "Audio won't even matter if there's no air in here." Nacen tried a few hand gestures: help, danger, and vacuum got no replies. He tried a few more of an obscene nature but nothing seemed to get the master of the ship's attention.

"This terminal might never have actually had audio... but surely he can see us," Camlo said, barely above a whisper.

He was right. They needed to do a better job of getting Folbix's attention. Nacen withdrew his plasma pistol. Shukernak gave a shout.

"Get out of here!" Nacen gestured with the pistol. Nacen set the small plasma coil to maximum charge and held it aloft at head height, directly in front of the terminal's aperture. He shielded his eyes with his left hand, and fired on maximum intensity into the small room.

***

For a long time, he felt only pain. It came from a long way off, some unknown font of agony. This was all he knew. But he held onto that pain, because it meant he was alive. After a while, as the pain became more familiar, he became aware of other sensations. He was breathing. His breaths came in short, ragged spasms, and there was some sort of tube in his mouth, down his throat even. But still he breathed. He wasn't unconscious in a bio-tank, or drifting over the great blue sun, he was here. Nacen Buhari was here.

Wait... where was here? He opened his eyes, only to realize they were already open and peering into utter darkness. He moved his hand to uncover whatever was obstructing his vision, but only tugged against restraints. His arms burned.

"*Kaha*. He's awake already? Somebody get the ship's medic," said a gruff voice beside him that could only be Shukernak's. There was a labored quality to it.

"No need to commit any more acts of heroism," another voice rasped from across the room. "They'll be around."

For a moment, Nacen had trouble placing it to someone he knew, then he realized Camlo was missing his usual cheerful tone. Would the blindness be permanent? What else was wrong with him? How quickly the simple gratitude of knowing he was alive had faded.

"There's only one person trying to be a hero, and he nearly got us killed..." Shukernak took in a deep breath before continuing. "Again. They still don't know how long we were breathing near vacuum."

"Will you lay off? He's still your captain."

"Relax, he can't hear us. And even... if he could, there's no way... he'll remember with everything... they've got him on," the voice of Shukernak said.

Nacen attempted to shift his weight to glare at Shukernak through whatever implements covered him. He managed only a minor nudge before something caught in his chest cavity and he settled back down, distracted by this new torment.

"He's lucky he didn't lose the hand," Shukernak drawled. "We still don't have any functioning bio-tanks... he could've ended up with a prosthetic, like you."

"Well if he'd told me his intent and let me fire the pistol, he wouldn't have those burns all over his..."

Nacen felt his heartbeat quicken, which in turn put strain on his already labored breaths. Camlo did not continue. A door clanged open in another room, and other voices filled the air. Nacen tried to focus on one in particular, to suss out some useful information, but the harder he tried, the more tired he became. He felt a relief of pressure around his head. Fresh air wafted around his temples and eyes in its place, but there was still only darkness to escort him back to sleep.

***

This time when Nacen was roused to consciousness, he was greeted by a harsh light. He greeted it in turn with a squint and a groan.

"They said you might be waking up soon," said Camlo's voice from somewhere in the sea of dazzling silver and white.

A loaded statement if I ever heard one, Nacen tried to say. What came out was a jumble of half-formed words strung together by a series of novel phonemes. He attempted to blink away his stupor and, failing that, tried to shield his face with his hands. No good. They were still restrained. Not to mention still stinging.

"They said you might not see again, either."

"Our medic sure says a lot for never being here," Nacen said, slurring a bit. This time, the words came out sounding more like they intended.

"He comes in regularly to check on us," Camlo said reassuringly. "So do a few others."

Gradually, his eyes' sensitivity to the light abated, and Nacen could make out hazy outlines around him. The figure that could only be Camlo lay in a bed one to the left and across the room from him.

"We must have been breathing near-vacuum for a while," Nacen said after a long silence.

"Just a couple of minutes, or so they told me. Folbix got the vents closed and sent in the emergency response team real fast."

"Oh, you helped get us out?"

"Actually, 'Nak and I passed out too. The Armads dragged us over to the bulkhead, though, and made sure we got treated first. Awfully nice of them."

"Yeah, very considerate." Nacen replied flatly.

Camlo watched him from his own bed, looking uninjured himself save for a breathing tube emerging from his mouth.

"I should have taken the shot," he said.

"Don't be foolish. Rushing in to save the day was my mistake. Fixing it was my responsibility," Nacen said.

"Yeah, well... protecting you is mine."

"I've fired my plasma pistol hundreds of times..."

"But never point-blank at a steel wall in a small room, with no armor or eye protection." Camlo finished for him.

"We were out of time, I had to act fast," Nacen stated.

"There's always time to talk out a plan."

Nacen opened his mouth to object again. This was not always the case but knew in this instance his cousin was right. This was no time to set a bad precedent by acknowledging it, however.

"Has Folbix been in at all?"

Camlo rolled back onto his back and stared up at the ceiling.

"No, just the doctor and some of the *Canotila* crew. Linasette was here for a while before your surgery. 'Nak got permission to leave just a few hours ago."

"That's good," Nacen said, regarding none of it in particular. He started sorting out how he wanted to confront Folbix. Partially this was an issue with misunderstanding and a gap in safety protocols, but he just couldn't shake the thought that there had been malice behind Master Rinkesi's actions. Incompetence could only explain the multiple failures up to a point, and Folbix was anything but incompetent.

"His name was Shal," Camlo said, as though commenting on the weather.

Nacen had no idea where that came from. He attempted to elucidate a succinct response to drive at the heart of the matter.

"What?" he snapped.

"He was the Armad who died on the *Asura*, back on Carnizad."

The neurons connected at the mention of his father's ship.

"Ah yes, the one Beskin shot to try to save us."

"It wasn't Beskin, he just took the blame so they might go easier on us. I played along, because... well, it made sense with us getting captured."

"Sure," Nacen agreed more out of reflex than any analysis. His head was still foggy.

"I've never learned the name of somebody I've shot." Camlo's gaze remained fixed on nothing in particular.

Camlo was clearly fixated on this altercation, which Nacen had chalked up as one of many that day which merely constituted their survival. This might explain why he had seemed off-kilter during the standoff in the exercise center.

"You were just doing your duty Camlo, under pretty difficult circumstances I might add," Nacen said. He tried to sound understanding, but his thoughts just kept returning to Folbix on the bridge. What had he been up to since Nacen was unconscious?

"I guess so," Camlo said, and let his head roll away from Nacen. "But the difference is they became our allies. And now Beskin is taking the heat for what I did."

"Two more Armads died from U.P. special forces, Cam. More could've died if we hadn't taken the initiative and attacked the lancers on their own turf while Basaul made repairs to their hauler."

"Justifying it doesn't make it better."

Nacen disagreed.

"Look, there's lots of things I haven't reconciled from that day, but this isn't one of them. You need to do what you have to in order to perform your duty," Nacen stated, leaving out that this was predominantly protecting Nacen's own skin.

"Are you saying I need to own up and apologize?"

"I don't think an apology will make much of a difference to the Armads. But do what you need to. Just make sure Beskin and I are around when you do."

"Sure, Nace," Camlo offered up a weak smile. They lay in silence for a while. Nacen's eyes soon grew sensitive to the bright light and he shut them. He drifted in and out of sleep for a while. When he was sharp enough, his thoughts would always return to the ship's master and the handling of the emergency. A sliding door interrupted Nacen's meandering thoughts.

"Ah, excellent, you are awake," noted an aging Stevari in a white robe. He swung up a case at his side and set it on a small table next to Nacen's bed. Many compartments clicked out, obstructed by the lid.

"I can see that," Nacen said.

"Well, that answers my next question," the doctor said agreeably, "but just so I can be sure our operations were successful, I will need to poke around a bit further."

"I'm not really in a position to stop you," Nacen said without mirth. The doctor chortled regardless.

"No, you wouldn't be. But do not fret, we will have you up and giving orders in no time. If you take it easy for a few days, you should be good as new."

"When can I walk out of this infirmary?" Nacen eyed the door before it reflexively shut.

"For your sake, Captain, you should really be here for two days." The doctor waved a menacing finger at Nacen.

"I said can, not should," Nacen huffed. "Please, for the sake of everyone on the ship, not to mention my sanity."

The doctor shook his head slowly and stood. For a moment, Nacen thought he would chide him and leave him shackled.

"I've done optical regenerative surgery for prolonged sunlight exposure, engine heat and radiation exposure, all as a result of failed shielding when traveling through quickspace. But never from a self-inflicted plasma wound. Fortunately for you, the procedure is the same for all causes. The skin grafts and regen baths are all fairly routine, and the damage to your lungs was light enough that a few hours on—"

"I'm glad I could give you some good practice," Nacen noted, cutting the doctor off before he could cross the line between polite discourse and revulsion at what his body had undergone. Flux rounds and plasma fire could be ignored, with experience and common sense, but as soon as doctors started screwing, sewing, and growing parts back on... Nacen tried to lose interest before he lost his breakfast.

"Let's give you four more hours rest and then I'll let you go on a trial run, or rather a walk. The hand bandages stay on, however." Another admonishing wag of the finger.

The next few hours passed quickly compared to the haze up until that point. Camlo departed, but Nacen was visited by most of the trufalci on board, even many of the Armads. Linasette visited on more than one occasion to report on repairs to the *Carmine Canotila*. Not once did he hear back from Folbix, nor the Armad leaders Basaul and Chalce.

***

The Sword and the Cipher

Nacen stumbled up the corridor of the *Lusterhawk*. Though the padded, restrictive gloves and headwear he sported were not particularly intimidating, his unrelenting forward gaze and lumbering momentum were sufficient to keep anyone clear so that his physical capability would not have to be tested. Hulking Armads and bustling trufalci alike gave way as Nacen neared the bridge. Behind him, Camlo and Beskin kept up a slow but uneasy pace as they tried to predict where they would need to be should their captain fall or a crewman not notice their captains' lurching path. Beskin had insisted on supporting Nacen in his convalescing state, and Nacen had taken the moment to assure his druvani that now was not the time to show weakness.

"Or intelligence, apparently," Camlo added, almost softly enough so the captain would not hear through his medical wraps.

But Nacen had pretended he could not. He stopped at the door to the bridge. He placed his hands in a suitably commanding position behind his back, straightened, nodded to his druvani, and limped slowly onto the bridge of the *Lusterhawk*.

The bridge held only a skeleton crew compared to the entrance into quickspace at Carnizad. Five Stevari manned the terminals and holoscreens around the perimeter of the circular room, and in Folbix's place in the center two junior crew stood conferring about something. Master Folbix Rinkesi was not among them. The duo on the platform stopped their confabulation and stared at Nacen as he made his way toward them, while the others merely pretended not to watch. Nacen recognized the bridge crewmen. Kezia was the senior of the two, Arav only on his second tour with the *Lusterhawk*.

"Hello, Kezia," Nacen nodded at the officers. "Could you please explain our current trajectory?"

Kezia drew herself up and stepped backward in order to bring a holoscreens into view.

"Sir. We are en route to Tantalos. Time to breach is two days, three hours, forty-seven minutes by the sundial."

"Your direct answer is very appreciated, trufalci."

"Certainly, sir," she snapped back.

"Now please tell me why our course takes us directly by the Urias passage in a few hours."

Kezia opened her mouth and did a slight double-take of the screen.

"I..."

"You're not sure why we're doing it, or you're not permitted to say?"

"It's not that, sir, it's just that..."

"Are you planning to exit quickspace via the Urias passage, contrary to my orders?"

"N–no, sir!"

"Then someone here please inform me why we are going out of our way to visit a passage we decided against?" Nacen announced to the room.

"Making sure my bridge crew is staying sharp and alert, eh, Captain?" a voice called out from behind.

"Something like that," Nacen turned and glared at the newcomer. Folbix had come, along with another half dozen trufalci with pistols at their hips. He blurred in and out as Nacen tried to stay focused on the master of the *Lus-*

terhawk.

"Medical sure did a number on you." Folbix glanced Nacen up and down, acknowledging the special gloves and helmet with suppressed glee.

"Indeed. I thank you for your quick action in recovering us," Nacen said, deciding to take the high road. Maybe it would lead to the answers he sought.

"Because of your daring signal with your pistol, thank the stars, we were able to react." Folbix circled Nacen and took his habitual place in the middle of the central platform.

"Indeed," Nacen said. Or had the desperate flare of plasma made it so Folbix could no longer ignore him?

"I confess, I was just finishing up in my private quarters and was going to come visit you in the medical bay, since I heard you were stirring," Folbix said.

"I had more important matters to attend to."

"Well, I apologize for not visiting sooner."

"Quite alright," Nacen waved a gloved hand dismissively. "What I would like to know now is—"

"Yes, the slight detour toward Urias... of course. In order to minimize the time out of our flight path, the decision had to be made while you were under," Folbix explained with an easy smile.

"So under what circumstances would you have informed me of this treachery?" Nacen interrupted before Folbix could get any further. "If the Armads had mutinied, I like to think they would have at least woken me up for it!"

"You misjudge me, Captain. Our route takes us close to Urias only so that we may deploy a scout drone through. If there are any other Stevari fleeing or attempting to regroup, this will likely be the one of the last sectors in which we may find them."

"A fine course of action," Nacen acknowledged, putting his bandaged hands at his sides. "But I cannot help but wonder what other actions you might take had I not survived the incident on the exercise deck."

Folbix stared at Nacen for some time before continuing. No one else dared to breathe, let alone speak.

"Are you implying I staged the incident in order to relieve you from command?"

"It is trite wisdom that one should never let a good crisis go to waste," Nacen said.

"I had nothing to do with the incident, and my response to seal off the area was a tough call for the good of the ship. Until you blinded yourself with a plasma pistol, I did not even know you were there," Folbix said defensively. "To think what I did merely contributes to your ongoing brashness. Frankly, you don't need me to put you in incredibly dangerous situations, you are perfectly capable of doing so all on your own."

What the master said made a vexing amount of sense, and Nacen had a sinking feeling that he himself had known it all along.

"You're right, of course," Nacen said, reigning in his anger as he spoke. "I guess I just wanted someone to blame for it all."

"Fair enough," Folbix shrugged. "The devil of it all, though, is that those

Armads who had the audacity to set up a heavy-caliber firing range on my ship would likely have died had you not intervened." Nacen slowly raised his bandaged hands up, as though justifying the injury to himself. "I have testimonials from bridge crew, the Armads, and your young druvani here for my report of the incident, and have already taken steps to ensure that such losses in communications do not result in such disaster again. We also have pan-atmo masks and oxygen tanks in all sectors of the ship."

"You have my thanks." Nacen felt the need to apologize as well, but he did not want to show any more weakness in front of the crew.

"I hope I have your trust, as well." Folbix glanced knowingly toward the astral maps on the holoscreens.

"Of course." Nacen staggered as he stepped off the platform but recovered easily enough. "Now I believe a return to my normal duties as captain should aid in my recovery, if you will excuse me."

Chapter 7

   A malaise hung over the crew after spending seven days over the great blue sun. Nacen felt that only he was truly aware of it, being himself on the up-and-up. He found convalescence a natural remedy for lethargy. But for the crew, there was none of that caged energy, that nervous buzz before a ship went starside. Even the grief at the losses at Carnizad seemed ground down by the routine. But perhaps this was for the best. After all, they were not marching to war. They were meant to be just another merchant ship, one of hundreds that day, that would be making a profitable trip to Daedalon Station.

   The change out of quickspace came rather undramatically, while a third of the crew was still asleep. One minute they rode blue crests, and the next a bright red dot shone in the middle of a suite of distant stars. Tantalos existed as a transit hub for the Unity. Most of the excitement in the system happened on a station orbiting one of two nearly lifeless rocks. Folbix would put the *Lusterhawk* in orbit, and Nacen would take the *Carmine Canotila* in for docking. Then Basaul's plan could truly begin. Whether cunning or idiotic, it all depended on the outcome.

   Nacen strolled around the *Carmine Canotila*, inspecting its repairs with literal fresh eyes. He felt more invigorated than ever as he stroked the re-worked and freshly painted crimson plating with recently unbandaged hands. Both he and the ship were fresh. Raw. After he was satisfied with the ship's exterior, he moved into the sleek interior through the rear ramp. The cargo bay was nearly empty, and preparation for the mission was still hours away. He navigated through the short, narrow corridors of the small transport and found the *Canotila's* pilot sitting in her designated seat already outfitted in her gray flight suit.

   "I can't let you fly around in the cargo bay, you know," Nacen said, taking the familiar seat beside her. "She's small, but not that small."

   Linasette gave a slight grunt of acknowledgment but remained focused on the streams of data taken in from the *Lusterhawk's* sensors. Nacen brought up the central holoscreens with an image of the Tantalos system patched together from known data. He pretended to be interested in the planetary specifications of two outer gas giants.

   "I've synced our Drovina homefleet sundial with Daedalon Station. It's currently five-thirty at night," Linasette said at last.

   "Good, not too dramatic of a shift. If that station ever sleeps at all," Nacen stated. "I've stayed on some planets where the time is changed from season to season."

   "Really? Why?" she asked, glancing at Nacen for the first time since he arrived on the small bridge.

   "I think they thought it was useful for some of their laborers."

   "Was it?"

   "Only in giving them something to complain about," Nacen noted. He felt the tension where a shared laugh might have been, and Linasette went back to studying her screens. Nacen did the same. A single red star lay in the center of the system. Two large gas planets circled the outer edge, just outside of the path of the quickspace passage. Nearer to the sun was a host of asteroid fields. Racing among them were two small, rocky planets which easily could have passed for asteroids had Linasette not tagged them. By now though, Nacen could hardly stand the silence. "Would you care to discuss anything before we brief for the mission?"

Linasette gave a slight exhale and her eyes glanced around, no longer focused on her holoscreens. She waved the screens into nonexistence and turned.

"It's tricky business trying to fool the Union Precept, Nacen."

"We're not. This is all an above-the-board business venture sponsored by the Extra guild."

"Call it what you want, but what you're doing is duplicitous. The Union Precept have surely gathered data on us over the years, and they are going to be alert after what they did to your father at Carnizad. Maybe not the individuals on the station, but everything is connected."

"You're right." Nacen slumped back. "Better to be honest. Why don't you open up a comms channel and we can ask them for their clandestine fleet dispositions?"

"Maybe if you asked politely," Lina suggested.

Nacen thought about what he would say to a Union Precept officer if he found himself face-to-face with one on the station. Most of the scenarios that ran through his mind ended up with his plasma carbine in one orifice or another. He broke off a few displays and gazed at the other ships coming out of Daedalon in the opposite direction of the *Lusterhawk*.

"What do you think they're up to?" Nacen asked the pilot, enlarging one display where a luxury ship was cruising toward one of the outer gas giants.

"Pointless to speculate," Linasette said flatly.

"Why?"

"Why do you care?"

"I asked you first." Nacen smiled. "Don't make me pull rank."

The pilot pulled a few strands of errant hair back into place by her ear. "I don't see how it matters, especially given our current situation."

"I think," Nacen said, suddenly and overly wistful, "they are a young, rich couple on a romantic getaway. Newly married, perhaps. They rented out the entire liner to show their love for each other and fill the entire emptiness of space with it."

"Seems a bit unrealistic," Linasette stated.

"How come?"

"I don't think anyone in the Unity is that romantic, or at least as romantic as you think you are."

"Wrong, Lina. By sheer statistics someone in the U.P. is bound to be a hopeless romantic like myself." As Nacen panned around to find other vessel of interest, footsteps echoed from behind.

"Oh, hello, Nacen." Camlo walked onto the bridge. "I hope I'm not interrupting anything."

"Not at all, Camlo," Linasette said.

"Just have a pre-briefing briefing," Nacen added.

"Good. I was having a tough time sleeping." Camlo stepped up and was immediately captivated by the big display of the system dominating the front of the bridge. "So, where exactly is Daedalon?"

"It's that second planet from the sun." Nacen zoomed in on the body in question.

"*Kaha*. People actually live on that rock?"

"Yep. Mostly underground in shielded facilities. Power is generated by Daedalon Station, which is where we're headed," Linasette explained.

"How?" Camlo asked.

"Orbital momentum. It'll be easier to explain once you've seen it."

The trio sat and watched the convoy cruise slowly toward the inconspicuous fleck of dust that was Daedalon. It seemed a testament to human determination to decide to live on such a wasteland. He was reminded how unfavorably the cosmos had stacked the odds against life developing in its cold oceans and barren balls of rock, to such an extent that no one had ever encountered an alien species. At least not to his knowledge. But the ingenuity and fecundity of humans had been more than capable of turning nature's hostility into hospitality. Humanity had been both successful and prolific, despite their own best efforts to hinder or eliminate themselves.

The *Lusterhawk* eventually joined up with a major traffic column headed toward Daedalon Station, a steady current of dozens of other ships. In reality, though, the ships were thousands of kilometers apart.

"At least we'll be able to hide in the crowd," Camlo said.

"Don't count on it," Linasette chided. "They probably started surveying us as soon as the light reflecting off our ship reached their station."

"Alright. Let's go make the final briefing." Nacen shook some life back into his legs and stood.

Nacen and Camlo went back to the cargo bay. Formerly empty, now most of the Armads and Nacen's crew occupied the small hold. Along with three Armads, Jeta and Shukernak were currently learning how to play 'masons,' a simple card game with a surprising amount of depth. Nacen looked out among the eleven Armads of his crew. Though tall, Nacen's eyes only came up to most of their chests. He stepped on the nearest compressor crate and cleared his throat.

"Alright everyone, listen up. By now we've all heard the plan. But there have been some small, last-minute changes. We will split into two teams. The forward team consists of myself, Beskin, Shukernak, Basaul, and his choice of two guilders. Any more than that and we're likely to draw more suspicion than we need. The second team, that's the rest of you, will guard the *Canotila* and will function as a relief force if needed. Ostensibly, we will be taking compressor crates to a delivery zone." At this, Nacen kicked the crate he stood on with his heel. "But in reality, we will be scouting out the station for a terminal with Counsel access. That's what the Unies, the Gloms, call the executive manifestation of their distributed intelligence network. We need a high enough code to access an interplanetary registry to ascertain fleet dispositions, store the data on our device compatible with Unity tech, and get back to the ship. And we need to do all this without alerting security personnel. There will be no communications not authorized by myself personally, encrypted or otherwise. We can't risk the Unity figuring out our true motives. I don't want this to get bloody, and I don't expect it to. Keep your eyes looking forward and your mouths shut and we'll get through easily enough."

Over an hour passed as the crew busied themselves in the *Lusterhawk's* starboard bay. The crew had lost so much money playing masons that the Armads appeared to be letting them win for the time being, in an effort to keep the Stevari playing. At last, Linasette pinged Nacen's earpiece and told him that the *Lusterhawk* received a signal originating from Tantalos II. Nacen, the druvani, and Basaul came up to the *Canotila's* bridge where Linasette was waiting for them.

"I'm listening in on Folbix's communications with Daedalon Station," Linasette informed them. "So far, we're just getting the same error message on repeat."

After a few minutes, Linasette was proven correct as a high, tinny voice chimed over the bridge.

"No shipment code received. You have been placed on watchlist yellow. Please proceed to the enclosed coordinates upon arrival. Place frigate in orbit at designated zone," the voice announced calmly.

What followed was a stream of data from the station, and a stream of curses from Nacen. "We needed to send them a shipping confirmation code? They could be firing on us now for all we know."

"Relax," Basaul said, "this kind of thing happens all the time. Unexpected deliveries, mix-ups with orders..."

"Potential terror suspects infiltrating your base?"

"All I'm saying is there's a protocol for it. Let's just follow it before you start taking evasive maneuvers."

"Very well. Carry on like everything is fine," Nacen sighed.

"Everything *is* fine," Basaul grumbled.

"That's the spirit."

As Daedalon Station became visible to the *Lusterhawk's* forward sensors, it appeared as a large moon in low orbit. Red light from the sun glinted off of its round surface. After reaching nine hundred kilometers out, however, they saw the station was actually separated into many levels, all shining gold and crimson with reflected light. Central columns connected layers of shielded glass and steel. Anchored into the columns were tremendous cables that extended all the way down to the planet.

"What's going on with the station?" Camlo pointed to the hologram as the station moved languidly in orbit. "It looks like a big jellyfish."

"The cables serve two purposes, Cam. The first is your basic space elevator. They ferry supplies and personnel between the surface and the station," Linasette explained.

"I'm with you so far. Long elevator rides."

Linasette nodded. "The cables terminate in what amounts to large claws hundreds of meters above the surface, which interlock with massive dynamo stations around the equator. As Daedalon Station passes over the planet in its orbit, the claws at the end of the cables latch onto the surface station handles around the equator and crank the lever. These in turn spin a dynamo below the surface, which stores the energy as mechanical motion as the dynamo spins, and gets converted into electricity through a turbine."

"And... you lost me..." Camlo rubbed at his temple.

"Call it whatever you want, it's effective." Linasette gave a shrug. "They have retro thrusters on the station to account for errors and drift so they can consistently latch with surface generators to make power."

"Won't the power station levers eventually pull Daedalon Station down?"

Linasette shook her head. "The energy the station loses on each pull is big, but not enough to impact the orbit of Daedalon. The end game is in about four hundred thousand years, the station and planet will be in geosynchronous orbit with each other. Locked in endless dance. *Then* no more power."

"This explanation is endless," Camlo drawled.

"Fine, engineering lesson over. But the economics of it are fascinating too," Lina said intently as Camlo's eyes lost all focus. "The power generated wouldn't even be close to financially viable, but the station existing in orbit saves enough money enabling trade vessels to ignore most of the gravity well effects. The power company actually *gives* money to people living on Daedalon proper."

"Well... how else are you going to convince someone to live there?" Camlo stated.

"Beautiful. Just the sight of it," Nacen said, admiring the seemingly lethargic drift of the cables over the planet's jagged surface. Then his gaze slid along the cables back to the station. It seemed sinister to him with its gold and crimson glow. "Somewhere in there is the link to getting the location of our homefleet."

Basaul grinned, and something in that expression chilled Nacen's nerves. "And vengeance for both our guild and our world."

"Here's the data chip," Linasette said, handing Nacen a black square not much bigger than his thumbnail. "According to the station specs, most of the processing power is located on deck one hundred twenty-seven. That's where I'd start."

***

"Alright, Captain Buhari, this is as far as I go," Folbix said over the *Canotila's* speakers. "We'll maintain this orbit until you return to us. Good luck."

"Thank you Master Rinkesi, and all aboard, for getting us here safely," Nacen said aloud, knowing his voice carried across all of the *Lusterhawk*. "We'll let you know before we're ready to leave."

"Looking forward to it," Folbix replied. "My visuals indicate there are no personnel or loose gear around the bay. Am I to believe this is the case before I open the bay doors?"

Was that some sort of dig against him? Nacen's temper flared for a moment, but then he realized this was probably part of Folbix's new protocols to avoid such disasters.

"You are correct, Master Rinkesi," Nacen said after a moment's hesitation.

"You are clear for departure. Without wood, the fire dies," Folbix said.

Nacen grinned before completing the chant and the *Carmine Canotila's* thrusters jolted them out of the frigate and into space. "Burning bright, the stars our prize."

The shuttle gave a hard burn for no more than thirty seconds, leaving the *Lusterhawk* behind, indistinguishable from the hundred-odd other ships circling Daedalon Station. Already now the *Carmine Canotila* slowed dramatically for its descent. Its target, according to the automated message they had received, was a solid section of wall approximately one third of the way up the lattice of scintillating floors. At the last possible moment, the solid wall opened up its nanite surface and enveloped the ship to pull it into the pressurized interior. After he was sure his ship had not gotten stuck in the wall, Nacen strode out in the small cargo hold of their shuttle. Shukernak was guiding the last crate over the transmat via hover drone.

"Okay, weapons and ammunition are in the compressor crates under our ghost field, correct?" Nacen asked.

"Righto. The Counsel won't know if we're smuggling in explosive or eclairs. I packed in something special for myself, too," Shukernak said.

"We're going for zero detection and zero casualties, 'Nak.'"

"Hey, it's just in case!" Shukernak raised his hands gingerly, the perfect imitation of innocence.

"Fine. In for a pistol, in for a plasma cannon. But I reserve the right to beat you over the head with whatever you brought, should the need arise."

Shukernak smiled and gave the Drovina salute, index finger and pinkie out over his right breast. They didn't have time to collapse the ghost field and check everything again, and he couldn't immediately scan the contents with the ghost field in place. Nacen knew they were in a pressurized environment now by the heavy clank the *Canotila* made on the station floor as it powered off its thrusters. He gulped. He hoped he appeared more confident than he felt.

Nacen pressed his finger to his ear. "Linasette, can you hear me?"

"Yes, Captain. You're coming in five by five," the pilot's voice chimed in his ear.

Nacen didn't like the idea of using the ship comms while within the station, but it was the only option they had in case of emergencies. Encrypted or not, the Unity would certainly be listening in. Fortunately, they had developed code words to circumnavigate this communications block.

"Excellent. The sooner we get this error resolved and our delivery made, the sooner we can be on our merry way," Nacen said.

The team gathered in a clump on the transmat. Rather than their traditional crimson robes of House Drovina that may have aroused suspicion, Nacen and his crew wore plain robes of brown and beige with no accents. These garments would signify their status as mercenaries with ties to anyone with enough currency. Beneath these they had donned recast armor of milky brown.

"Remember, Starkin, stay silent unless you are spoken to. You resemble any other human closely enough, at least as far as we can tell," Basaul said.

"I'll take that as a compliment. Okay, Lina, take us down." Nacen tucked in a loose corner of his robes.

In an instant, the six members of the team and two big crates were swept from the transmat of the cargo hold and reassembled just as they were in the interior of a wide bay. Five other ships were housed in the large space, in between the *Carmine Canotila* and the large set of doors that presumably led to the interior of the station. Before the group stood a hunched figure in a plum-colored robe. A great, bushy beard poked out from under a hood. The figure took a step forward and pulled back his hood, revealing two fluorescent blue eyes that looked up from below bushy eyebrows. The round, metallic eyeballs rotated as he looked the group up and down.

"Greetings. My name is Arban. I will be functioning as your escort this evening," the man said matter-of-factly.

"We don't need an escort," Basaul replied flatly.

"Hmm..." Arban stroked his beard. "Our station Counsel assigned me to your craft, so you are mistaken. Navigating Daedalon Station can be treacherous, regardless. I am here to make your job as easy as possible. We'll start with a cargo check, since your ship has already passed initial inspections. Standard security measures, I assure you." Before anyone could protest, a thin arm protruded from the hunched man's robe, and the plum fabric slipped down to his elbow. Arban cast his palm out over the nearest crate, splayed out his fingers, and cast his gaze upward. Nacen noticed odd little nodules under the man's skin on his knuckles, under his wrists, and on the pads of his fingers. The odd little man lacked the telltale signs of genetic alteration usually accompanied by one's being born into the Union Precept. Perhaps Arban's world was assimilated after his birth, or whatever they said in its place in the U.P.

Shukernak couldn't help but pass a nervous glance at Nacen. The captain returned the trufalci's look of worry with a deadpan stare, annoyed by his telltale anxiety. After half a minute, Arban repeated the process on the next crate.

"Hmm... raw materials in excess of three tons. Platinum, rhodium, and iron mostly. Everything appears to be in order," Arban said with a slight frown. Then his arm disappeared once again into his robes. "Follow me, and we will–wait!" The group rooted in place at the order. "You. Your left pouch at your hip. Remove its contents." Arban gestured at Shukernak's waist.

Shukernak stood frozen in place, not sure how to react despite the clear instructions. Nacen snatched the device from Shukernak's pouch, suspecting the worst. He withdrew a palm-sized device with a small screen.

"It's just a hover drone controller. For moving crates," Nacen said reassuringly, trying to hide his palpable relief.

"Hmm. Well, my security drones will take care of any necessary conveyance." With a flick of Arban's left wrist, four drones emerged from the large, slate gray doors at the end of the bay. They were built around a central chassis roughly the size of a man, albeit a legless one. They hovered on a sleek platform about a meter above the ground, with grav thrusters gathered around the base. In the middle of the chassis was a black band, no thicker than a hand's width, that wound around the circumference of the drone. Presumably, this was its sensory apparatus. Four huge servos sprouted from the torso, with a device on the end of each. They opened like a mechanical multi-tool, and claws extended out to grasp the handles of the crew's compressor crates.

During the brief moment they opened, Nacen saw that the approximations of hands also contained flux repeaters and some sort of plasma weapon, its coils currently inert. The drones hefted the crates with ease. "Let us proceed."

Nacen stared into Arban's mechanical eyes and pupils of ice blue dots. Did he know? Or at least suspect?

But Arban gave no indication, not a trace of unease, and led the group out of the bay doors into a long hallway with rounded sides and ceiling. Nacen, Beskin, and Shukernak brought up the rear. They followed the curving path around in a long circle. As they rounded one corner, the planetary cables came into view. They were even grander to behold from within Daedalon Station. From here, the cables stood like the trunk of some enormous tree, growing up and up until at last it appeared only as a thin line extending all the way to the planet's surface.

"Daedalon Station's cables are most impressive," Basaul said, gesturing to the other side of the shielded glass.

"Your compliment is well received, coming from an Armad. Your kind hold industry and craft very highly from what I have seen. Not like some others," Arban said with a slight turn of his head.

Nacen raised an eyebrow. Was that an insult directed at Stevari? The jab was nothing new, for oftentimes more material cultures looked down on those they called the Starkin. Still, he would take it over outright suspicion or hostility at this point. If Arban wanted to trust the Armads more than him, that was just fine. The conversation continued, and Nacen took the opportunity to increase the distance between himself and the front of the group. Beskin and Shukernak followed suit.

"Keep an eye out for a control room, maintenance station, anything that might have a link to the Counsel we could access," he said in a hushed voice.

On and on through the winding hallway they continued. They went down a large, gray elevator and began looping back. The halls were not crowded, but they did pass many other people. Among them they spotted haughty nobles of House Orizon in resplendent robes of blue, tan, and purple. Stoic Armads as black as coal also strode by, and hosts of Unity civilians went about their trade. Occasionally Nacen spotted a pair of Daedalon security drones on their patrol.

"Arban, you must satisfy my curiosity... how are the cables connected to the station?" Basaul asked with genuine interest. But Nacen detected more motive than simple curiosity.

"Ah, I see your mind is as keen as your eye! They are not actually physically bolted on, oh no. They are held in place by magnetic fields, powerful ones at that, and allowed to rotate in place slightly. Hmm... otherwise the tension in the cables could alter the course of the station. There are many factors that must be considered for long-term harnessing of the power at the equator."

"Fascinating. Do you think we may take a look at such an apparatus? To witness such a marvel would make our trip to Tantalos truly complete."

"Hmm... I suppose that is alright. Let us make a quick stop there, then we may proceed to our designated hold." Arban gestured at the elevator panel with his right hand. "Interestingly enough, our elevator does not use conventional cables or even magnetic rails for acceleration. The elevator uses the same artificial gravity system of the station but simply adjusts the rate as needed. Consequently, we may travel quite fast."

"Remarkable," Basaul acknowledged.

The group filed into a large elevator nearby, much larger that the first, about three meters deep by five wide. After a moment of silent communication between Arban and his artificially imbued Counsel, the elevator began moving. Something was most definitely wrong here. The elevator was going *up*. But the cables were on the bottom floor. Nacen took stock of his surroundings. Arban stood at the front of the elevator with two security drones on his flanks. The other two hovered behind the group. The crew was surrounded, but their compressor crates were right beside them. Could it be better to take a chance and seize the element of surprise here, or allow themselves to be captured and negotiate or fight their way out? No, there would be no way out after the Unity identified them and concentrated their forces. They needed to escape. Now.

Nacen looked down at the compressor crate interface and tapped a few keys. "Odd, something appears to be interfering with our compression field. I'm reading some radiation leakage."

"Hmm... funny. I do not detect anything." Arban glanced around with a deep frown.

Basaul gave Nacen a look that would have pierced tungsteel. Nacen kept his motions slow and steady, but he feared his pounding heart would betray him. Could the security drones monitor his vitals?

"Is everything alright, Starkin?" Arban said, a hint of mockery in his tone. "Do elevators make you nervous, or is it the confined spaces you cannot stand?"

"Heh, typical stargazers getting claustrophobic," Basaul added in an effort to defuse the situation.

With his right hand, Nacen keyed at the pad to unlock and unload a portion of the contents on top of the crate. Not the rhodium or other precious metals, but the weapon cache and several grenades hidden behind the sophisticated ghost field. With his left hand, he made a series of quick motions. The movement would hopefully appear as nervous fidgets to outsiders, but a message to those Stevari who knew the subtle hand tones.

Get ready to fight. Weapons coming. You two take the rear.

With a final tap to access the hidden index of the crate beyond the ghost field, the weapons materialized on top of the compressor crate. Directly in front lay his plasma pistol, which he snatched up and energized. Nacen left the remaining weapons and turned his attention to the drone immediately in front.

He raised the pistol, set it to roughly half of maximum intensity, and fired at the rear sensor band. The drone's blue hull shone with brilliant light as the plasma connected, but the drone spun before Nacen could snap off another shot at the weak point. He fired again, but the shot impacted on the drone's front ablative armor with little effect.

The drone's servo whirled about and struck Nacen on the shoulder. The end opened up, and Nacen saw a plasma coil whirring to life within. He pointed his own plasma pistol at the arm and unloaded into it, leaving the servo as a dangling rod of blackened steel. Already, however, the servo to his right had leveled a flux driver at his head. He ducked just as it unleashed a salvo that would have rendered him headless and got beneath the drone. He unleashed five shots where the anti-grav pedestal lay, and only stopped when he heard a detonation from within. There was another flash and his skin burned as though someone had set a hot poker to it. He rolled quickly to one side and only narrowly avoided being struck by the collapsing drone.

Standing up, Nacen had no time to take stock of the situation. He saw the other drone in the front of the elevator firing with both flux repeaters. He heard only a muted rumbling as his eardrums adjusted to the deafening roar of weapons being fired at point blank range. He aimed his plasma pistol to destroy the drone, but it was flung against the wall by Basaul. The Armad had seized one of the flux drivers and had put the butt of the weapon through the drone's sensor array. Again and again the Armad smashed the weapon into it, and each time more sparks flew. Finally it collapsed, smoke billowing from its former front facing.

In a moment it was over, and Nacen was still standing. He saw Beskin and Shukernak had destroyed the two drones in the rear, as instructed. Shukernak looked as though he had taken several flux rounds to the side, though fortunately the rounds appeared to have had gone straight through him. His enhanced blood would clot, and most of the major damage could be reduced until they got back to the ship for more intense medical treatment. Nacen's ears readjusted to the normal decibel range and he became aware of someone shouting.

"Cease fire! Cease fire!" Arban's panicked voice wailed. "What is going on?!"

"I could ask the same question," Basaul said, tossing the battered weapon aside.

Nacen swallowed and noted a bitter taste in his mouth. His right cheek was still burning, despite his body's protective nanites attempts to heal the wound the drone had inflicted. It was also becoming hard to breathe in the elevator, with the smell of molten metal and singed machinery crowding the stale air.

"Damned drones lit into me good, Captain, but I'll be alright. I can't imagine I look half as bad as you. Hope you don't have any upcoming dinner dates." Shukernak grinned slyly, which turned into a grimace as he stood and bore the weight of his injury.

"Only with your mother when we find the homefleet, and I'll be fine by then," Nacen said. He saw the two Armads with them, Loke and Hortz, were up and going as well. Like Nacen, they were singed badly by plasma from either the drone's hasty return fire or else their fiery demises. "Our escort here had no intention of taking us on your little detour. Did you notice the elevator was going up, not down?"

"I hadn't, what's that got to do with anything?" Basaul said.

"The cables are located at the bottom of the station, relative to our position anyway. Arban here was taking us somewhere else." Nacen turned to glare at the robed man. "Weren't you?"

"The Counsel had identified you as a threat. I was to detain you. That's all I know. Obviously it was right," Arban rasped.

"Shut up and stop the elevator. We need to think."

After a moment's hesitation, Arban complied. "Hmm... I will cooperate for now, for this is a useless enterprise. Every moment's hesitation allows the station to rally more security."

The squad recovered as best they could, and the Armads retrieved their hidden mass condensers from the other two crates. Nacen leaned against the wall to think. They had to get back to the *Carmine Canotila*, and fast. Who knew how many security drones the station had and were already closing in? Then again, this entire job would be in vain if they didn't get the information on Union Precept fleet disposition.

"It's a miracle none of us were killed," the Armad named Loke declared.

"I figured if we got the jump on them now, we'd have better odds than whenever they sprung their trap," Nacen said.

"Tell me then, genius, what are the odds on us getting out of here alive now?" Loke replied.

"Two point seven percent," Arban interjected.

"He wasn't asking you," Beskin said. "Besides, you're missing variables. Like our experience and resolve."

"Your fortitude and brashness are negligible factors," Arban replied.

Shukernak was now accessing the final ghost field, which transported out his personalized explosive microcaliber railgun. The flux driver variant was originally designed to be fixed on a stationary mount and manned by two soldiers. Shukernak then withdrew a small shield drone, with hovered at waist height as he set the elongated forearm of the ex-cal on top of it. The drone hovered, helping keep the heavy weapon aloft. "Well then how about my little friend, Betty?"

This setup allowed Shukernak to move and fire the automatic weapon solo. Still, the weight of the gun was exceptional, and the trufalci's bulging muscles were a testament to that fact. As the squad formed up in the elevator, Nacen's earpiece chimed.

"So, Nacen, I take it there's been a change in plans?" Linasette asked through the comm link.

"Yes," Nacen said, keying his earpiece, "we're going to need pickup on deck one hundred and twenty-seven. We'll find a way to let you in."

"It's getting out that concerns me. There are security drones coming in, those blue spherical numbers that hauled the crates away with you."

"I'm... intimately familiar with them." Nacen kicked one of the ravaged hulls at his feet.

"Yes, well, we're up to ten... no, twelve now."

"Hold tight. We'll see what we can do about getting you out of there. Until then, don't do anything to provoke them," Nacen insisted.

"Copy that."

The elevator continued to rise. The panel by the door indicated they were on floor sixty-three of two hundred and fifty-five.

"Alright, we're proceeding as planned. Let's go up to deck one-two-seven and get a hardwired connection to the station's Counsel. Lina said that was the most likely location for a viable connection." Nacen picked up a flux repeater and slapped his plasma pistol onto a magnetic patch on his hip belt.

"We can't just waltz out of the elevator. We just need to think of a plan of approach," Loke said. "Something that comes at it from a different direction."

"I think I know what you're driving at." Nacen grinned.

"I thought you were just smugglers! What is this about?!" Arban cried.

"We just need some information," Nacen said smoothly.

"Well here's some information for you," Arban sneered. "You're dead! All completely and utterly dead!"

***

Security drone C37.606 levitated near the elevator, its flux repeaters aimed squarely at the doors. It was joined by thirteen other drones, all surrounding the elevator at precise intervals. The hallway curved to the left and right, and of the many doors that locked behind them, one led to central processing. The hallway was punctuated on either side by pillars that curved up to the ceiling. Anything that would step out into the hallway could and would be filled with a thousand slugs in under a second.

Initiating alarm and response function marengo: total containment protocol. Orders received. Issuing request to planetary barracks to supply all available reserve troopers.

All guns remained locked on the doors. They opened, and the flux repeaters sighted in on the lone figure. It raised its hands in a pleading gesture, but no projectiles would fly unless the Counsel willed it.

"Don't shoot, don't shoot!" the lifeform cried. Counselors identified the lifeform as Master Arban, Class D ambassador of Daedalon Station. "They're bel—"

The drone to the right detonated in a surge of light that flooded C37's right sensor arrays. It smashed into the ceiling before hurtling to the floor, a section of the room which no longer happened to be there, C37 observed. It veered to the left and trained its guns on the smoked-filled space and fired into the gloom. The drone fired its repeaters at a cloaked figure emerging from the level below, but the figure's ablative armor managed to deflect the rounds before it ducked behind a column. Several more figures leapt out and dove for cover behind the curved pillars of the doorway. C37 maneuvered to fill in the gap where its ally had been eliminated. It laid down suppressive fire on the column to the right, and the plasma carbine that fired there fell silent.

Four of the remaining eight drones lined up to storm the position. They rotated their guns outward and drifted toward the columns, and the air became dense with the flux repeater slugs.

C37 detected a sound from behind and rotated to face it. Flux rounds screeched out of the hostile's support gun as it came barreling down the hall. The drone triggered all weapons to fire on the hostile, but nothing happened. Suddenly it lost balance. The walls spun and the drone hit the floor with a crash. C37 still had functionality of its rear engine and activated it to spin toward the targets in cover.

The lifeforms had charged out now, and the larger hostiles wielded huge flux drivers capable of penetrating a chassis with a single shot. Security drones were being shot down and smashed into pillars.

C37 unlocked its final functioning tool, a plasma torch used for repairing hull fractures in the station. It extended the servo, pushed its rear engine to full thrust, and flew toward a hostile in brown robes emerging from behind a pillar.

***

The drone seemingly came out of nowhere as it barreled down on Nacen with prodigious speed. He made to dodge out of the way, but it was too late. The security drone's plasma torch was no more than an arm's width away from cutting into him, but it was crushed and flung back by an invisible force. Basaul stood next to Nacen, brandishing his mass condenser.

"That one had some gumption." He laughed and, spinning the condenser around in his hands, smashed the butt of it into the drone's optical array. The lens shattered to pieces.

Nacen blanched. "I owe you one."

"You'd have done the same," Basaul grumbled.

"Maybe not so effectively, but sure. Alright, everyone, take up defensive positions. We have no idea how many more are coming for us. Arban, get these doors open."

The man gave no response. Nacen turned to find the man still in the elevator, though he was no longer cowering nor hunched over.

"Hmm... I have assisted you long enough, Starkin. That ends now," Arban said.

"Huh? What happened in the last five minutes? Need us to dispose of some more station security for you?" Nacen raised his plasma pistol and strode over to the man.

"I know what the Counsel allows me to know, and it has shown me more. Oh, so much more. You shall not be permitted to leave this station." Arban drew his lips into a line.

"If you know what your sick digital gods know, then tell me where the Drovina homefleet is before I send you to them."

"The Counsel cannot allow your homefleet to survive, not after discovering what they intended to do."

"What?" Nacen frowned. "We... my *family* are peaceful traders. To what are you referring?"

"If you are unaware of what your father meant to unleash, or what your brother now aims at, then you are a bigger fool than we had thought. How you got this far is a wonder to us." Arban's blue, fluorescent eyes seemed small and distant.

"Us? Who are you?" Nacen's eyes narrowed, and he lowered his pistol without meaning to.

"I can be many things. I am what the Counsel allows me to know. I am one of the station ambassadors of Daedalon. Had you been truthful from the start, I could have been your salvation. Now, I am your damnation." For the first time, Arban gave a toothy grin. "Be silent now. Your doom approaches. Greet it with some dignity."

"Okay, how do we get these doors open?" Nacen recoiled from the man and spun around.

"Give me five, maybe ten, minutes with our blue-eyed friend here and I can get him to change his mind." The Armad known as Hortz boasted.

"If there are reinforcements on the way, we don't have time for that. Besides, I doubt his Counsel will allow him to act against its interests anymore, even if you did half of the unsavory things you're planning."

"I have yet to see a material that an implosion grenade won't get through. As long as it's not shielded, we just duck through the blast zone after it's done its work," Basaul said.

"Make it happen." Nacen nodded.

Loke and Hortz gathered at the door and dug into a satchel. They huddled together for a few seconds before turning back to Nacen.

"You're going to want to get behind cover," Hortz said, kneeling by the doors.

"From the blast? How far?"

"No, from them!" Hortz pointed behind Nacen. He whirled to see several soldiers advancing up behind the pillars of the hallway curving to their right. Their armor was colored a burnt orange, with white stripes on the shoulders and helmet. The two-part helm separated by black slits marked them as Union Precept lance troops. Their armor housed all sorts of upgrades he could only dream of, the most relevant being its prismotion shielding.

Nacen ducked behind a nearby pillar just as a plasma lance singed the air where he had been a moment before.

"Hostiles! Everyone, take up defensive positions!" Beskin shouted from the left side of the hallway. *Kaha*. They were hitting his team from both sides. They would not be able to hold this position for long. Nacen leaned out from cover and sent three bursts with his flux repeaters at an exposed lance trooper. The soldier's prismotion shielding sensed and focused around the incoming barrage, deflecting nearly all of the rounds. Those that made it through bounced harmlessly off the armor's deflective plating.

From behind, Nacen heard a titanic screech of rending metal with a powerful rush of wind akin to a hurricane. The Unity soldier's plasma fire ceased for a stunned moment before picking back up. The implosion grenades had gone off, leaving a spherical hole in the wall and floor roughly three meters across.

"Cease your inaction, you incipient cowards, and stop them!" Arban shouted from behind a smoldering security drone.

Basaul leaned out of cover to snatch up Arban, but plasma fire made him think twice about retrieving the ambassador.

"We'll cover you, Captain! Get what you need and get out," Beskin said.

Nacen waited until he heard the distinctive whir of Shukernak's ex-cal before sprinting to the wide doors and jumping the gap. Plasma shots singed the door behind him. He landed hard and rolled awkwardly. Straightening his cloak, he stood and took in the small, rotund room around him. Rows of black computer servers lined the walls and rose to an elevated ceiling. Without a doubt, this must be one of the station's data vaults.

Nacen walked to the center of the room and stepped onto a raised platform. Servers rose above him like giants, silently watching his every move. He glanced around, surreptitiously tapping at the nearest of four control panels as though someone might demand he leave at any moment. In the hallway outside, a plasma grenade detonated, punctuated by a scream. That got him skimming the contents of the menus and submenus more hastily. But he found nothing useful in the first control panel.

He stepped quickly to the next panel. Having learned the general lay-out from the last panel, he searched through this one much more efficiently. Plasma and flux fire continue to ring out as the firefight his men would inevita-bly lose played out in the corridor. Beads of perspiration rolled down his face and dripped onto the screen. Nothing. He stepped to the next panel.

On the third control panel, Nacen finally found what he sought. Under material shipping requests, he found a fleet distribution log. It was not compre-hensive by any means and obviously did not include the Stevari ships among its annals of munitions, fuel, and rations. But it could be enough to track the activity of any Precept fleet giving chase to the homefleet. The logs also made special mention of something called the Void Protocol, which seemed an un-usual note for a database of fleet resources and other logistical concerns. He placed the data chip on the screen where indicated and began the download-ing process. Given the initial slow pace, he gauged he had roughly two minutes to go before the transfer was complete. The Stevari chip would interface with the Union Precept's node just long enough to take the raw data and carefully sever its connection with the Counsel to not be preemptively destroyed by it. He would not have enough time to play it safe and download everything from all the panels, unfortunately. This would have to do.

He checked the remainder of the third panel and the fourth just to be sure he didn't leave off any critical information as Lina's storage device fin-ished its work. There were yet more vague callouts to this thing called the Void Protocol. Was it a procedure, a ship, a program, a weapon?

The fourth panel did, however, contain access privileges to the entire station. Nacen scrolled over and added the chip to the list. To his surprise, it worked. The moment the transfer finished, he snatched up the chip, pocketed it in a secure pouch at his waist, and dashed off to the door. Once he returned to the homefleet with the U.P. fleet distributions, or rather if, he could give his family the edge they might need to escape whatever trouble they found them-selves in. This may be optimistic thinking, but it was better than showing up with a handful of Armads and a shrug.

"Okay, I've got what we came for. I've also granted us full security ac-cess to Daedalon Station," Nacen said over the comm link.

"Great. So now what?" Basaul demanded. "We're taking fire out here and it's getting worse by the minute. Your trufalci got hit by a plasma lance, but his gun took some of the damage."

"What do you think about taking a trip down to see the cables after all?" Nacen asked.

"Depends what'd you have in mind," Basaul said between two purrs of his mass condenser.

"My inclination is toward escape." Nacen peaked around the corner to see Unity troopers moving up. They were a stone's throw away from the entrance to the data vault now.

"There's something we can agree on," Basaul said.

Nacen led the move down the gap in the floor left by the implosion grenade. He landed roughly one level below, bending his knees to soften the blow, and rolled behind a pillar. The lancers had the elevator lobby entrance surrounded. What's more, the holes Nacen and the team had blasted to sneak up on the drones could soon be used to fire down on them.

"Everyone down, now. We're leaving in... ten seconds." Nacen leaned around the corner and prepared to lay down suppressive fire.

A gunmetal gray plasma carbine caught him in the forearm, and Nacen dropped his repeater, which skittered across the corridor. He was still partially behind the pillar and couldn't bring up the plasma pistol in his left hand quickly enough, instead grabbing at the nearest arm of the carbine's operator. He forced it over his shoulder and, bringing it down hard, felt the armor give in a very unnatural way. The lance trooper took the injury silently, and Nacen felt two quick but brutal punches to his side. His cloak absorbed most of the bone-shattering blows.

"Out of the way!" He heard another trooper shout as he dropped the limp arm. Nacen raised his plasma pistol as the Precept trooper swung an elbow at his face. The blow connected, and he heard a sharp crack. Stinging pain followed, and Nacen was knocked to the ground. He found he still gripped his pistol and fired three shots at the soldier who knocked him down, who fell in a heap as he fumbled for his carbine. Their armor, even with its prismotion reactive shielding for deflecting low-energy shots, was useless against plasma fire at this range. He lined up his next shot, but the lancer already had Nacen in his sights.

With a concussive crack, a mass condenser gun sounded off, and the trooper in orange and white was hurled off to the right. His helmet slammed into a pillar and he lay still at its base. With a sigh of relief, Nacen saw Beskin and Basaul rounding the corner, followed by Loke and finally Hortz dragging a limp Shukernak behind him.

"You can thank me later," Loke said. Plasma fire had already begun to pour down from the level above.

They ran to the elevator, and Beskin brought up the rear, firing his plasma carbine with unerring precision into the gaps in the ceiling. This kept the plasma fire off them, for the moment at least.

Nacen summoned the elevator with a few taps, and to his relief, it responded. "Someone get me a grenade."

"That's our last plasma," Beskin replied.

"So be it. We have to clear that elevator."

"And risk destroying it?"

"Let us do it," Basaul said. "It'll be a cinch."

"Fine, but if a single lance trooper's boot touches this hallway I'm chucking in this grenade," Nacen swore.

Basaul nodded and turned to help Beskin keep the troopers on the floor above pinned. The elevator doors opened, and Loke rushed around the corner first, flux driver ready. He lowered it dejectedly.

"Oh..."

A tremendous burst of plasma erupted from the elevator. Loke was incinerated instantly as the air around the entrance caught fire. The ensuing pressure wave knocked Nacen down. His vision flashed white and his ears rang. He shouted and barely heard his own words. He glanced at the elevator. It was entirely gone. Bits and pieces of its structure lay strewn around the lobby. The shaft was empty except for several large chunks of debris drifting aimlessly in all directions. It had been a desperate attempt by the Unity to eliminate Nacen's team. One that had nearly worked. He clenched his jaw. Nacen watched as a piece of the control panel drifted lazily upward in the elevator shaft. The drifting debris jarred his senses at first. How could they oppose gravity so effortlessly?

Of course. He thought back to Arban's explanation in the elevator. There was no gravity in the shaft. The elevators were controlled by grav plates, just like the gravity in the station. They could theoretically glide all the way to the bottom as fast as they wished. It was worth a shot. After all, it was their only option, other than wandering about to find another elevator, which could likewise be rigged with explosives.

"Get into the elevator shaft!" he yelled, repeating the order until he convinced himself he was actually shouting it as the ringing in his ears abated.

Beskin dove into the shaft without hesitation. Basaul and Hortz gave him a confused look. Were they not hearing him? Or did they not remember that the elevator acted on its own artificial gravity?

In lieu of blind faith, a demonstration would be needed. Nacen scrambled to his feet, grabbed his plasma pistol and flux repeater, ran to the elevator, and kicked off the side of the wall, downward into the abyss.

The Armads' surprised curses echoed in the elevator shaft. Nacen grabbed a support beam and glanced back up. Basaul, Hortz, and the unconscious Shukernak were now fluttering past him.

"Thanks for getting my man out of there, Basaul," Nacen said.

"We don't have time to write a song about it, Starkin. Move!"

Nacen aimed for a support beam about ten meters down the elevator shaft and kicked off. He timed this next leap better and was able to lunge off without the need to stop. He found there was a limit to how fast he could go without stopping, and he practiced treading this limit carefully. He gained quickly on the rest of his team. They had gone about thirty floors, he guessed, when a beam of plasma shot past him. He glanced behind and saw a half dozen lance troopers closing the distance. He didn't stop to turn around and fire back. Even if he was able to hit them, more would take their place. Speed was their greatest ally now.

"Beskin, do you still have that grenade?" Nacen asked over the comm link. His druvani, who was several floors ahead, or rather below, responded slightly out of breath.

"Aye, Captain."

"I need you to plant it behind a support beam. Set it to proximity detection, one meter with a... two second timer," Nacen ordered. More plasma shots flicked past.

"Aye, Captain." Beskin deftly slowed to a halt and set the grenade before leaping off again, barely losing pace. Nacen continued to dart around the shaft, spiraling farther and farther down with blurring speed. Plasma whined through the air around him, and several shots burned into his flesh. He noticed that Hortz had taken a few hits as well and was struggling to hold onto Shukernak amidst the bedlam. After a few seconds, a roar erupted behind him, and the plasma fire ceased. The grenade must have made its mark.

Soon he saw that the troopers had spread themselves out. At most only half of the squad had perished to the grenade. As Nacen and the crew completed their descent, he turned around and fired his carbine at them. Beskin followed suit, but the Armads were too concerned with safely slowing their descent. Regardless, they were no more fortunate at hitting their adversaries than the Precept troops had been, but they bought time for the Armads to get to a stop.

"Nacen, want to give us a hand with this door?" Hortz growled.

Nacen slammed into the floor with a rolling maneuver, not wanting to risk a slow descent even with the enemy firepower greatly diminished. He withdrew Lina's storage chip and held the chip to the door, but the door was not compliant. Perhaps it needed to be paired with the elevator via its control panel.

"Blow it open. You have an implosion grenade still, right?" Nacen said, taking aim at one of the lance troopers. He fired and connected dead center in the trooper's chest, who dropped his plasma carbine and began to drift.

"We're down to *way* too many lasts of things," Hortz grumbled as he set the grenade. "Setting to minimal range. Sorry boss, you're gonna have to crawl through." They backed off and the grenade sucked a hole in the door just big enough for Basaul to squeeze through. Beskin and Nacen scrambled behind.

Transparent walls curved up and around the massive room, gleaming with the light of the stars. The round hall, easily one hundred meters across, was a forest of huge cables. The diameter of each was roughly three times the height of a person. The cables extended through a flexible surface on the floor and each into their own dome in the ceiling. Nacen watched, mesmerized, as each onyx cable swayed slowly, held loosely in place by unseen forces. It reminded him of the angels of old myth who would descend from heaven, swinging censers from a long chain. These were certainly the planetary cables of which Arban spoke.

He felt a hand on his shoulder. It was Shukernak. He must have regained consciousness sometime during the flight down the elevator shaft.

"Now ain't the time to admire the architecture, Captain. Let's move."

One of the far cables had opened up to reveal a full squad of lance troopers. Before they could react, Nacen and the crew were already halfway to the nearest cable. They bounced slightly as they bounded across the pliable floor.

"We need to find one with a lift relatively close to the station," Nacen said.

"Preferably not one loaded with Unies, either" Shukernak added.

They closed the distance to the closest cable just as plasma fire began to whip past. Nacen hailed the elevator with the data chip.

"Okay, I'm going to hail a few more and hopefully we get one quick," Nacen said. "Keep me covered!"

Nacen leaned around the corner and snapped off a few bursts with his flux repeater at a lance trooper attempting to outflank, before running off to the next cable. They were spaced fairly close together, so the time for the enemy to get a fatal shot off was remote. As long as they didn't get too close, anyway. He requested the elevator and dashed to the next one, noticing the orange troopers blurring from cable to cable as well.

"Keep them off our elevators," Nacen reminded the squad over the comm link. Beskin and Shukernak fanned out and laid down suppressive fire with their plasma carbines. Basaul and Hortz were already advancing, unleashing their mass condensers on any figure ahead of them that moved.

At the fourth elevator, Nacen stopped. Out of the corner of his eye, he saw a lance trooper leaning around a cable. Unable to request the elevator with the storage chip, Nacen dove for cover. Plasma beams whisked by and sliced into the cable he lay behind.

"Captain, the first elevator is here, come on back!" a voice shouted.

Nacen looked back and saw a lance trooper emerging from the hole that the Armads had created in the wall. He fired off his flux repeater on full auto and managed to get through the man's prismotion-shielded armor through sheer weight of fire. The trooper collapsed, and his allies ducked back for the moment. Nacen slapped the weapon to his hip and sprinted toward the first elevator where his team was still gathered.

"We're leaving *now*, Cap!" Shukernak shouted.

Just a few more steps and he would be there. An entrance within the massive cable had opened up, and there the team waited. He felt a searing pain in his left leg. He went to take another step, but the leg failed him and he fell. Beskin darted out and grabbed Nacen's hand.

"I've got you!" he yelled. A plasma shot connected with Beskin's shoulder, and he lurched back, but kept his grip on Nacen. The pair went tumbling into the elevator where the team waited and the cable's access port slid shut. Nacen crawled to one side as enemy fire continued to pour into the closing doorway.

"Augh!" Nacen gripped at his leg. The shot had seared through the muscle and sinew of his thigh. It would be a painful healing process, should he be lucky enough to get the chance. So far his plan, or rather improvised outline, had gone terribly but had been successful. The next part was the most critical, however, and the most dangerous.

"Yeah, we made it!" Shukernak whooped.

"Barely. I'm going to need some quality time with your medi-drone when we get back to... wait... how is going down to the planet going to help? We're going right into the belly of the beast," Basaul said with a frown.

"Wrong. Well, actually you're right. But first we'll be going out through its throat," Nacen declared. He activated the comm link. "Lina, can you still hear me?"

"Yes, Captain. I've managed to keep our communications mostly intact, despite the Union Precept's jamming efforts," Linasette said coolly.

"Good. I wouldn't want you getting too bored up there. Listen, we need evacuation."

"Okay, just tell me where."

"One of the outer cables leading down to the planet."

There was a pause. Static. Did the U.P. manage to jam them after all?

"Clarify, Captain," Linasette said.

"We need you to intercept our elevator as we ride down the cable and pick us up. Get the transmats ready, and the medi-drone. Tell Master Rinkesi to get in position just below Daedalon Station, and it wouldn't hurt to have the *Lusterhawk's* medical bay prepped either," Nacen said. "This is going to get worse before it gets better."

"Wait, back up. *Intercept?*"

"Track my comms signal and target the cable, say... a quarter of a kilometer down planetside. Sever it with the rail guns. You're going to see five figures pop out of the elevator cable."

"...into space," she added flatly.

"Yes. Remember, a quarter of a kilo ahead of our position in the cable. I don't know how fast these cable elevators go, so adjust as needed. If you're too close, we're dead. If we reach the planet, we're dead," Nacen said, losing his patience a bit now.

"Thanks for the vote of confidence, Captain."

"If you didn't already have my complete confidence, I wouldn't have let you bring us to this station."

Nacen turned to face the group. All had wide eyes, save for Beskin. His hawkish features were rapt at attention.

"Alright, when this elevator severs, a couple of things are gonna happen," Nacen said.

"Yeah, I'm going to both wet and soil my pants," Shukernak said.

"We're going to be out in the vacuum of space for a few seconds. Maybe more than a few," Nacen continued, "but Linasette should transport us back on board the *Canotila* before we pass out from lack of oxygen or suffer an air embolism. Which reminds me, everyone needs to exhale all the air from your lungs as soon as you hear the cable rupture. If you don't, the air in your lungs will expand and rupture your lungs."

"I want to talk about trading in my robes for a pressurized suit at my next review," Shukernak said.

"Duly noted."

"Coming in for approach," Linasette said. "Ready up!"

Nacen exhaled deeply, felt his lungs run dry, and then exhaled some more. He reflected that this would be the second time in less than a week he would be exposed to vacuum. He had survived before though, if only barely, and now he had made the choice to be let loose into the inky void. That was better, right?

Several piercing snaps reverberated through the cable, followed by an enormous, creaking groan. Then the elevator picked up speed, and Nacen felt a rushing in his ears as all the air in the elevator was sucked into space. His first instinct was to breathe in the precious air, which he attempted out of reflex.

Riley O'Connor

Nacen felt his diaphragm contract and lungs ache, but he got no satisfaction. He opened his mouth wider to scream, but no sound emerged. Panic-stricken, he whipped his head around. Below him, his feet dangled in utter darkness. He could not find the red hull of the *Carmine* Canotila. Above him loomed Daedalon, the planet a muddy red ball spackled with dark clouds. Soon, the ruddy pallet of the planet began to fade to gray. Black spots appeared on the edges of Nacen's vision, and thin tendrils grew from the darkness. After a moment, he realized he was looking at the veins in his own eyeballs. Suddenly he realized how light and dizzy he felt. His heartbeat slowed. He closed his eyes. A nap would do him good.

Chapter 8

His lungs burning as he gulped in air, Nacen awoke on a hard surface. He opened his eyes to the interior of the *Carmine Canotila's* cargo hold. Camlo crouched over him.

"You were out there the longest, Nace. The blast threw you away from the main group. But we got you!"

It was all Nacen could do to muster a smile. He was extraordinarily light-headed. Objects in the room seemed to swim rather than snap back into focus. Linasette's voice came over the speakers, and Nacen heard her as though he were under a meter of water.

"...orbital cannons have ceased fire, but they are still loosing phase missiles on us. They've also dispatched fighters, and slower moving frigates are poised to cut off escape at all quickspace entry points."

Nacen felt dismayed that there was no time to head to the medical bay, in no small part to the aching in his head and burning in his lungs. As he stood, he was reminded of the intense burns deep in his left leg. He shifted to the right and collapsed in a fold-down seat on the wall.

Groaning, he was reminded as well of the burns along his face, seared over the flesh that had only recently healed. He was put at ease by the sight of the medi-drone flying between the seats, administering shots that would top off his blood supply's recovery nanites, adrenaline, and applying healing salves to the crew. He waited patiently for his turn, doing his best to block out his symphony of aches and pains.

"Did we make it back to the *Lusterhawk*?" Nacen moaned.

A nearby Armad nodded. "They scooped us up right after we got you aboard."

Another Armad hobbled up to Nacen. "Wow, you Starscum can really fly! Nice job getting the boss and the rest outta there. Damned impressive." He extended a huge hand, which Nacen shook weakly.

"Loke... didn't make it. I'm sorry."

"We know..." The Armad frowned. "But... you got what we needed? The fleet location?"

"We sure did. The death of your... our comrade was not in vain."

"Comrades," the Armad corrected. "We lost Trute in the firefight defending your ship."

Nacen didn't like the resent he detected in *his* ship. But still, the Armads had given it their all and had not come away unscathed.

"Brecca, I won't tell you again. Buckle up!" Basaul roared.

Brecca nodded hastily to Nacen and struggled into a harness. Beskin and Camlo sat down to either side of Nacen.

"Well, Beskin, you got him back in one piece. Even if that one piece has a few holes, and burns. I guess that means you got to stay a druvani," Camlo said jovially, "and getting shot out into space, I still can't believe you pulled that off!"

"It was all the captain's idea. I was nearly tempted to knock him out, after I heard what he had planned. For his own good, of course," Beskin sat back and allowed the restraints to envelope him.

At last the medi-drone reached him, and Nacen sighed in relief as its injections numbed him while the nanites did their work. Out of the corner of his eye, he noticed another Armad glaring at him. Chalce, standing a head taller than even his fellow Armads, glowered at him for a moment during a lull in his conversation. Oh well, now was not the time to deal with this. Basaul and the druvani could keep things in order for now.

"Beskin, Camlo, hold out here with our Armad friends," Nacen said. "I'm going to the bridge to get visuals on what's going on."

"But..." Beskin started.

"I insist. Keep an eye on Chalce and the other Armads."

Nacen limped his way to the bridge and slumped down in the seat next to Linasette with a harrumph. Linasette turned to look him up and down. She kept a straight face despite his open wounds and charred robes, her calculating gaze offering neither pity nor disgust. Nacen returned the analytical look. Her gray flight suit was pristine. He was glad to see her unharmed.

"I apologize if I bleed all over the bridge," Nacen said glibly.

Linasette gave a short laugh. "Sorry. I realized after I transported everyone in that I should have retrieved you first."

"Why is that?" Nacen's heart fluttered. These nanites could do strange things to a man's autonomic nervous system.

"You had the data chip," she replied.

"Oh, right," Nacen said. That made sense, he supposed. "So what's our status now?"

"Well we got back to the *Lusterhawk* before Daedalon got too many rounds off. Now our window to exit the Tantalos quickspace passage is shrinking fast. Fortunately, the Union Precept doesn't have many ships in this system. Most of their local fleet garrison may have been tasked with pursuing the homefleet."

"Okay. Here's your storage chip back. Let's see if we can plot a path for Folbix before we hit quickspace. The pilot placed the small device on a dashboard to her left. The holograms shifted, and a staggering array of information spilled forth. The lighted text grew and grew in number, until it more closely resembled a cascading waterfall.

Linasette raised her eyebrows. "Oh, you gave me all sorts of goodies. Let's see what we can parse here..."

Nacen studied the system display, despite understanding nothing, and allowed Linasette time to begin her analysis. Several red dots were in pursuit of the arrow representing the *Lusterhawk*. "You mentioned something about fighters earlier?"

"Yes, they're closing on us quite fast. The *Lusterhawk* is fast for a frigate, even a Stevari one, but those fighters have a lot less mass. It's going to be a close call. Folbix is firing all our stern-mounted weapons, but we have yet to score a hit. Okay, the *Canotila's* systems are perusing the data. It looks like the Union Precept has ordered some serious requests for fuel at both Mithrand and Fomalhaut." She paused briefly. "Heh, that's my old neck of the woods."

More sayings about woods. Where in the forest was the neck, anyway? Unity citizens must have been much more in tune with nature in the distant past.

"There appears to be increased traffic in most adjacent Union Precept systems," she continued. "Good news for us—we may be able to slip under the radar with some luck and ingenuity."

"Excellent," Nacen said. "Now where is the homefleet?"

"Patience, I'm getting to it." Linasette flicked rapidly through the holograms. "The homefleet escaped through the Ulastai system. That we know. The Union Precept tried to catch them there but failed. The next hints we get are reserve fleets from deep within Union Precept space being brought in around Astana and Yanenko. All of the fleets converge on Mithrand... here. If the homefleet was captured or destroyed, that's where it'd be. But dated just a few hours ago, we have more reserve forces being requested by Fomalhaut and the systems beyond."

Nacen sat quietly as Linasette plotted out numerous potential courses on the main screen. Most of them scattered and eventually halted, but a few possible paths converged onto one location: Fomalhaut. The central sprawl world of the Union Precept in the Prominar Rim.

"Now why would they ever consider heading to Fomalhaut? That's as deep inside Unity space as they'll likely be able to get," Nacen pondered.

"We'll have to worry about the details later," Linasette said dismissively. "It's a null point if we don't make it to quickspace. I have already submitted course suggestion to Folbix for the *Lusterhawk*. If all goes as planned, we *may* not be totally eradicated."

"Elaborate."

"Well, we can outpace the Precept frigates to quickspace, but those fighters are going to catch us for sure. Javelin classes I think. Very fast, and very lethal. But they won't continue into quickspace unless they want to run out of fuel over the surface of the blue sun and take a plunge into the photosphere."

Nacen and Linasette watched the display anxiously over the next ten minutes. They had caught the crew up on the situation, and all that could be done now was wait.

"One more thing," Nacen began, "the consoles I was searching mentioned something called the Void Protocol. Does that mean anything to you?"

"No, why?"

"The Unity seemed concerned about it, that's all."

At last the quickspace passage came into view, but so had the Javelins. Structurally, they were little more than a long dart. Three powerful engines were mounted in the rear, and racks of missiles bristled along the thin hull of the craft. The entire design minimized mass while maximizing thrust and weapon systems. The pilots lay with their heads facing the tip of the dart-like ship's bow, or else were entirely replaced by drones. Four of the Javelins had all but closed with the *Lusterhawk*.

"We're lighting them up. Still no confirmed hits," Linasette reported. The rear display showed very little of the action Linasette described. It was all too dark and too fast. The stern-facing flux support guns on the *Lusterhawk* fired with incredible precision but could do little against the Javelin's forward shields. Conversely, the two small rail guns mounted above the engines could easily dispatch the nimble fighters, if they could only hit one. Nacen felt powerless as they stood in his shuttle within the *Lusterhawk's* bay. But he was in no shape to walk across the length of the frigate in his current condition in the middle of a firefight.

"Lina, get Folbix to target one ship with both rail guns," Nacen commanded. "Have the second rail gun fire at the space next to the fighter. That way if they jink, we at least have a small chance of hitting them while they evade. Then switch up the second rail gun's trajectory randomly each time."

"Could work..." Linasette sent the instructions to Folbix's command crew. There was a brief respite as the pilot submitted the protocol to fire control on the bridge.

The pair watched with bated breath as the rail guns hammered at the fighter's positions with their new fire pattern. Each time the weapons fired off a slug traveling roughly a fifth of the speed of light, another followed fast behind. Each time they were disappointed as the fighter easily barreled out of the way of both shots.

"We have missiles locked on to the *'Hawk*. Thirty-six in all. According to our specs, that's just under one third of the Javelins' total capacity. Twenty seconds to impact."

"The good news just keeps on coming," Nacen said. "Let's see what Folbix can do."

As the phase missiles arced in for their final approach, the *Lusterhawk* fired its starboard engines, then those on the port side in an attempt to throw off any missiles already straining the limits of their maneuverability. Only two were tricked by the maneuver and quickly locked back on track. At twenty-five meters, the *Lusterhawk* fired out a volley of magnetic chaff that saturated the area behind the ship. The particles rushed toward the missiles. On contact, they released a powerful electromagnetic field that disabled their target's guidance and detonation systems. Those that were on a direct path bounced harmlessly off the hull. The missiles not directly aimed at the ship continued on their current course, destined to wander the stars indefinitely.

Nine missiles hit the rear of the frigate, the first three of which were deflected by the shield with little to no effect. The remaining six collided directly with the hull and delivered their payload. Carefully serrated portions of the armored hull were turned to slag as explosive payload punched into the engine compartment. Much of the air was vented into space before the damage could be contained. The *Carmina Canotila*, though relatively safe in the ship's starboard bay, was still rocked by the impact.

"Six direct hits to the engine room," Linasette replied.

"But it could have been worse?" Nacen asked doubtfully.

"Technically, yes, we could all be dead. But then at least we wouldn't have to worry about being stranded inside the great blue sun."

"*Kaha*," Nacen swore.

"The ship has contained most of the damage and we still have diminished control of some of our engines."

Suddenly, Linasette's lips curled into a smile. Nacen wasn't sure whether to be elated or horrified at that. His eyes followed her gaze and he saw what caused her amusement. On the rear screen, one of the fighters began to deviate off course. It began to spin wildly, and Nacen saw bits of cosmic flotsam and jetsam fling off its spindly hull. It had been hit by one of the rail gun projectiles.

"We got one!" Nacen whooped.

"Quite," Linasette said. "Our chances just increased dramatically."

"I'll take it."

"We have enough momentum to get us out of quickspace. If the remaining missiles don't reach us first."

Nacen nodded. This was all out of his hands now. "Do we have more missile glitter?"

"Cute. There is plenty of magnetic chaff left, if that's what you mean," Linasette replied. "The next round of missiles is away. They have fired another third of their... no... no, they've now fired their *entire* payload. They're not taking any chances with their Javelins now susceptible to our rail guns."

Forty-two missiles streaked toward the Stevari ship through the vacuum of space, rocket fuel spreading them into a more dispersed attack formation. The Javelins had learned much from their missiles' last encounter.

"We're going to make it," Nacen said, though his gut was telling him the opposite as he watched the horde of signatures flying swiftly toward his ship like a volley of flaming arrows. "We're going to make it. We're going to make it."

The invisible outline of quickspace shimmered against the background of the stars on the *Lusterhawk's* forward display. They were on a direct path for the center. Despite one reactor being down and several thrusters completely destroyed, they were maintaining a steady course. No acceleration or deceleration was needed, at least not yet. Just as the missiles closed for their final approach, a thick sheen of chaff deployed around the stern. Twenty-nine missiles detonated prematurely or drifted off course.

The *Lusterhawk* was just four hundred meters short of the passage when the remaining thirteen missiles connected to the hull. The shields flickered in forlorn defiance before disappearing. The lights illuminated the horrified faces of the crew for one last instant before they blinked out. But still the frigate catapulted through, spurred on through quickspace by the long forgotten will of its creators.

Chapter 9

Red light bathed the cabin. Nacen brushed his hand up off his moist forehead and up through his auburn hair, as though he had to feel his body to believe it had not been disintegrated.

"We... made it," he stammered.

"Very observant of you, Captain." Linasette was already tapping on the holographic keys. "There is critical damage to all sectors, but the *Lusterhawk* is functional. For the most part. Both reactors are down, so we're running off stored power alone. We have controls, basic life support, and... it looks like that's it. Emergency shielding is... responsive, but I don't know the capacity. We could have a few days, we could have minutes.

"We made it," he repeated, smiling at Linasette, finally believing in the meaning behind the words again.

"Oh, ye of little faith."

"So... we're at the mercy of whoever we come across in Nabomir," Nacen said rhetorically, ignoring the pilot's jab.

"I am afraid so."

"How far out are we from Fomalhaut?"

"Over five days. That's if nothing else goes wrong and the shields hold up."

"Alright. I'll go try to explain what happened, then we can meet up at the *Lusterhawk's* bridge to discuss our options with Folbix. Or lack thereof." Nacen rose from his seat, shaking considerably. The last few hours had been incredibly trying, and the adrenaline was just now leaving his system.

Nacen wound his way through the narrow hallway to the shuttle's cargo hold, racking his brain for the right phrases to mitigate the peril of their situation. Maybe mitigation was the wrong way to go. Before Nacen rounded the corner, he heard the raucous din of a quarrel. He entered the cargo hold to find the entire crew unstrapped and at each other's throats. In the center of the room, Shukernak was shouting up at Chalce. Beskin and Camlo had completely lost control of the situation, if indeed they ever had it at all. Nacen took in the scene for a long moment.

"I have good news and bad news." Nacen leaned against the bulkhead. He had hoped his authority and promise of information would be enough to still the room and continued on, and to an extent it had. "The bad news is there isn't any good news. We're very nearly dead in space and still days from our destination, with no idea what is on the other side awaiting us or if we can even make it there. Also, the Union Precept surely has ships coming after us from Tantalos and the stars know where else."

Chalce was the first to react, redirecting his ire from Shukernak to the captain. "All of that effort? And for what? We just delayed the inevitable end of this foolish journey! It was a failure from the onset!" Chalce raised his hands to get a rise out of his fellow Armads.

"Is this what Loke and Trute died for?" one shouted, rising to the call.

"That's not true, and it's not too late. As for our friends, we all knew it could end that way." Nacen took a step forward and straightened. He was feeling much steadier now.

"You know what happens to war criminals in the Unity. We'll be placed in permanent stasis with no hope of release. At their mercy to be interrogated, tortured, or killed." Chalce slammed his fist into his palm for emphasis.

"You were right. Is that what you want me to tell you? Well I can't. Because if there was any chance of rescuing my family, then I would do it all over again," Nacen said calmly. He could sense familiar anger rising up in him.

"Then you Starkin are as foolish as I thought." Chalce stormed out of the cargo hold and into the *Lusterhawk's* bay. Several Armads followed him.

Basaul turned to Nacen. "This is indeed regrettable, but I will not go back on my word. My men and I are with you until the end."

Nacen bowed deeply. "Thank you."

Basaul grunted and turned to go. "Let us plan what repairs we can make to the *Lusterhawk* here in the stellar tunnels, so we may better be prepared when the Precept navy meets us."

"Good thinking," Nacen said. "We should have at least a few hours before any frigates in Tantalos catch up, assuming they entered quickspace after us. Coordinate with Master Rinkesi's bridge crew."

The next few hours through quickspace were dismal. The crew repaired what they could with their limited access to the ship, but their work was mostly relegated to ensuring existing damage did not worsen catastrophically. The shields held back the radiation of the blue giant, and it appeared they would continue to do so for another day or two. The exterior of the ship was pockmarked with scorch marks and gaping holes where armor had been penetrated. Entire plates of the serrated hull had been shorn away.

But still, the crew persisted. The Stevari did what they could to keep themselves and the Armads entertained throughout the journey. On their few breaks they sang songs, danced, and told tales of daring quests. The Armads were eventually lured out of sulking or constant work with games of masons. They had also taken quite a liking to one of Camlo's songs, which he had first performed by jumping atop a mess hall table quite unexpectedly.

Now is no time to be quiet and hushed,
Life is too short to be silent or blushed.

Ah, now I see! Your eyes, they do glisten!
Now sit back, relax, and carefully listen,

To the tale of a gentleman angered over spilled drink,
And the reveler who kicked it in no mind to think.

Tell me young pup, he said, why should one prance amok?
It's simpler by far to sit or to walk.

And why do you sing with such reckless cursing?
Your speech you should save for productive conversing!

Riley O'Connor

The reason is clear, he replied to the gloomy old man,
Not everything needs contrivance or plan!

A song is quite more than pitches to hear,
More cheerful than frequencies inside your ear.

Don't fret or lose hope over prior refrains,
Just keep singing and dancing, if you've got any brains!

When a bard or a minstrel strikes up their score,
It's your duty as people to stand up and roar.

So raise your mugs high, hold your flagons aloft,
Sing yourselves hoarse and give reason to quaff!"

The Armads had roared in delight with each subsequent verse. Nacen patted the druvani's seat jovially as he climbed down off the table. "Well done, cousin. I couldn't have done it better myself."

"That's because if you tried, you would have torn open your wounds. We really do need to get you and these Armads to a proper medical bay."

"I'll be okay," Nacen said. "Besides, the medical bay is still in Tantalos along with half of the stern."

"All we can do is wait then," Camlo said.

"In some ways it's worse than being fired at."

"Well, I'll have to disagree with you there," Camlo raised his metallic right arm poignantly as he took a drink from his mug.

The second day tumbling through the photosphere of the great blue sun passed slowly. In the hours before calculated shield failure, every crew member was now required to wear a protective suit over their normal gear.

It was during the dawn on the second period of perpetual daylight that Nacen was called to the bridge of the *Lusterhawk*. He terminated his morning meditation with one final exhale and headed to the bridge in his clunky over-suit. He arrived to find the bridge crew in their familiar positions around the circular room's perimeter. Folbix stood in the center with Linasette. Both of them could have honestly been mistaken for children next to Basaul and Chalce.

"Good morning, everyone." Nacen said, hoping that no one would point out it couldn't technically be morning within a star, and besides could by no rational definition be considered good. A muttering chorus greeted him.

"I have some urgent updates," Folbix was studying a screen of ship vectors intensely and began in a tone as though he had just revived Nacen's childhood dog, only to accidentally back over it on his way to inform him. "We have two Precept frigates on our tail. Under normal circumstances we could outrun them, but half our engines are out and we're mostly relying on momentum built up before we were hit at Tantalos. They'll catch us in a matter of hours."

"And we're in no shape to fight them," a bridge officer announced through her radiation suit, trying to sound helpful.

"Naturally. So... what's our next move?" asked Nacen.

"There's a passage out of quickspace two hours away. I advise we take it." Folbix said.

"Any significance about it?"

"It leads to the Chosan system. Unity space, of course. Days away from Fomalhaut and probably a dead end."

"Why there then? Why not just keep going and hope for..." Nacen was coming up empty. Surely there was something that could save them. A friendly Stevari ship? Rampaging deepsun raiders? Surely it couldn't end like this. Lots of ships met their end in the depths of the blue sun. Just not *his*.

"When I said we should take it," Folbix gave a deep sigh and turned away from the screens. "I meant you."

"A transport the size of the *Canotila* isn't meant to travel through quickspace. Any Stevari child knows that," Nacen said.

"It would only be for a few hours. Your shields should be able to hold until you can reach Nabomir."

"Now you're just making these up," Nacen said in an effort to lighten the mood. Folbix's facial muscles maintained their downward orientation.

"The Nabomir passage, leading to the system of the star of the same name, per Unity standard practice, is not likely to be heavily defended based on the evidence of your stolen data."

Well that certainly beat any of the options Nacen had in mind, all ending in certain death.

"If they didn't want it stolen, then they shouldn't have left it so heavily guarded on a secure floor," Nacen pointed. One of the bridge trufalci cracked a grin behind her radiation-resistant visor. There. Finally. A smile.

"If you could manage that, who knows what you can manage," Folbix admitted.

"Your idea is absolutely nonsensical, but it's far better than anything I've got so I'll play it out," Nacen said with a forced smile. "How do you propose we give the frigates the slip?"

The bridge trufalci lit up another screen. This one showed the *Lusterhawk*. Or what looked like a discarded jigsaw puzzle of the *Lusterhawk* after someone gave up on it halfway through.

"The *Lusterhawk* still maintains some offensive capability. Though we cannot fire point defense systems, lasers, or... well almost anything, we can fire what missiles we have left manually. We'll fire them out in all different directions, some of them drifting off and others on a course toward the enemy frigates. The *Carmine Canotila* light reconnaissance and transport specialty craft will fire one engine only in a ploy to appear as one of those errant missiles."

Nacen raised an eyebrow. "I have a few questions."

"Proceed," Folbix indicated, "but know we have less than an hour before we need to act."

Nacen held up a placating hand. "It won't take but a minute. First, what are the odds this actually works? I mean that you get through to Chosan and we make it through Nabomir?"

Folbix cleared his throat. "There's no reason it shouldn't work. As long as our shields hold out for a couple more hours and the U.P. doesn't look too carefully at the failed missiles."

"Very well. Last question, who came up with this hairbrained scheme?"

The radiation suits turned expectantly to Folbix. The master of the *Lusterhawk* nodded to the bridge trufalci who had answered Nacen's question earlier.

"That was me, sir." Her sheepish grin returned. "It was the best I could do with our limited resources."

"Nonsense, this is brilliant. What's your name, trufalci?"

"Lavinia, sir. Lavinia Lee."

"Someday, Lavinia, in the near future if the stars are with us, we will meet again under happier circumstances. If you've haven't been promoted at least twice by then I will be having strong words with your commanding officer." Nacen smiled at her, and winked at Folbix. "Everyone, I would like to thank you for your service... these last few weeks in particular. It has truly been an honor."

"I hope your time aboard the *Lusterhawk* has been to your satisfaction, Captain," Folbix said. Nacen could not detect the usual acrid way the master of the frigate pronounced his title, but Folbix may have just been too tired to put in the extra effort. "I am sorry we have to depart under these circumstances."

"Master Rinkesi, I did not ask to be placed under you for my first command. But I could not have asked for a better frigate," Nacen bowed slowly. "Please surrender when you reach Chosan. The Unity I know may show mercy on you."

"I do not intend to die for any hopeless cause, however noble. I trust you intend the same," Folbix said.

There was a round of handshakes and salutes, of praises to the Drovina homefleet and to each other, made more awkward by the radiation suits, and then Nacen departed. He made his way to the *Canotila* and verified they had all the provisions they would need for a two week journey. Soon the transport was ready, and all within her knew what was expected of them in the coming hours. Nacen stood in the cargo hold, looking out through the rear ramp at the interior of the *Lusterhawk*. He heard heavy footsteps behind him.

"How much longer do we have to wear these suits?" Basaul asked, tugging at his ill-fitting radiation suit. It was the largest size the Stevari offered, not having Armads as regular crew members. "We have more radiation resistance built into our skin, anyway."

"It's standard protocol," Nacen said absent-mindedly. He realized this answer probably wasn't very satisfying. "Besides, it's not something you want to risk if the *Canotila's* shields don't cut it. Being inside the great blue sun is a bit harsher than on a rocky planet with minimal atmosphere."

"I know all that, it's just... yes, fair enough."

The pair fell silent for a long moment.

"I just can't help but feeling this is the last time I'll see the 'Hawk, and everyone on it," Nacen said.

"Don't get sentimental on me now, Starkin, they've made it this long and they don't have far to go before they can put up a white flag," Basaul said with a grim smile.

"I mean us. Where does this end for us, as a light transport going up against... *kaha* I don't even know anymore."

"Oh. Well, it's true we don't know what awaits us out there," Basaul fumbled for his next words. "But then the universe is so big, who really does anyway? The best you can do is well... your best."

"I just wish I could have seen the homefleet again. Growing up, it was all I knew. We traveled all over the great blue sun, saw so many worlds, but I was always home. When I left to make it on my own, I didn't really know how much I was leaving behind until it was gone. If I'm going to die somewhere, it should be there." Nacen closed his eyes to the bay doors, tired of looking at the ship interior.

"Don't think about dying at home, think about fighting for it. Wherever that might be."

More footsteps echoed from behind, lighter this time.

"In this case, it happens to be some back-curtain system in the Prominar Rim," Camlo said.

"In any case, the fight isn't over yet. Don't fret or lose hope, right, Camlo?" Basaul asked sternly.

"If you've got any brains." Camlo offered a weak smile.

"Okay, let's see what the *Lusterhawk* has left in store for these Lunies," Nacen murmured, turning and stepping into the cargo hold.

"We're approaching Chosan and breaking vac in two minutes," Linasette said. "Last chance to get things stowed away."

Nacen took his place on the bridge after ensuring all his crew and the Armads were secured in the cargo hold fold-down seating.

"Captain Buhari," Folbix said over the bridge comms.

"Yes?"

"I realize that if this works, we're sending you to the mercy of the Nabomir system. Know that with you lies all our hopes, and our confidence," Folbix said with finality.

"We will do our utmost to see this through," Nacen returned. That was surprisingly touching of Folbix.

"Lavinia's words, not mine. Thought you should know."

"Oh. Yes, well... thank you."

Nacen was spared the need to think of a more graceful reply by his pilot.

"We're back in the vac in ten, everyone," she announced.

Nacen gazed out the doors. Where normally a unique signature of constellations lay before him, now he looked out onto the roiling sea of the great blue sun. How long would the *Canotila* survive out there?

"Alright, pressure in the bay is at vacuum. Opening bay doors. *Lusterhawk* missile silo is on standby." Linasette reported.

"You know, I think I was too hard on Folbix." Nacen said to the pilot alone as he leaned back in the flight seat. "I mean, thinking he had it out for me? I guess I've just been under a lot of pressure."

"We all are." Linasette noted, tapping away at the virtual keyboard.

"Inertial dampeners are maxed out. Port engine is silent. We're ready to go full bore with starboard."

"Right."

A wispy trail began to cross along the great blue sun, a rippling wake of sputtering white barely visible as it chopped along the swirling surface of the star.

"First missiles are away. Here we go," Linasette said. Steady fingers rocked forward slowly, then lunged forward all at once.

The *Carmine Canotila* shot out of the hangar. The blue sea now stretched from horizon to horizon. It *was* the horizon. Nacen couldn't help but smile at the whoops and hollers from the cargo hold. Wispy streaks trailed out all around them. Nacen saw on one screen some of the several hundred missiles aiding in their escape. The craft swam amongst them for a short while, keeping a safe distance, as Linasette steered about to orient the ship toward the coordinates of Nabomir.

Most of the missiles now began to curve back toward the *Lusterhawk* and the two Precept pursuers behind. Then another tiny star was born miles above the great blue sun. It gave a slight wink and then was gone. A few more winked briefly into existence before being extinguished.

"What is happening?" Nacen asked, more in wonder than in fear.

"Missiles detonating prematurely," Linasette said, giving her captain only the smallest sliver of her attention as she navigated.

"Why?"

"I don't..."

Linasette's eyes grew wide. Nacen's question was not so much answered as it was made less relevant. The next thing Nacen knew, the craft was shaking hard. It shook for a long time. Too long.

"What the—"

"Missile impact," Lina reported as she fumbled at the controls.

"Folbix, that treasonous swine!" Nacen cursed. "I should have known that he was plotting to kill me as soon as he started dishes out the compliments. I never should have let my guard down after the shooting range disaster. That scum of the—"

"It was just one missile," Linasette said.

"Only one knife in our backs?" Nacen sneered.

"Tell that to Caesar."

"Who?" Nacen asked, not really caring but just annoyed at Lina's distraction.

"Nobody. The missile could have been the Precept's doing," Linasette noted. "We weren't targeted instantly. It took a while before the missiles started detonating and crashing into each other. Fast-hacking older technology is definitely within the Unity's capabilities. The missiles could have malfunctioned from magnetic interference from the great blue sun, too. Never attribute to malice which you can attribute to incompetence."

"That doesn't apply when people are out to kill you," Nacen said. The screens had gone suspiciously blank. "What's our status? Are there any more missiles?"

"What is happening?" a voice shouted from behind. "Are we being boarded?"

Nacen saw Camlo panting hard at the bridge's ingress.

"Get back in your restraints, Cam, we're not done yet," Nacen commanded. "Just a little mishap."

"Just a..." Camlo began skeptically. "What does that even—"

"Back! Now!" Nacen jammed his index finger at Camlo, and the druvani flinched and retreated as though Nacen had brandished his pistol.

"A fraction did survive and are on their way to the U.P. ships, so our cover still may be intact. It doesn't look like there are any more around us," Linasette gave a sigh of relief. "Furthermore, we're running with minimal power to one engine and no minimum shields, so we'll be very difficult to detect. Just on forward momentum alone, we should still be able to reach Nabomir in a few hours. Though when we get there, our options will be extremely limited."

"We should be fine with radiation suits alone for a couple of hours," Nacen said, then faltered. "Right?"

"We'll want to get tested either way," Linasette concluded.

Nacen tapped at a few icons on the screen. Thankfully they still had power.

"What are you doing?" the pilot asked warily.

"Updating our loyal crew," Nacen replied.

"Would you like me—"

"I've got it under control," he replied defensively. "I can be tactful."

In a stunning feat of restraint, Linasette returned to her navigation screen without rolling her eyes.

"Attention, passengers of the *Carmine Canotila*... we have just suffered substantial engine loss due to an undetermined incident from the..." Nacen deactivated the intercom and leaned over to Linasette. "Wait, can we communicate with the *Lusterhawk*? Ask them what happened?"

Linasette shook her head. "I tried. It's either damage or electromagnetic radiation is blocking us."

Nacen nodded and keyed the controls again. "An indeterminate incident. We are en route to the Nabomir system and will arrive in..." Nacen looked at Lina imploringly. She mouthed a response. "In five hours. In the meantime, we will repair what we can and prepare for an encounter with hostile forces." Nacen keyed a few icons. The intercom shut off and his flight straps retracted. He stood and stretched. "Time to go make myself useful."

Nacen met with the crew and explained what had happened. They identified some areas where welding could patch things up, but for the most part, the damage had been done and isolated. The time was spent mostly cataloging and cleaning the few weapons they had aboard. Eventually the team broke up into smaller groups to either chat away the time or play the Armads' favorite card game, masons, fast becoming a Stevari pastime as well.

"Good news." Linasette's voiced chimed through the cargo hold. "The *Lusterhawk* made it through their egress and the Precept frigates just followed them in. The diversion worked," Linasette announced over the intercom.

"Well, with mixed results," Nacen said softly so only the game of masons could hear.

"Now the bad news," Linasette said.

More of it? Nacen kept to himself this time.

"Our last engine has given out. We're down to minimal control with retro thrusters on the wings. But we should have enough momentum to get us to Nabomir."

Nacen set his cards down. He needed that last bit of news as a reminder that this was no time for games. "We all have our rad suits, armor, and weapons. We have justice on our side. Whatever we find on the other side of quickspace, I know we will be prepared for it. Until then, if you have any concerns... come to me. I will be up on the bridge."

The room gradually returned to its gentle clamor of conversations and games. Nacen returned to the bridge and walked through scenarios of what they could expect at Nabomir, even going so far as to create detailed lists of protocols and prerecorded messages in case time was an issue. Still, Nacen caught himself reflecting on his time on the *Lusterhawk*. His short career as a captain had been entirely within its holds—until now, of course. He recognized his most recent paranoid thoughts of Folbix's betrayal as childish. After all, the plan, not even born in the mind of Master Rinkesi, had risks and unknowns. Nacen did not like the present situation one bit, but he had to admit they were still flying free. At last the *Carmine Canotila*, its hull unshielded and twin engines inert, rounded on the Nabomir passage rising from the depths of the great blue sun.

Linasette used the few remaining retro thrusters to orient the transport toward the invisible passage out. Nacen did not need to remind her that if she missed, they would be plunged into the blue star with no way to escape. But she and the computer worked in perfect tandem, making minute adjustments to steer the craft through the sputtering photosphere. The passage came on them suddenly, opening like some infernal portal to unknown depths. Some atavistic instinct within Nacen leered at this, but he clamped his jaw shut and waited.

The *Carmine Canotila* emerged from the passage with a momentary burst of light. The ship maintained its current course, having few other options.

"No hostiles detected in the immediate vicinity, Captain," Linasette said. "System is unchanged from our last update. There is one hot gas giant orbiting a class K star, with two terrestrial planets orbiting farther out. Not detecting a whole lot... wait a minute..."

The pilot set her fingers flying at the keyboard and images magnified across the helm. The system, barren at first glance, was alive with vessels traveling to and from the rocky interior. Small trade ships, long and elegant, sailed alongside massive freighters. The small ships, some even smaller than the *Carmine Canotila*, were a splendid, colorful mixture of the varieties one could expect to see over decades of flying. The freighters, on the other hand, were a case in point that beauty didn't matter one bit for functioning in the vacuum of space.

The bridge door opened, and Nacen saw his druvani enter behind Basaul. They gathered around the images with curiosity.

"Let's send the closest frigate a hailing signal," Nacen ordered.

The pilot did so, and the bridge became tense as the crew waited for a return message. Camlo struck up a conversation speculating as to the origins and owners of some of the vibrant merchant ships. After giving more than adequate time, it became obvious the lead ship had not acknowledged the *Carmine Canotila's* attempts to establish communications, nor had any in the fleet sent their own request. They sent out more hailing signals, this time to any ship that looked remotely Stevari in origin. They waited patiently for the next few minutes, still adrift on their current course.

"Captain, we have a signal. Patching it through now," Linasette said, her voice monotone but enthusiastic.

"You do not seem to have control of your engines," the voice said. It was male, high-pitched and a touch highfalutin. "We take great sorrow in seeing fellow Stevari in trouble, but we cannot afford to lose time to stop and assist in your repairs. We are contract-bound to resupply Precept fleets, and any delay is unacceptable. We do, however, wish you the best of luck in restoring your systems. I am sure that Union Precept ships will come to... assist you... before you should expire."

"Figures," Camlo muttered. "Typical Orizon snobs."

"Silence," Nacen hissed. He tapped an icon to record a message. "Surely you could spare a single ship with sufficient materials to repair a fellow Stevari's ship?"

A few more tense minutes passed as they waited for a return.

"Oh?" the bombastic voice stretched out the word to an insult. Nacen winced. "Where was Drovina when our homefleet came under pursuit by the deepsun pirate Blood-Shines-Under-Moonlight? Or during the height of the Battle for Synar? Or at the interstellar conclave of the Seven Millenia War? You cannot pick and choose when it is convenient and when it is not to participate in Stevari affairs. Until your house accepts its responsibilities among the proper houses, you will remain relegated to the shadows."

Nacen swallowed his pride and prepared the next outgoing message.

"Then let's start now," he pleaded, ignoring the jabs. "My homefleet could be destroyed in a matter of days, if it has not been already."

The wait was slightly shorter now as the ships roughly converged on the same page.

"I am deeply sorry, but as I said before, the present moment is simply not feasible."

Nacen slammed his fist against the dash and cursed.

"Wait," Linasette said, "one of the ships adjusted its course. They could be on their way to help us."

After a tense minute or two, a communication request was received. Nacen nodded for Linasette to open it, and the pilot complied.

"Greetings. This is the Union Precept heavy liner *Etrusca*. We have received your request and are en route to retrieve you."

"Retrieve?" Basaul scoffed. Nacen instinctively shut off the communication pickup. "These guys are Uni. The only thing they'll want to retrieve is a bounty."

"Let's give them a chance. Besides, they could very well be our only way out of this system."

"I'm all for it," Beskin said. "They're a commercial craft. There's always the possibility of boarding action and taking the ship for ourselves."

"It's decided then, we'll accept their offer. As for the boarding action, I'd like to see if we can resolve this peacefully. The *Etrusca* is a big freighter. They likely have a crew of at least fifty. Then again, we took everything a Unity space station could throw at us and got off fairly easy. If we could fight our way to the bridge, and assuming they didn't scuttle their own ship before we got control, we could take the *Etrusca* all the way to Fomalhaut and reunite with the fleet."

"You said it yourself, if there was any chance at rescuing your family, you'd take it," Beskin noted.

Still, Nacen didn't like the plan. It had a lot of risks involved. Too many. But the reward would be staggering if they could wrest control of the ship. But as a Stevari, Nacen could not take up arms against a host willing to take him and his crew in at their time of dire need. Nacen switched on the comms and prepared a message to send back. "Greetings, *Etrusca*. I am Nacen Buhari, Captain of the *Carmine Canotila* and son of House Drovina. We are most grateful for your response. We will be on standby for your intercept."

Less than a half hour later, the bulky *Etrusca* was upon them. The ship swung around to take in the Stevari shuttle as they moved along their unchanging course. The Unity merchant vessel set itself to travel just slightly slower than the *Canotila's*.

"What are they doing?" Camlo exclaimed as they watched on the bridge. "We're going to crash!"

"Well we have no way of landing, so they're getting ready to catch us," Nacen said, raising an eyebrow. "They're going just a bit slower than us to bring us inside their hangar, then must plan on using their anti-grav fields to slowly bring us to a stop."

"If you say so." Camlo shifted uncomfortably.

The *Etrusca* dominated the screen now, only a few kilometers away. They faced the engines, jets of blue against the dark, metallic brown of the ship. The predominant shape of its structure would have served the *Etrusca* well in many environments, Nacen noted, particularly as a block of skyscrapers in a bustling metropolis. The creators appeared to have enjoyed the orthogonal design so much they made every portion from identical chunks and tacked it all together in a tremendous aversion to good taste. A set of retractable plates slid open to reveal generous hangar space.

"It looks like it's getting ready to swallow us whole," Camlo said.

"That is the desired outcome." Linasette reactivated the communications link. "*Etrusca*, we are nearly inside your aft hangar bay. We're counting on you to slow us down so we don't get flattened."

"Copy that, Starkin," a relaxed, gravelly voice replied. "We'll let you down gentle."

"So you've pulled this maneuver before?" Nacen asked hopefully, ignoring the double meaning of being let down.

"In practice, not as such," the deep voice returned, though no less confident, "but the Counsel has many times, and it shall guide my hands."

The Sword and the Cipher

"Why am I not relieved..." Nacen muttered to himself.

The *Carmine Canotila* passed through the opening in the hull and flew through the bay, coming close to scraping the ceiling. For nearly twenty minutes, they crept along the ceiling of the hangar as the *Etrusca* slowed both its own speed and, using its internal artificial gravity, slowed the *Carmine Canotila* until at last it struck the far hangar wall with a gentle bang and glided to the floor with another.

"Well, I suppose a couple more dents won't hurt." Nacen stood with a great sigh. "Let's get working on repairs. Druvani, suit up in your best attire. Let's give them a warm welcome."

"Suit up, as in recast plate?" Camlo asked. "And warm as in plasma fire?"

"No. Formal and amiably, respectively." Nacen turned to exit the bridge. "We're surrendering."

Chapter 10

Compressor crates, gargantuan sheets of scrap metal, and small transport craft neatly filled the spacious interior of the *Etrusca's* rear hangar bay. Nothing threatening lay in the neat arrangements of cargo, material, and tools. The bay appeared to be merely a neglected but tidy portion of a prolific trader's inventory, or perhaps this area had contained recently offloaded goods. The ceiling of the room was nearly forty meters high, enough to accommodate a small ship such as Nacen's own along with at least one more stacked atop. Though the exterior of the ship was a dull brown, every surface of the interior was a pristine white. On the opposite end of the hangar was a set of winding stairs that led up to a gantry and a set of doors. Below the gantry was a largo cargo bay door, closed at the moment.

Nacen, his druvani, Basaul, and Chalce stood at the foot of their ship awaiting the arrival of the *Etrusca's* crew. Basaul shifted uneasily. "The last time I waited for Gloms before a deal, they were bringing me coffee. Now look at me, begging for my life after a shootout alongside the Starkin. I can accuse you of many things, Nacen, but not of leading a boring life."

"So, does anyone know what their commander wants to do with us?" Chalce inquired.

"I'm guessing they want to toss us in the brig until they can turn us in to a proper U.P. authority," Nacen said, lifting his heels in anticipation.

"If we're lucky, they'll toss us into space so we don't have to undergo torture." Basaul frowned and flexed his fingers.

"Lucky? How is that a good outcome in any way, shape, or form?" Camlo replied.

"Have you not heard of what the Gloms do to enemies if they get direct access to your brain? There's a lot of places you don't want them poking around, and I'm not just talking about where you keep your embarrassing mishaps and secret lovers. I expect the worst, and prepare for it. It's the wisest course of action, and the most likely," Basaul said.

"You've watched too much Unity propaganda," Nacen chided lightly, attempting to cover up his own similar trepidations.

While they awaited the *Etrusca's* welcome party, Nacen put his crew to work. Though they would need better equipment and supplies, Jeta and Shukernak went about the preliminary assessment of the holes and dents around the exterior, and damage to retro thrusters. The trufalci would be busy a long time, even with four Armads assisting them in the repairs.

Eventually, the white doors parted and five figures entered the hangar bay. In the front, a man in robes glided purposefully down the gantry. He was flanked, two on each side, by armed guards. These were no Union Precept lance troopers. In their flowing light blue robes over serrated armor of glossy white, they more closely resembled the Stevari than any Precept troops Nacen had ever seen. They carried small, bulky flux weapons with thick barrels. Whatever the fierce guns were, Nacen did not want to be on the receiving end.

The guards wore white helmets with smooth faceplates. Any sensors or visors were completely hidden.

The man between was tall and lean. His lithe form swayed rhythmically beneath his blue robes as he walked. Unlike his guards, his own flowing garments were fringed with gold. Instead of a firearm, the man carried a tall staff which clanked on the staircase with every other step. The leader made his way gracefully across the hangar bay floor, weaving languidly around crates. He stopped at no more than an arm's length from Nacen. For his part, Nacen admired the man's courage; his own men and women could easily be concealing a knife or explosive device.

His features were that of a handsome man approaching middle age, but not the flawless perfection that most in the Unity defaulted to. He had long, curly brown hair with a neatly trimmed beard. Rather than the usual compact ears, Eberwik's were rather large. His cheekbones were pronounced and made his face look a bit gaunt. Nacen was reminded of a character from old paintings in an era on Earth known as the renaissance. There were an inordinate number of paintings featuring this singular man, though Eberwik did not have the thorny crown present that Nacen recalled on many of them.

"I am Bogdan Eberwik, lord of the *Etrusca*. Welcome to my humble realm," the man said, raising his staff and free palm in a welcoming gesture.

Nacen found it odd for a member of the Unity to refer to the ship like a sovereign nation, and he its royalty. Regardless, Nacen dispensed with his own long line of practiced formalities and gave a deep bow. Eberwik gestured to Nacen's ship with a flick of his wrist.

"You seem to be having some trouble getting around," Eberwik said.

"We were hit... during a firing accident," Nacen replied. This was technically true.

"That's an awful lot of damage for an accident. Did you inadvertently collide with a moon?" Eberwik tilted his head slightly.

"Our mother ship was suffering from extensive injuries and we were struck by a wayward missile," Nacen said honestly, hoping he wouldn't have to go into any more detail.

"Very well. Tell me at least, why would the Union Precept be after a simple merchant vessel? You clearly wish to evade capture."

Nacen could see he was not going to escape this line of questioning with convenient omissions. As before with the Armads, he decided to stick to the truth. "My homefleet was unjustly attacked by the Union Precept navy. We seek to find them and assist in any way we can, so long as there is breath in my lungs."

He felt no inclination to mention the fact that most of his crew yearned for revenge.

"Now that's a proper introduction! I'd be happy to bring you aboard and help you in any way I can."

Nacen blanched. "We accept your gracious hospitality, of course. But if I may be so bold, why are you so ready to help us?"

"I believe there is a certain amount of risk one needs to take to be successful in business. Ferrying large quantities of goods about provides a decent enough income, but it does not carry a particularly high amount of prestige. I see some very beneficial outcomes in escorting you to your forlorn little cause."

"Thank you!" Nacen said, nearly out of breath with excitement. "You will receive great payment when I return, and more if my homefleet can safely be on our way!"

"Of that I have no doubt," Eberwik said with a wry grin. "I will not question you further, but you will need to relinquish your weapons while onboard my ship."

"That seems only fair."

Eberwik gave a gracious nod. "My guards will show you to your quarters. It would by my distinct honor if you would join me for dinner."

Nacen looked to his druvani beside him, standing nervously at attention across from the *Etrusca's* guards in their slick, faceless helmets. "We would be delighted," he said, for all of them.

***

Following the guards through the orthogonal, wide corridors of the ship, Nacen paid close attention to his surroundings. With a few deft taps on his earpiece, and hushed tones when he could, he communicated details of the local landscape back to the *Carmine Canotila*. Small differences and inconsistencies with the other crew doing the same primitive but clandestine mapping could be sorted out later on the bridge.

With a three day journey to Fomalhaut at full burn, he and his crew could get a good sense of the layout of the ship. Knowledge was power, and Nacen would go out of his way to obtain information that could be even remotely helpful in the future. He held a small compressor case in his right hand containing nothing but toiletries and a few changes of clothes. Beskin and Camlo followed behind with similar luggage.

The guard to his right signaled for Nacen and the druvani come to a halt. The rest of the crew, Armads and all, had been escorted to separate parts of the crew quarters.

"These will be your quarters," the guard beckoned inside with his short flux driver.

The room was extraordinarily spacious for ship quarters. It was filled with rich cloth of deep blues and purples. Two large beds lay at opposite corners of the room, and against the walls stood a writing desk, dressers, and cabinets of genuine wood. It appeared to be oak, given the light shade.

"Stay here and wait for me," Nacen said to his druvani. "I just need to get changed into my formal wear."

"You misunderstand, Captain. This is your bodyguards' room. Your quarters are up ahead."

"I will not be separated from my druvani," Nacen wrinkled his brow. "Surely you can accept this as a cultural difference?"

"We speak for Lord Eberwik. You are to be escorted to the first class cabins."

"First class? Not a bad way to go, Nace," Camlo said, shoving his way past Nacen and the guard into the lavish suite. "I'll just have to settle for the lesser digs. Just don't piss anybody off in the meantime, and we'll see you at dinner."

"I don't like this," Beskin said flatly. "Everyone has been far too accommodating."

"Neither do I. But as much as I hate to say it, Camlo is right. We are at Eberwik's mercy here. I will see you at dinner."

Nacen turned and, with some reluctance, followed the two guards down the gleaming white corridor. He continued to map the surroundings, and as his escort led him through the massive ship, his eagerness to meet up with his allies and view the complete puzzle of the ship's interior grew. Why would one trader require so much space? He must rent some of these spaces out to rich tourists.

The guards halted outside a nondescript white door. With a wave of the guard's gauntlet, the door flicked open.

"Your quarters, Captain," he said plainly.

The interior was magnificent. The room was furnished in silks of deep red, and luminescent panels behind velvet drapes gave the illusion of a sun setting on a summer's day. Dressers and cabinets of authentic mahogany stood in the corners, and a chandelier hung from a ceiling patterned with elaborate millefleur.

"We shall retrieve you for dinner in one half hour."

Nacen gave them a brief nod and the door whisked closed. He shrugged his compression case onto the bed and collapsed into a nearby chair to relax. As he sank into the plush exterior, his thoughts drifted back to the first contact in the Nabomir system.

He was grateful for the assistance. But why had the *Etrusca* turned back for them when no one else did? He would do his best to put his suspicions aside for now. Thoughts of family entered his fatigued mind, unable to keep up necessary barriers now that he was out of immediate danger. The sting of his mother's death had faded long ago, as she died when he was still a child. Though House Drovina sported some of the grandest, most sophisticated technology the galaxy knew, it had been caught unaware by a malicious but natural strain of virus. The infectious disease killed a sixth of House Drovina before a cure had been found. Now, it was not knowing whether his brothers and sisters were dead or alive that gnawed at him.

Even his father, Yoska, may still be out there. The bold movements of the fleet certainly had his fingerprints on it. Nacen's eldest brother, Zura, was certainly a top pick for command if something happened to their father. His sister, Zelda, just a year older than he, was the only other sibling on the homefleet during the time of the attack, insofar as he knew. The rest had the titles and comforts of colonial governors or diplomats amongst the far-flung factions of the great blue sun. All but himself.

Nacen rose and changed quickly into his formal robes. He wrapped a dark sash over a crimson tunic and breeches. As he was tying his bootlaces, another stylish but antiquated portion of his formalwear, he heard a knock at the door. The guards must be early to check on him. He stumbled off the chair and took a few uneasy hops, being careful not to trip on the unlaced second boot.

After straightening himself, he pressed the button to open the door. It whirred open.

"Look, you can..." he began, then stopped after he saw who stood there.

Linasette had one gloved hand placed on the door frame, the other on her waist. She wore a glamorous emerald dress that showed off her shoulders, aspects of her that Nacen had never seen. A thin, silver necklace dangled at her neck. Only her short, pale blonde hair seemed to remain unchanged.

Nacen, dumbfounded, stepped out of the way to make room for her to enter. She brushed past him, taking her right hand and running it across an antique cabinet. Nacen's gaze inexorably followed the thin, elegant finger as the hand made its journey along the furniture and back to her waist.

"Hello," he said, finding it difficult to come up with anything fitting to say.

"You clean up nice," Linasette looked him up and down, "but you're a slow dresser."

"I have a lot on my mind," Nacen replied earnestly. The statement, though true moments before the pilot showed up at his door, was now patently false.

"Well, forget about it for now. Relax, enjoy yourself while we have the opportunity. I don't know if you've noticed, but this place is practically a luxury cruise liner," Linasette mused.

"It may be extravagant, but we're still prisoners. Don't forget we have no weapons."

"You heard Eberwik. As long as we pay our way, we're free to go when we please."

"Color me unconvinced."

"The only color I see is red," Linasette raised her eyebrows slightly.

Nacen ignored the comment and sat down to finish tying his boots, painfully aware of his partially blushing face. After the task was done, he adjusted his sash and moved on to the laces on his tunic.

"I see no reason you cannot enjoy yourself, but be on the lookout for anything suspicious. Check in with the *Canotila* and tap out layouts covertly if you cannot send in vocal descriptions. We're looking for distances and relative locations of junctions, doors, and locations of interest. So far we've only been exposed to a small portion of a large ship."

"Aye, Captain," Linasette leaned against the dresser, hands behind her back as she admired the chandelier.

"I'm worried about the crew, having us all separated. What's more, I don't like being apart from my ship."

"I agree wholeheartedly, but it's not like there's anything we can do about it. We have a couple of days before the *Canotila* will be in good flying order, and another day or two after that before we arrive at Fomalhaut. Just do what you normally do when I'm flying, and enjoy the ride." She gave a coy smile that set him blushing again.

"I'll see what I can do," he managed to say.

Both of their attention was drawn to the sudden opening of the doors. Two guards stood there in silent expectation, their faces unreadable behind their white faceplate. Nacen made the final adjustments to his tunic and waited for them to speak.

The Sword and the Cipher

"I suppose dinner is served," Linasette said.

***

The dinner table formed a wide crescent along the dining hall floor. Above, brilliant chandeliers of glittering silver sparkled as they illuminated the long room. Nacen had been seated near the middle of the table, across from Eberwik and several other men and women in formal attire he had not met yet. To his left sat Linasette, and to his right Basaul and Chalce.

Nacen would not have ever been able to picture the Armads in formal-wear, but here they sat as a testament to Eberwik's apparent boundless wealth and imagination. Basaul and Chalce wore black suits that appeared to have been perfectly fitted for them. The rich fabric conformed to craggy skin and bulging muscle alike.

"Not a word, Starkin," Basaul grumbled.

"About what?" Nacen said, making an obvious point to look far away from Basaul's garb.

Jeta, Shukernak, and the Armad crew had forsaken the formal din-ner for their own informal meals in the hangar while they worked on the ship. Eberwik had silently made it clear this was to be a command personnel only meeting. The crew would be allowed to feast at future meals. Beskin and Cam-lo were allowed to attend, only in their capacity as bodyguards, but then were not even allowed weapons.

"Thank you all for joining me for dinner tonight," Eberwik raised his goblet and gestured grandly across the table. "It is not often we use the dining facilities to their full capabilities, and so we welcome you to our humble ship with what offerings we can provide."

Nacen eyed his own food suspiciously, though the spread looked de-licious. Slender slabs of red meat had been seared to perfection, alongside a large dish of harvested vegetables of greens, reds, and yellows. Exotic fruits had been delicately placed alongside pastas of extravagant color and smoth-ered in steaming sauces. A spongy mountain of what looked like baked choco-late of some variety lay in the distance, covered in whipped cream and dusted with dark powder.

"Nothing synthetic touches the head table," Bogdan Eberwik said. "The crew will eat prehydrated confections, but only because they prefer to scrimp and save. I prefer, however, to live as good as I can while I can afford to. As my guests, I extend to you the same courtesy."

"You are a magnanimous host, Lord Eberwik." Nacen bowed his head before touching his food. He noticed that Chalce was already eagerly digging in. "We are honored to be your guests and humbled by your hospitality."

In short order, Nacen was introduced to the man on Eberwik's right and the woman on the left. The woman had short, straight red hair with streaks of gray. In an age of technology that could nearly eliminate the signs of aging, the gray stood out almost as an act of defiance.

"I am Ofelia Erdene, the master of ordnance and grand accountant," the woman stated.

"Those positions seem somewhat incongruous," Nacen grabbed a piece of nearby fruit and sunk his teeth into its juicy interior.

"They are, but I am quite adept at accounting, so I took over when our past master of ordinance had a… an occupational incident. What is either field but keeping track of expenditure?"

This drew a round of chuckles from those nearby. The man to Eberwik's right seemed very familiar and bore a striking resemblance to someone Nacen once knew, though he could not put his finger on it. He was tall and had a pointed nose and stark, light blue eyes. His blond hair was long for a man, braided and tied in a ponytail in the back. He had the pointed ears of a Stevari, although he could not pinpoint the exact house. Like all Eberwik's personnel, he wore sky blue robes.

"Altan Nergi, captain of the guard here on the *Etrusca*, and your humble servant during your stay. Tell me, Nacen," he spoke in a manner of sincere curiosity, "what's a Stevari of House Drovina doing stranded in Union Precept territory?"

"We were traveling through on a trade mission when we were attacked. Now we only seek to reunite with our homefleet."

"That may be tricky when your homefleet is destroyed," Altan said cautiously while sawing into a filet.

"Surely, you jest," Nacen said, with as much congeniality as he could muster.

"Not at all," Altan placed the meat in his mouth and chewed sumptuously. "I speak of the future, of course, not the present. But of certainty, nonetheless. Whether or not you make it there is of no consequence. The Counsel defended us against the rampaging fleet, and soon the fleet will come to an end. It has more than enough data to reach this conclusion. It was merely a matter of marshaling the resources, and now it is simply a matter of time."

"Not everything that your Counsel predicts comes true."

The man gave a shrill laugh which seemed to shoot up Nacen's spine and fill him with rage. Still, that laugh really struck a chord with Nacen. There was something familiar and haughty about it.

"Of course not, Captain," Altan said and swallowed the morsel. "It is up to its loyal servants to make it so."

"So tell me, how did you become the captain of the guard for our esteemed commander here?" Nacen asked, deciding to push the matter of the laugh.

"Lord Eberwik prefers the aforementioned title to the more standard rank of commander or captain." Altan set down his wine glass. "But I delay. It is a dull story, but one that deserves to be told I suppose. I began life as a poor street urchin on the colony planet Renata. I have no memory of my parents, you see. Eventually, the planet was assimilated into the Union Precept and the Counsel brought us a modicum of prosperity. I was blessed with a future then. Prospects of a job, a family, a life worth living. But rather than simply embrace these new treasures, I decided to fight for them. That's right, my first act as a new citizen was to join the Federation of Worlds, or the U.P. as you know it. I started as a lowly lance trooper, though the noble and capable warrior class is far from lowly in spirit and reputation."

"How virtuous," Nacen noted. He started in on his entree as the guard captain continued. Conversation elsewhere at the table had lulled, and now most ears were directed at Altan.

"Eventually I worked my way up to the rank of squad leader of a unit of drop troops, known to ourselves and the enemy as the Iron Rain. I had over seventy combat drops under my belt, dozens of victories against Xandra and even a few pirate asteroids. During one mission, we were sent on a drop on a colony world. It was a rainy, swampy, miserable hellhole. Just like the one I grew up in. Except these fools, the prideful bastards, didn't want to submit to Precept rule. We killed three million on the first day. This just validates their own incipient feelings of superiority, and they fight on. Well now the Iron Rain gets called up to secure key ground locations. Maximum destruction orders: nukes and all. You know what I did?"

Nacen and Linasette shook their heads in tandem.

"Well, I refused. The Counsel might be infallible, but we as individuals are still permitted to make our own choices, our own mistakes. How else does one grow? Well, the next thing I knew I was back to square one on a new planet. I should say square zero for, like as when I was a child, I had nothing. So I went back to doing what I knew and became a hired gun. I just traded masters, the Union Precept for Lord Eberwik."

"One all-knowing being for another, eh?" Nacen said with a lopsided grin.

The table chuckled cordially, and Altan laughed again, that shrill laugh of his that dug at Nacen's nerves and memory.

Then it clicked. Altan Nergi was not who he claimed to be. He not only resembled the look of some of those of House Orizon, he was indeed from the very house itself. Nacen had seen him at the negotiation table during Stevari meetings before. He was an up-and-coming officer if Nacen remembered correctly. His name… eluded Nacen. What was he doing as the head of security on a U.P. merchant vessel?

At this point, Basaul joined the conversation. The man had barely touched any of his food, despite his reputation for having a voracious appetite.

"So tell me, Commander, what has the Union Precept been told about the attack on the Drovina homefleet and Extrata guild?"

"That's Lord," Eberwik said, a hint of annoyance seeping into his polite demeanor. "And the official story is quite simple. According to the Counsel, your house initiated the attack when you brought hostile weaponry of the Xandra Colonies into friendly Union Precept territory. When confronted and offered the choice to stand down and surrender, Yoska Buhari fired on our fleet. Only in his last moments of life did he realize his mistake and order his remaining ships to flee. Now they are led by a new steya, Zura Buhari, who cleaves a bloody path through the Union Precept."

"My brother…" Nacen exhaled.

"So it is true. Tell me, Nacen, why do you believe your fleet is headed to Fomalhaut?" The commander chewed while he awaited the answer.

"I've been asking myself the same question since we deduced their route," Nacen said. "It doesn't match our earlier projections of an elaborate escape. If they had wanted to escape, they could have tried to by now."

"I agree, as does the Counsel," Eberwik said.

"Perhaps, despite their actions, they do not wish to flee," Ofelia said with a frown. "Perhaps the Starkin merely seek an honorable death."

"That's a grim depiction of Stevari honor." Linasette chimed in. "I have lived with them for years now, and they value life and prosperity above all else."

"That's right," Nacen said. "Killing solves immediate problems: saving oneself, or preventing the deaths of innocent people, or loss of property. But it doesn't stop the idea that set your enemies on their path. It only justifies their hatred, or sense of justice. Fighting fire with fire only spreads it."

"An interesting theory, if not overly simplified. Values change when people get pushed to the edge. Repression is a funny thing," Eberwik said. "Even a virtue can be turned into a flaw. Patience can turn to indecisiveness. Kindness to weakness. Strength... to brutality."

"There's some people out there that just need killing, no way around it," Chalce said between bites of red meat.

Nacen could bear the conversation no longer. "Enough about theories. What are *you* planning, Lord Eberwik? To hand us over to the U.P. at the first opportunity?"

The table fell silent.

"Please, I have no intention of selling you out to the military," Eberwik said. "You may stay as long as you wish, then you may leave at your own discretion."

"So why did you help us, and continue to help us?" Nacen asked. He was honestly grateful, but this did not help to alleviate his suspicions.

"Because you will help us stop your brother. But such talk is not befitting of the dinner table. Please, let us continue along a more polite course of discussion."

The meal eventually concluded with hushed small talk and formal farewells. Nacen retired to his bedchamber but did not undress. His head swam with the knowledge that the homefleet was still alive, and that his oldest brother was at its helm. But this was all from the word of Eberwik, whose actions became more suspect by the minute. After a few minutes of anxious waiting, he opened up an encrypted comm channel with Linasette.

"Lina, we need to meet up. Something isn't right here," he sent.

"I know the idea of going up against your brother isn't ideal, Nace," she replied. "But maybe there's a way out of this that can save the homefleet. If we could just—"

"Not that. Fog lies heavy in this place. Eberwik speaks many truths, but he isn't being entirely honest with us. Do you recall that captain of the guard, Altan Nergi?"

"With that laugh? Of course. Why?" the pilot asked.

"He's not a hired gun, he's Stevari. An Orizon officer."

"Why would he lie? He had that whole story..."

"I don't know, but I intend to find out. Meet me by the *Canotila* in twenty minutes. I'll have everyone in the crew meet us there."

Nacen took up his travel case and changed back into his crimson combat robes, donning his cloak as well. He regretted not having his tried and true recast armor, but he would have to make do with what little he had. If there would be a firefight, they had likely already lost anyway. This was purely a mission of reconnaissance. He reached deep into the case, found two short daggers, and tucked them into his boots well out of sight. Still, better to be prepared.

***

Nacen made his way back down the corridors and did not encounter any guards. He descended the staircase down into the hangar bay and walked the length of it to where the *Carmine Canotila* lay. He was surprised to see it in much better shape already. He spotted Jeta and Shukernak sitting on the extended rear ramp, sipping some hot liquid in big thermoses. A data pad sat next to her on the ramp. Nacen was not able to bring his own into the *Etrusca* proper.

"She's looking beautiful. You're doing good work."

"You can chalk a lot of that up to the Armads, sir," Jeta said. "They may look it sometimes, but they're not dumb. They learn fast and work faster."

"Where are they?"

"Inside the ship's private quarters," Jeta gestured with her head, and her curly black hair went tumbling.

Shukernak smiled. "As soon as Basaul and Chalce got back from your hoity-toity dinner, they went back there and started fighting up a storm. Hence our break here. The reactor still needs a lot of work, and we haven't even started on the primary engines. But Eberwik's crew are letting us have any raw materials we don't have on board, and their precision manufacturing is top notch."

"Very charitable of them," Nacen noted. He nodded at Jeta's data pad. "May I?"

Jeta nodded her consent, her mouth still full from the thermos.

"Suspicious as all get-out is what I call it." Shukernak slammed his own thermos down and concealed a belch.

"It's not the only thing…" Nacen opened up the rudimentary diagram the Armads had been building of the *Etrusca* with the crew's reports out of the basic layout. The crew quarters had nearly been mapped out, as well as neighboring hangar bays and maintenance areas, thanks to Jeta and Shukernak. But huge swathes of the freighter remained unknown. Nacen perked up at echoing footsteps behind him. It was Linasette, Camlo, and Beskin. All had arrived as instructed.

"Alright, Nacen, what's up?" Linasette asked.

"Yeah, I was just laying down for a nice nap." Camlo stretched and gave a soft yawn.

"We need to plot out more of this ship. Linasette, you take the bottom holds. Beskin, you take the bow. Camlo, you'll take the stern. I'll try to gain access to the bridge. Just stroll about casually, no need to arouse more suspicion than we need to."

"There's quite a bit of my mattress that could use mapping." Camlo yawned again. "Plus, I think I can do it fairly discreetly."

"This is serious," Nacen said. "Commander… *Lord* Eberwik is certainly playing the part of the gracious host, but he's hiding something. I just haven't been able to ascertain what. For starters, the captain of the guard is a Stevari... from House Orizon."

"What, really?" Jeta gave a crooked frown.

"Why would he be on a Uni ship?" Shukernak asked. "I mean, aside from the great food, comfortable quarters, ample space, good—"

"I'm not sure about that yet, either." Nacen said.

"Forgive me for not brimming with skepticism. Oh, and I was going to say *coffee*," Shukernak drank deeply from his steaming thermos.

"Well then, let's work together and shed some light on the situation. You have your orders. Do what you can tonight, get a good night's sleep, and we'll get to work again tomorrow."

Chapter 11

The remaining trip to Fomalhaut was scheduled to take fifty-five hours. During that time, Nacen was to partake in lavish meals in the banquet hall, stroll along the showcase hallways of the *Etrusca*, and enjoy as much personal time in his estate room as he desired. He was often accompanied by either Camlo or Beskin, but generally his crew stuck to their cabins, roamed what parts of the ship they could, or assisted in repairing the *Carmine Canotila*.

Occasionally, Eberwik would join in for a meal, and he and Nacen would converse for a long time. Nacen shared stories of growing up on the homefleet, and on one occasion, he recounted his adventures in fighting the deepsun raiders. Eberwik told of his fantastic trips around Alpha One, the great blue sun, to Nacen. If even half of them were to be believed, then the *Etrusca* was the envy of any admiral to have in their fleet. In recent years, the *Etrusca* had gone on daring refuel missions to Synar, but its history dated back long since Eberwik's tenure as captain, back nearly as far as the founding of the Union Precept.

During the intervals, Nacen read in his cabin, reviewed their diagrams of the *Etrusca*, and walked the winding corridors of the freighter. The bridge was located aft, but deep within the hull as if to seclude it. Nacen found that two hallways were the only way to gain access to this centralized command area. Each one was watched by a pair of guards, short-barreled flux shotguns clutched about their waists, that rotated every three hours. The armory of the ship was likewise defended, as were certain areas below in the bowels of the ship. Otherwise, the majority of the vessel had been successfully laid out by Nacen and his crew. Munitions and cargo lay toward the bow, while the crew, armory, and guard barracks lay topside: dorsal, as Lina would insist on saying.

After the third day's breakfast aboard *Etrusca*, Nacen went back to the *Carmine Canotila* to check on repairs. He found Jeta with two Armads, Traver and Brecca, enjoying steaming cups of coffee. Traver, he knew because he was the shortest of the Armads, with one of the shorter tempers to match. Brecca had a more pronounced crest above his brow.

"Hello, Captain," Jeta said cheerfully, raising her cup in acknowledgement. Nacen felt the Armads' eyes on him. "To what do we owe the honor?"

"Just checking in. Have you seen our esteemed pilot today?"

"Today?" Jeta scoffed. "The last twenty-however-many hours have been a blur for me. We got the ship nearly vacuum sealed, interior refurbished, reactor running. Just a few hundred more odds and ends and we'll be ready to fly."

"Good, good. When was the last time you saw her then?"

Jeta considered again. "Maybe... early yesterday? She came in once to see if the reactor was ready after you gave your orders to scour the ship, which it wasn't at the time. We haven't seen her since."

Nacen nodded and turned to go. "Thank you, and good work on the ship."

Jeta saluted with her thermos and took another swig. "Good luck on your search. A ship won't do us much good without someone to fly it!"

Nacen nearly scolded the trufalci for forgetting that he was perfectly capable of flying his own ship, but he held his tongue. He exited the bay, taking a brisk pace up the steel gantry. He decided to check Linasette's room again. Perhaps she was merely asleep and had disabled notifications. It wasn't like Lina but, then again, very little on this ship was business as usual.

He knocked loudly on the metal door to her quarters, and after no one had answered after a minute, he attempted to open it. It complied with a swish.

Linasette's room was equally as extravagant as the rest, but themed in dark forest greens. A dark bronze chandelier hung from the ceiling, and lush carpet lay across the floor. Apart from a bag on the bed with some scattered belongings and clothing, there was no sign of the pilot anywhere. Now he was getting worried. Nacen decided to do a deep search of the room.

He scoured the cabinets, dressers, and end tables to no avail. The bathroom was no success. All he found was normal clothing and sundries one would expect for a week-long trip. Nacen started turning pillows, seat cushions, and lamps. On his sweep of the floor, he found a small object below the bed. It was Linasette's earpiece, no bigger than Nacen's little fingernail.

He picked it up and turned it over in his hand. It was undamaged. The most likely explanation was that it landed there by mistake. But Linasette was anything but careless. It seemed to Nacen that it was placed there intentionally, or perhaps landed there after a confrontation. Either way spelled bad news, though Nacen had no clue as to why either of these events could have happened.

Then he heard a slight whispering, starting as a mere fluttering of the air until he recognized it as a barely audible voice. He inserted the earpiece.

"...no intention of letting any of us go. I don't know what Eberwik really has planned, but it does not involve our best interest."

It must be a preset recording. He listened to the message until it looped back to the beginning.

"I hope this message has fallen into the right hands, because it may be our only hope. Eberwik is currently jamming my communications, ever since I managed to slip the guards and go below decks. There is a massive storage area in the underbelly of the ship, but it's not cargo. It's people. Hundreds of them, maybe even thousands. They're frozen, locked in some kind of induced sleep and kept in mechanical pods. I have no idea what twisted purpose this is for, but I fear we may find out. The guards followed me back to my room, but I... they're here. Please, whoever finds this message, tell Nacen. We have to get off this ship by whatever means necessary. Eberwik has no intention of letting any of us go..."

From there, Linasette's message repeated. He pulled out the earpiece, flung it on the ground, and ground it to dust into the carpet with his bootheel. Nacen put his face in his hands. All the suspicion and confusion and helplessness turned to anger within him. Was the entire galaxy against him and his little ship? He kicked at a dresser. He severed a wooden limb and it slumped forward. He began to pace, barely resisting the urge to lash out at whatever was nearest him. This was no time for meditation.

But how to proceed? He needed the *Etrusca* to carry him to Fomalhaut but couldn't trust they would let him go, or allow him to speak with his brother. As to the people in the bowels of the ship, Nacen could make neither heads nor tails of what could motivate Eberwik to do such a thing. Nacen needed to get the crew together before it was too late. He needed a plan.

Nacen heard footsteps down the hall. He exited the room and quickly set to walking in the opposite direction.

"Something the matter?" a cheerful voice shouted.

Nacen turned and saw the voice belonged to the captain of the guard, ostensibly Altan Nergi.

"Uh, no," Nacen began, "I'm just checking in with my crew. Making sure everyone will be ready to go when we reach Fomalhaut."

"Everything alright?" Altan asked, appearing genuinely concerned.

"Yes," Nacen answered, hoping his smile would conceal his urge to grab the Stevari and shake him until he divulged his real name and where the pilot was being kept. "Linasette doesn't appear to be in her quarters. She's probably on the *Canotila* or getting a morning jog in."

"That seems plausible. If you need anything at all, please let me know."

"Of course." Nacen left out the part about calling Altan a two-timing snake. "Actually, do you know where I can find your commander? I wish to speak with him."

"Lord Eberwik is currently preoccupied. May I forward a message?"

"When would I be able to see him next?"

"He will be at lunch in an hour," Altan said.

Nacen nodded his acknowledgement and turned to go. The Stevari's true identity continued to grate at him. Then he remembered his father shouting something at a House Orizon representative during a particularly heated meeting. Cease your infernal palavering... what was his name? Nacen tapped at the walls as he strode down the corridor, tapping along with the cadence of his father's long lost words. Cease your infernal palavering... cease your infernal palavering...

"Cease your infernal palavering... Lash Procah!" Nacen shouted to himself in triumph.

***

"She just disappeared?" Jeta wrinkled her brow.

"It sounds like she was kidnapped," Beskin said evenly, though the slight frown betrayed his calm disposition.

The entire crew had gathered in the *Carmine Canotila's* hold at Nacen's request. The interior hull had been magnetically sealed to allow for no electronic communications in or out. The cargo hold was filled with Stevari and Armads among the stacks of compressor crates. The crew had become accustomed to the busy cargo bay, though it now seemed crowded in comparison to the sprawling hangar bays and magnificent bedrooms of the *Etrusca*.

"Abduction is precisely what I suspect," Nacen said. He had withdrawn a dagger from his boot and was toying with the point. "She was taken just after she made her discovery of the silent populace in the lower holds of the *Etrus-*

ca. I can only speculate as to what Eberwik is doing with hundreds of bodies below the ship."

"Please don't," Jeta said.

"Maybe it's not so bad," Basaul shrugged with his massive shoulders. "He could be planning on colonizing his own planet."

"Or they're slaves in some sort of black market," Jeta snapped.

"Would you really want to be a part of either one? Look, the fact that the captain of the guard willfully lied to us about his own background shows they don't want us to know," Nacen reasoned, spinning the dagger in his left palm now. "I don't want to count myself among the sleeping ranks down there, if that is what's being planned."

There was a clamor as a dozen voices rose to give their opinions. They wanted to mount a rescue mission. They wanted to abandon the pilot and flee. They wanted to storm the bridge and take over the ship. They were all drowned by a rumbling baritone.

"So what do you propose, Captain?" Basaul asked.

The cramped room hushed as Nacen stabbed the dagger into the work bench and leaned forward.

Chapter 12

"Okay, now ease into it. If you go too hard, you'll shave off too much and we'll have to replace the whole section." Shukernak stood a nervous vigil over Brecca. Camlo waved at him from the corridor outside. This had to go just so. The Armad held a whirring blade and was delicately posturing the tool to shave off an excess portion of the *Carmine Canotila's* new starboard wing to achieve symmetry.

Repairs to the craft had begun to slow as the tasks increased in complexity. Some critical parts had been damaged beyond simple repair, and parts had to be custom manufactured to replace them. Many of the crew had now moved on to more cosmetic fixes while portions of the engines and control systems were still being replaced or retuned. Nearly every small extremity had to be replaced: fins, rudders, antennae, sensors. Shukernak let his thoughts drift back to the banquet hall where just yesterday he had enjoyed a lavish feast for breakfast. Stevari rations were exquisite but could not compare to the smorgasbord that Eberwik had put on. If Nacen was keen on mapping out the *Etrusca*, Shukernak wanted to be the one to discover the meat locker. Or, failing that, the larder where the coffee beans were kept. He could fit a lot of grounds in just one compressor crate.

Shukernak put his attention back on Brecca's cutting. The Armad had complete and utter control of the blade. Until he didn't. The diamond-tipped saw tore into a flap, severing part of the wing. Shukernak swore and cut the power, but not before the damage had been done and the component ruined.

"You idiot, now we have to start all over!" Shukernak wrenched the saw from Brecca's hands.

"Well how do you expect me to work, with you leering over me like that?" Brecca countered.

"I expect you to not screw it up." Shukernak turned away. He crouched down and jumped off of the crimson wing onto the steel platform that now supported the ship.

"What did you say to me?" Brecca's nostrils flared as he stepped toward Shukernak.

Shukernak, now on his way to get new material, turned back. "Oh, so *now* you can hear, eh?"

Jeta, who until this point had simply ignored the two men's boisterous jabs, set down her plasma torch. The trufalci rose from her spot beneath the *Carmine Canotila* by the rear hatch and looked on. Camlo stepped out of the hatch beside her. Armads were beginning to take notice as well.

"I *understand* that you and the rest of the Starscum would be long dead without us: fixing your ship, fighting your battles, fixing your ship *again*." Brecca squared up against Shukernak. The trufalci was big for a Stevari, but still stood nowhere near as tall as Brecca.

"I don't deal in what-ifs, and I can fight just fine without the likes of you." Shukernak put his hands up into clenched fists.

Brecca dropped his own hands and laughed in amusement. The deep laughter echoed across the spacious hangar. At last he stopped and blinked away a tear.

"You think so, do you?" Brecca asked, staring the big trufalci down.

"I know the bigger they are, the harder I get to whoop them," Shukernak said.

The Armad sneered and turned away in disgust, but suddenly whirled back around with one fist flying. Shukernak stepped back to dodge but did not escape Brecca's impressive reach. The man's rock-hard fist collided with Shukernak's right cheek and sent him reeling. The trufalci recovered quickly, circling around the Armad, looking for an opening. He lunged, aiming a right hook at Brecca. The Armad blocked it, but this was not Shukernak's true target. Shukernak threw a quick jab at Brecca's side, where his genetically toughened exterior was weaker. The punch connected, and Brecca grunted in pain. He retaliated by slamming Shukernak square in the gut.

Shukernak saw Jeta step forward to intervene, Camlo reached out to stop her.

"Don't... Jeta..." Shukernak managed to say.

"What, are you all crazy?" Jeta tried to shove past Camlo, but he held her back.

"Trust me, Jeta," Camlo insisted. "It has to go on a bit longer."

"Move it, or *both* your arms will be artificial before we leave this ship," Jeta said.

Camlo held fast. Every member of the crew was watching the brawl play out on the platform now.

Shukernak and Brecca had both hit each other more than was fair. They wavered but circled each other with the same vigor with which they had started. Shukernak went low, below Brecca's reach, and grabbed at his legs. Brecca staggered but did not fall. He kicked free and sent his heel colliding with Shukernak's ribs. Shukernak yelped as Brecca bent over him. The diamond-tipped saw was in his hand.

"Why is no one stopping this?" Jeta struggled hard against Camlo's arm.

Brecca powered on the saw, which quickly spun up to full speed, and hefted it above his head. At last Jeta broke free and ran to them.

"Let's see if I can get this right on the second try!" Brecca shouted, barely audible over the deafening whine of the saw.

A hand reached out and grabbed Brecca's wrist. It was the guard captain, Altan. He deftly switched the saw off before disarming the Armad.

Shukernak lay on the ground, panting. It was fortunate the captain had gotten there when he did. To her credit, Jeta had attempted to intervene, but Brecca had come way too close to taking things too far. The entire crew was gathered around the guard captain now, but they didn't look grateful or happy that Shukernak had been spared the fate of the ship's wing. Shukernak stood, carefully angling himself to cut off Altan's path out of the hangar.

"You're lucky I was passing by when I was," Altan said, setting the saw gently on the platform. "I'm surprised you weren't able to defuse this matter yourselves."

Camlo stepped forward, rubbing the back of his neck with his tungsteel

The Sword and the Cipher

hand.

"You're right, we should have been able to," he said. As he spoke, Beskin stepped up behind the guard captain, brandishing something in his right hand. "It's just that everyone has been under a lot of stress recently."

"Perfect understandable, but still, I would feel personally responsible if anything were to happen in my hangar. Next time there's a confrontation like this, take a deep breath and—" Something flashed in Beskin's right hand, and a needle slid into Altan's unarmored neck. "Take... a nice, relaxing..."

Altan hit the platform with a thud.

Shukernak turned and glared at Brecca. "The saw? Really?"

"Your captain told us to make the fight convincing," the Armad shrugged.

"Not *that* convincing!" Shukernak rubbed at his stomach.

"It worked, didn't it?" Brecca said.

"Are you two insane?" Jeta turned on Beskin. "And you! Did you just kill that guard?"

"Lash is merely unconscious. My apologies, Jeta, not everyone could be privy to this stage of the plan," Beskin said, placing the long syringe into his pocket. "Hortz, Perido, get our new friend here inside the ship."

The two Armads complied, and the rest of the crew followed them inside the hatch. After it had been sealed and the guard captain propped up against a compressor crate, Beskin withdrew a second syringe and carefully administered another shot to the man's neck. They waited.

"Are you sure you didn't kill him?" Jeta asked.

Beskin did not respond. He eyed the guard captain, searching for some sign of response. After a few seconds, the man's nose twitched. Then he grunted uncomfortably.

"Brecca, get a glass of that Ambrophyta you Armads are so fond of," Beskin ordered. "Jeta, get on the ship's computer and load up the scrambling program you worked on with Linasette a while back."

"The one to disrupt close-range signals? Linasette did most of the work on that one. It's just a slight modification of the magnetic field induction the ship already uses to block enemy interference."

"That's the one," Beskin said.

The guard groaned as his eyes flickered open to the storage bay of the trade ship. Shukernak sat beside him, taking the opportunity to rest from his bout with Brecca. The rest of the crew had been sent back out into the cargo bay, to give the illusion of normality.

"Welcome to the *Carmine Canotila*, Lash," Shukernak said.

"What... who... address me by my proper title, wretch," he demanded.

"Which is?" Shukernak held up an impatient hand.

"Altan Negri, captain of the guard of the *Etrusca*, in service to—"

"Enough. Jeta, run the program. Narrow coordinates to just this portion of the cargo hold." Beskin indicated a little circle around the cargo hold that contained himself, Shukernak, and guard captain. " Maximum interference."

"What?" the guard captain blinked. "What are you planning on doing?"

"Done," Jeta said.

"I say again, what are you planning?" he demanded.

"Relax, it's done," Shukernak said. "Now remind me, what is your name?"

"I uh…" the man blinked hard again. "That's beside the point. What have you done to me?"

"We're not quite sure yet. Nacen's hypothesis is that there was some kind of neural override acting on you, forcing you under Eberwik's control." Beskin paused, waiting for the guard captain to correct him, to speak the full title of *Lord Eberwik*. The correction never came. The man only offered up a blank stare. "It could have been done by an invasive chip, or short-ranged signal from a control panel, but whatever it is… it appears to be disabled while we are within the ship's privacy screen. Psychoactive conditioning could also be a factor, but there is nothing we can do about that in one afternoon."

"You can stand, you know," Shukernak said.

The man shifted his blank stare to the trufalci and did as he suggested.

"Ah, why yes, thank you."

"So, tell me about your childhood," Beskin said.

"This is neither the time nor the place. You must free me at once, and maybe Eberwik will go easy on you." The man strode about the small cargo hold, trying to find a clear path between the parts and crew to get to the rear hatch.

"Nothing about growing up on a planet called Renata?" Beskin asked. "Humor me."

"Never heard of the place," the man replied fretfully.

"Have you ever been a part of the Precept military? Lance trooper, drop forces, drone operator, anything?"

"Don't be absurd, I'm a Stevari lieutenant of House Orizon."

Shukernak perked up. He shared a knowing look with Camlo. Had the captain been correct after all?

"Why should we be concerned about Eberwik? Because he is your commander, your lord?" Beskin ventured.

"No, because he's a madman and no doubt seeks to imprison you as well."

"Tell me your name." Shukernak rubbed his chin. Now this was an interesting development.

"My name is Lash Procah, and you would do well to remember it," Lash said with a haughty frown.

"Sure, just as soon as I give you something to remember." Shukernak cracked the knuckles on the right hand and rose to meet Lash, but the action sent a ripple of pain down his side and he resumed his seat.

"Our apologies. Of course we will remember. You do seem to have recovered some of your cognitive faculties," Beskin said.

"Yes, it would appear so. I thank you, fellow traveler. I had been under Eberwik's control for so long, I had forgotten… well, everything worth remembering."

"It seems the modified interference program functions as intended. Let's get it loaded onto five of our handheld devices. That's one each for Shukernak, Jeta, Camlo, myself, and Lash here. The Armads will be on guard duty, finishing the last critical repairs to the ship."

Lash was hardly paying attention. He was examining his hands, turning them over as if seeing them for the first time.

"If what you have said is true, you have my eternal gratitude for freeing me from that interminable link to this madman's ship."

"Well, then, you're *really* not going to like the next part of the plan." Shukernak grinned inwardly as he grabbed one of the small, black field generators in the cargo hold. "Beskin, what was the captain's passphrase again?"

***

Several hours passed since the meeting with his crew, and Nacen decided it was time to catch up with the so-called lord. The lavish banquet hall normally hosted twenty or so people between the crews of the *Etrusca* and the *Carmine Canotila*. When Nacen entered, however, he found Bogdan Eberwik seated at the head of the table alone. Eberwik was sawing into a thick steak and finished his bite before he acknowledged Nacen and bade him to sit.

"We passed the Dorsaline quickspace lane with no issues," Eberwik said. "I thought you might like to know. A security drone had a few questions for me, but nothing I could not handle."

"It seems we're making good progress toward Fomalhaut," Nacen sat down and helped himself to a bowl of greens.

"I have received news from Fomalhaut, in fact, from another Union Precept drone. The Precept navy has finally converged on the homefleet's location. It seems your guess that Fomalhaut would be their location has proven correct. But even now the noose tightens, and Zura will not be able to escape. When we pass into the Fomalhaut system, I expect you to tell your brother to stand down."

"And then we can leave with the homefleet." Nacen played with his fork, twirling it the bowl of greens and spearing bright vegetables with its prongs. He eyed Eberwik cautiously. Eberwik continued to eat, saying nothing. "You know, Zura was always an impetuous one. When we were kids, he would always be the first one to suggest sneaking off to the star dome during a lecture. We'd go and sit under the stars, either talking about what the future would hold or playing the strings. Sometimes he'd run off to obscure parts of the ship without telling anyone at all. He was a wanderer among wanderers, never able to keep still and rarely doing what he was told. He did what he did to hold his own interest, even lying on occasion. It's funny… how willing people are to deceive those closest to them."

"It would seem you and your brother have more in common than you admit. Do not think I have not noticed what you've been up to." Eberwik set down his silverware and interlocked his fingers. "I have simply allowed your reconnoitering to continue because it is of no consequence. Your pilot got a little too adventurous, so I detained her for her own good."

"You will release her after we comply with your wishes?"

"If that is what you want. She is inconsequential to me, though potentially quite valuable to the Precept navy," Eberwik said. "I am afraid I have been less than forward with you, Captain. You see, all I asked is that you pay your way. *Your* way is a high price, however, Prince of Drovina. I cannot permit you or your crew to simply leave. You will come to the bridge with me, say your piece, and if you are fortunate, your brother will stand down. I want what you want, a peaceful end to this whole affair. War may be good for business, but annihilation is not."

"You want what, my ship? You won't have it," Nacen blurted.

"I do not want your ship, Drovinian. I want its crew. Specifically, you. As the last prince of a lost fleet, you make quite the collectible. The information you will provide shall be of some value as well, of course. And let's not forget what you'll get in return."

"But I'm not the last prince, if that archaic title even really applies here, there's still Zura," Nacen said. He put the pieces together as he finished saying the words. Even if the Union Precept allowed the remnants of his homefleet to live, they might not allow Zura the same privilege.

"Now you see your homefleet's peril. I am not your enemy. We both seek the survival of your people."

Nacen remained silent, transfixed by horror and rage in equal measure. "What do you want with us? With all those people down below?" he stammered at last.

"Effectively? Immortality. Knowledge beyond what I myself as one man can possess. New peaks of both pleasure and pain. In sleep, you shall fight in the immortal halls that our ancestors sang of, and dine in palaces of impossible dimensions, be torn apart and put back together in a thousand ways. In waking, you shall serve as one of my elite guard… or possibly my court minstrel."

"Why are you doing this? Are you trying to please your depraved Counsel? Are you trying to join with it?" Nacen asked in disgust.

"Alas, no. No living entity may truly merge with the Counsel. But my status as a mere man will not prevent me from reaching such lofty stations, or perhaps beyond. Each mind I take and shape, I grow more powerful." Eberwik began pacing the length of the table, running his hand along the back of each chair as he did so. "I have eyes everywhere. I am my drones. I am my guards. I am *Etrusca*. Soon, you will be too."

"I won't be your plaything, not like Lash," Nacen said.

"We shall see," Eberwik stood up and beckoned to the entrance of the hall. Guards streamed in from every corner of the room, four from each entrance. They surrounded Nacen, flux shotguns raised. Resplendent in their blue robes and gleaming white armor, they stared at him from behind their faceless helmets. "Now, please, let us proceed to the bridge. I have someone you may be interested in speaking to."

Nacen rose slowly. He found himself calmer than he had been in the last few days, despite the twenty-odd shotguns leveled at his skull. This was all to be expected once he confronted Eberwik. Well, not the revelations about how mad the so-called lord really was. But that simply made sticking to the plan all the more important. Nacen allowed Eberwik to lead him out of the room, with guards swarming about like flies.

Eberwik apparently did not want him bound by chains or cuffs for his interaction with his brother, and besides, this was wholly unnecessary with what must be a third of the ship's guard contingent on either side of him. Nacen walked freely down the corridor, clenching and unclenching his fists. Had his crew been able to get in position? He glanced at the guards around him. Everything had collapsed so fast. His unease was amplified by the fate that awaited him should he fail. In all his scouting of the ship, he never could have imagined what Eberwik was doing. He thought of Linasette. Even if the commander stuck to his word and released her, what awaited her at the hands of the Union Precept? Surely they would not look fondly on a defector.

Nacen stared down at the tiles of the ship, replaying his decisions since coming onboard the *Etrusca* in his head. What could he have done differently? His hands shook from the stress of clenching them, and he reopened them. After all his cunning and planning, the grim realities of the situation were finally catching up with him. As the forbidden corridor to the bridge came into view, Nacen straightened. He had done all he could. Now he had to accept what lay ahead.

The bridge was located aft of the ship, accessed by two carefully guarded corridors. The guards, headed by Lord Eberwik in his long, slow strides, led Nacen into the bridge. The room was large, and characteristically square for the *Etrusca*. Consoles and alcoves of control panels lined its edges. A central, raised platform dominated half of the command room. Control panels were manned by a score of men and women in blue uniform. High alabaster walls rose above them.

Eberwik walked up a short staircase in the middle of this elevated platform and beckoned Nacen to join him. The guards spread out, eight around the platform and four on each corner of the platform. The rest went out to patrol the corridors.

"Welcome to the bridge of the *Etrusca*, Captain. You should consider yourself privileged. Very few visitors get to see this far into the ship." Eberwik gave a haughty grin.

"Hmm," Nacen grunted. He was still too furious with Eberwik to give him any sort of satisfaction.

"Well then." Eberwik turned and activated a forward display. The familiar blazing sea of the great blue sun raged below them, fading into blackness above. "At present, we are nearing the lane for Fomalhaut, mere minutes from seeing what's become of your homefleet."

They waited in silence. Nacen stood with his hands behind his back, not acknowledging Eberwik but staring intently at the display, willing his long lost homefleet to appear.

"This is for the best, you know," Eberwik broke the silence at last. "What I am orchestrating here is the best possible outcome for you that the Counsel has seen. Would you rather perish in a disastrous fleet battle? See your friends and family destroyed? There was no way you were ever going to get back to your homefleet and still evade the Union Precept navy. Surely... surely you must see that?"

Nacen's gaze remained squarely at the screen. How many frigates had made it through? Would he see his father? Suddenly being trapped aboard this hideous freighter didn't seem like such a bad end, not if he could help the homefleet in some way. But would it make a difference? If the Union Precept had really cornered here, why not just snuff his people out?

"What will you say to him?" Eberwik said, his voice dripping with amusement. "Will it be a plea of rationality, of sanity? Or will your last words to your brother be a mere heartfelt goodbye?"

"My words will be exactly what he needs to hear, and nothing more." Nacen maintained his forward gaze.

Eberwik scoffed and turned to face the front of the bridge as well. Soon the branching, dancing lights on the screen faded. The arcing prominence of the great blue sun vanished and was replaced by a multitude of stars amidst the black. To the left, a bright blue star dominated the system, appearing mostly white.

"Connect me to the flagship *Exemplar*," Eberwik commanded. "This is Lord Eberwik of the *Etrusca*, coming in to assist the Precept fleet stationed here at Fomalhaut."

"Ah, hello, *Etrusca*," a high baritone voice answered in a lackadaisical tone after a long delay. "We expected you hours ago. You are slated to refuel the *Iron Templar*. Coordinates to follow. What's been the holdup?"

"We recently acquired some additional cargo," Eberwik mused. "We shall be communicating to the head of the Starkin fleet soon. Please inform the ranking admiral in command of this."

"I'm afraid that's above my paygrade, Commander. I'll patch you through to the flagship, but that's all I can do."

"Very well. Attached are my clearance codes. All I need is a few seconds to get the admiral's attention."

They waited in tense silence. Nacen noticed most of the crew were no longer actively working at their stations. Finally, the screen changed. Blackness covered it like the deepest night. Then a voice spoke, harsh and callous.

"This is Admiral Sorkitani. This better be worth my time, *Etrusca*, I have a war to win," the pitiless voice announced. "I hardly need my munitions topped off."

"With all due respect, Admiral, my aim is to help you end this misunderstanding," Eberwik replied. "I have within my custody the youngest son of the late steya, and brother to the current one who is making a mockery of your fleet."

The black screen suddenly disappeared to reveal a woman of minor stature compared to the stoic men standing behind her. Medals stood pronounced on the left breast of her green uniform and gilded straps lay on her shoulders. Her short, copper locks flecked with grey were tucked into a bun. She topped it all off with a deep scowl. "You have my attention, Commander."

Eberwik took a step forward and stood with his palms out. "I propose we allow the brothers to speak, to allow Nacen here to negotiate with Zura to stand down and leave the system."

"You are not familiar with the current situation I see," Sorkitani noted. "Zura holds the planet of Fomalhaut hostage, along with fifty-two billion souls. If we fire upon him, he will bombard the planet. We estimate his claims of casualties in the thirty to forty percent range to be most accurate. This is of course unacceptable."

"Surely my honored guest could get his own brother to stand down?"

Admiral Sorkitani exhaled sharply. "It is worth the attempt, I suppose. If you succeed, I will ensure our navy provides double the commission you were paid for the refueling mission."

"Make it tenfold and we have a deal," Eberwik said, a little too casually.

"Withholding information? Transporting fugitives of the Union Precept? I could easily make it treason, instead," Sorkitani chided mirthlessly. "We have contingency plans we are currently working on besides this. You are in no position to barter."

Nacen noticed a slight twinge at the corner of Eberwik's mouth. "Of course, Admiral. You have my utmost apologies for—"

"This concludes our business." Admiral Sorkitani glanced to the side, distracted by something off-screen. She whispered to someone and turned to face Eberwik once more. "Good luck, Commander. Our citizens are depending on your actions here. My second in command will be listening in."

"Thank you, Admiral. I will not disappoint." Eberwik gave a curt nod as the *Exemplar's* bridge disappeared from the main view.

"Are the lives of your friends and family on the homefleet and billions of Union Precept civilians worthy enough motivation for you, Captain?" Eberwik asked. "Even if you and your crew are to stay here with me?"

"If this is the only way I can save my homefleet, then this is my duty. This was the oath I swore to my crew when I first set us on this mission," Nacen said.

"You've got conviction, another quality I admire." Eberwik whirled and pointed at the man sitting to his left. "Patch us through to the lead Starkin ship."

"Yes, Lord," the man replied. Nacen found himself wondering how that particular crewman had been acquired, or if he had come aboard of his own free will. "The *Burning Stag* is ignoring our hailing frequencies."

"Send them a still image of our bridge. Let them know who we have."

"Yes, Lord," the man tapped at the console's holographic keyboard. "It is done. The fleet is a bit farther out than our friendlies, so we will have a greater delay to contend with."

The bridge was still as they waited for the signal to travel to Fomalhaut orbit and back.

"Okay, depending on the length of their... hold on, we have a communication request."

"You are who you say you are." Eberwik gave Nacen a grin. He stood aside and beckoned Nacen to take his position at the front of the dais. The Stevari captain complied, clasping his hands together behind his back. The screen flicked on again to reveal a man strikingly similar to Nacen. He had the same auburn hair, but his short curls lay just below his ears. His face was slightly more worn with age, and he had a saturnine look to him, though this could have been from the recent tribulations of the fleet he now led.

Zura wore a crimson tunic over dark brown breeches. Over him flowed a familiar white cape with gold filigree. The last time Nacen had seen this particular raiment was on the shoulders of their father.

"You're a difficult man to find, brother," Nacen said with a smile. He kept up the smile for a while, but eventually dropped it as he waited for Zura to receive and return the message.

"Nacen, you offend me. I left plenty in my wake for anyone to locate me during my little trip," Zura smiled back momentarily before slipping back to a more passive expression to await his brother's reply.

"The Unity certainly have taken offense," Nacen said.

"As they are wont to do. Tell me, how much money has the Union Precept promised you to betray us?"

"Now it is my turn to take offense," Nacen said. "Like you, myself and those under my charge have been placed in less than ideal circumstances. We came to rescue you, not bring about your downfall."

"If you have come to parley, then the two are one in the same," Zura said bitterly. The eldest son stood straighter, if such a stance were possible, and the gleaming raiment shifted on his shoulders. "After what happened to the fleet, to our father, at Carnizad, this can only end in blood. Now that you are captive, my only hope is to do more damage to them than they have caused us."

"Me? What about me could change this conflict for the better?"

"Father said you were the key. Or rather that you *had* the key."

"To what?" Nacen asked.

"The Void Protocol. Our ace in the hole against an attack from the Unity. Ironic, given that the possession of such a weapon is what caused them to attack us. Heavens know how they found out about it," Zura said.

"I honestly have no idea what you're talking about," Nacen blurted.

Zura paused and glanced at unseen figures in his ship. "Now is not the time to speak of such things. Besides, it is useless to belabor the point of you being here since you've been captured."

"No, I will hear of this now," Eberwik interjected, stepping behind Nacen and into the screen. Nacen waited uncomfortably by Eberwik for their message to arrive and for Zura's to return.

"I am under no such oath to you, Uni lapdog," Zura said, pulling his cape about his shoulders.

Bogdan Eberwik pulled out a stubby flux pistol and, taking a step toward Nacen, leveled it at the base of his skull from an arm's length away. "You are under your oath as kin to this Starkin, you filth. I will not be dishonored in front of the fleet and denied my fortune."

Eberwik glared at the bridge camera during the transmission time. Nacen knew Eberwik would not shoot him, not after he had divulged his plans. Still, the gun made him uncomfortable. Family reunions could be so awkward.

"Then that is your choice, Commander. We must all make our own choices. This is mine."

The screen was replaced by the Drovina fleet in orbit around the sprawl world of Fomalhaut. The communication had been terminated.

Nacen had no words. Zura would throw his life away so casually? That, or the Void Protocol was more important than he realized. But how did it pertain to this situation? And what did Zura mean by Nacen having the key?

"It would be foolish to kill you simply because your brother will not comply." Eberwik lowered his pistol. "We will simply have to try another way. Perhaps I can make some subtle touches to your psyche and have you infiltrate your brother's ships..."

Nacen glanced surreptitiously about the bridge. There were twelve guards in all, and twenty or so crew. Now was probably the time to spring his trap.

"The one who spots the splinter in another's eye fails to see the beam in his own," Nacen said. He stared at Eberwik, who stared right back. Then Nacen flung himself to the floor, covering his eyes. Upon hearing the phrase, four of the *Etrusca* guards in white armor leapt into action. They lobbed grenades in the middle of the room which emitted a bright flash of light, temporarily blinding anyone not shielding their eyes. The remaining eight guards staggered about and looked around bewildered for their targets, hardly suspecting those within their own ranks.

Shotgun blasts went off in rapid succession. The crew's cries of panic reverberated throughout the chamber as they sought cover. The eight armored guards fell one by one from the concussive flux spread fired at point blank range.

Nacen blinked and saw Eberwik trying to get his bearings. Nacen swatted his flux pistol away with a sweeping kick. Eberwik lunged for him. Nacen kicked out again, nailing the man in the jaw with a sickening snap. Eberwik drew a dagger from his gauntlet and held it out as a warning. As he clambered up, he slipped on a patch of blood and the knife fell from his hands. The nearest guard knelt to help Nacen up.

"You!" Eberwik shouted. "Kill him!"

"Sorry, I don't take orders from you." The guard removed his helmet. Shukernak stood smiling over Nacen and, grabbing him by the shoulder, hefted him up with his enormous strength.

"Blue suits you," Nacen said jovially.

"Aww shucks, Captain, you're just saying that because we saved your ass," Shukernak said.

Nacen laughed. "Does that make it any less true?"

Eberwik was lying on the floor, propped up by one elbow. Blood seeped from his mouth. "How? These guards are all under my control!"

"They were. You had total control of my crew, since they willfully planted themselves into the *Etrusca's* systems in your guard barracks. But our devices lay in wait to scramble your control, lying dormant for a code phrase. As soon as they regained control, they assumed their order to take the bridge. Which as you can see," Nacen spread out his arms. "They have achieved."

"You fool. You and your pathetic homefleet will never leave the system now," Eberwik growled.

"I'd say you have a rather poor record at predicting outcomes at this point. Wouldn't you agree, Camlo?"

"Oh, yeah," Camlo said with a grin, stepping on the platform to join Nacen, Shukernak, Beskin, and Jeta. The Stevari crew, having secured the bridge, had doffed their helmets to reveal their true identities. "I'm glad to be out of the *Etrusca* network. It's like I had no control over what I was doing, like everything had this weird compulsion to do it."

"I know I won't miss it, even if it means back to taking orders from the captain," Shukernak said.

Beskin leveled his flux shotgun at Eberwik. "Orders, Captain? Shall I terminate?"

"No. I am not like my brother. Spilled blood only deepens the pools of hatred." Nacen took a seat at one of the consoles and, after some searching, brought up a holographic projection of a map displaying the levels of the *Etrusca*. At last, a complete image of the entire vessel.

"What do we do now, then?" Camlo asked.

"We have one more detour to make before we head back to the *Canotila*," Nacen said. "We need a pilot, after all.

"If you wouldn't mind, Captain, I have some friends in the cryopod storage below." A fifth guard strode up to Nacen's console. He tossed his helmet to the ground. The Stevari's ponytail had been undone, and lustrous blond hair spilled out onto his shoulders, braided in portions. He had a long, proud nose that suited him well. He seemed to smile with his entire face, and his eyes shone with rich emerald irises. The familiar features, before seeming strange and foreign on a Unity guard captain, the Orizon Stevari wielded in style.

"Lash," Nacen said, "you made it. It's good to see you at last."

"Likewise, Son of Drovina. I apologize for anything I've said in the last few days unbecoming of an officer of Orizon, or for anyone I've killed for that matter. I've been on the *Etrusca* a long time."

"Well let's put an end to that unfortunate tenure, then. We can see about setting you up with a small ship onboard the *Etrusca*. Of course, we'll need to—"

Lash held up a hand.

"Please, that is unnecessary. For rescuing me, I shall accompany you back to your homefleet. If even half of what I've heard is true, then House Drovina could use the help. Besides, my greatest chances of returning to homefleet Orizon are beside my fellow Stevari."

"I thank you, Lieutenant Procah," Nacen said.

"Please, we are both officers of respectable homefleets. Though we may indeed be rivals from time to time, there was a time the homefleets were all one. It is long past, but not forgotten. We are all family. You may call me Lash."

"I extend the same courtesy to you." Nacen bowed deeply to Lash.

Though he wished he had his digital pad on him to access the ship's layout they had constructed, he had long since committed the essential passages to memory. He could lead his crew into the bowels of the ship. Surveying the disorderly bridge, he found some armor in decent condition and strapped the major pieces on with Camlo's help. He also picked up a discarded flux shotgun. At last he turned to his trufalci. "Shukernak, escort Mr. Eberwik, please."

"That's *lord*," the man spat, "and I am not setting foot off my bridge."

"I don't see you in control of a bridge anymore, let alone a ship. I guess that settles both points," Nacen said.

"And if I refuse?"

Nacen nodded to Shukernak. The trufalci rose from the body of a security guard, holding a hard, slender baton. With a flick of his wrist, it doubled in length and gave a crackle of discharged electricity.

"Oh, I'm gonna enjoy this..."

Chapter 13

The alabaster walls of the *Etrusca* rushed past as Nacen and the crew ran to the lower decks. Working from their patchwork map, they jogged through the interior of the ship. Their progress was quick, though hindered slightly with the weight of the unconscious Bogdan Eberwik on Shukernak's back. They encountered no resistance so far, but Nacen doubted their journey would stay that way. He could see they were nearing the ship's dungeons as they approached a large, reinforced steel door where the map's boundaries stopped dead. It remained closed in their presence.

"Alright, wake him up," Nacen said reluctantly. Camlo jostled Eberwik, and when he got no response pinged his communications net instead.

"Wha–where am I? Where have you taken me?" Eberwik demanded of Nacen.

"Relax," Nacen said, "you're still on your ship. We're leaving as soon as we get our pilot back."

"The only way you are leaving is in a body bag," Eberwik growled as he rubbed at his head. "Or possibly out of an airlock."

"Well, we can agree on a method later," Nacen said. "For now, we just need a little help from you and your men."

"You will get nothing from me."

"Okay, I get the picture you're trying to paint for us. But right now, it's your life for my pilot's. I think that's a pretty fair exchange. *Kaha*, I'd say it's generous with how I rate you right now." Nacen waved his pistol with authority.

"How do I know you will keep your word?"

"You're alive still, aren't you? Want to stay that way? Keep being useful."

"Hold on." Eberwik closed his eyes. The doors slid open with a groan. Metal grating and stairs led down into the darkness below.

"Jeta, can you access the ship's network to keep these doors open?" Nacen asked.

"I can try. No telling whether it will hold or not, though," Jeta slid a gauntleted finger down the edge of the door's groove in the wall.

"That will have to do." Slowly at first, then with growing boldness, Nacen led the group down the stairs. After thirty paces or so down, Nacen took a furtive look around. The room had a low ceiling, and the far wall extended further than Nacen could reasonably see. The expanse was filled with row upon row of what appeared to be data storage banks. Each was slightly taller than Nacen and no more than two meters wide. Nestled in between several stacks in each row was a large pod with a clear top, its contents dark and foggy. To the right sat a large control unit, multiple stands for holographic keyboard overlays out in front of three large screens.

Nacen immediately took note of seventeen hostile guards in various defensive positions around the room. Most were partially hidden behind pods. The guard closest emerged from a databank and held up a cautioning hand.

"Halt!" the figure barked, raising his flux shotgun.

"How mundane," Lash noted.

Nacen turned to Eberwik, currently being muscled down the staircase by Shukernak. "Anything to say, Commander?"

"Stand down, all of you!" Eberwik ordered. "Let us not turn this into a bloodbath. The Starkin shall take what they came for and leave."

The guards shared a few looks, puzzlement clear from their slow motions. Gradually, they each stood up and lowered their weapons.

Nacen took a few hesitant steps forward. Some of the guards stepped back, but most remained at ease. "Alright, where are you keeping Linasette down here?"

"Miss Derada is located in the holding zone. Take the main corridor straight ahead," Eberwik instructed. "After about fifteen terminals, you will take a left. There will be a sign over a side corridor marked transfer bay. Follow that corridor down six perches."

"A bit less than one hundred meters," Lash clarified.

"This had better not be some sort of trick," Nacen eyed the adjacent corridors.

"I assure you, at this point, I merely want you and your crew off the *Etrusca*."

"Come now, where's that famous Precept hospitality?" Nacen moved the group down the corridor. Beskin, Camlo, Jeta, Shukernak, and Lash fanned out along the sides, ready to bring their weapons to bear at a moment's notice should the guards try anything. As they passed each pod, Nacen could see that most contained a person, barely visible beneath thick, tinted glass. They passed dozens of these pods on the way to their destination.

Unable to contain his curiosity any longer, Shukernak peered into the nearest pod. "So these guys are all your slaves, or what?" He tapped gently on the glass.

"No, they were acquired perfectly legally through proper channels or signed themselves over willingly," Eberwik said.

Shukernak nodded, only half listening. "Mmmhm. Sure. So they're all sleeping?"

"Not exactly," the commander of the *Etrusca* explained. "They are in a deep, cryogenic state. Unlike most cycles of sleep, their brains are quite active. Most of their consciousness is running in simulations. Generally, they are completely unaware they are in stasis at all."

"Okay. So they just don't know that they're your slaves. Got it." Shukernak kicked at a pod's base as the group turned the corner for the holding bay.

"My own crew is down this hallway." Lash tilted his head to the right.

"We'll retrieve them on our way back," Nacen assured. "I don't want us splitting up."

"Very well."

Two men stood guarding the double-sided door to the holding bay. Their weapons already holstered, they waved the Stevari masquerading as guards through. The doors slid open, revealing a small, circular room. Even so, the room looked imposing, with a ceiling twice the height of the corridor and crammed with computer banks and data storage. In the center lay Linasette, unconscious on a long white table. Despite this, she was manacled to the table by her forehead, waist, wrists, and ankles. A woman in a form-fitting white coat stood with her back to the door, and turned as it whisked open.

"Lord, I'm sorry, the specimen is not quite ready. I wasn't expecting you for at least another hour."

"The specimen is ready, all right. Ready to get out of here. Release her restraints," Lash insisted.

The technician looked Lash and company up and down, noticing the white armor and blue robes on all but Nacen. "Why is your guard speaking to me like that?" she asked of Eberwik.

Eberwik gritted his teeth. "They aren't my…"

"There's been a temporary change in management. Now please, release the prisoner," Nacen said.

"Lord Eberwik, what is going on here?" the technician asked.

"Okay, enough of this," Shukernak said, withdrawing his flux shotgun from the magnetic sling on his back and taking several steps forward. "Release the lady, now."

"'Stand down, 'Nak." Nacen stood in front of the trufalci and extended a firm hand. "Waving your gun around isn't going to solve any problems."

"Really? Because it's worked pretty well so far."

Nacen returned the remark with a hard stare. Shukernak hesitated a moment. His eyes flicked from Nacen, to the technician, then to Linasette lying on the table. He lowered the weapon.

"Eberwik, help us out a bit," Nacen said, "before I let Shukernak call the shots again."

"Petra, please. This is a sensitive situation," Eberwik stepped to the foot of the bed and placed his hands behind his back. "The sooner we do as the Starkin wish, the sooner they will leave."

"Very well." The technician wrinkled her brow and turned to the console on the wall. She began typing at the holographic keyboard. "The specimen, she…"

"Linasette," Nacen corrected.

"*Linasette*," Petra said, "should be awake any moment now. It may take her a few minutes to regain full muscle functionality."

Nacen looked her up and down. She appeared to be unharmed but had forsaken her green gown for a blue medical one. "Why did you want her anyway?"

"First was to keep her from going where she wasn't supposed to, but beyond simple security, it is for the same reason I wanted you," Eberwik replied. "You are a rarity. You are the son of the steya of a dying house. When your homefleet is gone, you will be a priceless artifact. She, on the other hand, has a perspective many of my clients will be interested in. She lived in the Unity and had a promising future in the Precept navy. She chose to walk away from it all."

Nacen disregarded Eberwik's words. He didn't care for the rationale behind the madness and regretted asking the question. "Okay, here's the plan. First we get Linasette walking, or carry her. Then we're going to find Lash's people, then hoof it back to the *Carmine Canotila* as fast as possible. We'll round up the Armads and get out of here. Last I checked, the *Canotila* was more or less functional, just missing a little paint here and there."

"Understood," Beskin said.

Nacen faced the commander of the *Etrusca*. "You'll stay with us until we're back on our ship."

"Fine. I just want you out of here," Eberwik said.

"Well, we're in agreement there."

Several quick snaps behind Nacen drew his attention. The cuffs restraining Linasette's unconscious form had been unlatched and retracted. The pilot blinked several times. Her eyes darted about the room, not appearing to focus on anything in particular. She raised her right hand to rub at her left wrist, and her face registered surprise when the limb moved freely. She rubbed her shoulders next and finally looked up at Nacen with a smile. When she spoke, her words slurred and she seemed distant. "I was just about to break myself out, you know... I had the guards lulled into a false sense of security."

"You'll have to excuse the bravado of my rescue, then," Nacen said with a smile.

Camlo came around to the other side of the chair. "You're referring to how we saved you, right, Nace?"

"Right... let's just agree to make this the last rescue today." Nacen crouched and allowed Linasette to throw her arm over one shoulder. Camlo did the same on her opposite side. "Can you walk?"

"Should be able to handle it fine," Linasette said as Nacen and Camlo guided her off the chair. She placed one foot on the ground and stumbled forward. They got under her arms and prevented her from planting her face into the deck. "Or not... thanks."

"No worries," Nacen said, "just make sure that after we get you out of here, you get us off this damned ship."

"I should be fine by then."

Eberwik walked cooperatively with them now, flanked by Beskin and Camlo, with Shukernak looming from behind. Lash led the group, darting back and forth between the rows with suppressed energy. Just when they had nearly reached the turn that marked the halfway point back, he stopped and stared down the bank of pods.

"We're here," he said in little more than a whisper. Without looking back to see if Nacen and the crew followed, he walked down a dozen pods. He placed one hand reverently on a pod, paused, and walked to the next. He repeated the process for nine pods.

"We need these nine pods activated, and the Stevari within them released," he called back.

"It's always more and more with you Starkin, isn't it?" Eberwik sighed and closed his eyes. He gave a brief smile, which Nacen alone appeared to be disturbed by, then his face became contorted with mental effort for a moment. A series of sharp clangs echoed down the line, nine in total. As the lids lifted and slid back, Nacen suddenly saw a resemblance to old coffins in which people were traditionally buried on terrestrial worlds. The old, slate gray could also easily have been replaced by the dusty stonework of a sarcophagus.

"Rise, children of Orizon, rise! It's been far too long since I've felt your names on my lips," Lash called out. He grinned wildly as he dashed from pod to pod, grasping the edges and peering inside before moving to the next. "Bosha, come, there are so many songs to sing before they are forgotten! Mingo, it's been many nights since you've sipped a fine Stevari wine worthy of your sharp tongue. Come! Ha! I see you there, Phantine. Do not be shy, it is our destiny to ply the stars once more!"

As he finished his celebratory rounds, Lash's frenetic movements slowed. None rose from the pods.

"Come on, let's help them up and get moving," Nacen said. "We don't have time to spare, and this place makes me uneasy."

"Maybe they suffer from some muscle degradation or sleep paralysis?" Camlo suggested.

"Impossible," Lash said. "They are taken out of the pods every few macrocosmic days for routine servitude. Most of them are used as staff in the kitchens, or as musicians during feasts. I wonder if they ever recognized me as you did, Nacen."

They waited respectfully, but there was no movement within the pods. Nacen peered into several. Each contained the body of a Stevari, their flesh still rosy with their lifeblood. But they did not stir, nor even respond to touch.

"I'm sorry, Lash, but they're not getting up," Nacen said. "We need to go."

"No!" Lash cried and pointed to Eberwik. "This is *his* doing. Wake them. I said wake them, fiend!"

"There are certain risks when one withdraws from the deep, artificial sleep of the cryobanks," Eberwik frowned. "While unlikely, it is possible and indeed most regrettable that this unfortunate mishap has occurred to your entire entourage."

"You did this intentionally, you miserable butcher!"

"They appear to have indeed perished. I am sorry, Starkin."

"Then you will join them!" Lash pushed Nacen and Camlo aside and jammed the barrel of his shotgun beneath Eberwik's jaw. The commander did not recoil.

"Lash, stand down! We need him as a hostage!" Nacen shouted.

"No, he must pay for what he's done. We cannot allow this man to live."

"We'll never make it off this ship if you kill him now. Yes, he deserves it. But don't condemn us because he condemned your friends. Look at him, he's not some admiral or senator. He's a trader, born into a vast empire, so desperate to make something of himself he's gone through these extravagant measures to give himself purpose. Do not hate him. Pity him, and spare him."

Lash stared into the commander's eye, his finger dancing on the trigger.

"You're right. *Chodra*," Lash swore, letting his weapon fall. "You're right. I'm sorry."

One by one, Nacen's crew filed out back into the corridor until only he and Lash stood by the pods.

"We need to go," Nacen said again.

Lash gave a solitary nod, still looking at the open pods. "I'm sorry."

The Stevari worked their way back through the labyrinthine databanks and back to the entrance. Guards from the *Etrusca* in their polished white armor and blue robes regarded them suspiciously and trailed them from a long way off. Nacen and his crew plodded on warily, always making sure Bogdan Eberwik was secure within their ranks. Nacen glanced uneasily into a cryopod he passed. A blurred image of a woman, forever lost to time, lay on the other side of the glass.

By now, Linasette had regained full use of her limbs, and the group quickened their pace as they approached the steep staircase leading to the main corridors of the *Etrusca*. As Nacen placed his right foot on the bottom step, he paused. The group continued their brisk pace to the egress. Beskin was the first to take notice.

"Captain? Something wrong?" Beskin raised the butt of his shotgun to his shoulder.

Nacen grimaced. "I just feel guilty."

"Regarding?" Beskin asked. By this point, the rest of the crew had stopped as well.

"Everyone we're leaving behind."

"We can't save everyone, Captain. The best thing you can do is get your crew out of here. As your druvani, I intend to make that happen."

"I know... it's just... after almost becoming Eberwik's plaything, I can't stomach the thought of what these people must be going through."

Eberwik stepped forward, shrugging off Shukernak's grip. "Now see here. I am permitting your vile crew to get off of my ship with all of your lives intact. A remarkable deal, it seems to me. I acquired these people through perfectly acceptable channels. Lieutenant Procah here was given as a ransom to broker a peace deal on Synar. The alternative for most of these people would likely be indentured servitude or death. Wouldn't you prefer this?" The commander glared at Nacen, who cast a sideways glance at the control panel.

"Uh, I hate to say it, Nace," Camlo said, tightening his grasp on the foregrip of his shotgun, "but we're outnumbered in enemy territory. Let's get back to the *Canotila*."

Nacen held up a stern hand. "In a moment." He backtracked to the control panel and, after a little difficulty, brought up the status menu. A notification popped up, letting Nacen know that he did not have the proper credentials to access this particular set of menus. Fortunately, he thought, he had someone on hand who did.

"Eberwik, come over here please."

"Why? Your ship is up the stairs," Eberwik stated with dismay.

"Because I asked nicely. And it's the last time I do so. We can make this trip back to the ship much more inconvenient for you."

Bogdan Eberwik scowled and approached the monitor. "System settings? What are you muddling around in here for?"

"How many people do you have locked up down here?" Nacen inquired.

"I fail to see..."

"How many?!" Nacen exclaimed.

Eberwik sighed. "Four hundred and twelve."

"Enter your credentials. I want to see for myself," Nacen said.

"If it will get you out of here, fine." Eberwik placed his forefinger and middle finger on the top-left corner of the screen, and a blue light played across the display. A graphic appeared asking for a passcode. Eberwik impatiently jammed in an eight-digit code and stepped back. "There you are. Four hundred and twelve subjects. Satisfied?"

"The system reads four hundred and one."

"Ah, well, you've depleted the count by one," Eberwik said, gesturing to Linasette. "Plus the nine that perished in the awakening process, and my former guard captain."

"It would appear so," Nacen said, probing around in the maintenance settings. There was no obvious system shutdown or self-destruct mechanism. The death of Lash's team had made up his mind. Even that was a better fate than to live in this stasis, where one was periodically called on to serve against one's will.

"What are you doing?" Eberwik asked.

"Checking on a few things."

Eberwik paused. "Those people are not your crew. Your crew is here."

"True enough." Nacen navigated through the coolant monitoring. He selected a program for emergency override. That seemed promising. "Shukernak, get him back. Prepare to proceed to the ship on the double."

"Your will be done, Captain." Shukernak grinned and placed two huge hands around the commander's arms. He lifted him up a few stairs. Out of the corner of his eye, Nacen saw several of the *Etrusca's* security forces take a few steps closer.

"Here we are. Emergency shutdown."

"You fool! That will…"

"Cause you to lose all of your subjects? A shame." Nacen tapped through several verbose override warnings. He turned and glared at Eberwik. Beside him, Lash nodded encouragingly at Nacen.

"Yes, but…"

The bright white lighting of the control bay was suddenly bathed in dull red lighting.

"Shutting off the coolant will cause the system to overheat…" Eberwik continued. He was interrupted yet again, but this time by a calm, masculine voice over unseen speakers around the facility.

"Your attention please. Reactor systems have experienced major failure. Initiate manual shutdown of reactor or critical release will be imminent. Fifteen minutes and counting."

"Which will rupture our fusion drives if we don't shut them down!" Eberwik shouted over the repeating automated message. "Do I really need to tell you that that is very, very bad?!"

"Fifteen minutes? Sounds like *your* problem," Nacen said. "Let's go, double time."

"Fool, you know not what you have initiated!" Eberwik shouted, his eyes wide. "This will destroy not only this portion of my craft but perhaps the entire ship, which you are still on. Many more troops on the *Etrusca* will converge on you, and we will take control of that ship you are so eager to get back to. If you want to see your comrades survive this, you'll let me deactivate that override!"

"It sounds like we'll have to fight them regardless. Come on, we're moving out," Nacen said to the crew.

"You're not going up this staircase, let alone to your ship!" Eberwik tried to squirm free of Shukernak's grip but found he was clasped far too tightly. He looked around wildly, gnashing his teeth and groaning in frustration. Nacen ascertained his next move too late.

"Take them all out, now! Fire, fire!" The commander bellowed.

The air became saturated in accelerated flux shrapnel as the encroaching guards unleashed their shotguns into Nacen's crew. Most of the shards were deflected by the Starkins' pilfered armor or embedded harmlessly into the plating, but some found bloody purchase in cracks and joints.

"Up the stairs, now! Back to the ship! Return fire only when you can do so safely!" Nacen roared over the din.

Shukernak flung Eberwik around as he ascended the staircase, blocking many of the incoming projectiles. He was clothed in a nanofiber mesh uniform, which did precious little to halt any shots. In short order, Commander Eberwik was torn to pieces by his own guards' firepower. Shukernak let the mottled body fall as he backed up the staircase.

"*Kaha*, they fragged their own leader just to get at us," Shukernak said.

"Stow the talk and hustle, 'Nak!" Nacen shouted, forgetting about shooting back for now in favor of putting distance between himself and the advancing fusillade. The Stevari managed to get to the top of the stairs more or less intact. As Nacen ascended, he was relieved to see the doors still open. He beckoned his crew through as shots peppered the stairs behind them. "Status report?"

"Got hit in the side and under the shoulder," Shukernak strained to say, "but I'll live."

"Our communications are being jammed. I cannot contact the ship," Linasette added.

"Let's just hope they're holding up their end of the plan," Nacen said. If there was anything wrong with the rest of the squad, they didn't share it. Beskin took up the rearguard, laying down cover fire whenever he saw movement behind them. The rest maintained a quick pace, set by Nacen and Camlo to the front.

In the distance, shouts could be heard. The captain and druvani navigated the group through several corridors, pausing only once to dispatch an errant guard who had wandered onto their path. The guard, running in the opposite direction, was splayed out with a quick shot by Camlo, whose flux shotgun barrel was raised as he rounded every corner.

"It's fitting that Eberwik died by the cryobanks he valued so highly," Lash said as he ran beside Nacen.

"I'm not entirely convinced he was killed," Nacen replied.

As they rounded on the entrance to the ship's hangar bay, they spotted two guards, one to each side of the sliding doors. They stood crouched down, peering into the hangar beyond. Nacen and Camlo fired on them, but they were outside of lethal range. The guards stumbled into the corridor to the left, out of the line of fire. Nacen sprinted headlong to the doors, and making sure the adjacent corridors were clear for the moment, took stock of the situation in the hangar.

The *Carmine Canotila*, his precious sanctum in this hostile universe, was surrounded by white-clad troopers in the blue robes of the *Etrusca*. Nacen counted nearly thirty men and women. The closest figure was perhaps ten meters from the ship. The entire Armad contingent of the Extrata guild, at least from what Nacen could make out, was holding them off to the best of their ability. Two fired flux drivers from the rear cargo hatch of Nacen's ship. The rest had taken up various defensive positions around the *Canotila's* perimeter, after they apparently had raided Nacen's armory. They directed flux repeaters and mass condensers at anything that so much as twitched. Basaul could be identified by use of a pilfered flux shotgun. He was fighting from cover to cover to stop the encroaching Unity advance.

"This is the bulk of the garrison. It appears we're in for a fight," Nacen turned back to his crew. "We should clear a way to the ship, then take off. Beskin, follow me. Jeta, Shukernak, and Lash, flank to the left with Camlo. We'll provide cover fire for your advance and vice-versa. Lina, you stay with me. On my signal, we go in."

The crew formed up. Nacen walked to the front and raised his hand when he slipped and nearly fell over. He pressed a hand to the wall to steady himself. The surface rumbled and a deep thundering echoed from the halls from where they had come. At least one of the reactors must have detonated. That would suffice for a signal.

Chapter 14

Nacen strode out onto the railed landing, immediately eyeing an *Etrusca* trooper pointing a long rifle at the Armads. Before he could get another shot off, Nacen sent him tumbling over the rail with a blast from his shotgun. Whether or not the shots penetrated was made irrelevant when the marksman slammed into the deck ten meters below. Nacen was already on the stairs down to the hangar floor with his druvani close behind. He fired again, forcing the nearest guard into cover as he made his way down, and his crew did the same to other immediate threats.

Still, flux rounds pierced the stairs as Nacen ran down. He hit the ground and staggered behind a small fighter craft to his right as shells whipped through the air. Beskin was on the other side of the craft, with Linasette crouched between them. Camlo and the rest of the crew had gone left as planned. After a few seconds, they began to fire on the guards along Nacen's path.

"Alright, Beskin, let's advance. Linasette, stay close behind me," Nacen ordered.

"Without wood, the fire dies," Beskin said.

Linasette nodded, eyes locked straight ahead. Nacen forgot that the pilot had rarely seen ground combat. He would need to watch over her carefully. Noiselessly, Nacen whirled around the drab fighter and made his way to a group of crates. In this environment, combat was a matter of keeping the enemy pinned. Running haphazardly between cover could lead to an untimely demise at the point of a flux shotgun or repeater.

Nacen chose his path carefully. He reached a stack of crates and thrust his shotgun over the rim. Sure enough, a guard had sought cover here. Nacen dropped him with two fast shots. He ducked as the guards on the other side returned fire. He and Beskin returned the salvo blindly as Camlo, Shukernak, Jeta, and Lash advanced.

After repeating the bloody procedure three times, Nacen found himself only a short sprint from the *Carmine Canotila*. He rounded a compressor crate and nearly ran into yet another guard, this one's shotgun was leveled at Nacen's chest. Before the man could fire on Nacen point blank, an object swung in and connected with his helmet. The trooper was flung far to the left. Basaul knelt over him and collected something from the unmoving troopers' waist.

"Thanks, I needed more ammo for this thing," Basaul said gratefully, brandishing his new shotgun. There was blood on the stock.

"No, thank you," Nacen stood in shock for a moment before he realized where he was, and promptly found better cover.

"You've made plenty good on your word that we would have vengeance on the Unity. This is a good start." Basaul said. "Chalce and two others have planted explosives on the opposite end of the hangar bay by the retractable doors in case you can't get them open remotely."

"Good," Nacen paused to gather his bearings. "Do we have time to wait for them?"

"Of course. Both Chalce and I have remote timers to detonate the charges. When that happens, anyone and anything not bolted to the floor is going to be blown into space along with all the air in this room. Give him a few minutes."

"You've done well, but I won't rest easy until this place is far behind us," Nacen said. "Camlo, I need three plasma carbines out here now."

"On it, Nace." Camlo sprinted into the interior of the transport.

"What's your status, Basaul? Anyone down?"

"Two injured. No casualties," Basaul replied.

"Excellent," Nacen took note of his own borrowed armor. It was chipped and cracked in at least a dozen places. "At least we..." Nacen's ears perked up at the sound of more shouts at the entrance. The *Etrusca's* garrison had rallied and was now pouring into the hangar. He could see ten guards moving down the staircase, with more streaming out every second. The big cargo bay doors were opening, as well.

"Uh, what was that you said about the majority of them already being in the hangar?" Shukernak said.

"Get the plasma support gun and lay down suppressive fire," Nacen ordered. "Buy us some time to take off."

"Oh, I'll give you enough time to take a light vacation. Maybe somewhere tropical. What's that verdant world your dad was always yakking about? Zelenista?"

"Not now, 'Nak!" Nacen fired his shotgun at the line of incoming troopers to little effect. Camlo slid into cover next to the captain and thrust a plasma carbine into his hands. "Thanks. Make sure Beskin gets the other one."

"Already done," Camlo said. As if to support the point, a shot fired off nearby felled a trooper halfway down the staircase.

"Permission to stop getting shot at?" Linasette asked with dismay.

Nacen turned, shocked to see that the pilot was still here. Her unflappable demeanor was as steady as ever. "Granted. Go get our bird ready to soar. But wait until 'Nak is laying down suppressive fire on that hangar entrance first."

"Ah, I remember now, it was Salinar!" Shukernak exclaimed, returning to the hangar bay hefting the plasma support gun. "Yoska could talk about those beaches endlessly. I've practically been there myself."

"I said stow the chatter!" Nacen ordered, taking aim at a heavy weapons team setting up a small flux cannon on the railing.

"Aw, but Betty likes it when I talk to her."

"Betty?" Nacen fired at the heavy weapons team but did little except to delay their setup. They fumbled with the cannon's stand under his fire, but it was inaccurate at so long a range.

"Now don't act like you and Betty aren't acquainted." Shukernak tossed his hover drone in front of him. At the same time, he hoisted his plasma support gun up into the air. Before the heavy weapon could clatter to the floor, the drone flew underneath, affixed itself under the barrel of the gun, and hovered in place. "Alright, sweetie, time to say hello."

Shukernak fired a stream of plasma rounds into the heavy weapons team. The flux cannon was dismantled by the fire, and the operators turned and fled—no doubt to return with other firearms. The trufalci then swept across the stairs and took out three guards as they descended. There was little he could do about the guards that had already made it to the floor, however.

A blur out of the big cargo door caught Nacen's attention. Some sort of drone had entered the hangar. It traversed the high ceiling in fast, wide loops. "Druvani, focus plasma fire on that drone! The others can keep the enemy pinned."

The drone's wild path so far above made this a difficult task. Nacen breathed in to shout another order when a luminous globule soared into the middle of his ranks. It exploded next to an Armad, turning him into ash and knocking over a pile of crates. Stevari and Armad crewmen scrambled for new positions of cover against this new aerial foe, but there was little that would protect from above. The Unity infantry fire had picked up, and now Nacen could see trails of plasma lances. Another plasma burst rained down from the encircling drone, this time striking the ship directly above Shukernak. The damage appeared negligible, but Nacen wasn't sure how long the craft could sustain that kind of firepower.

Nacen peered out of cover and fired several shots into a guard running between crates. The fourth shot penetrated at the shoulder, and the man went down. Nacen glanced up at the ceiling. The drone's cannon was preparing another salvo.

"You're back!" an Armad roared from behind. Nacen turned to see Chalce's monstrous hulk behind him.

"I could say the same," Nacen said. "It seems neither of us is easy to kill."

"Let's not test that further." Chalce began striding purposefully to the *Canotila*.

"Agreed." Nacen turned to follow. "Everyone, into the ship! We're getting out of here!"

"Someone get Traver's remains!" an Armad yelled.

"There's not enough time, or remains!" shouted another. "Run!"

Jogging up the sloped walk into the cargo bay, Nacen made a point to avoid the spray of the plasma light support gun that Shukernak was still putting out. "Pack it in, 'Nak!"

Nacen made it into the cargo hold just as a high-pitched whine reverberated through the bay, followed by the ping of a round ricocheting off the ship.

"He's been hit!" Jeta yelped. Shukernak was on the ground, bleeding profusely. Another marksman must have made it past the suppressive fire to set up somewhere in the hangar. Around him, Armads and Stevari were filtering into the *Canotila*. Lash walked up the ramp backwards, firing methodically back into the hangar. Jeta and Beskin grabbed Shukernak by the arms and dragged his limp form inside. A trail of blood followed. Camlo lugged the plasma support gun, still hovering on the drone, back inside. That was everyone. Nacen gave the order to close. The cargo hold ramp rose, still being pelted by enemy fire.

"Jeta, get the medi-drone and see to Shukernak. Chalce, detonate the explosives, we're getting out of here for good."

Nacen rushed down the narrow corridors of the *Carmine Canotila*, shoving everything to the back of his mind but the current necessities pertaining to their escape. When he arrived on the bridge, he saw Linasette going through ship diagnostics.

"Nacen, I'm glad you're here," she said. "We're taking a lot of damage from something out there. Looks like high-energy plasma. We need to take off while we still have the ability."

"Chalce is setting off the explosives. Any second now. Then we're out of here." Nacen leaned on his empty seat rather than sitting. Nacen tuned his earpiece to the Armads' comm channel. "What's going on? Why haven't you detonated the charges?"

"I have. It's possible the Gloms deactivated them," Chalce said warily, sounding like he did not want to believe it himself.

"Well then, we're as good as dead." Nacen exhaled deeply. "Let's talk solutions. Get up here with Basaul." Nacen heard their thundering footsteps, and the two Armads entered shortly after. Both had lacerations and puncture wounds from flux rounds from the firefight. Basaul had several plasma burns on his right side.

"Let me see the detonator," Nacen said, holding out a twitching hand.

Chalce complied with a frown. "I don't see how that..." Nacen turned the device over in his hands. There was a piece of shrapnel embedded in the back, and he held it up for all to see. "Doesn't matter, Basaul's didn't work either." Chalce handed his overseer's detonator over as well. Nacen pulled the trigger. Nothing.

"*Kaha,*" Nacen swore. "If those explosives don't go off, we're finished." Nacen's mind raced with possible solutions that didn't involve the *Canotila* as singed wreckage. He came up with a desperate few, and nothing realistic.

"Too bad that reactor blowing didn't take out the whole ship then," Chalce said.

"We'll have to go back and manually set off the hangar door charges," Nacen said with grim finality. "I'll go with Beskin. Basaul, choose your three best men to come with me. Tell them they won't be coming back. Lina, you have the bridge. Command of the *Carmine Canotila* will go to Camlo. Take orders from him, and—"

Linasette turned about swiftly in her seat. "I cannot accept that."

"I mean... my cousin is far from an ideal candidate, but given the circumstances..."

"That's not what I meant. Captain, what if we had the *Etrusca* detonate them for us?"

"Why would they do that?" Nacen asked.

"What Chalce said gave me an idea," Linasette began. "We altered the *Etrusca's* systems to cause an internal overload that destroyed the reactor. What if we attempted to do the same thing, but made it look like we wanted to destroy the other reactor?"

"I'm not following," Nacen crossed his arms. They were wasting valuable time.

"Right. We gain access to their system and override their safety checks to destroy their remaining reactors. I saw the passcode that Eberwik entered.

That would either destroy the whole ship or leave them dead in the water."

"Space," Nacen corrected.

"Figure of speech," Lina countered. These damned Unity sayings were not aiding in his understanding. "Also, this is neither the time nor the place."

"I like it." Chalce pounded a heavy fist into his palm.

"Then you'll love this next part. We don't actually try to destroy the reactors, just program our attack to appear so. We take the trigger signal for our charges, disguise it as the backdoor shutdown for our virus, and upload it to their maintenance system."

"Can we do that?" Nacen asked.

"With our advanced network and a little panic on their end, it's possible. At least in theory."

"Okay, my turn to be confused." Basaul held up a hand. "What will this whole runaround actually do?"

"It means when they go to counteract our virtual attack, if they're smart, they will find our masked signal disguised as a shutoff switch. By flipping that switch to save their reactor, they'll be setting off our charges for us." Linasette bit her lip. "Assuming they haven't destroyed the explosives themselves... and assuming they fall for it."

"That's a lot of assumptions," Nacen rubbed at his left temple. He did not bring up the additional assumption that Lina had actually executed the programming correctly.

"Indeed. In addition, we don't have long before that drone starts doing serious damage to the ship." Linasette glanced back at her myriad diagnostics. "I estimate four minutes before we take enough to damage to prevent us from taking off, at the most. Assuming they don't hit something critical first, or the guards closing on our ship don't have their own plans."

"I won't pretend to understand the nuances of your Starkin software," Basaul said, "but it sounds like our best shot."

"Okay, you've got two minutes to send your signal. We need to prepare for the eventuality that it doesn't work and make it to the explosives before that drone takes out our ship." Nacen walked to the bridge entrance.

"I will make it happen," Linasette gave a weak smile. "I hope you won't need it, Nacen, but good luck."

"To you as well. Without wood, the fire dies." Nacen gave the sign of House Drovina.

Nacen nearly ran into Camlo as he strode out to the cargo bay where the crew was huddled.

"Nace! We're taking fire back there. The ship won't hold much longer."

"I know, Camlo. Get to the bridge. Assist Linasette if she asks for anything. But I need you to remain there." He placed a hand on his cousin's shoulder.

Camlo stuttered for a moment, then straightened. "Sure thing. But what are *you* doing?"

"Making sure those explosives go off."

In an instant, Camlo understood. He gave a solemn nod and turned to the bridge. Nacen entered the cargo bay as a large thud shook the roof.

The Sword and the Cipher

"Been happening every twelve seconds," Perido said. "Could set your watch to it."

Shukernak lay where Nacen had last seen him, his chest and head elevated as a medi-drone was sealing up a massive chest wound.

"Marksman, heavy-caliber," Jeta said, not looking up from Shukernak. "The slug missed his vitals, but he's not in good shape."

"He's always been a tough one."

Jeta scoffed, but Nacen could hear the distress behind it. "More lucky than anything."

"That too."

Nacen found Beskin standing at attention in the corner. He held his plasma carbine in one hand and was inspecting a series of plasma grenades in a bandolier around his shoulders. He must have anticipated what had to be done.

"Bad news, Beskin," Nacen said.

"I noticed the explosives hadn't gone off." Beskin pursed his lips.

"We have one minute before we pass the critical point where we cannot manually detonate them and still escape. Linasette is working on an alternative, but I'm not hopeful."

"Where the needle goes, the thread will follow." Beskin finished checking the last plasma grenade and gripped his carbine with both hands.

"I will join you," a bold voice said from behind. Nacen turned to see Lash standing in the shadows. He snatched up a plasma carbine and drew a knife from somewhere Nacen had not seen, pressing the flat of the blade to his chest.

"No," Nacen said outright. "I need you here as a representative of Orizon. If we do our job, this will not be the *Canotila's* final fight. If worst comes to worst, we will need someone to return to the other houses and warn them about what happened on Carnizad, and what will doubtlessly happen on Fomalhaut."

Lash grinned mirthlessly and shook his head. "You forget, I am your honored guest. As for my position in House Orizon, I outrank you."

Nacen stared back into Lash's unblinking eyes. Would that he had more time to convince Lash of the futility of this petty revenge. But he did not.

"Fine," Nacen grunted.

"I've chosen my men," Basaul said. "Or rather, they volunteered. Hortz, Brecca, and Perido will accompany you."

"You've all been made aware of the objective?" Nacen asked. The Armads returned gruff nods.

Brecca, the one who had talked back to Nacen after the escape from the elevator on Tantalos, shrugged. "I appreciate the opportunity. Didn't quite get my fill of killing Gloms back there."

Basaul chuckled. "You always offer a unique perspective, Brecca. May the guild be with you."

"And with you," the three Armads said in unison.

Nacen stood before the cargo hatch with his chosen few. He reflected on the recent path that had brought him here, the last moments of his life: his begrudging acceptance of the office as captain of a pitifully small trade ship, his harrowing travels with his new crew, the sight of seeing his homefleet again briefly over this freighter's display, everything he'd ever known and loved torn apart before learning he had the chance perhaps to save it. How torturously small that hope seemed now as he stood just a few paces from his doom. It seemed that every step of the way, destiny had made his choices for him. What else could he have done but give his utmost effort to preserve his ship and crew, to reunite them with his imperiled homefleet?

"Basaul, get your men out of the way and prepare to lower the hatch," Nacen instructed. "As soon as we slip out, raise it again and don't let it down even if your mother herself knocked."

Basaul nodded gravely and stepped to the control panel. The crew cleared out to the side hallways. Nacen withdrew two plasma grenades and set them to low energy, high flash.

"I know this isn't how most of you anticipated our final moments together, but I count myself fortunate to have made it this far, and to have fought with you all at my side. With our help, the rest can make it one step closer to freedom." Nacen checked the synchronized timer on the ship's computer. Ten seconds until they were past the point of no return. He exhaled deeply. "Lower the hatch."

"Belay that order," Linasette said smugly over the ship's speakers so all could hear. "The *Etrusca* has taken the bait. No need to—"

The charges went off in a single, focused detonation directly into the reinforced hangar doors. Air began to pour out into the vacuum of space, first in a leak and then like a hurricane. The two main engines of the *Carmine Canotila* fired up. The crew gave three cheers as inertial dampers kicked in and they felt the craft accelerate. Plasma rounds scored and singed the hull, but the ship shot unabated through the hangar and blindly plunged into the Fomalhaut system.

Chapter 15

It took Nacen's heart a few minutes to stop racing and to come to terms with the fact that the *Carmine Canotila* was gaining distance, and that he was in fact still on it. After raucous applause and cheering, Nacen had the crew stand down and return their weapons to the armory. Anyone who wasn't responsible for repairs or in dire need of medical attention was given permission to get immediate rest. Nacen anticipated sleep would be hard to come by if events in the system escalated but, despite his own desire for sleep, he now stood in the bridge with Linasette and Camlo.

"There's not a lot of time to celebrate, unfortunately," Linasette said as she cobbled together a network of images of the Fomalhaut system. "Or write a research paper on what I did back there."

"It was excellent work. I should allow you more time to play around with our tech."

"I make time when I can."

"I'm just glad we made it out. Emphasis on the *we*," Nacen said with a sigh.

"I wouldn't have anyone else as my captain," Linasette said, with a brief glance at Camlo, who whipped his head back and forth between Nacen and the pilot. The druvani's jaw dropped.

Me?! He seemed to mouth silently.

"Where is Beskin, anyway?" Linasette continued.

"He's receiving medical attention for wounds he had not reported to me until after the emergency intervention was called off," Nacen said. "Noble, but foolish."

"As noble things often are. I heard Shukernak was injured. What's his condition?"

"Unconscious but stable. The medi-drone is still patching him up. Betty hasn't left his side."

"Betty?" Linasette furrowed her brow.

"Never mind." Nacen waved a hand. "How long before we reach the homefleet?"

"We have approximately two and a half hours running at a forty-five percent burn with a moderate deceleration curve, which is about all we can muster right now given current damage to the *Canotila*."

"That will do," Nacen said. "We can see about more extensive repairs when we rendezvous with Zura. What can you tell me about the fleet operations in the system?"

Linasette brought up a summary, some of which Nacen had read before. Fomalhaut was a bright azure star, which gave off an incredible amount of heat when compared to similar K-type main sequence stars. The blue light shown through a dense field of dust orbiting close to the star, probably caused by the star swallowing up some of its own planets eons ago. The passage from the great blue sun hung on the outside of the Fomalhaut system within a massive ring of dust, heavily guarded by U.P. ships. Nacen did not have to guess that this would be more than enough to destroy the small Stevari fleet, should they make a run for it. They had not seemed to notice, or perhaps care, that a single small transport had fled a freighter that recently passed the blockade. What horrified him was the fleet grouping near the center of the system.

Linasette zoomed in to the verdant planet orbiting the star. "The Drovina fleet consists of five worldships holding an unknown number of smaller vessels. This does not appear to be the entire homefleet. Either a large portion of the homefleet has been destroyed, or they were simply not part of this fleet. As you know, Stevari worldships are comparable to a large Precept cruiser in terms of military capability. Size-wise they're comparable more to their largest battleships."

"Yes, the *world* is more a description of its function as the home to our civilians. Our first priority must be to answer the question of what happened to the rest of the fleet," Nacen said.

"Agreed." Linasette nodded before continuing. "Stevari ships are in orbit around the large terrestrial world of Dagon, in a long orbit around Fomalhaut A. There were dozens of deep space military installations, too."

"Where are they now?" Nacen leaned forward and narrowed his eyes at the display.

"Still there," Linasette assured him. "Mostly debris, though. Zura appears to have made short work of Fomalhaut's defenses. Which is saying something, given what I know of the place."

"Beyond visual diagnostics?"

Linasette nodded.

"After my second tour flying F66 Strixes, I lived on reserve fleets patrolling core Unity worlds," Linasette explained. "I spent a few months running defense drills around Dagon and the military installations your brother has since removed from existence."

"Any thoughts on the attack? Was it smart to go in this close to the planet and have to wipe out those installations?" Nacen wasn't worried about Linasette switching sides, but he didn't want any conflicts of interest affecting her work.

Linasette shrugged. "Fine by me. They had lousy coffee anyway."

"Sounds like we did them a favor, then," Nacen said blithely.

"When will they learn..." Linasette shook her head slowly in mock disappointment. "Now, Fomalhaut is a major hub for the Union Precept. Not only for trade, but for information. Dagon is a nexus planet. It forms one of the many cores of the Union Precept's distributed networks for the Counsel. Its tendrils spread out to every planet from here to the Synar in one way or another."

"So it's quite valuable to them," Nacen postulated.

"That's an understatement. Aside from the industry here, both software and hardware, it's one of the most densely populated planets in the Union Precept. The size and landscape of the planet Dagon allows it to support a massive population, roughly fifty billion at the latest count. It's far from hostile borders and one of the safest places to live. At least, it used to be," Linasette said. "There's a lot of important people down there. Beyond this solar system with two more rocky, mostly uninhabited worlds, lay two more stars of the Fomalhaut system. This rare grouping classifies Fomalhaut as a trinary star system. It makes the day and night cycle fairly hectic as well."

"Sure." Nacen rubbed at his chin, still examining the orbiting homefleet. "Let's get ready to open communications with Zura. I want to let him know we made it out alive and that we're coming to see him."

"The *Burning Stag* appears to be the new capital ship." Linasette changed the view on the central holographic to center around a large Stevari frigate. "It's the ship in orbit closest to Dagon. I will go ahead and request an audience. We should get a return signal back in..." Linasette brought up another screen with the flick of her wrist. "Three minutes at the soonest."

Nacen nodded. "Good, we need to be sure to—"

He stopped short as heavy footsteps hammered outside. Raised voices came through the door to the bridge. Nacen looked at Camlo. "Were you expecting anyone?"

His druvani shook his head rapidly.

Nacen approached the door and it whisked open. Basaul had been arguing with Chalce, the two having stopped before the entrance to the bridge. The second in command towered over even the overseer. "What has he done to earn anything but our scorn? He only saved us from a problem he placed us in in the first place." Chalce stormed off toward the private quarters.

Nacen glanced at Basaul, expecting the boss to follow his subordinate. But the Armad was looking ponderously back at Nacen. Basaul stepped toward the captain until he was so close that Nacen had to crane his neck up to maintain eye contact. Basaul inspected his features with a meticulousness Nacen had not observed in the man before. Nacen glanced away and, trying not to appear rude, stepped aside so that the Armad might make his way through the tight corridor of the ship unimpeded.

"Captain," Basaul started. Nacen perked up. He could not recall the Armad addressing him by his official rank for some time. "I have something to show you. Something, I think, I should have shown you a long time ago."

"If you insist," Nacen said, though his genuine interest belied the words. "Lead on."

When the pair had reached the Armads' quarters, Basaul knelt down in front of a large, steel lockbox. Nacen recalled seeing it when the Armads first unloaded their luggage on Carnizad. Basaul entered a code on the keypad. "We found this in the *Asura*. The Gloms missed it, as it was concealed in the very matter of the floor itself." The Armad withdrew an object, shrouded in red cloth, a bit longer than the length of Nacen's forearm. "We may have missed it ourselves, had we not been exceedingly thorough in our mapping of your father's ship for salvaging parts. I apologize for not giving this to you sooner. It should belong to you. I just wanted... we wanted to be sure you could be trusted." Basaul gingerly removed the fabric, which fell noiselessly to the floor.

In his rough hands, the Armad now gripped a strange object. It was a large chunk of what appeared to be the metal floor of a ship, but roughly hewn from its original position using a plasma cutter or similar tool. What distinguished the lump of scrap metal from utter garbage was what appeared to be the hilt of a sword protruding from one end.

"This is no ordinary blade, as we found out. To be hidden within the ship itself..." Basaul said in awe.

An alert pinged in Nacen's earpiece. He ignored it. With a slow reverence, Nacen reached out for the blade embedded in scrap. "Indeed. It's a phase blade, and an ancient one at that. Its alloys are able to change frequency and composition to bypass most matter at the will of the Stevari who wields it. When detecting softer material, such as flesh, the blade may harden to cut and stab, but can alter to pass through even the densest metal." Nacen hefted the object in his hands. On its own, the blade would be light and well balanced, but embedded as it was, the weapon was entirely useless. Nacen placed his right hand on the hilt and grasped firmly. He exhaled deeply, then pulled.

The sword did not budge.

"The hilt could be encoded to function only for the original bearer." Nacen frowned and turned the cumbersome object over in his hands with difficulty.

"That seems likely," Basaul grumbled. "Too bad. Such a weapon could have proven useful."

"Indeed. We shall bring it along with us to the *Burning Stag* and see if my brother can make use of it. Regardless, thank you for returning this relic to House Drovina. I will see that you are rewarded for doing so."

Basaul nodded. "Worry about getting us out of the system first. As you have said, violence will only ever beget more violence. I wish to reestablish the Extrata guild. Perhaps one day, with the proper alliances, we can regain our former status on a more prosperous world."

Nacen's earpiece chimed its alert again. It was Linasette. Better to not keep her waiting.

"Thank you, again, Overseer. I have matters on the bridge to attend to once again. I shall keep you apprised of the current situation."

Basaul nodded, and the two parted ways. Nacen made his way to the bridge, slower than he knew he should be. He gripped the scrap piece of floor in both hands, inspecting the pommel jutting out of one end. It was plainly made of a dull bronze color, as was the round dome that made up the cross guard. Aged leather crafted from the hide of some long-forgotten beast was wrapped around the hilt. With a wave of realization, Nacen finally recognized the object from his youth. This was his father's blade.

"Talavaar Bhaganadi..." he muttered, looking the hilt up and down with fresh eyes. Not for the first time, he wished his father were here. Here to deliver the sword in person and free it from its prison. Here to offer up words of wisdom. Here to show Nacen the way forward. But perhaps this artifact would do as a solemn reminder of his father's legacy, and of the steyan that came before him.

The alert chimed again, shaking Nacen from his thoughts. He cradled the unwieldy object uncomfortably beneath his arm and proceeded to the bridge, where he found Camlo and Linasette rapt in conversation. Behind them lay a single holographic image, frozen on Nacen's brother Zura.

"No, no. That's clearly not his plan," Camlo insisted.

"Let's wait until Nacen takes a look before we jump to conclusions. It is his brother, after all," Linasette countered. "Nacen, finally. We got a prerecorded message from Zura. It's... somewhat disheartening."

"Where were you?" Camlo's eyes drifted lower. "And what are you doing with a chunk of the ship?"

"This is my father's sword: Talavaar Bhaganadi. It's a phase blade. Basaul bestowed it onto me just now," Nacen said, gripping the hilt proudly.

"It doesn't do you much good embedded in that hunk of metal," Camlo noted with a pout. "Why don't you withdraw it?"

"It doesn't activate for me," Nacen said.

"Eh, just as well. I mean, a sword? When are you going to use that?" Camlo wrinkled his brow.

"It's more a symbol of office, Camlo," Linasette offered.

"Indeed, but let's focus on the problems at hand. Grant me power to spot friends from spies..." Nacen walked up, reciting the old rhyme, and reversed the video on the display to the beginning, "...and tell the truth from honest lies."

Zura stood on a raised platform in his own ship, the Burning Stag. He held back his gleaming white cape with one hand and stared hard at his audience.

"I saw the Union Precept fleet bear down upon us, Nacen. Our father foresaw their murderous intent, but I tried to reason with them first. Muteness was their response to my parley, silence in speech but deafening in their treacherous surprise. It took my breath away, and in the short span of that astounded respiration, I witnessed the death of a thousand vessels and a thousand thousand lives." Now Zura gestured wildly with his free hand, pacing with an odd cadence about his stage. "So did I learn of the Unity's vicious purpose, dear brother, and with greedy eyes I watched them set about their dark work. Only by the will of our father are we alive at all. Now is the hour of our judgment, brother. Shall we spend it in our death throes? Shall we beat back against an endless tide? No. Now we are in position to bargain. To ensure our survival rather than to gamble it. Join me and we shall bear our people into eternity." With one last cast of his dark eyes, the transmission ended.

"Our communications are being monitored, that much is certain," Nacen pointed at his brother's hand on the screen. "See how he holds his cloak in his left hand? Palm out, two fingers displayed. In addition, despite what the message says, he has no intention of surrendering. If he thinks himself unable to slip past the quickspace blockade, he will do as much damage to the planet and opposing fleets as possible. See how he paces to the left when he speaks of bargaining, and to the right when he recounts the Unity's destruction of our fleet?"

"I assumed that was just for show," Camlo noted.

"My brother is not one for trivial theatrics. Every word and every action in that speech, bombastic as it was, was chosen and executed for a purpose. In any case, his request to rendezvous was genuine. Let us proceed to the Burning Stag. As much as I wish to know more, I will refrain from further communications until we can meet in person."

"We should begin deceleration in twenty minutes. It doesn't seem like the Unity is doing anything to stop us... even if they could at this point." Linasette lowered the video of Zura and scrolled around her layout of the Fomalhaut system. "Our escape either took them by surprise, or they don't think it is worth pursuing a single trade ship."

"They have bigger concerns. Like Zura threatening fifty billion of their citizens," Nacen remarked.

"Yes..." Linasette agreed. She opened her mouth to continue but must have thought better of it.

"I'll go brief the crew. Let me know if anything changes." With one last sidelong glance at his pilot, Nacen departed the bridge with his druvani in tow.

"There's a lot of factors in play right now, Camlo," Nacen tapped his index finger on the hilt of his sword as he walked, feeling the weight of the embedded blade now. "My brother is walking a tightrope, and I have no idea how I fit into his plans. I'm also having misgivings about some of the crew."

"Well you can trust me, Nace," Camlo said.

"I know, Cam." Nacen returned his thoughts to his brother. It had been so long since they had met face to face, and much had happened to both of them in the meantime. How could he approach this diplomatically? Nacen and Camlo walked in silence for a time.

"You went back for her. Linasette, I mean. You care about her," Camlo said at last.

"I care about all of my crew. I would have done the same for any of them," Nacen said earnestly. He almost added *except maybe for 'Nak*.

"Yeah, but I doubt you would've blown up a ship for them," Camlo said. Nacen was silent. He hadn't really thought about that with all of the other action that had happened in the meantime. But it wasn't an entire ship, just part of a very large one. "Look, I'm not saying it was a bad decision, and I know it's not my place to criticize your decisions. Just... next time, remember you're watching out for all of us. Things might not end so nicely next time."

"You're right, Camlo. Before Carnizad, I wouldn't have been so quick to respond with violence. Thanks for putting things in perspective for me."

"Would you really have made me captain? If you... you know..." Camlo trailed off and glanced away.

"I believe that's what the chain of command called for at the time."

"So you think I would make a good captain?"

Nacen paused and thought about his next words carefully.

"Stevari tradition is clear on the subject: you would temporarily inherit command should I perish, with a permanent promotion to be reviewed at later convenience," Nacen said, straining under the effort of lifting the entombed blade. He tightened his grip on the sword hilt. What would his father have said to him if he were here? "Yes, Camlo. You would make a very good captain for the *Carmine Canotila*."

Chapter 16

"You seriously want me to carry this for you?" Camlo swept a sweaty palm through his thick, auburn curls before he grabbed the hunk of scrap metal that Nacen held.

"Yes," Nacen said with finality as he did one last inspection of his crew. The signs of battle had been cleaned away, uniforms patched up, and damaged weapons replaced.

"So the plan is to give Zura some options for remodeling his floor?" Shukernak tried to sit up from a crate, but he clutched his abdomen and grimaced instead. "Personally, I think something in onyx would look better."

"It's a phase blade," Nacen said with an exasperated sigh.

"Then why don't you just—"

"I've been told. Anyway, it's good to see you back on your fee... well, your butt anyway. You stay here and protect the ship while we check out the *Burning Stag*."

"I wouldn't miss another chance at a fight." Shukernak shrugged. "I'm coming with, even if I can only carry a pistol."

"These are our fellow Stevari. There will be no fighting this time," Nacen drew his crimson cloak about him. "We're just going to have a little family reunion and discuss our options. If all goes well, we won't have to fight again at all."

"Yeah, well... I usually bring a *pie* to my family reunions," Shukernak said, nodding to the plasma carbine on Nacen's back.

"Well, I'd rather not be caught unawares. Again. We arrive in less than ten minutes."

The crew dispersed to make last-minute preparations and idle banter. Nacen approached Shukernak. The trufalci folded his thick arms across his chest. Even sitting, Shukernak was an imposing figure. "I need to know I can count on you out there. This is a very delicate situation. We can't afford to slip in a joke at an inopportune time, or lose our calm when the debate gets heated."

"...And by we, you mean me, right?"

Nacen pursed his lips as he thought of a reply that could reassure the trufalci and at the same time conceal Nacen's very real concerns.

"Why do you... you son of a..." Shukernak's eyes widened. "You read my file, didn't you?"

"As the captain of the *Carmine Canotila*, I have a right to know the history of my crew," Nacen asserted. Looks like subtlety was out the airlock.

"No, those are just the logs. My record on the *Canotila* is pristine. Anybody can attest to that. You accessed my personal records. Back when Yoska was captain, the *only* captain as far as I'm concerned, he said he had those wiped. Look, what I did back then, it still gnaws at me when I think of it. That's why I don't. Your father cleared the record, but no amount of forgetting or forgiving can clear my conscious. Mistake or no, I killed those Stevari. There's no one else to blame."

"I read the whole report, 'Nak. There were other trufalci there, you weren't the only—"

"And they get to live with that. I have to live with what I did." The trufalci narrowed his eyes, staring Nacen down. "Can you?"

"Shukernak, me knowing doesn't change what happened, and it doesn't change how I think of you either. I want you on the mission. Truly."

Shukernak's firm jaw softened a bit. "You actually believe that, don't you?"

"I do," Nacen said.

Shukernak exhaled deeply. Nacen braced himself.

"You won't regret it. Sir."

"Good," Nacen said. "Take it easy until we land, and leave Betty behind. We won't need her where we're going."

"Yeah," Shukernak said with a laugh. He stopped when it became too painful to maintain. "I bet you believe *that* too."

Nacen watched him disappear into the armory. Most of the crew was loitering in the hold, some watching their destination on a holographic image projected from the wall. The five remaining worldships were there. In space, where all that mattered was thrust and mass, the outlines of the vessels against the planet were beautifully and defiantly curved. Was this all that remained of the homefleet, or were the others somehow safe elsewhere beyond quick-space?

Even among the sleek Stevari frigates, the *Burning Stag* stood out. In his long tenure as captain, Zura Buhari had left his mark on the vessel. He had a reputation for taking on dangerous missions and excelling in their execution. As a result, the *Stag* had many modifications. The most noticeable was the two additional thrusters it housed by the stern, allowing it to make harder burns for longer. Parts of the armored hull had been scrapped to decrease the overall mass, making it even faster. The slimmer hull gave the craft a vaguely serpentine look compared to the other worldships. Nacen knew that a staggering array of weapons lay beneath that hull, concealed in all manner of crevasses and bays. The *Burning Stag* was a blockade runner and fortification smasher. The man at the helm was equally adept at both destruction and diplomacy, though he generally preferred the former.

Nacen had spent the last few days going over what he would say to his brother, even before he was alive and here at Fomalhaut. A thousand thoughts swirled in his mind. He wanted to shout at Zura, to call him out on his recklessness and endangering the homefleet by taking them so far into U.P. space. He wanted to scold the wanton destruction in Unity systems. Nacen wanted to throw Zura out of an airlock for all he'd done, for making a mockery of their father's trust, and do it before he condemned them all to oblivion. But Nacen wished nothing more than to embrace his brother. For he understood his brother's actions, however monstrous, and regretted not having been beside him when the difficult decisions had been made. Nacen's anger, usually so ready to take control and guide him to action, had been tempered by sorrow.

Nacen trusted he would know what to say to his brother when the time came. They had drifted apart since adolescence but, if nothing else, their rivalry could have been called intimate. In school, they competed over grades. In military lessons, they competed over martial and tactical skill. Zura continued the competitive relationship by attaining an officer position on the *Burning Stag* and eventually command over the craft. At some point, Nacen had dropped the rivalry, more out of complacency than out of maturity. His interests drifted into piloting, reading, and music.

The *Carmine Canotila* touched down on solid metal, and Nacen's musings ceased. He stood from his seat in the cargo hold and addressed the crew, currently at ease about the open space. "Keep your weapons on you, but do not draw them. I'm not expecting any aggression here, at least not in a combat sense, but I'm weary of being surprised. Stay close to me, and be ready to move back to the *Canotila* at a moment's notice."

"Aye, Captain," Basaul said. His Armads nodded along with their overseer's acknowledgement.

"Yes, sir," Jeta said. She, Shukernak, Beskin, and Camlo made the Drovina sign of loyalty across their chests.

"I may as well take the opportunity to rub elbows with the other houses," Lash said. "I shall accompany you as well."

Though the pilfered flux shotguns had proven useful in the tight confines of ship corridors, Nacen had ordered them left behind in the armory for two reasons. First, they had expended a good deal of ammunition during the last firefight and had no stores of their own for the weapons' munitions. Second was the fact that they were indeed Unity weapons, and Nacen didn't want to cause any undue suspicion aboard the *Burning Stag*. He imagined his presence was already slight suspect, having successfully maneuvered through a substantial portion of the Union Precept in the Prominar Rim relatively unimpeded.

"Hopefully our new host treats us a bit better than our previous ones," Basaul said, securing his looted shotgun to his harness.

"The bar for hospitality has been set quite low," Nacen acknowledged.

Basaul shrugged. "If your brother is half of the leader you have proven yourself to be, I have no doubt your homefleet will survive this day. Knowing you are both cut from the same cloth of the man who sacrificed himself for his people leaves me hopeful."

"Well, he did what he needed to do when it counted," Nacen said.

At Nacen's signal, the hatch opened. He found himself in a much smaller space than that of the Unity's sprawling hangar bays. The space, just big enough for a shuttle like that of the *Carmine Canotila*, was significantly dimmer than the harsh white light on U.P. ships. Rather, a diffuse glow originated from every surface of the room. It left each object in the room clear and crisp without straining the eyes. Brighter lights pulsed slowly around the ceiling, giving the illusion that the visitor beheld a corridor lit by lanterns.

Four druvani in crimson armor greeted Nacen at the exit of the cargo ramp. They carried compact plasma carbines strapped to harnesses under cloaks of midnight black. Behind them stood a tall vehicle which Nacen recognized as a maintenance drone. It towered over three meters high, with little of the artistic flair that defined other Stevari craft. Several men and women in gray jumpsuits milled about, retrieving tools from the ever-changing configuration of the maintenance drone. At first they appeared interested in Nacen and his crew as they descended the ramp, pockmarked by flux rounds and plasma.

However, as the captain stepped onto the floor of the *Burning Stag* for the first time in nearly a decade, he noticed their concern was only for his ship.

Nacen could sense the druvanis' unease at the appearance of his ship. The repair crew's amusement was more obvious, their quiet laughter and flippant remarks barely disguised. The armor plating that the *Etrusca* had provided stuck out from Stevari craft like an ill-fitted suit so as to mock the familiar design of the transport. Even some of the mustard yellow Boromite hauler plating was visible in areas. In addition, the top had been scorched black by the deluge of plasma from the aerial drone. Weaker connections or those sections that had been subjected to repeated strikes had even been partially melted. The bright red hull shone through in places, but Nacen now saw that the shade of red was too bright and did not match the rest of the ship. However, Nacen had left Linasette with instructions for the ship's reconditioning, and he had no doubt that the pilot's pride in her ship coupled with her slavish attention to detail would see the return of the *Carmine Canotila* to its true form. If not today, then soon.

Before Nacen could give orders to the Stevari milling about the bay, the lead druvani approached him. "Welcome home, son of Drovina." The soldier made the sign of the homefleet, index and little finger pointed across his chest. "We shall see to the repairs of your... ship. Worry not."

Nacen returned the gesture. "Your welcome is much appreciated. I am honored that my brother sent his most trusted warriors." In truth, Nacen was a little irked that Zura didn't bother to come himself.

"Steya Zura awaits your arrival. He sends his apologies, for he did not know when to expect you and has many matters that require his attention." The druvani turned, his fellow guards following the same smooth maneuver, and began at a brisk pace to the interior of the ship.

Nacen glanced about and hurried after the guard, his crew in tow. Jeta and Linasette, as well as the Armads Chalce and Hortz, stayed behind to observe and direct ship renovations. The corridors winded and twisted throughout the frigate. The friendly lantern light effect danced perpetually ahead like a warm and inviting guide.

"I wasn't expecting a warship to be so..." the Armad named Perido started to say.

"Cozy?" Brecca finished.

"This is nothing," Nacen said. "Had our current situation not been so perilous, we would have been greeted with song and dance, and then we would be on our way to the great hall for a feast."

"Because of your rank?" Perido asked.

"No, all guests of the steya are treated as such."

"Ah. Well in that case, I'll take a tall mug of coffee, black, whatever soup you have on today, and a steak. Medium-rare," Perido added with finality. The crew gave a few light-hearted chuckles at this. The druvani of the *Burning Stag* ignored the banter and pressed on.

"Zura is not in the command center?" Nacen asked as the group passed by the double doors to the most secure part of the ship.

"The captains of the homefleet are holding vulakaat," the druvani said without breaking stride.

The Sword and the Cipher

"When will I be able to see my brother?"

"The steya informed me you could enter whenever you arrived."

"Ah, excellent."

The group followed the swift druvani through the meandering corridors. Basaul caught up to Nacen and leaned over to him, speaking softly.

"What is this vulakaat? Are we walking into a trap?" Basaul asked.

Nacen would have grinned if not for the weight of the situation.

"For once, no. It is an emergency meeting of house leadership, literally meaning a touching of heads. There is no set limit for the duration of vulakaat, but it must always end in decisive action."

After several more curving corridors, the lead druvani turned and swept his gaze across Nacen's group. "Before we enter the vulakaat, you must relinquish your weapons."

"Not going to happen." Nacen shook his head. "The amount of times we've been ambushed or taken prisoner in the last week defies belief."

"I am afraid I must insist," the druvani said. His hand shifted a nearly imperceptible amount toward his plasma carbine. Nacen stood fast, staring the druvani down. At that moment, the doors whisked open and a figure cloaked in white came striding out. As it drew nearer, the hood was thrown back and revealed a shock of thick, auburn hair.

"Manfri, Manfri… there is no need to enforce such rigid protocol here. Why, after what my brother has been through, I would be shocked if he did not go everywhere with that…" Zura's eyes flicked to Camlo's waist, where a sword hilt protruded from the scorched metal he held in both hands, and deftly back to Nacen, "…rifle of his."

"But, sir, the vulakaat…"

Frowning, Zura placed his hand over his breast.

"I would sooner lop off my right hand at the wrist than doubt my brother's good motives." Zura turned and embraced Nacen. Initially taken aback, Nacen returned the embrace. Zura's arms tightened around him. At last, his brother pulled away. "My heart is light as a feather to see you return safely in these troubled times, Nacen. Thank you for joining us."

His brother was gaunter than Nacen remembered, which was no paltry statement. Zura had always been about a hand taller, but his larger physique was thinner now. The gleaming white cloak seemed to weigh heavy on his lighter frame.

"It is an honor to see you again, brother. I am overjoyed to see the man who helped save the homefleet," Nacen accidentally let a little sarcasm bleed into his tone. He was glad to be home, but Zura's snatching of the title of *steya* irked him. Their current position, trapped at a Unity nexus world and surrounded by half a dozen fleets, was a testament to his brother's brash attitude that Nacen knew all too well. Though Zura was not currently covering up his communications using the doublespeak codes, Nacen knew he always had ulterior motives. "I am saddened to officially hear of our father's death. I never gave up hope that he might still be alive."

Zura lowered his head.

"Yes, he perished in the fleet action over Carnizad. But it is by his actions we are here today. And not just you and me!" Zura gave Nacen a little jab with his elbow. "Your little escape from the *Etrusca* took the Unies quite unaware. Congratulations. I knew you wouldn't let that tacky freighter be your grave."

"How could you leave me like that?" Nacen asked sincerely.

"I knew the little rat wasn't going to shoot you," Zura scoffed. "I could see it in his eyes. He was desperate. I was right, wasn't I?"

"Yes, but not for the reasons you think. I never gave him the chance to pull the trigger. I had a trap of my own set," Nacen said.

"See? I knew you would pull through. He was no match for the Stevari of Drovina, the sons of Yoska!" Zura clapped his hands before placing one on Nacen's shoulder. "Sometime, you must regale me of the entire experience in lavish detail. But for now, we have our own plans to formulate. You have missed much but are still in time to witness the results of vulakaat."

"I am most intrigued as to how we will get the homefleet out of this predicament."

"Of course, but first I must ask if my eyes deceive me. Is that father's sword?" Zura asked incredulously. "The Blade of Rushing Waters?"

"Your eyes tell you true, brother. Talavaar Bhaganadi has been reunited with Drovina," Nacen declared proudly.

"What a pair we make." Zura smiled broadly. "One with father's raiment and one with his sword. Or at least the hilt."

"It seems he also left you with his ambition. The new steya, eh?" Nacen raised an eyebrow.

"Ah, I have merely taken up the role thrust upon me," Zura said humbly. "Tell me, the sword... how did you come across it?"

"It was found by the Armads who we've been traveling with." Nacen told Zura of their chance meeting with the Armads and their escape from Carnizad. He summarized their travels through Union Precept space. Zura nodded silently along, grinning slightly whenever Nacen made mention of the destruction they had left behind.

"So father never bestowed it on you? Interesting. One could make an argument that it should be passed onto the steya, then." Zura stroked his chin.

"I believe he consciously left the blade for me." Nacen shifted his weight to block Zura's view of the hilt in Camlo's grasp.

"Intriguing that he would hide it rather than bestow it onto me in his final moments. Concealing it must have been a move born out of desperation more than premeditation." His brother broke out in a wide grin. "But who am I to question father's motives? Our dear departed mother knew him best, and even she admitted to knowing only half the man!" Nacen caught a lingering in Zura's gaze at the sword's exposed hilt. "But alas, I forget myself. Vulakaat awaits! I can permit your druvani to enter, but the rest of your fine crew must remain out here." Zura turned his brother about and began walking him down the ingress, gesturing at his men and women to follow.

"What of my newest guest, Lash Procah? He is an officer of House Orizon and surely may at least spectate." Nacen said, stopping in his tracks to glance back at the crew.

"Is that so?" Zura asked with exaggerated incredulity. "I apologize, Procah, I did not recognize you in the garb of Drovina. Welcome aboard the

Burning Stag."

Lash gave a bow. "It is an honor to be present on such a renowned craft. If your exploits are to be believed, and I have heard them from very reputable friends, the *Burning Stag* may be counted among the most prestigious of all Stevari vessels."

"You are far too kind, sir." Zura returned Lash's bow, not quite as deeply. "But alas, I cannot allow you into our humble ceremony as a foreign power."

"To be allowed to witness Drovina vulakaat at such a critical juncture could be an important development in our houses' relations," Lash reasoned.

"Nacen, you didn't tell me you brought a diplomat aboard!"

"I owe your brother a great debt, Steya." Lash started in a serious tone that was unwilling to risk whether Zura was being facetious or not. "My intentions are only to open doors that have remained closed for too long."

"I'm afraid traditional must hold sway here," Zura said with a frown. "Regrettably, only fleet commanders and their druvani are permitted in. I'm sure Nacen can fill you in on the particulars later."

Zura beckoned Nacen into a large room. Beskin and Camlo followed, the younger druvani covered in a film of sweat from the exertion of lugging around a section of the *Asura's* deck.

The magnificent hall rose to nearly fifteen meters at its apex. The walls' visuals had been adjusted to resemble fine oak boards, with crimson tapestries hung by golden rope. Torchlight flickered in iron sconces, but no heat emanated from them. Around the edge, the tiered seating for the audience had been retracted to make more room on the main floor. Nacen's own meditation and performance room on board the *Carmine Canotila* had been designed in pale imitation of this grand space.

The area was now occupied by four immaculately dressed Stevari, each flanked by a distinct pair of druvani bodyguards. The four were locked in conversation and paid no heed to the new arrivals. Only when Zura strode up to them and outstretched his hands to speak did they cease their arguing.

"As vulakaat draws to a close, I would like to introduce you to a fellow captain. He may be able to offer some useful input toward our current dilemma." Zura stood aside, clearing a space in the circle.

Nacen stepped forward, but before he could speak, one of the other captains interrupted. "A captain, eh? It is good to finally receive some reinforcements. Tell us, what is the name of your craft?" He was portly for a Stevari, but he carried his weight well. He bore a full but well-groomed beard.

"The *Carmine Canotila*," Nacen said with a proud bow toward each captain. "I am Nacen Buhari."

"I apologize, I was not aware we had a worldship with such an appellation in the fleet," the Stevari said in vain sincerity.

"I am afraid I must correct you. The *Carmine Canotila* is a trade craft… a small scout shuttle. My original frigate, the *Lusterhawk*, was abandoned by necessity on our way to meet you. I possess no armaments that could harm a battleship, and I bring you fewer than a dozen soldiers." Nacen's hands fell to his sides.

"A shame."

"Please, friends, please." Zura held up a hand in supplication. "Nacen does not join us for strength of arms, but for his insight. He was always a clever one."

"Clever enough to be the only son of Yoska still going on trade missions?" the stout Stevari said with a chuckle.

"He found his way here by himself," Camlo said, his face reddening, "and he did it without wrecking every system he went through."

"Hold on, now. It seems our tongues are getting ahead of our manners. Let me cool your tempers with warm greetings," Zura said. He walked up to the outspoken Stevari captain, who now tugged uncomfortably at his black robes. "This is Captain Danior Tosque, commander of the *Wayfarer*."

"An honor to meet you," Nacen bowed again, deeper this time.

"Please, the honor is mine. I'm afraid I must apologize for my earlier comments. The situation has me forgetting myself." Captain Tosque bowed his head.

"Next we have the adroit officer in command of the *Faith Immutable*, the incomparable Captain Leander Medios." Zura gestured to a short but fierce-looking man. His head was shaved, and he bore no garments around his thick neck and arms. He wore tight-fitting maroon robes and dark knee-high boots. Leander pounded a fist into his palm and bowed to Nacen.

Zura continued his path around the circle of officers. "This is Captain Timbo Belim. He is a new addition to our ranks, but he has proven himself many times in the current crisis at the helm of the *Nivasi*."

"A pleasure," Timbo said with a flourish of his right hand and gave the slightest of bows. He was a tall, lanky man. Captain Belim wore the white robes of a craftsman rather than a uniform befitting a man of his rank. The last captain must have perished very recently.

"Lastly, but certainly not the least, we have Florica Tengrin. Another somewhat recent addition. Her first official mission was to scout ahead to Carnizad. An ill omen... but she has commanded the *Trishula* admirably ever since that fateful day."

Nacen bowed deeply to the woman, who returned the gesture. Her straight, raven hair fell in waves on the pauldrons of her black impact armor. Nacen found it intriguing that she had donned her combat uniform, rather than the formal robes the others carried about their shoulders for the ritual meeting. Another thing he found interesting was her name. Far back in the annals of Nacen's mind, it rang a bell. Dusty and nearly forgotten was the chime, but clear.

"Tengrin... I recognize the name..." he started.

"From my mother's work, no doubt," Florica gave a weak smile. "She was a musician of some note. She often played the clariphone at official festivals. She likely performed on the day of your father's coronation."

"That was it!" Nacen exclaimed, forgetting the current solemnity of the situation. He felt the years slide away. He was back in the great hall of the *Asura*, a boy of twelve. He was lying beneath a cedar tree, grasping his dulcinet and paying close attention to the instruction of a woman. Deftly she would climb a scale and return back down to her starting note. Patiently she waited as Nacen clumsily attempted to mimic her instruction. Patiently they repeated the process. "She was one of my music tutors onboard the *Asura* in my youth."

"Yes, she was an exquisite musician. You were lucky to have her as a teacher," Florica said politely.

"I feel lucky now, as well, knowing we are in the capable hands of her daughter. Perhaps she will play for us once more when we have found peace." Nacen smiled congenially.

"She... perished at Carnizad." Florica glanced to the floor.

"Oh. We lost too many Stevari that day."

"Indeed," Zura said, taking back the conversation. "It is to that subject of conversation we must regrettably return. As you are all aware, we are in orbit above the nexus world of Dagon. It is no accident that we find ourselves here. Rather, carefully planned after we fled the massacre at Carnizad."

"Many more lives would have been lost if not for the intervention of the steya," Florica said.

"Yes," Zura nodded once. "Father realized what the Unity's aims were immediately and devised a plan to get out as many souls as possible while sacrificing his own life."

"A noble man until the end," Danior said gravely.

"I'm afraid I must interrupt here," Nacen said. He could bear waiting no longer, and needed to be more familiar with their current predicament if he was to be any use. "I know many ships were lost at Carnizad, but to what extent has House Drovina been destroyed? And why do none of our beacons shine over the great blue sun?"

The captains looked at each other, as though frozen by simultaneously asking and granting each other permission to speak. At last, Zura turned back to Nacen.

"The disaster at Carnizad was terrible, as you know, but does not spell the end of our house. The survivors and those Stevari within range convened an emergency vulakaat after the attack. We chose to deactivate our beacons, to eliminate any risk that the Union Precept navy may be able to track us. It was then that we, the survivors here before you, swore an oath to avenge those lost."

Nacen was awestruck. These were not the shattered remnants of the homefleet, but those blinded by revenge.

"What did you hope to accomplish?" he asked plainly. This was the best he could muster for now.

"Simple... To prove that there are consequences for attacking House Drovina," Captain Tosque said.

"It sets a dangerous precedent to allow empires to attack us with impunity," Captain Medios said sternly.

"We cannot always flee at the first sign of danger, brother," Zura added.

"Fine, granted. Though I will point out that many ships of the homefleet did learn lessons and chose not to join in your... raid. But I ask again, what do you hope to accomplish here? Wanton violence?"

"What we have done so far may seem like simple raiding, but it has all been feints and distraction to lead us to this point," Zura clenched his fists. "Now the Unity knows what it is like to feel threatened, to know existential fear."

"Surely the entire Unity cannot wish us destroyed? You would turn them all against us?" Nacen asked. He was desperate for some rationale he could work with, for any desire for peace... or failing that, stability.

"This is not a matter of weights and scales, Nacen. It is a matter of principle. We do this so that future generations may have security." Zura smiled now, and that placating veil of fraternity only turned Nacen away further. "However, we do find ourselves pinned prematurely at our destination, surviving only because the Unity does not want to see their nexus world's population culled and the surface irradiated for years. Now before we cast our final vote as to our decision, I have one more factor to introduce. This comes courtesy of my brother."

Zura gestured for his druvani Manfri to step forward.

"Nacen recovered Yoska's phase blade, a weapon given to us long ago by allies within the Colonies of Xandra as a sign of mutual respect and interest," Zura explained, pacing a slow circle between the group of captains now. "I believe this sword contains the Xandran script for a weapon I once heard my father call the Void Protocol."

Here Zura paused and raised a hand as though holding Dagon in the palm of his hand.

"By launching the Void Protocol on Dagon before we bombard it, we can all but ensure casualties up to ninety-eight percent by bypassing their defenses. Dagon is protected by a sophisticated planetary defense grid. Not only the population, but the infrastructure will be annihilated. If this is to be our final stand, I will make sure the Unity suffers for their ill-gotten victory. If we are lucky, the weapon will spread to neighboring systems and cause untold damage to their infrastructure as well."

"So you want to go ahead with your suicidal plan just because we can kill more of them? What does it matter if none of us survive?" Florica bared her teeth as she questioned the steya.

"What you think of the plan is irrelevant. Zura is steya, and his word is law in times of crisis," Danior insisted, glowering at Florica. "I will gladly lay down my life for the homefleet."

Nacen crossed his arms and tapped his index finger against his gauntlet nervously. Danior Tosque's grim determinism coupled with his blind obedience made him a capable warrior to be sure, but a potentially disastrous policy maker. For vulakaat to succeed, if indeed it hadn't already failed, he would need the support of the captains.

"Steya Zura, I recognize we are in a tough spot, but we may have other options," Nacen began. "Could you elaborate on how this Void Protocol works?"

"Aye," Captain Leander Medios said. "How do you know this sword of which you speak holds this great power?"

"Circumstantial evidence, but evidence nonetheless," Zura began, clasping his hands behind his back. "You all recall our dealings with the Colonies of Xandra? Simple sojourns into their space, a few trade missions to open up future commerce. As you know, these expeditions were very profitable, for both us and the Xandran. After one of these expeditions, nearly a decade ago by the sundial, I noticed Yoska began carrying around an old artifact of the fleet: Talavaar Bhaganadi, passed down through various families. Our father was no practicing swordsman, nor had he ever worn the sword before, though he surely learned the finer arts of swordsmanship in his youth as we did. In truth, I had never seen him wield any blade on his person. But here he was bearing an ancient phase blade as though he was a practiced blademaster, so much so that it eventually became associated with his very office of steya." Zura took a breath with parted lips as if he intended to continue, but did not. He looked about expectantly. It was Captain Timbo Belim who broke the brief silence.

"A fascinating development indeed, but there appears no evidence that the Unity descended upon us because we possessed a piece of sharp metal," Timbo said with a frown.

"Because you are missing one final confirmation. In my father's last moments, he passed the mantle of steya on to me. He explained the operating principles of the Void Protocol to me, and told me to watch for the return of the key. I firmly believe father never wanted us to use this weapon. But then I doubt he knew the Unity would ever learn of its existence. They obviously have, hence their predation of the fleet and destruction of the steya and his ship."

Zura stepped over to Camlo, who still held the portion of uprooted floor in his hands.

"Well, the key has been returned, and now I shall hold the power of..." Zura paused and gripped the hilt with his right hand, raising his left as if to hold back applause. He braced himself and pulled. "...Talavaar Bha—"

Zura stopped and glared down at the immobile hilt. He gripped it with both hands and yanked. His muscles strained beneath his white raiment. Camlo struggled to maintain an even footing. After a third and even more strenuous attempt, he stepped back and exhaled forcefully.

"I do not understand, all the signs were there. Father gave me..."

"Perhaps it was not meant for you," Captain Florica Tengrin said simply.

Zura did not turn and face his captains, but he glowered at the disobedient sword hilt. "It makes no sense. Father left command for me. He told *me* about the key." He whirled around at Florica. "That sword is *mine*."

"Then why does it resist you so?" Florica asked.

Leander stepped up besides Zura. "Perhaps it requires a warrior with greater strength. Stand aside." Captain Medios gripped the hilt and pulled, his great arms flexing with strain. Camlo gave a shout and stumbled forward onto Leander. Though taken aback, Leander did not fall but shoved Camlo back. "Perhaps your father alone was meant to wield the sword, Zura. Perhaps he did not expect to die at all. Perhaps... his final sacrifice was just a failed, desperate gambit to save his own skin and leave us all to die."

"Insolence!" Zura shouted. "I will not be mocked, and I will not stand to have my father's name besmirched so!"

"Gentlemen, please," Florica Tengrin strode forward. "There is no point arguing. Perhaps this process requires a woman's touch. It was no secret that the old steya was fond of my mother." Florica placed one hand delicately on the hilt and grabbed the pommel with the other. Silently, she pulled. After a moment she stepped away.

"Well, it's worth a shot," Timbo Belim said, stepping forward himself. He pulled up his long, white sleeves and approached Camlo. With a great, exaggerated effort, he yanked on the sword's hilt, but to no avail.

"Well that leaves only one," Danior Tosque did not try to conceal his smug grin. "It *is* I who was in Yoska's service the longest. It would seem my loyalty and resolve have paid off at last." Captain Tosque approached Camlo, who braced himself yet again. The captain grunted for a long while attempting to extract the blade. At last his shoulder's slackened. "Alas, it was not meant for me."

The vulakaat was suddenly silent.

"Why doesn't Nacen try?" Florica mused.

"Please." Zura blanched. "It was in his possession for hours, maybe even days or weeks if he is not being truthful as to when he acquired it. Surely he has attempted it."

"It's true," Camlo blurted. "He tried... a lot."

"You see? The blade will not withdraw for anyone," Zura declared. "As acting steya, I claim it as my own, as my birthright. There may be something wrong with the blade in how it has been stored in a piece of the *Asura*."

This was not good, Nacen thought. This weapon of his father's, this gift or curse imbued on Talavaar Bhaganadi by the Colonies of Xandra, seemed poised to doom his people... not save them. Nacen cared not for titles or accolades now, only for the preservation of the homefleet. He had seen what the illustrious mantle of steya had done to Zura. Silently, Nacen stepped forward.

"The plan shall continue," Zura commanded. "This false lead changes nothing. Everyone, return to your stations. We shall content ourselves in leveling what we can of the planet and destroying the biggest piece of the Union Precept fleet we can manage in our final moments."

Nacen stood a few paces from Camlo. He closed the distance slowly and lay a gentle hand on his cousin's shoulder to alert him. Then he delicately placed his palm on the hilt of Talavaar Bhaganadi, wrapping his fingers around the grip. The leather was worn and soft.

"When the time comes," Zura continued, "we shall turn our ships on the surface of Dagon and destroy our ships, irradiating the planet. In our death throes, we shall have our revenge!"

Nacen pulled, and the blade came free.

Chapter 17

Nacen held the blade aloft with a single hand. Lantern light danced along its fine edge. The sword was not even a meter long, barely longer than his forearm. After a while, he became aware of the heft in his hands. He lowered it, inspecting the blade as he did so. Distant torchlight flickered off of subtle etchings. On both sides, the blade was engraved with a snake and a hawk. One side depicted the hawk grasping the snake in its talons. On the other, the snake lashed out at the hawk as it flew by. There were further designs and patterns hidden in the fine engravings of their feathers and scales. He wondered how far down the details went.

"Talavaar Bhaganadi..." Nacen said breathlessly.

"You... how..." was all Zura could utter. The captains of the homefleet looked on wordlessly.

"Yeah, go Nace!" Camlo shouted in jubilation.

It was Captain Tosque who composed himself first, snapped back into reality by Camlo's outburst. "We will have our moment of glory, as the steya has ordered. This changes nothing." Tosque nodded once, forcefully, to emphasize the point.

"Does it not?" Nacen asked, tearing his gaze from the engraved blade. He turned to each of the captains in turn as he spoke, striding in front of each of them, ensuring they each had their chance to look upon the blade. "How do you measure the cost of one life lost, how to extrapolate that into the thousands? However it is done, it is a mighty sum indeed. A great debt. It could be ignored, as we might flee from our assailants lest we who survive suffer the same fate. The debt could be compensated in revenge, every ship destroyed paid for by the destruction of a greater number of rival vessels. Down the list of charges we could go, blood for blood and life for life. But this only creates a debt that both sides can never fill, save for the utter destruction of the other, and then only because there are none left to carry on that hatred. No, our loss cannot be redeemed in any act of destruction, no matter how violent or just. It must be repaid by those of us who carry on the memory of the lost. Every breath denied to the dead must be taken back, in that I am in agreement with you. Not from our enemies, though, but from ourselves... in joyous pursuits. The songs sung by each soul plucked too soon from the homefleet, should be plucked across our strings until they snap from use. This will be the best revenge, to live a worthy life."

Zura wiped his hand across his forehead, composing himself at last. "Do you want to know why father put you in charge of his old trade frigate? Because he knew you couldn't handle the burdens of command. Where he saw the light of command on my brow, he looked at you and saw listlessness. He knew you weren't ready. I know you will *never* be ready. That blade falling into your hands was just another one of your long list of mistakes. This has been a surprising turn of events, granted. But we shall continue with my plan regardless. After all, I am still the steya."

Though Nacen may have been furious at the accusation before, this baseless claim only vexed him now. This was not the time for another sibling feud.

"He put me in charge of the *Lusterhawk* so that I might follow in his footsteps, brother. To set me on the path, not to turn me away."

"I led our people here, and I lead them now." Zura's eyes flared, but his anger had seemed to have diminished. Nacen needed to capitulate for now, to not seem like the threat that Zura perceived him to be. They were all allies, here, no matter what happened.

"I do not dare question the legitimacy of your leadership, Zura," Nacen said, lowering the sword. "I only wish to provide council."

"I apologize then, for my hasty words," Zura replied. "I think I speak for all here when I say we merely wished the blade for ourselves."

Nacen needed to think of another option, something other than a last stand. Something to rally the captains behind. But he needed information. "Tell me then, how do we even deploy this Void Protocol? What is it, some kind of virus?"

"Somewhat, though you're thinking on too high a level," Zura explained. "The Void Protocol plays against the very basic operations of the Counsel. You see, as a result of encountering challenges, the Counsel is constantly adapting and propagating. But this, in turn, creates more problems to solve: the more worlds conquered leads to more worlds that must be ruled. What the Xandrans have done is tweak a few core parameters for the Counsel, for within it lay the seeds of its own destruction. The only permanent solution to the entire endeavor is to cease the effort entirely. All we need to do is plant it. There are a number of centers where the Counsel operates on Dagon. We just need to get in, find a place to access one of its networks, and activate the Void Protocol. Don't you see? It was the Xandran's plan all along, or at least some sect within it. Dagon is a nexus world. The protocol will spread to all of the worlds around it, not unlike your virus metaphor, and then all the worlds bordering those in quickspace, and so on for a hundred worlds. Maybe more. The Unity just forced the plan forward. So what if the Colonies don't get their opportunity to strike at the Unity like they wanted? We have a chance to repay what they did to our fleet tenfold."

"Incredible. What if we used this power as an opportunity to slip through the Unity's grasp one last time?" Nacen asked.

"You think we have any chance to get out of here?" Zura's voice rose in anger yet again. "I will humor you. Say by some fantastic feat and at immense cost some of us do escape, how long will it be before we are hunted down again?"

"I can't tell you those odds," Nacen admitted, "but if we stay here and wipe out this planet, our odds of survival are zero."

"I alone am the acting steya of Drovina, and you will follow my command." Zura pointed an accusatory finger at Nacen.

"You will be the steya of a house of ashes," Nacen protested. He looked to Florica, the only captain still making eye contact with him. "Surely, Captain Tengrin, you see the folly in this." Nacen looked imploringly into Florica's hazel eyes. He saw tinges of cherry red he had not seen before. She hesitated a moment, glancing over at one of the other captains. Who, exactly, Nacen could not tell.

"The young captain is right," she said, timidly at first. Nacen's heart fluttered. Had she really just said that? She straightened and looked around poignantly. "There are alternate options available. Options without the impetuous, incendiary touch of his brother."

"You will address me by proper title, and without your grandiloquent invectives, if you wish to maintain your own." Zura's eyes were wide and his mouth was drawn tight. "You stand with my brother, but you are alone among our circle. Do not forget that your command may be relinquished. In emergency situations as this, I have that power."

"And who would you replace her with?" Leander Medios said. He framed his question boldly, a contentious statement more than an expression of curiosity. He stood firm, arms crossed, as Zura approached him.

"Your chief lieutenant, Rasamun, is quite competent... perhaps he would appreciate no longer being in your shadow. My lead druvani, Manfri, would be eager as well." Zura stood over Leander, speaking softly now. "I have a number of officers under me who could easily replace *any* should the need... arise."

Leander kept his gaze pointedly ahead, avoiding Zura's, and spoke plainly.

"Sir, it is my analysis that a tactical strike at a vulnerable point in the Precept fleet and careful deployment of this Void Protocol... could prove a useful enough distraction to allow some of the fleet to escape."

"You would toss away certain glory for a small chance to flee?" Zura said. "Even so, you two still account for less than half of what remains of House Drovina. Even at full strength, your plan has no chance of success."

Behind the steya, Timbo Belim cleared his throat. The newly minted captain stood in stark contrast with his white artisan robes. Zura's head turned slowly until he could barely be seen peeking over the thick, white cape that draped over his left shoulder.

"Something to add, Captain Belim?" Zura spoke in a deliberate calm now, stressing the man's new title above all else. Timbo Belim's eyes darted over to Nacen, then back to Zura. He moistened his lips with a quivering tongue.

"I am indebted to you, my steya, for my recent promotion," Timbo managed to say.

"Good," Zura said with a menacing smile. He whirled to face the captain with a flourish of his cape. "It is good to see my most loyal captains remain at my side. Even with these cravens threatening to abandon our attack, we should have more than enough forces to assault Dagon, especially while they distract the enemy fleet."

"I... I was not finished, Steya." Timbo stiffened as Zura took two steps toward him, but he stood his ground. "I am indebted to you for my recent promotion, but Captain Medios has more experience in combat than all of us combined... certainly more than I could ever hope to attain. To do the people of the *Nivasi* justice, I must side with him." Timbo glanced around, appearing to be suddenly aware of where he stood in the circle, and nervously stepped over beside Leander.

Nacen remained in the center of the circle, holding Talavaar Bhaganadi out for all to see. He wanted to thank the captains who had sided with him and Florica, to drop to his knees and praise them. But such an act would not do, not at this moment. He would stay silent for now and let the captains deliberate. He glanced over at Captain Tosque, now the only captain on Zura's side. He held a loose fist up to his mouth, propped on his chin, appearing to be content in surveying the scene.

Zura was silent. He was difficult to read at the best of times, but he was now a complete enigma. His rage subsided, Nacen figured he had either re-signed himself to the changing momentum, or his anger had only ever been a show to keep the captains in line. His hands had withdrawn beneath his white raiment. His eyes had settled on the sword Nacen gripped in his right hand.

"It seems I stand alone in support of the steya." Captain Tosque sighed and looked pensively around the room for a moment. "I would like us all to recall the last few days. Ever since Zura was thrust into the position of steya, he has kept us alive. He alone made the hard decisions that saw us narrowly avoid destruction. He gave us the option to strike back instead of flee with the rest of the homefleet. We flew through quickspace, smashed blockades, all without losing so much as a frigate. Protocol dictates that in extreme situations as these we relinquish power to the steya, and so far this has worked. Howev-er, within this dire situation, we appear to be locked within one direr still. I shall stand with the families, for to do anything else would be to act against my own people. My steya, I hope you appreciate the predicament we are in and do not consider us too harshly."

Zura pondered this for a moment. His face was still an unreadable mask of calm. Nacen wondered what his brother could be thinking. Did his placid expression reflect an accepting mind or belie raging currents beneath?

"It takes the mark of a good leader to recognize when he is beaten." Zura walked back to the center of the circle, no longer standing between his captains. "Though I still disagree, I recognize when I am outnumbered. To commit half our forces to either plan would be folly. You have given me little choice but to join you."

"Of course you remain steya," Danior Tosque assured him, "and will remain so if and when this conflict resolves. This is merely a disagreement in tactics, nothing more."

The other captains were quick to nod their assent.

"A disagreement in tactics, eh? Well, no matter. If everyone here is resolved, then I declare the vulakaat concluded." Zura placed his hand on Na-cen's shoulder, and Nacen flinched slightly. "Brother, you shall bear Talavaar Bhaganadi onto the chosen ship when the time comes. As the *Burning Stag is* the fastest frigate, you may remain here by my side to prepare for the attack."

"There is no place I would rather be." Nacen smiled, feeling tears force their way up.

Zura grabbed him in a hug, jostling his sword arm.

"I am glad to have you returned to the fleet," he said. "Back to your ships, captains. As soon as you are able, form into the inclined diamond forma-tion, with the *Burning Stag* at the center. We shall loop around the planet and accelerate toward quickspace. As the enemy fleet moves to intercept us, we will move from refuse chevron to needle attack pattern and strike at our target. I will flag a suitable ship, and the *Burning Stag* will lead the boarding action."

The captains nodded in agreement.

Florica gave the sign of House Drovina. "Without wood, the fire dies."

Every captain, including Nacen, echoed the salute.

"From the houses, ashes rise," Zura returned. Nacen frowned at this turn of the Drovinian phrase.

Everyone was now filing out. Beskin and Camlo stood by the entrance awaiting him. Nacen took another look at his sword and tucked it firmly within his belt at his waist. He followed after the captains and their attendants, catching Florica's eyes.

"Thank you, for siding with me," Nacen said softly when he had formed up.

"It is I who should be thanking you, Captain," Florica replied. She slowed to walk beside Nacen as they exited the hall and back into the meandering corridors of the *Burning Stag*. "I had proposed many different plans of escape, but after Zura stood his ground, no one even attempted to side with me. You tipped the scales."

Nacen shrugged and tapped at the hilt of Talavaar Bhaganadi at his side.

"I think it was mostly the sword."

"I wasn't going to mention it, but..." Florica grinned. "I jest. You sell yourself short."

"I assure you, my modesty is entirely false." Nacen grinned.

The procession of captains and druvani passed into the hallway, and Nacen saw his crew waiting. Lash and Shukernak stood amidst the throng of Armads, noting the different uniforms and style of dress robes on each passing group. Their bemused expressions turned concerned as Nacen and Florica emerged, the last to exit. Lash was the first to speak, if his abrupt muttering could be classified as such. The Orizon cleared this throat and tried again.

"Nacen, you have the sword. How?"

"I'm not sure. It could be that the sword was set to release on a timer, or perhaps on close proximity to one of our worldships. But it only withdrew for me, and only now..." Nacen trailed off and pulled the blade carefully from his belt. "It is called Talavaar Bhaganadi, the Blade of Rushing Waters. It is one of the last true relics of the homefleet."

The Armads gathered closely to get a better look at the sword. The dim, atmospheric lighting played marvelously off of the hawk and serpent carvings on its surface.

"The time was ripe. I knew you had it in you," Basaul said, his thick jaw set firmly in a grin.

Shukernak took a step forward, not to get a better view of the blade, but to look Nacen straight in the eye.

"So... I'm glad you overcame your stage fright and managed to whip out your fancy sword in front of the other nobles, but what are we doing now? I'll grant you that it's very shiny, but how's that supposed to help us?"

Nacen filled in his crew on the details of the Void Protocol as they headed back to the *Carmine Canotila*, as well as the plan to unleash the logic bomb on the Precept fleet through a suitable interface. The crew listened intently, occasionally asking for clarification or making an exclamation.

One by one, the captains and their druvani peeled off for their individual ships. At the end of the row, Nacen's crew turned in to find the *Carmine Canotila* true to form. Singed and pockmarked plates had been shed like an old skin, and the bright red curves of the sleek craft now stood proudly before them. The crew filtered past him, eager to get back to the ship and prepare for their mission. Nacen was locked in place, gazing up at his ship. Not some ancient trade ship he had been relegated to, but *his* ship. His resentment had been just like the ill-fitted armor plates, artifices he had placed on the ship and nothing more.

A grunt beside him snapped Nacen to the present. He looked to his left. Camlo had only become more glazed in sweat since the vulakaat. His pale skin was significantly redder as well, though to his credit he did not appear out of breath. He was still lugging around the piece of the *Asura's* floor in which the phase blade had been trapped.

"Camlo, were you carrying that debris back this whole time?" Nacen asked. He already knew the answer but wanted to hear Camlo's rationale.

"My last orders were to carry this, and that's what I'm doing," Camlo remarked.

"Right," Nacen dragged the word out in amazement at Camlo's stubbornness. "You realize you could have just dumped it anywhere after I retrieved Talavaar Bhaganadi from it?"

Camlo blinked. "Of course! I just… thought it would be rude to leave it lying around."

"Well, chuck it by the ruined ship plating. That's all junk now, anyway."

"Yes, Captain." Camlo set the piece down next to the heap.

"Seeing the ship like this reminds me of our first assignment," Nacen said. "Do you remember, Cam? It was our first trade mission. I was so afraid that this ship and the *Lusterhawk* were going to be my grave. Before I even set foot on them. I thought, how could my father consign me to a merchant ship?"

"I never knew that. Personally, I was excited. You seemed like a great captain, and I was eager to put my training to use."

"*Seemed* like a great captain?" Nacen chided.

"Well, you proved it quickly enough," Camlo said with a weak grin.

"The funny thing is, even though the *Carmine Canotila* could very well be my end now, I don't dread it like I did before. I'm proud to be captain here. Really, I wouldn't wish for anything else. I hope we make it out to find the *Lusterhawk*, as well."

"I'm glad, Nace. I wouldn't want to be anyone else's druvani."

One of Zura's technicians strode down the ramp after the group of Armads had clambered past holding a few small parts. She stopped short of Nacen.

"Ah, welcome back, Captain Buhari the Younger. We are nearly finished with the repairs to your ship." The trufalci wiped at her form-fitting technician robes and sent a smattering of ashes and solder to the floor. "Fortunately for you, we have plenty of staff on hand and spare parts for the smaller ships of the fleet."

"You have exceeded all expectations, and in short order. Very well done, Trufalci."

The woman nodded gratefully and returned to the repair drone.

Nacen felt more perceptive now, cognizant of every detail of the *Carmine Canotila*. His footsteps echoed off the ramp where over a year ago he had taken his first impatient steps into the cargo hold. Nacen passed through to where the crew had begun to settle into their tasks. They talked excitedly about what had transpired on within the *Burning Stag* and of what was to come. The conversation lulled as soon as Nacen arrived. Shukernak, his back to the ramp, still chattered on.

"I'll tell you where he should have put that sword, right up Zura's—"

"May we see it again, Nacen? In this light?" Perido interrupted.

Nacen nodded curtly and withdrew the sword from his belt carefully. He held it in outstretched hands, to allow anyone a chance to see should they desire. The bright lights of the cargo hold illuminated the etchings on the blade's surface as he turned.

"Marvelous," Perido said.

"A fine weapon, if not a little small," Hortz added.

Beskin had stayed close to Nacen all the way back to the ship, never intruding to ask if he may see the weapon. Now he looked on with amazement. "The etchings have changed since I saw it last," he said. "The last time I saw your father wielding the blade, the hawk soared magnificently on one side and the serpent slithered along the other. Now it seems they are locked in battle. So the wielder can alter the blade for combat, so does the blade itself change to adapt to its master."

"I am blessed to be its wielder now. All thanks must go to Basaul and the rest of you whom we were fortunate to find on Carnizad."

"Nonsense! All we gave you was a piece of a ship," Basaul said. "It was you who claimed the blade."

The man's words were kind and true, no mere false flattery. But they must now be tempered with the reality of the situation.

"Now the blade has allowed our commanders another path, away from the ashes and glory that Zura dreamt for us. No longer shall we prepare for an attack on Dagon to lay waste to its populace. As I am sure you have by now heard, we are to rally and head toward quickspace."

Many of the Armads, not privy to the details of the plan, gave an uproar.

"I would sooner die in battle with my feet on solid ground!" Diat shouted.

"The Glom fleet will crush us for sure!" Kurt yelled.

Other Armads echoed these sentiments until a deep voice rose above all others from the back of the hold.

"Hasn't it been your plan all along to die for your homefleet, Captain?" Chalce, who had been leaning silent against the far wall until now, spoke. "Has your resolve for sacrifice weakened now that you've seen the enemy?"

"I said I was willing to die for it, not *with* it," Nacen said.

"I fail to see the difference." Chalce sneered and gazed back out the rear hatch, appearing to lose himself in the undulating lights.

"There is a weapon, one that resides in the very blade I carry now," Nacen announced over the din in the cargo hold. "Zura heard my father speak of it and seems to know its workings. It contains a virus, one bestowed in secret by the Colonies of Xandra, a program that can subvert the operations of the Unity's Counsel."

"But to what extent?" Chalce demanded. "For how long?"

Nacen frowned and gripped the hilt tightly.

"I do not know," he admitted softly.

The clamor in the cargo hold rose again.

"We cannot hope to escape their fleets, even in a hindered state!"

"Our brothers have died in vain, and with this plan we will join them!"

"Enough," Nacen demanded in a voice hard as tungsteel. "We have our orders. This is our best chance to leave the system. Any plan has risks and uncertainties. Come, there is work to be done on the *Canotila* before we form up with the other ships."

"You heard him," Basaul ushered the crew along, splitting them apart from their clusters in the cargo hold. "Finish checking the repairs, pack in the tools, calibrate your weapons. Come on, come on!"

Nacen caught the eye of Lash Procah. The Stevari now sported Drovinian recast armor and robes of scarlet and brown. His blond hair had been fashioned in many thin braids that lay across his shoulders. Lash uncrossed his arms and walked up to Nacen, the slightest of smiles on his face.

"I regret to say we have no Orizon blues for you to choose from," Nacen said earnestly.

"Oh?" Lash glanced down, and his smile turned into a mocking frown. "It's probably for the best. If I were wearing the cerulean accouterment of my Orizon rank, I would be far too elegant for the Stevari of your homefleet to withstand. The distraction could prove a fatal tactical disadvantage, your soldiers not being able to tear their eyes from me."

Nacen would normally find himself wryly smiling at such antics, but present matters now weighed heavily on him. There was still much to do as their time drew short. Besides, a part of Nacen thought that Lash, at least to some extent, may have actually believed the outlandish claim.

"I would not ask you to go to battle for me, Lash. This is not your homefleet, and not your fight."

"Where am I to go?" Lash asked rhetorically. "I've been hitching a ride on a U.P. trade frigate before this."

"Take a single fighter to the Unity and surrender," Nacen suggested. "They have no present quarrel with House Orizon that I know of. Surely you can locate the Orizon beacons and find your way."

"I do not doubt such a plan could work. We Orizon are shrewd and diplomatic. We have good standing with the Unity, and I may be able to negotiate my return. My homefleet may be a long ways away, and the beacons' range near limitless if you know how to look, but you're wrong about one thing."

Lash's expressive face hardened, his usual theatrical aspects taking on those of stone. "This *is* my fight. Not because House Orizon owes anything to Drovina, or would even support you in such an endeavor if they did. The Unity has taken away my family as well. Bosha, Mingo, Phantine, Menowin, Leonora, Hester, Geary, Rhoda, Kezia. My druvani, my trufalci... my family."

"I am sorry they perished, Lash, and all the sorrier that it was I who spurred us on, denying you time to issue any last rites."

"That is a foolish apology. It was the only call you could have made."

"Regardless, my offer stands," Nacen said. "I am sure Zura could spare something."

"I'm flattered, but that is unnecessary, Nacen." Lash shook his head. "Make no mistake, I am with you to the end."

Lash's exaggerated smile returned. He gave Nacen's left pauldron two firm pats and turned to leave. Nacen turned to make his way to bridge. He had one more person to check in on. He methodically turned each corner, taking in the interior of each room he passed. The armory, where he had first tested the plasma carbine he carried to this day. The barracks, where he spent his first restless night agonizing over his poor fortune. How pitifully small those concerns felt now. At last, he stood in front of the bridge door. It whisked open at a pulse from his short-range comms.

"Welcome back, Captain," Linasette acknowledged as Nacen entered. She did not turn from her displays. "Major repairs to the engines and armor are nearly complete. The *Burning Stag's* crew estimates no more than fifteen minutes to finish final repairs. Jeta will want to make her own checks as well, of course."

"Excellent. We have plenty of time. We're staying here until we deploy with the rest of Zura's strike craft and transports for our target."

"Good."

"I have to admit, I thought you would be a bit more surprised," Nacen said, pointedly gripping the phase blade's hilt at his waist.

"You'll have to excuse me for snooping, but I was on your communications channel the entire time," Linasette admitted. "I had to make sure you were not in any danger."

"Ah," Nacen said. This made sense. He had forgotten that Linasette normally followed the movements of all members of the crew when they were outside the *Canotila*.

"May I see it?" Linasette asked, rising from her chair.

"I'm sorry?" Nacen replied.

"Talavaar Bhaganadi, your sword," Linasette clarified.

"Oh, yes, of course." Nacen withdrew the blade carefully and held it before the pilot. Her eyes ran slowly along its edge.

"May I?" she asked, holding out her hands.

"I, uh..." Nacen was taken aback. No one had asked to hold the weapon up to this point. It was his, after all. He supposed it couldn't hurt anything. "Sure, just for a moment. Be careful."

"Of course," Linasette said. Slowly, she took the hilt from Nacen's hands and held the blade flat atop her right hand. She held it aloft, nearly reaching the ceiling in the small bridge. She seemed almost to be waiting for something. Then she lowered the sword back to Nacen. "Thank you. It is an elegant weapon."

"Yes, it is." Nacen tucked the blade back into his belt, making sure it was perfectly secure. He wouldn't be letting anyone else hold Talavaar Bhaganadi anytime soon. It was too critical for the upcoming plan for anything to happen to it.

"I am glad you were able to persuade the other captains to your side," Linasette said after a moment of silence. "I am also most curious to see the effects of this Void Protocol."

"We've got a long way to go before we're able to even think about using it.

"I am not worried, I have docked inside Union Precept battleships hundreds of times. Granted they were not shooting at me, though."

This forced a laugh from Nacen.

"There's a first time for everything." Nacen turned to go. "I will be in the barracks, if anyone needs me. Be sure they knock first."

"Meditating?" Linasette asked.

"You could say that."

***

Nacen gripped the hilt of his phase blade firmly at first. He swung it in a wide arc around the center of the empty barracks, then alternated between stabbing the air and slashing. With each strike, he focused on one aspect of the swing until he was content. The grip felt worn and smooth in his hands. The blade was light and well-balanced with the hilt. The air hissed as he pierced and slashed at it.

He sent a signal to the barracks storage, and six small drones rose from behind a crate. They spread themselves out in a ring around Nacen. The small drones were meant to be used for target practice, but Nacen figured this qualified. He slashed out at the drone directly in front, and it nimbly shot to the side. Sensing the attack, the other drones began flying about in a clockwise pattern. Each had its own unique series of movements which changed every few seconds. Nacen studied them all for a few cycles, then locked on to one. Just after it switched patterns, he thrust out at where he thought it would be. The drone was skewered on the end of the blade. The other drones quickened their pace, as if frightened by the demise of their comrade. Nacen focused on the next drone, studying its patterns before lashing out again. They had gotten faster, learning from Nacen's movements even as he learned from them. This was a lot easier with a gun.

Nacen continued the dance, losing track of the time as he managed to fell one drone after another. Eventually, only one remained. By now, Nacen was covered in perspiration and breathing heavily. He allowed the drone to return to its resting place and stood surveying the barracks. The sword had made quick work of the drones, after he managed to hit them anyway, completely bypassing their magnetic shielding and tungsteel chassis.

Content for now, Nacen lifted the blade and turned it downward toward his belt. Inadvertently, the carved images caught his eye as he prepared to put the phase blade back. The hawk was frozen in time and space, locked in perpetual struggle with the serpent. Eternity seemed to pass along the blade's edge. Awareness of the passing time slipped away. The seconds elapsed into minutes, which in turn passed into reverie.

Finally, Nacen slid the blade home. Then, with only the faintest realization of having made the decision, Nacen withdrew the sword once more. The images had faded away. Only a dim reflection of Nacen's sharp features could be seen in the blade's reflection.

He adjusted his grip and slashed Talavaar Bhaganadi into a cup that a crewman had left on a crate, focusing his goodwill. The blade passed through it without leaving so much as a crack in the clear glass. Exhilarated, he then cleaved the phase blade through the flux driver he had set aside when he had first entered the barracks. The blade passed through it, but this time severed the weapon clean in two. Nacen stopped short of the full swing, and after recognizing what he had done to the gun, gazed with trembling eyes at the sword. The hawk and serpent had returned.

Nacen slowed his breath, and his racing heart slowed in turn. Until he could learn to master the properties of the blade, he would stick with what he knew. He secured the sword to his belt and made his way back to the cargo hold. On his way, Basaul nearly plowed him over.

"Nacen, there you are," Basaul rumbled. "My men are ready. I must admit, though we are ready to wage proper war on the Conglomerate navy, many of us wish we could have spent more time with your fleet."

"Thank you, Overseer." Nacen smiled. "We would happily welcome you as brothers after what we have done together."

"Speaking of brothers..." Basaul frowned. "How was your brother elected steya, anyway?"

"He wasn't elected," Nacen clarified. The pair began a slow pace toward the cargo hold. "My father was, however. Every twelve years, the baroni, the various nobles of the fleet, gather and vote to elect a steya. Most major captains and governors of frontier worlds and trade posts are baroni, though not all. Conversely, there are many older Stevari who no longer hold command but rather work and teach in various trades, who still maintain the rank of baro."

"It is too bad we cannot elect a new leader. Get some fresh blood in the mix."

Nacen raised an eyebrow. "Who are you suggesting?"

"Someone brave, noble, not only a warrior but a scholar," Basaul paced around the room ponderously, and Nacen straightened a little. "A leader of men, who has proven himself in battle time and time again."

"Yes?" Nacen urged him to continue.

"I was hoping they could nominate *me*." Basaul gave a wry grin.

Nacen chuckled and shook his head. "I'm afraid you wouldn't meet the requirements."

"Because I'm an Armad? Or because I wasn't born in the homefleet?"

"You're too tall," Nacen teased. He stepped aside and let Basaul enter the cargo hold where his men awaited. Nacen saw Jeta and Shukernak chatting in one corner, and Camlo and Beskin were inspecting their weapons in another.

"Do all homefleets choose their leaders as such?" Basaul wondered aloud.

"No, each has their own traditions. Though we are all descendants of the first homefleet, of the first steya, or so the stories say. Many of our rivals seem to conveniently forget our shared ancestry. I myself forget, you have not traveled among us long and do not know our traditions," Nacen said. By now, he had attracted the attention of some of the crew, Armads and Stevari alike.

"True. You have told me about your people through your songs, and more importantly your skill in combat," Basaul replied earnestly.

"Listen, then, to the tale of the first steya, whose name is long forgotten," Nacen said to all in the cargo hold. Basaul nodded for the captain to continue. The idle chatter died down as Nacen began in an audacious tone.

> "He was a warrior born,
> Taught to fight, ne'er to mourn.
> Since mother's arms been torn,
> Corsair ships his sire.
> From black abyss they came,
> Howling some wicked name,
> Death and plunder their claim,
> Their helm he'd aspire.
>
> With each vessel struck down,
> So grew his dark renown,
> O'er brow they placed a crown.
> Thus he earned command.
> Often he pushed their luck,
> Jewels of empire they'd pluck,
> At golden fleets they struck,
> Treasure lumped in hand.
>
> He sat atop his throne.
> The loot did ever shone,
> On all he'd ever known.
> He longed for a place,
> That which he never knew,
> Yet hunger in him grew,
> Long was peace overdue.
> He must cease this chase.
>
> He toasted for good health,
> Fled far and wide in stealth.
> In trade regained his wealth,
> With no more bloodshed.

He'd given up his hoard,
And thrown away his sword.
Order had been restored.
All he broke was bread.

The sun peeked through the dome.
No more in death he'd roam.
At last he'd made his home
In every nation.
Robes covered up our scars.
No longer behind bars,
We're free to roam. The stars,
Our destination."

The room was silent for a time after Nacen uttered these last words.

"It is good to know that other homefleets will carry on that tale, among others. That your traditions will not die here today," Basaul noted gravely.

"It is... a slight comfort," Nacen agreed. "I count you Armads now my kin, even more than some Stevari of the homefleet."

The cargo hold was still for a long time. Slowly, Armads and Stevari broke off to finish their tasks in silence and contemplation. Nacen began inspecting the crates in the cargo hold. The heaviest were to go in the back, lightest in the front. Some of the stacks violated this and did not leave enough room in between. Several minutes into his inspection of the hold, he received a triple mic tap from Linasette, the covert signal of trouble.

"Yes, Lina? What is it?" Nacen transmitted.

"It's the ship, Nacen, we cannot move," the pilot reported.

"Why would we? We're remaining here until we make a move for quick-space." Nacen stood up from his inspection of the transmat by the rear ramp and looked around.

"Sure, but we are locked in place right now. I believe the *Burning Stag* is keeping us in place with its artificial gravity."

"That doesn't make any sense," Nacen replied. "Why would they do that?"

Outside in the small hangar bay, Nacen saw the trufalci technician he had spoken to earlier addressing someone in the hallway. He was nodding vigorously.

"Uncertain," Linasette said calmly. "All I know is that we are not going anywhere for the time being."

Nacen peered into the corridor. His eyes adjusted and he saw several figures in red recast plate and midnight black cloaks. Zura's druvani. They held plasma carbines at the ready. The trufalci technician beckoned to two of her remaining comrades, and the three of them hurried out of the hangar. The druvani entered, spreading out around the entrance.

"Uh... Lina?" Nacen began, keying his earpiece as he tried to organize his thoughts. This couldn't be what it looked like. The druvani raised their plasma rifles and began advancing the short distance to the *Carmine Canotila*.

"Yes, Captain?"

"Close the rear access ramp, please."

"Why?"

"Just close it. Now," Nacen added. He began backing away, into the interior of the cargo hold. There was a bright blue flash and sparks shot out from the wall to Nacen's right. He ducked behind a compressor crate as sparks raked across his face, singing his flesh as the embers died. "Now!" The room was all shouts and scrambling. Armads and Stevari alike dove for cover or retreated to the interior of the ship. "Now, now, now!"

Soon, the flashing ceased and the interior amber lights of the cargo hold were all that remained. Nacen stood. The wall and crates around him had been marked black by the impacts of plasma.

"What's going on out there?" Nacen heard Basaul's voice from somewhere in the *Canotila*. "I wasn't expecting any action so soon!"

"Nacen, I have eyes on the exterior. Zura's men tried to get access to the ship. Druvani by the looks of it," Linasette reported. "I have also disabled any transmat access from the outside."

"Excellent."

"Not to alarm you, but they are bringing in something else. It appears to be a drone with a large plasma torch. Ah, blast. I lost visuals."

"Okay, so Zura has troops out there and they want in." Nacen opened up the communications with his druvani as well. "Any ideas of what to do?"

"I suggest we open communications with them," Linasette sent.

"No point," Beskin transmitted.

"Why not?" Nacen asked.

"We *know* what they want. The sword. And it doesn't sound like it's up for discussion."

Chapter 18

The hull sang with a deep whine as Zura's men and women cut deeper. Nacen had formed the crew up in defensive positions around the cargo hold after arming themselves. Armads took what cover they could behind crates and columns, hugging flux shotguns close to their chests. Jeta, Beskin, Camlo, and Lash had positioned themselves toward the back with the longer ranged plasma weaponry. Nacen crouched behind a crate, pretending the screech in his hull was merely the cry of some distant animal. Something he didn't have to deal with. What could he do? He was cornered in Zura's own ship with no means to escape and certain death outside. He wished desperately that Zura could have simply stated his problems in the vulakaat, rather than going along with the plan until he could turn on Nacen, which undoubtedly appeared to be the case now.

Nacen sent out another request to open communications with the *Burning Stag*. There was no response.

"Such a shame that they fixed up the *Canotila* so nice only to wreck it again," Shukernak said. He set down his ex-cal's tripod, then thought better of it and moved it back a few steps.

"Yeah, I'm sure they feel awkward about this whole mess." Camlo looked away from his carbine's sights for a moment to speak, but was now focused back on the rear of the cargo hold as though Zura's men could break through any second.

"Why is he doing this now, anyway? I thought he was on our side," Jeta said through gritted teeth.

A few heads turned to Nacen expectantly. Nacen ignored them, staring straight ahead at the hull opposite him. He willed the screeching to stop, to be anywhere else but here. He clutched his plasma carbine and closed his eyes. The tearing at the hull continued unabated. He heard it all around now. Like it was coming from his gut. From his bones.

"He waited," Nacen said at last.

"Waited? What?" Jeta asked, wide-eyed.

"That's what threw me off." Nacen opened his eyes and surveyed the hold again. The crew had the room locked down. They could survive for a few minutes, maybe. Assuming Zura's druvani didn't have anything for a breach and clear scenario: stun grenades, explosives, drones. But they would have something. "He waited. Zura was always the impetuous type, just like our father. His plan to hit the Unity as fast and hard as possible had Yoska's name all over it. It's not like him to hold back and be silent, to lie and misdirect. He waited for a time when the captains were gone, and now he's trying to take the sword from us so he can carry out his initial plan."

"It appears he's learned some new tricks as steya," Camlo said.

"Indeed."

"Well whatever happens, we can't let him get the sword," Camlo looked up from his carbine sights.

"Why not?" Nacen asked. He looked down to the floor, dejected.

"Because... we can't!" Camlo said. "Let's just use the transmat to get out of here and attack these guys from behind. They'll never expect us to attack right now."

Shukernak snorted in derision. "Why not just blast a hole in the hangar and shoot the stupid sword into space?"

A hole in the *Stag*. Space outside. Freedom.

"Perfect," Nacen said, thinking of the worldships which had surely taken positions in the diamond formation by now.

"Whose plan was perfect?" Camlo asked.

"Both. Neither."

"Okay, well, the captain's lost it," Shukernak said without mirth. "Who's in charge now? Beskin, or one of the Armads?"

Nacen ignored the trufalci.

"Lina, can we get in touch with Captain Tengrin on the *Trishula*?" he asked over their short-ranged comm link.

"Well, our outward communications are being jammed, but since we're physically in contact with the Stag, I could try to hitch a ride on its carrier signal to get out to the homefleet."

"A simple yes will do. We're short on time."

"Well then... probably?" Linasette replied.

"Patch me through to Tengrin then, if you can. Tell her it is grievously urgent."

"Aye, Captain. Give me a little while."

Nacen directed his attention back to the cargo hold while he awaited Florica's reply.

"Listen, everyone. I'm working on a way out of this mess, but I need silence. If Zura's men get through, hold them off as long as you can. Even just a few seconds could make the difference we need. Be prepared to fall back and seal yourself off in the interior."

"Difference between what?" Camlo asked.

"Patience. You'll see."

They returned to their stations around the hold, guns poised at the rear hatch. The grinding screech continued.

"You Starscraps have any good battle songs?" Basaul muttered over the din of the plasma cutter.

Nacen shook his head slowly. "The taking of a life is not done lightly by Stevari. It is a terrible act, done out of necessity at best. It is nothing to ponder on or glorify. There is enough murder and hatred across the worlds joined by the great blue sun to sustain itself, it does not need us to carry it along too."

"Alright, I was just curious," Basaul said defensively.

"I've got one I've been knocking around," the Armad Brecca chimed in from the front of the hold.

"Do go on..." Basaul grumbled sarcastically.

Brecca stepped up on a short crate and cleared his throat theatrically.

"There once was a Starkin named Zura.
Bring his fleet to its doom he was sure ta.
He got really bored,

And tried takin' our sword,
So we blew him out of an airlock and ruptured his aorta."

Silence returned to the cargo hold, all but for the ceaseless plasma cutter.

Suddenly, Shukernak erupted with raucous chortling. Nacen thought the big trufalci had broken into tears for a moment. Several Armads joined in, and soon the entire hold rocked with laughter.

"Well we have to make it out of here now," Shukernak said as his chest still convulsed. "The homefleet needs that in its annals."

"That was quite the battle hymn," Nacen said at last.

Brecca gave a deep bow and stepped off of the crate. A few crew members started clapping. Nacen set down his plasma carbine for a moment and joined in the applause. He was interrupted by a chime in his earpiece.

"Zura? What's going on? The *Burning Stag* should be in position by now." The voice could only belong to Florica, the captain of the *Trishula*.

"Wrong brother," Nacen stated, more gloomily than he meant to.

"Nacen? What's going on over there?"

"Well, there's been a change in plans."

"I'm listening," Florica shot back pensively.

By now, the plasma cutter had made it clear through one small portion of the hull. Flickering white light flooded the interior, turning the cargo hold into a collage of bleached ghosts and sharp shadows. The cutter began its slow but inexorable sweep toward the port side.

"Well, and I'm just speculating off of the facts as I see them, but I believe Zura was not a proponent of our modifications to his plan."

"Of course not. Some resistance was to be expected, but he eventually shifted support to our escape attempt. There's no reason to suspect he's gone back on his word."

"Well, judging by the sound of the heavy plasma cutter breaching through my ship's hull, he wants Talavaar Bhaganadi. Presumably so he can have his heroic last stand."

"Zura's troops are attacking your ship? Are you absolutely certain?" Florica's voice rose an octave by the time the transmission ended.

"Beyond any doubt. He's ignored all of my communication requests, but I know what he wants. I estimate we have two minutes before they breach our cargo hold. Three or four if we're fortunate and can actually hold them off." There was a long silence on the channel. "Tengrin? Hello? Lina, are we being jammed?"

"No, I'm thinking. I take it you can't simply fly out of the hangar?" Florica asked.

"We're locked in by the hangar doors."

"Can you ram them?"

"Artificial gravity is preventing us from taking off. We could maybe get a couple of G's in before getting critically damped."

"That may be enough," Florica mused.

"Enough for what?"

"Send me your coordinates on the *Burning Stag* and make sure your crew is in a secure area, sealed off from Zura's breach."

"I also believe he may have one or more of the captains still on his side. We'll know soon if they break off from formation to join in on Zura's assault on Dagon." Again there was silence. "Hello? Florica?"

Nacen disconnected from the dead connection. *Kaha*. All he could do was blindly follow her orders and wait. She sounded like she was going for some kind of rescue attempt. How she planned to do that was anyone's guess. Personally, Nacen preferred being the one handing out the blind orders. He accessed the *Carmine Canotila's* location on his pad and passed them along to Lina for transmission to the *Trishula*.

"Okay everyone, listen up." Nacen stood and addressed the flickering shadows of his crew around him. "I need all of you to seal yourself off from the main interior: barracks, meditation room, kitchen, wherever you can."

The room filled with short confirmations, though he heard some grumbling dissent mixed in. The crew mostly agreed with Nacen's sentiment that this was preferable to eating a plasma grenade, however.

"Why?" Brecca asked directly to Nacen's face as he strode by.

"I can't say," Nacen said. It was frustrating, but better than stating to the crew his own total ignorance of Florica's plan. He could guess at what Florica intended to do, like launch a sortie to come breach the hangar and pull out the crew of the *Canotila*. But then he didn't want anything coming back to haunt him. At least this way, he could fall back to trying to surrender to Zura's breach team without any of his crew needlessly giving their lives.

The Armads thundered past him along with the Stevari crew. The hold had been emptied except for Beskin and Camlo, their cloaks bathed in the blazing light of the plasma cutter now at the apex of its journey across the rear ramp.

"Let's head to the bridge. If Zura's troops make the breach before Florica can do her magic, I'll formally surrender myself and my sword, if Zura is feeling merciful."

"He's your brother, Nace," Camlo protested. "Surely he'll accept your surrender."

"He hasn't so far." Nacen turned and made his way to the bridge. He made sure each room was locked and properly sealed on his way. One door was still open. Using its exterior control panel, Nacen triggered it to close. The dark red slab whirred to the side but caught on something. Nacen looked down.

A massive boot prevented the door from closing all the way. Nacen glanced back up, and Basaul's scarred face now stared back at him.

"Between you and me, Nacen, what's going on?" Basaul said in a low, gravelly voice. "I think I've earned that much."

"I honestly don't know, Basaul," Nacen spoke softly. "I'm acting on Florica's orders. She disconnected in a hurry before I could ask for any follow up. Just know, if Zura's men get in before Florica can do whatever she's planning, I will surrender myself and the sword."

"Not if we can help it." Basaul patted the flux shotgun he still gripped in his right hand. The weapons would be extremely effective in such close quarters, but such endeavors were doomed to failure at their current odds.

"Just... stand down. Please. I do not want any more conflict between brothers here," Nacen replied.

Basaul grunted in what Nacen hoped was confirmation. The door slid shut as he withdrew his boot. One less thing to worry about. Nacen finished the short walk to the bridge, his druvani in tow.

"How are we looking up here, Lina?" Nacen took his usual place in the seat beside her.

"There is nothing to see," the pilot said. As if to reinforce the point, the holoscreens displaying the camera inputs showed only darkness. Their exterior cameras hidden and recessed as they were, had apparently been destroyed.

"What are our options right now?"

"We can sit tight and prepare to be boarded, unless you feel like lowering the ramp and letting Zura's troops in." Linasette paused. "If any of your people believe in a higher power, now would be a good time to pray."

If it had been any other person on the ship, Nacen would have assumed they were joking. Nacen often struggled to tell the difference between her rigid Unity demeanor and grim humor. He preferred to be more obvious with his own.

"They're so close to cutting an opening in, I'd hate to make them feel like they had wasted their time," said Nacen sardonically. "Do we have any other options? What about weapons?"

"All exterior weapons were temporarily disarmed during repairs. Now Zura's troops have taken plasma torches to our rail guns' coils and shoved a thermal charge down the barrel of our aft flux support gun," Linasette stated, "and there's the obvious hole being cut into our rear hatch."

"Naturally," Nacen said with a frown. "What if we—"

A violent quake jostled Nacen in his seat.

"Zura?" Camlo said from behind.

Nacen looked back. Camlo and Beskin had their carbines at the ready. Either they were unphased or had quickly recovered from the tremor.

"They must have finished the breach and entered with explosives," Nacen rose from his chair, careful to brace himself in case of further shaking. "Let's go meet them."

"Hold on. They're close but not quite through," Linasette snapped through a series of diagnostic screens.

"Then what was it?" Nacen asked.

"No, that can't be right," Linasette said incredulously to herself.

"I'm growing weary of asking what is or is not happening."

Another tremor rattled the cabin. This time, Nacen was prepared for it and grabbed the back of his seat.

"Captain, it appears that the *Burning Stag* is under fire," the pilot said. She continued changing her holoscreens in vain.

"Under fire?" Nacen balked. "But the nearest enemy ship is light minutes away, beyond the maximum engagement range of even the longest—"

"It's the *Trishula*. It's firing at the port side of the *Stag*. Nothing massive. It's mostly short-range plasma and low-caliber flux, if the *Canotila's* analysis is accurate."

Another quake shook their shuttle, stronger than any before it.

"That didn't feel low caliber. What is Florica doing?" Nacen wondered aloud, his eyes wide.

"That is because the impacts are so close. Unusually close... if I could just... got it." Linasette exhaled in relief. "They missed one."

"One what?" Nacen asked.

One of the anterior bow cameras showed... nothing. There was only black. No, that wasn't true. There were pinpricks of light. Nacen blinked and almost cried out in surprise. This camera had functionality and was looking into the inky void of space, dotted with stars. For a moment, Nacen was too shocked to realize what this meant. Linasette must have accessed Zura's cameras feeds, or brought up past logs when the *Canotila* was free in open space. Then a huge object drifted into view, quickly concealing the eternal night with a huge wall of deep maroon.

"Come with me, to thee I'll show my soaring city in the sky." A familiar woman's voice from the comm link shook Nacen from the trance that beckoning darkness had on him. The way was clear, but there was still the bay's artificial gravity holding them back.

"Zura's men have breached our cargo hold, Captain. Orders?" Linasette's hands lay poised over the controls.

"What are you waiting for, an invitation?" Florica chimed in again. "You must not have received my instructions. I'm shortcasting coordinates directly to your ship now."

It was now or never.

"Go," Nacen said. "Full acceleration."

The ship jumped forward as soon as Nacen had uttered the words, and he felt the shudder of the inertial dampeners kicking in to minimize acceleration on the interior of the craft. But the distant object that could only be *Trishula* did not grow closer, nor did the walls of the *Stag* diminish. They were locked in place between deliverance and damnation. Flak began to hammer the hull like rain. Nacen felt himself strain every muscle he had under the tension of the situation. Then suddenly, he laughed. First a snort, and then a full fit of laughter.

"What? What is so funny, Nace?" Camlo asked. Nacen was unsure whether the tense worry in his cousin's voice was due to their shared peril or the absurdity of his outburst.

"It's... it's just..." Nacen took a moment to compose himself. "It must be quite a sight from the Unity's perspective. They chase Zura halfway across the Prominar Rim, and as soon as they catch us, we light into each other."

"Oh, right." Camlo let out a tense, uncomfortable laugh but stopped after Beskin glanced at him. Nacen's own uncontrollable laughter lasted a short while longer.

Linasette remained focused. Her fingers tapped away, deftly monitoring and altering the reactor controls for maximum generation and thrust.

"We *are* making progress. Every millimeter farther we get, Zura's artificial tug weakens."

"How... how long do we have before we're free?" Nacen sighed and wiped away a tear with a gauntleted finger.

"Our reactors cannot keep this up indefinitely. If we're not free in the next... twenty seconds, our engines will have peaked and we never will be."

Nacen was about to ask for more information but thought better of it. He would let the pilot do her job. Two shots rang out in the ship interior, muffled by the bridge door. Nacen turned instinctively, plasma pistol in hand.

"I wouldn't go out there, Captain," Linasette said. "The cargo hold is still compromised. There's precious little air out there."

Nacen eyed the door warily. No more sounds came through. He couldn't decide whether that was a good sign or a bad sign.

The *Carmine Canotila* continued its aching crawl, getting imperceptibly further from the *Stag*. Were they even gaining any distance now? Just out of reach, the *Trishula* drifted past.

Florica's worldship began to slow down.

Wait, no. The *Canotila* was getting faster!

"Ha! Yes! Well done, Lina!" Nacen whooped. Then he reigned in his enthusiasm. "Are we good? We escaped?"

"Yes, Captain," Linasette gave a rare smile. "We are good."

"Good. Proceed to Captain Tengrin's coordinates."

"Already underway," the pilot replied.

"Excellent. Let's get situated on the *Trishula* so we can patch up our rear."

Upon finishing its broadside of the *Burning Stag*, the *Trishula* turned and sped back towards the formation of the three remaining frigates. It slowed just enough for the *Canotila* to gain on it. Linasette found the designated ingress for their small trade ship and swiftly darted inside. After the ship touched down, Nacen confirmed that breathable air and adequate atmosphere existed outside the ship before leaving the bridge and making his way swiftly to the cargo hold. Or at least what had been the cargo hold.

The small hold comprising the stern of the ship no longer contained much cargo at all. What few compressor crates, racks, and shelves remained lay strew about the floor, mangled or dented. The large, oval gap in the rear door was the likely candidate for the rest of the cargo's disappearance. Though Nacen was grateful he and the crew survived the ordeal, a part of him reeled at the loss of the majority of his cargo. These valuable metals and goods were meant to be sold across the Prominar Rim. But more goods could be acquired later, and the homefleet had suffered startlingly worse losses than a few compressor crates laden with osmium ore, platinum nuggets, and radioactive portmantonium bars.

Hearing tentative footsteps, Nacen turned around. Jeta and Shukernak approached, wide-eyed as they surveyed the scene. Behind them, Armads looked over their heads.

"Is everyone okay?" Nacen asked as more crew filtered into the cargo hold.

"Yes, we're all still here and in one piece," Jeta said.

"What happened to Zura's men?" Nacen asked. "Some surely must have been on the ship after they breached."

"They uh… didn't buckle up for the trip," Basaul patted his flux shotgun.

"Right…" Nacen glanced around the hold warily for any bodies or objects he had not seen before. He found none. He sighed. They would have made useful prisoners. Nacen opened his mouth to chastise Basaul but decided against it. His men here may not take kindly to such castigations. Nacen would pick his battles.

"I should be able to get that hole patched," Jeta said. "It won't be pretty, but 'Nak and I can use some of the steel we have in one of the remaining crates to get the rear ramp sealed."

"Good. Please proceed. You have my permission to access whatever stores you need. Lash, you and the Armads stay with them," Nacen ordered. "In the meantime, I need to meet with Captain Tengrin and see what confounded havoc is ruling out there."

***

Captain Florica Tengrin was waiting in the corridor outside. She wore the same dark battle attire as in the vulakaat. Her raven hair spilled neatly in tresses over black plates, and crimson sleeves poured from the armor. She was flanked by no fewer than twelve druvani. Nacen wondered how she got here from the command bridge so quickly and why she had come herself. A portion of his curiosity was dispelled when he saw the transport drone off to the right, hovering just above floor level. It was a modified Stevari T7 transporter, better known as a Forelle, its crew compartment completely open to make room for more seating and fast embarkation.

"Welcome, Nacen, to the *Trishula*: the divine instrument of the gods' own hands with which we wrought our enemy's destruction."

"It is a pleasure and, quite honestly, a debt that I shall endeavor to repay." Nacen bowed to a level commensurate for such a grand welcome, and a little deeper for the rescue.

Florica beckoned for Nacen to follow her into the Forelle transport drone, and he complied. She sat in one of the four empty seats at the front of the open-topped vehicle, while Camlo and Beskin obediently piled in with the *Trishula* druvani in the back. Nacen gripped a rail as the drone silently accelerated. The wide corridors of the *Trishula* bore little resemblance to those of Zura's ship. These walls were brightly lit with pulsating blue light. Nacen felt as though he were riding beneath an iridescent ocean. He supposed the illusions of the beating waves and fleeting eddies were meant to evoke calm and comfort.

"I thank you for getting us out of Zura's grasp," Nacen spoke loudly over the hum of the drone and the air rushing in his ears.

"You're welcome. Before we begin our escape, my repair crews will do what they can for your ship." Florica nodded congenially and kept her gaze on the undulating waves above as Nacen stumbled for his next words. He hesitated, wondering if he should simply stop at expressing his gratitude.

"Did you have to do it so aggressively, though? Now the U.P. has seen our own ships fire on each other. They have seen dissent within our ranks, within our leadership."

The Forelle whipped down the corridor, strafing around obstacles and personnel as necessary. Florica kept her eyes forward.

"The Union Precept can take it however they want. If it causes them confusion, then so much the better. Zura started this when he went back on his word and tried to enter your ship to take your sword, and possibly your life. I am merely responding with necessary countermeasures."

"When you phrase it like that, treason sounds downright reasonable," a gruff voice said. Nacen looked around for the source but could not find its speaker.

"Slide over, Captain," Florica ordered.

Nacen complied and was surprised to see the form of Captain Leander Medios materialize beside him. The captain, or rather what appeared to be some sort of holographic projection of the captain, sat right beside Nacen. It was full color, and aside from the fuzzy outline and occasional flicker, it was entirely lifelike.

"Hello, Captain Medios. Glad to have you... aboard. As to your comment, you may call Captain Tengrin's actions whatever you wish, but she saved my life."

Leander waved a hand through Nacen's shoulder as though he meant to slap it were he were here in person.

"Relax, I'm with you," Leander said assuredly. "Captain Tosque and Belim, on the other hand, have been ignoring our hails. They are holding position in formation, though. It's possible they are being jammed or simply do not know with whom to side."

"Has Zura responded to any communication requests?" Nacen asked. He became self-conscious of his shouting as the rushing air diminished. The drone appeared to be slowing.

"We are trying, but so far we have achieved nothing," Florica said.

"We'll keep trying, but the critical path here is getting Nacen up to speed and his ship and crew ready to play their part," Medios spoke through a speaker in the transport's front cabin.

The Forelle now slowed to a walking pace and soon stopped in front of three large crates in the hallway. Nacen glanced about, curious as to why the drone had chosen here to halt. Large doors stood on either side of the corridor, appearing to lead into the ship interior. An unseen Stevari barked orders up ahead. Florica's druvani began sweeping over the rail of the transport. Camlo and Beskin clambered down to join them, making a point to stand between them and Nacen. The druvani withdrew several khaki-colored plates from the side of the Forelle and set to work lifting the large crates.

"I apologize for not having these ready at your bay when you arrived, but it was a fairly last minute arrangement, and we are stretched thin on munitions as is," Florica said, leaning back in her seat. "Due to the nature of your present charge of managing a scout shuttle, I am under the impression you have no means to assault a fortified position. We'll get these crates delivered to your ship. They contain a few assault drones, as well as twenty-two nanito grenades. The assault drones can remotely advance and detonate, even utilizing remote transporter mats to surprise the enemy. The nanite grenades target all synthetic and metallic materials in a two and a half meter blast radius, though that can be set smaller. They'll pick most matter apart at the molecular structure. Both are excellent for destroying static positions and emplaced weapons. May they serve you well."

"I am familiar with all tools of the homefleet and will use them as aptly as I would my dulcinet," Nacen replied. He smiled to himself. He could put these tools to excellent use when they reached their target ship. The smiled vanished. *If* they reached their target.

"Good. We will do our part in getting you where you need to be," Florica said reassuringly, as if reading the anxiety on his face. "We will move into position shortly. If we have to attack without three of our worldships, then that's what we'll do."

"The plan remains the same no matter how few worldships we have," Leander stated. "We will make a break for the quickspace passage, and when the Unity intercepts, we go for the highest tier command ship in the local area. As soon as we breach the zone for maximum point defense damage, we will deploy everything: fighters, bombers, troop transports, and chaff."

"Timing the spread to minimize casualties of our transport craft," Nacen affirmed.

"Precisely." Florica picked up where Leander had left off. "Once we have penetrated the hull, the transports will file in and the worldships will retreat... for the time being. After unleashing the Void Protocol, the worldships should be able to slip back in unopposed by the target ship. Other ships may still have the capacity to fight, but we'll mostly evade until we get our troops back on board."

"And if Nacen fails to activate the sword?" Leander asked. "No offense, kid, but I expect the worst and plan for it."

"None taken," Nacen said. He blinked in surprise as the Forelle kicked off again. Evidently the munitions crates had been loaded on.

"If that is indeed the case," Florica began gravely, "which is a non-zero possibility, granted, then the worldships will simply retreat and attempt to make it out of the system."

"Alone against Precept blockades and the massive fleet?" Leander scoffed. "We'd be better off landing on Dagon and trying to assimilate peacefully into the population."

"You know, I've always wanted to be a baker," Nacen said blithely.

"You might want to put your career aspirations on hold, Captain," a hard, feminine voice said from somewhere on the drone. Another hologram? No, he knew that voice. It was Linasette. Why was she listening in? Nacen read equal confusion on Florica and Leander's faces.

"It's alright, she's my pilot," he said.

"Captain Buhari, please maintain control of your crew," Florica stated sharply. "This conversation is strictly a command matter."

"This cannot wait," Linasette said, urgency creeping into her voice. Her figure materialized on the seat opposite Nacen, next to Florica.

"Proceed," Nacen said. Florica shot him an irksome look.

"The audacity..." she muttered.

"Zura, sir, has begun his attack," Linasette said.

"What? But we're not even in range of the Unity fleet, nor are we near enough to Dagon's surface to attack." Nacen straightened and tried to maintain his composure.

"I do not know what to tell you, but I am seeing twenty... no, twenty-one troop transports taking off. They're... wait a minute."

"Lina, what's happening? Talk to me."

Beside the pilot's holoimage, Florica's expression darkened with the realization of what was transpiring.

"What's going on?" Leander asked to no one in particular. Creases appeared in his forehead as he furrowed his brow in vexation.

"They're headed... here. To the *Trishula*. I wasn't sure at first, but it's the only explanation for their trajectory," Linasette announced.

Was Zura so zealously uncompromising that he would invade this ship to get Nacen and the sword back? But it appeared that the question of *would* had been answered. Now it was all a matter of means and method. According to homefleet specifications, he had the largest garrison of trufalci and druvani. The *Burning Stag's* forces were well-drilled in assaults and boarding actions, and now they were on their way here.

"Was this all a ruse? Did Zura get Nacen planted on the *Trishula* to use the Void Protocol on the homefleet?" Leander sneered. "End him, Tengrin. End him and take the sword. We'll continue with the plan without these traitorous brothers."

"Don't be absurd," Nacen said defensively. He shrank back, briefly forgetting the captain's form was merely a projection.

"That doesn't make any sense. Cease this madness, Leander," Florica said quickly. "Nacen's plan is what turned the captains against Zura in the first place. Zura had nothing to gain by going along with our plan of escape before turning on us. This is a move born from desperation."

Leander paused to consider this. His frown remained prominent, but he bowed his head.

"Very well. This seems the most likely explanation. Please forgive my haste. I shall move into position to assist in your defense."

The drone began to slow. They appeared to be in one of the corridors outside the hangar bays, though Nacen could not tell which one in particular.

"I'm afraid we're out of time," Florica shook her head slowly. There was a cold, analytical look in her eyes. "It's not just Zura moving in. Most of the Unity fleet is approaching now. It's just as Nacen feared, they've sensed discord and are moving to take advantage of the situation while they can."

"Then we all rally against Zura, then make our dash to the great blue sun," Leander said stoutly, his projection straightening.

"According to my bridge command, the Precept ships are closing too fast," Florica replied. "The closer they get, the tighter the net draws. Here is your stop, Captain."

The transport drone stopped by a nondescript hangar door. The druvani piled out and began unloading the crates.

"Thank you. We proceed as planned, then," Nacen said, breaking his silence. The statement was just as much a question.

"With Zura bedeviling us from within?" Leander said with incredulity. "The *Burning Stag* easily has enough garrison to overwhelm the *Trishula*, let alone with the potential might of the *Wayfarer* and *Nivasi* against us."

"All we need is enough time to get to the battleship," Nacen said, holding up a fist for emphasis. "When the Precept fleet envelopes us, Zura's plan is shot, and there will be no point in continuing his attack on us."

"Zura still needs to get past my batteries, and the *Trishula's* interior is far from defenseless," Florica said, bristling as she gripped her seat. "I am deploying my druvani and trufalci to defensive positions. I will redistribute them where needed when Zura's boarding positions have been determined. Nacen, ready your own troops and standby for further orders. I may need your help in repelling this breach. Your brother's forces outnumber mine by more than three to one."

"Yes, Captain Tengrin. In the meantime, I will attempt to contact my brother and negotiate our way out of this," Nacen said.

"You may try, but I won't be holding my breath."

"May the next time we all meet in person be under better circumstances," Nacen said, standing and placing an armored boot on the lip of the drone compartment.

"They will be," Florica said. She met Nacen's gaze intently. Nacen knew out of all the commanders of the homefleet, he could trust her the most. She had been the first to stand with him and the plot for escape. This feeling he had now wasn't anything like affection or admiration, though. It was a melancholy pit in his stomach, that this would be the last time he would look into those eyes. He hoped his instinct was wrong.

Leander gave a slight scoff as Nacen hopped off the Forelle.

"Without wood, the fire dies," Nacen said emphatically, giving the sign of Drovina.

"Burning bright, the homefleet flies," Florica said, returning the gesture.

Leander's image remained seated facing away from Nacen. He wasn't sure whether it was a technical limitation of the projection or if Captain Medios didn't deem him worthy. Nacen turned to Camlo and Beskin, who were helping Florica's druvani haul the crates into the hangar bay. He followed them closely, eager to lay eyes on his ship again.

"I didn't catch much of what you guys were discussing up there," Camlo said as he guided the last crate through the door, "but I think I heard enough."

"We'll likely be confronting Zura's troops in real combat. Are you comfortable with that, Cam? And you Beskin?" Nacen asked.

"Comfort forms no part of duty. I will see you come to no harm while I yet live," Beskin said as he set down the crate.

"My custom carbine was in the hold when those *chodras* blew most of our cargo to the black," Camlo said. "I'm going to have to try out one of the new models sometime. May as well be now."

"Let's hope the rest of the crew shares your feelings," Nacen said.

The crew had made good progress sealing off the rear door, but there had simply not been enough time to complete it yet. They would need more time to get the hull sealed and the most severe damage from the *Trishula's* close range batteries patched. To Nacen's relief, several crewmen from the *Trishula* stuck around to help with the repairs. They brought more raw material and plasma torches for the breach to the rear hatch.

"Captain!" Nacen saw a big figure emerge from the *Canotila*. Thinking at first an Armad managed to fit into Drovinian battle regalia, Nacen now recognized Shukernak's silhouette. "Captain! You brought me new toys. Assault drones and nanite grenades? You spoil me."

"You are correct, 'Nak," Nacen nodded. "But I will be divvying them up before the assault."

"You know, me and Jeta—"

"I am keenly aware of all my crew's capabilities," Nacen shot back. "You will get what is suited to you. Is the crew aware of the unfolding situation?"

Shukernak rolled one shoulder and grunted. "Lina may have mentioned something."

"This isn't the time for equivocating, 'Nak."

"Yeah, yeah, she briefed us. Zura's men are coming for us again, and they mean business this time."

"Good. Get geared up then, you're with me," Nacen walked toward the *Carmine Canotila*, accessing the ship's communications as he surveyed the damage. "Listen up everyone. As you know, the shock troops of the *Burning Stag* are headed here, likely with the hostile intent to retrieve the sword I now possess. Everyone not absolutely essential in patching up the ship is to arm themselves and group up in the hangar. Immediately."

Nacen strode past Florica's druvani loading the munitions crates onto the *Canotila*. He watched Armads arming themselves to the crest with shotguns, flux repeaters, knives, and other implements with wicked edges or drills. He watched his druvani stock up on supplies, crimson impacting cloaks fluttering about in their haste. He grasped the hilt of Talavaar Bhaganadi, still firmly at his side. Nacen felt like all the events unfolding now were coalescing around him, drawing in closer to suffocate him. Then he felt guilt, a gnawing at his stomach, for being at the center of the cause for which Stevari were about to fight each other. Then yet more guilt for the sheer egoism that this was all about him.

He armed himself with his plasma carbine and fixed his pistol to the magnetic holster on his right hip. He cast these thoughts aside. This was no time for doubt, or guilt, or hesitation. He stepped back into the cargo hold and walked to the transmat by the rear access door. He slid a hand down the wall of his ship. There was an indent from a flux round there. So many times across so many worlds people had tried to do his ship harm. Never in all his paranoid ruminations would he have thought it could be his own people. His own family. After spending a few minutes calibrating his weapons and stocking up on ammunition and grenades, he descended the ramp back out into the bay.

Roughly half the Armads were present, including Basaul. They jostled and jabbed at each other, reveling in the calm before the storm. Basaul quickly straightened and stood at attention, his Armads falling into an even line next to him. Beskin, Camlo, Jeta, and Shukernak all formed up in an arc around their captain. Lash was leaned up against a landing strut in the umbra of the *Canotila* and sauntered over. Basaul looked uncertainly at the casual circle around Nacen, shrugged, and joined it.

"I know this isn't what most of you were expecting when you signed up for trade duty on the *Lusterhawk*. But this is life or death. Zura's troops are most likely here to get this sword." Nacen jostled the hilt in his belt for emphasis. "If he gets the sword back, he'll go through with his plans to destroy our fleet with as much of the Unity as he can. We are the only ones standing in his way." Nacen paused as the last of the Armads emerged from the ship into the docking bay and fell silently in line. Chalce formed up with a slow, calculated stride. "We tried diplomacy, and we nearly got blown out into the vacuum for our troubles. You can rest easier knowing it was my brother who delivered the first blow. We shall deliver the last."

"Gloms... Starscum... I got no problem killing soft-skins," Brecca announced, "and neither does my new friend, here."

Nacen glanced to the Stevari to the Armad's right, thinking he meant Lash for a moment, before Brecca cocked the action on his flux shotgun. Soft-skins. That was a new one for Nacen.

The other seven Armads murmured agreement. Beskin stood at attention. Nacen was certain that the druvani would sooner throw himself into the vacuum of space than disobey an order. He was less sure about Camlo, Jeta, and Shukernak. Would they be able to fire on men and women of their own homefleet when the moment came? For that matter, would he? Yes... he had faith in himself that he would do what needed to be done.

"We're with you, Nacen. Wherever you call on us to go." Camlo's rose a half octave when he spoke, and he gripped his carbine tightly.

"I know we can't just surrender your sword, Nacen." Jeta shook her head. "This just... doesn't feel right. No matter what way you spin it."

Shukernak put a gentle hand on her shoulder. He and Nacen met each other's eyes. Nacen left what lay between them unsaid. Like he said in the cargo hold before, Shukernak's past crimes, accidents, whatever they had been... had no bearing on the current situation. The trufalci had proven himself since then, and doubtless would again.

Nacen received a communication from the *Trishula*, but the transmission was silent when he answered. Were they being jammed already? But the enemy ships hadn't even...

A distant blow hammered the hull of the *Trishula*. The faint knock of metal on metal was followed by another strike, then another. After a dozen more knocks in the span of an eye blink, Nacen lost count.

Chapter 19

"Suppress that hallway, I don't want any more getting through!" Nacen shouted over the thunder of pounding boots and distant flux cannon fire. He crouched behind a monolithic repair bot, the same model used in the repairs of the *Canotila* before, which the Armads had turned on its side and dragged into the hallway. This makeshift cover blocked one side of the only entrance into the cargo bay occupied by his ship. The other side of the wide arch was blockaded by five heavy crates. Both were being pelted by pot shots from trufalci in black robes and crimson armor on either end of the hallway.

The corridor outside the docking bay wound around the ship starboard along the outside curved edge, making it difficult to get off any useful long-range fire. Enemy squads had made rapid progress by alternating covering fire against Nacen's makeshift position and darting into the next available cargo space, and so on down the line. Nacen's crew had found their reluctance to fight fellow Stevari had disappeared under the frightening speed and pressure of Zura's assault.

To his right, Camlo took a moment to vent the coils on his plasma carbine. As his squad's suppressive fire waned, three Stag trufalci made a dash for the next bay up, only three bays from the one housing the *Carmine Canotila*. Nacen cursed silently as he resumed his even cadence of pinning plasma fire down the far end of the corridor. Several concussive bangs rang out from the cargo hold, drowning out the thud of three bodies hitting the floor. To make up for the lack of decent firing positions at Nacen's own position, the Armads had moved into the adjacent cargo bays. It seemed that this move suited them fine, as their mass condensers and shotguns were only lethal at close range.

"We need to clear out the bays close by before they get enough troops to launch an assault on our position," Nacen said aloud.

"Agreed," Beskin said.

"Chalce, take your men and move up the other cargo hold. Stay there until further orders," Nacen instructed over the Armads' hard communications link.

"Too risky," Chalce replied. "There's too much fire coming from this corridor that you can't see."

"Basaul is already three bays up on the other side," Nacen countered with a tinge of annoyance. He squeezed in two shots against a sprinting Stevari. Though he appeared to hit, the cloak swirling around the druvani's armor diverted the rounds just enough to turn them into a glancing blow, allowing him to pass into a cargo bay unimpeded. The trufalci following behind him was not so lucky. A well-timed shot to the head from Beskin sent him tumbling to the ground.

"Well I'm not the overseer, and he's not getting pounded by a flux cannon," Chalce grumbled from his position in the adjacent cargo bay.

Nacen closed his eyes for a moment in an effort to stop his patience from hemorrhaging.

"We'll see about providing you some additional firepower," Nacen took a moment to vent his own plasma coils and turned to Shukernak. "How do you feel about paying those Armads a visit and giving them a little pep talk?"

Shukernak ceased his volley of plasma light support gun fire. "Just say the word."

Nacen expected an even distribution of Zura's men around the hull, with a higher concentration at the stern to take out the engines, or perhaps the ventral side to strike at the command center hidden deep in the underbelly of the *Trishula*. But it seemed as if all of the transports that made it past the blink missiles and barrage of flak had landed in or around the docking bays.

"Nacen," Captain Tengrin transmitted over the ship's comm link. "Nacen, can you hear me?"

"Five by five, Florica," Nacen said back. "What's the situation in your end?"

"I've been trying to reach you since the breach. Do not get bogged down in a firefight, do you hear me? Get on that tradeship of yours and get out of here. Fly in a defensive orbit around the *Trishula* until we can get these interlopers out of here. My squadrons will keep the enemy fighters off you. We've already taken out most of their fliers. I will not risk losing you and the sword."

"That's going to be tough considering we're already repelling boarders," Nacen stated boldly. "We're staying here to defend your ship and all the civilians who cannot help themselves."

"What?!" Florica yelped over the communications. "You're in a firefight? Now is not the time to be noble. Leave now. My household troops are attempting to relieve pressure on the docking bays, but I can only do so much. There's an army gathering between my crew and yours. Whatever you're dealing with now is only the beginning."

That gave Nacen pause. Though the breaches were all over the ship, it would make sense they would converge on Nacen's position after they confirmed his location. It was probably only going to intensify from here.

"That's a direct order from your commanding officer."

That settled that, then.

"Will do, thanks for the warning," Nacen chimed back. He fired off a final burst of plasma and lowered his rifle. "Pack it in, 'Nak."

"That's a funny way of saying go," Shukernak said.

"We're moving back to the *Canotila*," Nacen transmitted to the Stevari squad and Armads' comms simultaneously. "Everyone fall back to the ship right now. New orders are to get out of here and do laps around the *Trish* until it's safe to come back."

"Can't do it, Captain," Basaul replied. The Armad's words were reinforced by the pounding of a flux cannon, which sounded much closer than it had just a minute before. Metal shards peppered the cargo bay in front of Nacen where the Armads now cowered. Their ambush point had become a death trap.

"*Kaha*," Nacen swore. "Shukernak, give Basaul and his men covering fire until they can make it back. Beskin and I will cover Shukernak's rear. Camlo, take everyone else back to the ship and get ready for dustoff in two." Nacen swung around to the crates at his rear. Chalce, Hortz, and Perido did not appear to need much convincing. They were already running pell-mell back to the bay. A smattering of flux rounds followed in their wake, but the Armads made it back unscathed. Jeta and Camlo laid down covering fire as the Armads threw themselves over the barricade.

"Finally came to your senses, eh?" Chalce shouldered his mass condenser, not seeing the need to use it anymore.

Nacen gritted his teeth. Until now, he had not considered Chalce a liability, but now his impetuous criticism was bordering on insubordination. He hoped Basaul would set his right hand man straight.

"Orders from above," Nacen explained, taking cover behind a crate as flux rounds whizzed by from the already advancing red and black trufalci.

"Works for me," Chalce shrugged. His tone was cold and distant, even in the buzz of combat.

Jeta and Camlo shared an uneasy glance, then led the Armads back into the bay. At this moment, the high-pitched whirr of Shukernak's plasma support gun filled the air as he saturated the opposing hallway.

"There's too much firepower on our position, Captain!" The relentless pounding of flux rounds on metal nearly drowned out Basaul's shouts completely, even over the comm link.

"Hold on, we'll try to relieve some pressure," Nacen urged.

"Okay," Basaul replied, "but you'd better—"

The Armad's reply was lost in a hail of flux cannon fire.

"Beskin, on my mark we release two plasma grenades down that hallway," Nacen said. "I'll go short and left, you go far and right. Maximum lux."

The druvani nodded in understanding, releasing a grenade from his satchel with his left hand while he continued to lay down suppressive fire to the rear. Nacen felt himself calm slightly as his body's nanites absorbed some of his excess adrenaline. After a moment, he felt his heartbeat slow.

"Now." Nacen dropped his plasma carbine on the crate after firing one last shot down range. He whirled around to the fallen repair bot and, quickly gauging the best trajectory, twisted the top on the plasma grenade and lobbed down the corridor. Beskin's grenade followed in a longer path. They bounced out of sight, their clatter drowned out by the mass of gunfire by Basaul's position.

The grenades detonated, filling the wide corridor with a blinding light and frenetic discharge of plasma arcs. From the residual glare rushed Basaul, followed by Brecca, Kurt, Diat, and Phyl. All five were halfway back to Nacen's position when Zura's troops resumed their curtain of fire. The shots were hastily made, taken on the go as the enemy Stevari rushed up to the next bay. Few connected with the fleeing Armads, and those that made contact did little more than superficial damage. Brecca was the first to round the repair bot, followed by Kurt and Phyl. Nacen turned to pick up his covering fire of the opposite hallway beyond the barricade of crates. As he reached for his rifle, something in the distance caught his eye, and he instinctively dove for the ground, abandoning all plans of retrieving his carbine.

A flash of light filled Nacen's vision and a deafening clang echoed off the crate in front of him. He felt his bones rattle at the impact. There was another flash. The enemy must have set up a heavy weapon in the short time he had taken his eyes off the corridor. He blinked and he could see again. He got his sight back just in time to see Kurt reach the repair bot. Diat followed, but as he dashed around the structure, the flash came again. A massive, hyper-accelerated round punctured his armor and blew clean through his chest. Diat's momentum carried his now lifeless body forward, slamming onto the deck. Nacen stared at the clean, gaping hole in his torso. Only one weapon could leave a mark like that. They were flanked by flux cannons now.

"Back to the ship, we can't hold here anymore!" Basaul shouted.

Nacen felt a tug on his arm. Beskin had both their carbines slung over his shoulder and was helping Nacen to his feet. Nacen staggered up and regained his bearings. He kept low to avoid the devastating flux cannon fire. Their opportunistic barricade was coming apart under the sheer force of the barrage.

"Confirmed, everyone fall back. Stagger your retreat, fire pattern windsong," Nacen ordered over their comm link. "As soon as everyone is on the ship we're getting out of here."

Nacen fired his plasma carbine in long volleys down the hallway as his crew ran. The gun would soon overheat, and the coil might be fried permanently. But this didn't matter, he needed as much firepower as he could get out in this short window of vulnerability. As soon as he got an alert from the carbine, he turned and broke for the hangar. Beskin followed close, the last man to leave the hallway.

Nacen broke into a run in the cargo bay and did not stop when the transmat brought him onto the ship. He narrowly avoided crashing into Basaul as he rounded a corner. He slowed his pace slightly only when he was nearly to the bridge.

"Jeta, what's our status?" he asked through their shared communications. "Is everyone aboard?"

"All crew is now present and accounted for, Captain," Jeta replied. "Except for one Armad, he…"

"Diat. I know. Tell everyone to get strapped in. We're dusting off in less than a minute."

The doors to the bridge whisked open. Linasette was typing frantically at her keyboard display. Diagrams of ship components flew up on the screen and fled almost as soon as they appeared.

"Lina," he said as he settled into his co-pilot seat, "get us out of here. Now. I'll tell Florica to open the bay doors."

The pilot remained silent, typing frantically at her holographic keys.

"What's wrong?" he asked, sensing the pilot's unease.

The typing ceased for a fraction of second. "We can't take off right now."

"What, did someone develop a fear of flying recently? Because I happen to have an acute fear of being shot right now." Nacen's voice raised to a higher volume than he meant it to. If it bothered his pilot, she showed no sign.

"There's something wrong with our engines," Linasette said. Nacen noticed the chill in her voice and felt real panic grip him. He slumped back, stunned.

"What?"

"They just won't start. It could be any one of a thousand things, or more, considering what the *Canotila* has been through in the last few weeks."

"But we repaired them on the *Etrusca* and they worked just fine, then got further repairs just a few hours ago," Nacen said, dumbfounded.

"Yes. Who helped us to complete those, again?"

"Eberwik... and then Zura..." Nacen felt his heart skip a beat. "Oh, *kaha*. It's sabotage."

"That seems likely," Linasette agreed, not losing focus on her task. "If it was a common mechanical issue, our ship's diagnostics would have found it by now."

"Well let's figure it out. I don't believe I need to state the alternatives."

"Jeta and Shukernak are already on hardware inspection."

"Good, the last thing I want to do is report to Captain Tengrin that—"

"Captain Buhari, what are you still doing here?" Florica demanded sharply through their comm link.

Nacen winced before replying. "It's the *Canotila*, Florica, she won't take off. I think we've been sabotaged."

"Zura?"

"Yes, most likely when his crews repaired our ship."

"My trufalci are on their way to relieve you, but they're encountering heavy resistance at starboard. Zura's chief druvani, Manfri, is reportedly leading the assault himself."

"We'll get out, don't worry," Nacen assured the captain of the *Trishula*, though the words sounded hollow in his own ears. Nacen signaled his restraints to unlatch. Swiftly, he wound his way back to the cargo hold. The only thing that puzzled him was why the *Canotila* was able to leave the *Burning Stag* at all, considering Zura's crew made their repairs while they were still aboard. "Everyone except trufalci, exit restraints and prepare to defend the ship. We need to see to some last-minute repairs."

The communications channel was silent. There were no confirmations, begrudging or otherwise. Very strange. Could the sabotage have affected more than just the engines? Nacen frowned as he rounded the last corner into the cargo bay. He saw everyone was already out of their restraints, but something was off. They were silently huddled around the door leading to the engine room.

"What is going on here?" Nacen demanded to anyone who would listen. "Why aren't you armed? Zura's trufalci are at our doorstep." No one so much as glanced at the captain. Nacen shoved himself past a motionless Camlo and squeezed between two Armads. "What is going on here? Did Jeta and 'Nak figure out what was wrong in the engine room?"

"It's not just the engine room where something is wrong, it's the whole damned ship." Nacen instantly recognized Chalce's booming voice. He stepped through the tight corridor and spotted Shukernak on the other side of the small engine room visible from the entrance. The trufalci was deathly still, his gaze locked with something in the corner. He was covered in a sheen of sweat, though the room was kept at a comfortable temperature. He held a flux driver low at waist level.

Chalce spoke again. He was definitely in the engine room with Shukernak and Jeta. "Everyone is content to follow you around, listening as you save us from one problem only to get us in another. We've all been applauding as you march us to our death. Well I've had enough. This is where we start calling the shots, and the first is that you can stay here on this ship. Come on, brothers, join me! We are evenly matched in numbers, and in these close quarters can easily beat these Starscum."

"Chalce, stand down," Basaul ordered from somewhere behind Nacen. His voice wavered, as though he lacked conviction. Like Nacen, he was likely in shock at what he was seeing. Or was he considering Chalce's plea?

"What's your plan here, Chalce? No one is going to join you." Nacen called, trying to fill the small space with authority to cover the uncertainly and fear he felt. "Beskin, Camlo, get out into the cargo bay and defend the *Canotila* by any means necessary. Take Lash and three Armads with you. Bring the bay entrance down if you need to. Linasette can give you additional firepower with the *Canotila*."

Nacen took a hesitant step in the engine room, his hand wrapped tightly around the hilt of Talavaar Bhaganadi. Chalce was wrong about one thing. If it came to his crew versus Chalce and any foolish enough to join him, they would sincerely regret the choice of close quarters in which to mutiny.

"My plan?" Chalce called out. "First, we'll leave you to Zura's wolves out there. Anything he wants to do to you will be fitting punishment enough. Then when the remnants of your fleet are engaged with the Gloms, we'll leave out the back door. They don't have anything against us Armads, at least once we've dissociated with you."

"Sounds like you've been thinking about this for a while." Nacen shifted in the direction of Shukernak's gaze to find Chalce standing in one corner. To Nacen's horror, the Armad had Jeta pinned up against his body with his left arm, her neck caught in the crook of his elbow. The trufalci was gasping for air, her hands gripping Chalce's forearm in a futile act of resistance. Her pleading eyes were wide with fear. In his right arm, Chalce held a flux shotgun. When Nacen entered, the barrel of it shifted from pointing at Shukernak to himself.

"Jeta, are you okay?" Nacen asked slowly. He knew it was a stupid question. He just wanted a response from his crewman, to know desperately that he wasn't too late. Jeta did her best to nod with Chalce's forearm around her throat. Nacen's heartbeat raced, and he gripped the hilt of his phase sword tightly.

"It wasn't supposed to happen this way, you know!" Chalce shouted. "No one was supposed to notice the engine trouble, and you would go down fighting Zura's men!"

So this is what Nacen got from all his dedication to keeping his crew alive. All the sacrifice, and this is how they repaid him. The bile within him grew until he wanted nothing more than to draw his phase blade and run Chalce through. Would it know to pass through Jeta and leave her unharmed while delivering a fatal blow to the Armad? Did it feel his rage?

"Rarely does reality take the course of our desires. It is up to us to adjust to these changes, not reject the path completely." Reciting the ancient Stevari saying calmed Nacen, reigning in his anger even as he tried to induce an effect within Chalce. He loosened his grip on his phase blade and raised his hands in supplication.

"Chalce, what do you plan to do now?" Nacen asked simply but deliberately. He hoped to gain time to consider his next few actions.

"Zura's plan will continue, and we'll get out of here alive. It's a win for everyone." The Armad pointed the wavering tip of his gun at Shukernak, then back at Nacen. "Well, nearly everyone."

"By my plan, I am taking a calculated risk with a comparatively peaceful action, however slim it might be."

"Your naive plots will kill us all the same!" Chalce raised the shotgun ever so slightly.

"What did my brother promise you?" Nacen asked. He took one slow step toward Chalce.

"He promised me nothing but the fruits of his own plan. I act on my own, though it is for the interest of all. Tenfold vengeance against the Unity? A hundredfold? What does it matter knowing that we honored our fallen dead?"

The Armad's life, maybe all of their lives, rested on how he answered Nacen's next demand.

"Tell me what you did to the engine, and go and join my druvani in the bay. Hold off Zura's forces until we can get the engine repaired. It is not too late to redeem yourself."

Nacen heard the unmistakable cracks of flux driver fire outside the ship. How many were his crew up against? How long could they hold?

"Despite what you might think, killing Starkin does not please me," Chalce frowned.

"Then how about saving your fellow Armads?"

"From the peril that I placed them in..." scoffed Chalce.

"One step at a time," Nacen said. "That's all any of us can do, right?"

Chalce opened his mouth as if to speak. He glanced down at the weapon in his hands. Jeta took in a desperate draw of breath as Chalce loosened his grip on her, if only slightly.

"We can start by putting the guns away. Shukernak, can you start?" Nacen asked, directing a calm hand in the trufalci's direction. The man's stance hadn't budged since Nacen had entered.

"The only thing moving is going to be my trigger finger," Shukernak said earnestly, as though imparting some great truth.

"Jeta is going to be okay," Nacen said to the trufalci. "But you have to listen to me. Do you trust me, 'Nak?"

"What?" Shukernak's gaze darted between his captain and Chalce. "But, Jeta..."

"She'll be fine. But you have to trust me. There's a lot of fighting going on out in the bay, Shukernak. I need my heavy weapons specialist out there."

Shukernak gritted his teeth, and with one last hard look at Nacen, lifted his rifle. "Jeta... I, I have to go. The captain said you'll be alright. You will be, right?"

Jeta once again nodded under the strain of Chalce's grip. Shukernak's jaw quivered, and the big trufalci looked as though he might charge at Chalce. Then he turned and stomped out of the engine room.

"There. Already better," Nacen soothed. "Now, what's our next step?"

Chalce lowered the shotgun excruciatingly slowly, as though he might take the motion back and turn the weapon against Nacen at any moment. The captain remained perfectly still, maintaining eye contact with Chalce. Nacen kept his features as neutral as possible. His mounting stress was amplified every few seconds as projectiles ricocheted off the exterior of the *Canotila*.

"Good. Now show us what's wrong with the engine."

Chalce released Jeta, and the trufalci staggered forward, clutching at her throat. She bent over, gasping for air. The Armad dropped his weapon and looked down at his hands.

"Chalce. We're in a hurry." Nacen fingered the hilt of his sword nervously. "What did you do to the engine?"

"It's not the engine, it's the reactor." Chalce shook his head and approached the big, sleek cylinder that dominated the room. He crouched by a junction box at its base and opened up a panel. "I pulled one of the containment rods that regulate power generation and prevent cascades in the reaction, and replaced it with a dud so your system would think they were all in place. Without it, the original reactor won't start."

"You've been planning this for a while," Nacen said grimly.

"Since just after Daedalon Station, in Tantalos, when I first had a moment to familiarize myself with your systems without interference."

"How do I know you didn't just sabotage it in another way? Destroy the ship with a... what did you call it, cascading reaction?"

"If I wanted you dead, I could have done it a dozen ways by now," Chalce uttered in a monotone voice. He finished his work in the panel and shut it gently.

"Then I'll give you what you wanted, a fight. Grab your shotgun, let's go." Nacen jerked his head to the left. Jeta balked.

"You're not seriously..." Jeta swept her arms in a furious arc. "He just nearly killed me, maybe even you! He just admitted it! You can't trust him!"

"If we can't trust each other now, we're all dead anyway," Nacen said.

Jeta eyes' flared and she rose as if to scream at Nacen, but she bit her lip. "Fine. I'm going to stay here and confirm the reactor is fixed. I'll have Lina run diagnostics. If all is well, we could be airborne in a few minutes."

"I'll see that we stay alive until then."

"You'd better." Jeta eyed Chalce as he left. If looks could kill, Chalce's guts would have painted the engine room.

Jeta's frustrated words steeled Nacen with resolve as he followed Chalce out of the room. Had he betrayed his own crew by forgiving Chalce? Was he a fool for giving the Armad a second chance so soon? It seemed to Nacen that he didn't have much of a choice.

Suddenly he became very aware of the weight of the plasma pistol on his right hip. The ship was soon to be fixed. Why not finish the traitor here and limit the risk to the rest of his crew? The short walk back to the hold seemed to drag on for minutes in Nacen's mind. It was moments like this that he hated. The boredom of endless quickspace could be lessened through study or entertainment. Fighting got easier with experience as well. But these decisions where his crew's lives balanced on his own decisions weighed on Nacen's mind. Only the thought of his next steps, the necessity of survival, could break his tormented cycle of uncertainty.

He reminded himself that Chalce need not be left entirely off the hook. He could always confer with Basaul and discuss a reasonable punishment. But *kaha*, what was a reasonable punishment for this?

Chalce picked up a shotgun and lumbered onto the transmat. He looked back at Nacen, and the captain felt as though he was seeing a new face. The man looked Nacen in the eye, not past him. Perhaps for the first time. Chalce said nothing as he disappeared from the hold. With a sigh of exhaustion, Nacen followed him out and the pair materialized below the ship.

Chapter 20

The port side bay of the *Trishula*, which had seemed so empty and calming when Nacen first arrived, had become a hectic place. The previously comforting, undulating light on the walls now served as a disturbing backdrop as muzzle flashes and plasma bursts played across them. Nacen and Chalce dashed quickly forward to take cover behind a large silichrome container. Judging by the thick, black liquid oozing onto the floor out of several punctures, this was a fuel tank. Not an ideal choice.

His crew had fought their way back across the bay and were now nearly to their makeshift position at the entrance. Zura's trufalci in their crimson armor sporadically popped up and took quick shots at Nacen's men from the other side of their former improvised bastion.

"I'm going to group up with Basaul and get in better range," Chalce said.

"Stay with me for now," Nacen said. "Help me get to Camlo. He should be just ahead."

Chalce nodded. Nacen brought up his carbine and snapped off a volley at a trufalci firing at the Armads' position. The trufalci ducked as Nacen's plasma scorched her cover. The Armads took the opportunity to peek out and return fire with shotguns and repeaters.

"Now!" Nacen brought his carbine to his chest and set off at a sprint to his left. He ran left, crouching low, until he spotted Camlo. He didn't stop until he slid down next to his druvani. Chalce crashed down to Camlo's right.

"Good to see you, Nace," Camlo clutched his plasma carbine close. At Chalce, he only stared. "Beskin is about four meters up. He has the explosives. We're keeping Manfri's troops behind cover for now. I think Florica's men finally caught them from behind. It's only a matter of time before they group up for an attack or bring some heavy weapons to bear, though."

"Good. Keep me covered while I move up to Beskin." Nacen peeked up over the barricade. The trufalci continued their game of cat and mouse with the Armads, neither side committing to an engagement. It seemed that Camlo's assessment was correct: the enemy Stevari were indeed holding back until they received reinforcements in the form of heavy weapons or more bodies. There was a very limited window in which Nacen could strike, if at all. He nodded back at Camlo, who readied his carbine.

This time, the trufalci were ready. Their flux rounds nipped at Nacen's heels as he, Chalce, and Camlo bounded across the hangar to Beskin's position. Behind him, Chalce cried out. When the pair reached the druvani, Chalce was holding his left shoulder. Dark blood seeped through his fingers.

"I'll be alright," he said.

"We'll patch you back up when we get back to the *Canotila*," Nacen promised. "Beskin, status report. Transmit to Basaul's crew as well."

"Right. We used all of our high-density chemical explosives getting out of the *Etrusca*." Beskin opened up a black satchel at his waist. "However, we still had a few fairly high-yield plasma charges. These are the last ones we've got, so we need to make them count. A hot burn could bring down that arch. Or at least give us some more time to retreat."

"Good work. Make it happen," Nacen replied. "Let's get the Armads to move up with us so we can plant the charges. Camlo, stay here and provide covering fire."

Camlo opened to his mouth to protest.

"Your role is just as critical as ours. Beskin, Chalce, and I won't make it without suppressive fire from multiple angles."

"Chalce?" Basaul asked over the comms, sounding genuinely perplexed. "You let him out of the engine room alive?"

"Yes, he stated his willingness to work with us and helped fix the issue," Nacen said defensively. "Is that a problem?"

A moment of silence hung between them.

"That will remain to be seen," Basaul stated simply. "We'll hold our current positions and keep the *Stag* soldiers pinned until you move up."

"Hold on, Basaul, Lina is trying to reach me," Nacen said apologetically.

"Nacen, I have an update," Linasette announced in Nacen's earpiece.

"Can it wait for when my brother is not trying to kill me?" Nacen peeked around the corner and fired on Manfri's barricade. There were definitely more trufalci there now than the last time he checked.

"Afraid not. The Precept ships are nearly here. One third of their fleet is headed to Dagon. I estimate we have nineteen minutes until we are in their maximum threat range and they fire missiles. The remaining ships are staying put around the quickspace passage."

"No, no, no," Nacen stammered aloud. "This is far too soon."

He couldn't believe it, or at least didn't want to accept it. The plan was already unraveling before his eyes.

"Want to bring us up to speed?" Beskin asked with a raised eyebrow.

"Just more people coming to kill us," Nacen said hotly.

"I could have guessed."

Nacen nodded. "We need to escalate our plans." The captain jumped on the Armad's comm link. "Basaul, the U.P. is moving into engagement range. We need to end this now. Deploy all of your grenades and let's get these charges planted. Send two of your men right. My druvani and I will take out the left side of the arch. I will send Chalce to you with the explosives."

Nacen split the charges into two clutches of plasma bombs. Half he left in the satchel Beskin had given him, which he slung around his shoulders. The other half he gave to Chalce, who took them gingerly in his big hands. Nacen stood to fire upon the barricade again, but a flash of light caused him to shrink back down immediately. The whine of a plasma light support gun filled the room. Curses and exclamations from the Armads flooded the communications link. Correction, two plasma light support guns.

"Get ready to lob grenades," Nacen transmitted to the entire crew. "We go on three. One, two..."

A shot thundered out from behind the barricade, and a ghostly trail of white smoke streaked across the bay. A tremendous explosion shook the hangar, and Nacen felt a blast of heat from behind. He glanced behind and saw a maelstrom of debris flying from the *Canotila*.

"They're moving up!" Beskin warned. He leaned out from behind the crate and fired on a target Nacen couldn't see.

"Nacen, I can survive maybe one more of those rockets. A bad hit, and the Canotila is done for," Linasette urged in his ear. "You and the crew need to make it back here now."

"I can't without bringing down this arch, or they'll just hit you again before we leave!"

"Remember that trust thing we talked about? Trust me. We need to leave right now. Jeta is nearly done patching the reactor. Your Armad friend really did a number on it."

"He's not my—"

Nacen felt a tug around his shoulders. He pulled away but was knocked to the ground. He looked up, ready to meet his end at the barrel of a flux driver. Instead he saw Chalce standing over, gripping Nacen's satchel bag. He stood with all of their remaining charges.

"What are you doing?" Nacen blurted.

"New plan." Chalce took off running.

"*Kaha!*" Nacen shouted. "What is he doing? Cover fire, give him covering fire, he's got the charges!"

"Filthy traitor!" Basaul roared over the earpiece, not that Nacen needed its assistance to hear him. At his lead, the Armads hurled their grenades at the barricade. Some fell short and obscured the space in front with shrapnel, forcing the trufalci down. Two made it over, wreaking unknown havoc behind the makeshift fortification. Still Chalce ran headlong into the acrid smoke and enemy gunfire. The plasma light supports had been too concerned with the Armads' position, and Nacen got a clean view of the leftmost gun. He placed the gunner's head in his sights and fired. There was a brief flash of light and burst of crimson, and then the gun fell silent.

"Where is Chalce?" Nacen cried over the comm link. "We need to get those charges planted and get back to the ship!"

Nacen thought he saw an Armad by the barricades, but there was too much intervening fire, as well as debris kicked up from the grenades. Smoke still billowed in from behind him from the initial rocket that had struck at his ship. Too much time had passed. Chalce had doomed them all.

"Everyone back to the ship now!" Nacen ordered. "Split into your designated pairs and fall back, deergallop formation!"

Nacen saw the obscured bodies of two charging Stevari fall near the barricade. He fired his plasma carbine at a misty shape and that made the count three. More appeared every second. Nacen heard a flurry of flux repeater shots over the din by the barricades. He realized that Chalce was still alive.

He realized what Chalce meant to do.

"Down! Everyone!" Nacen flung himself by the nearest crate and jammed his eyes shut. He hoped everyone else had the sense or blind obedience to do the same. The back of Nacen's eyelids flared red as dazzling light filled the bay and tremors rocked the floor. The pressure wave felt like a small building had collapsed on him, even from a dozen meters away. The aftermath of the enormous plasma burst was punctuated by the miserable screams of those unfortunate to get caught near the blast but not instantly incinerated. Nacen forced himself to his feet and stumbled into a sprint to the ship. He did not look back.

Chapter 21

The hollow shells of Zura's boarding craft covered the hull of the *Trishula* like barnacles on an old galleon. Nacen leaned back, trying his best to enjoy the view from the relative safety of the *Carmine Canotila's* flight path around the ship. He had never thought his command chair had felt more comfortable than it did as he looked out at Florica's ship from his own position at the starboard side. Still, he could not shake the guilt at abandoning the Stevari of the *Trishula* to Zura's invaders.

"Continue our present evasion course, nothing fancy," Nacen instructed his pilot. He leaned against his seat, tapping his finger while eyeing the outline of the *Trishula* for any movement. "Keep us out of sight of the *Burning Stag* when possible. If I never lay eyes on Zura's ship again, it will be too soon."

The downside of the presently safe position in the shadow of the *Trishula's* starboard side was that it afforded a clear view of the distant but rapidly approaching Union Precept navy bearing down on the homefleet. The vast emptiness of space felt a lot more crowded now.

"Eight minutes until we are in maximum threat range of Union Precept, Captain," Linasette chimed.

"Thank you," Nacen said solemnly. He turned his attention to Lina's displays and the Precept fleet. They had nine battleships to Florica's two worldships, four if they could still count Tosque and Belim's support. The worldship *Asura* could have dwarfed any of the craft, but his father's ship was doing nobody any good on the roiling surface of Carnizad. In addition, the U.P. had seventeen cruisers, roughly one hundred frigates, and an unknown number of strike craft. "How long does that give us until first impact?"

"It will take roughly two minutes, thirty seconds for their missiles to reach us from max threat range, a bit longer for projectiles."

"Suspect the worst and hope for the best," Nacen said, mimicking something he had heard from Beskin. Or had he heard it from Medios? "Let's see if we can improve on that. Has Captain Tengrin responded to our requests?"

"No. She appears to be jammed again."

"Apparently Chalce's sacrifice wasn't the coup de grace we could have hoped for."

"Likewise, Zura is not responding to our transmissions," Linasette noted. "Perhaps Captain Tengrin has managed to jam him back?"

"The only thing jamming him is the stick up his own ass," Nacen exhaled and ceased his idle tapping on his vambrace. "Put us through to Captain Medios. We may as well group up in case Zura tries something even more desperate."

"On it." Linasette tapped at her holographic keys like they might disappear at any moment. "The *Faith Immutable* has been hailed."

Nacen stared at the screen ahead, but he no longer saw the physical ships there. He saw only the *Trishula's* hangar bay in his mind's eye, filled with fire and smoke and blood. Two more of his crew had died to get them out of that crisis. What had Nacen given them in return? One more deadlock in which to perish. What was it all for? Had Chalce's words finally got to him?

"We're receiving a signal," Linasette said.

"Patch Medios through. Thanks." Nacen blinked hard and took a seat.

"It is not Captain Medios, it is Danior Tosque of the *Wayfarer*."

"Interesting..." Nacen raised an eyebrow and the transmission opened, but no video came through. Either Tosque preferred to project his voice exclusively, or the man had something to hide. He supposed one did not preclude the other.

"Ah, Captain Buhari, the err... Younger. It is about time we spoke. I've got Zura blathering away about launching another brazen attack on our own forces, by whom I mean yourself and Captain Tengrin, meanwhile I am simply trying to prepare my ship for battle with the enemy navy. Captain Belim is nearly daft enough to go through with Zura's plan and attack Captain Leander Medios. Can you imagine? A boarding action on the *Faith Immutable*? Medios has been at the helm longer than Belim has been sucking air. Even his best haven't half the experience of the majority of Medio's trufalci."

Nacen and Linasette shared a puzzled look.

"Where does that leave us?" Nacen asked.

"Don't play coy with me. You are a Buhari after all," Tosque drawled. "Come now. What are your terms, man?"

"Terms?"

"You're going to make me say it then, are you?" Captain Tosque muttered. His dejection was plain even with the audio feed alone.

"Say what?"

"Very well. I, Danior Tosque, captain of the *Wayfarer*, do hereby formally surrender to you, Captain Buhari the Younger. There, is that what you wanted?"

"Uh... yes? Thank you for your formal declaration," Nacen said at last, trying to force a little conviction into the words. They were never formally involved in any conflict, as far as Nacen knew. "Let us join forces and enact Captain Tengrin's plan. Nothing has changed, except for the exclusion of the *Burning Stag*."

"Ah yes, our brazen offensive on the Precept navy. We are ready to proceed. I take it this was the cause of the rift between you and the current steya?"

"At least in part, yes," Nacen said. "Regardless, his actions have shown where his allegiances lie, and they are not with the people."

"Not to worry, my boy, not to worry! I shall marshal my forces and inform Captain Belim of the change in leadership."

Nacen jumped in before Danior could utter another syllable. "I am in your debt, Captain Tosque, thank you, but please let me inform Captain Belim." Nacen didn't want Belim getting the wrong idea from any of Tosque's embellishments, but also couldn't risk being jammed again.

"Leading from the frontlines, eh? Very good, very good... perhaps I was too hasty in my judgment of you. Tosque out."

Nacen could have jumped out of his seat and danced back to the cargo. The support of Tosque was a huge shift in their favor, and bringing Belim into the fold would effectively make Florica and himself commanders of the homefleet for now.

"Do we have contact with the *Trishula*?" Nacen asked.

"I am afraid not," Linasette replied. "Your brother is still jamming their signal. We would not have been able to speak with the *Wayfarer* had Tosque not initiated contact with us first."

Nacen supposed that even if they lost the *Trishula*, the plan would have to move forward.

"So we cannot speak to the *Nivasi*, either?"

"Correct."

Nacen folded his hands in front of his face. Hopefully Tosque would spread the word to Belim. He realized there was one more captain he needed to speak with.

"Put us in contact with the *Burning Stag*. Let's try this one more time."

"I don't know what you're planning, but good luck," Linasette said.

"Thank you," Nacen replied, grinning to himself. Danior Tosque had given him an idea.

"Nacen?" Zura sneered his brother's name as he appeared on screen in his white cloak. He was standing in his usual place at the helm of the *Burning Stag*. Behind him, purple banners lay still against gleaming walls. "Congratulations. I see you're still alive. Contrary to what you may think, I don't want to kill you. Have you come to your senses at last?"

"Yes, I have," Nacen said. "I surrender, brother."

The smug look on Zura's face was just as infuriating as Nacen had imagined.

"I cannot say I'm surprised," Zura preened. "I see you and your band of rogues were put in your place by my cunning surprise attack. Even now, my druvani Manfri closes the noose around your traitor captain's throat."

"I do not wish to see any more bloodshed. In fact, I never should have thrown out your plan," Nacen put all of his bountiful supply of sorrow and regret into the words, though this was not the true source. Indeed, he was sorry. Sorry he had not run Zura through with the phase sword the moment he had pulled it free, and had the captains swear fealty to him then and there.

"I see you have at last given in to reason during your inevitable defeat. Though my foe's demise is quickly approaching, there is still time for me to dispense justice. I shall have Manfri execute Florica Tengrin on her own bridge. In this, your fault in what occurred here may be forgiven, should you wish it." Zura spat out these last words, the venom in them belying any compassion. Forgiveness by his brother seemed as though it could just as easily mean a flux slug to the back of the head.

"You are merciful, dear brother," Nacen said.

Zura appeared taken aback by the praise. He stared long and hard at Nacen, until at last he abandoned his scrutiny and began pacing the high platform at the center of the bridge of the *Burning Stag*. "Naturally, I cannot allow you to maintain possession of Talavaar Bhaganadi. Come back to the *Stag*, and return it to its rightful heir. I shall lead the assault on the poles of Dagon to unleash the Void Protocol personally. You may command the last stand of the homefleet while Manfri oversees the planetary bombardment."

"As you command." Nacen bowed his head. "Please, allow me to serve to my greatest potential. Permit me to speak with Captain Tengrin. I may be able to persuade her to stand down and spare our house of yet more pointless bloodshed."

"Granted. If you get her to surrender, perhaps I shall spare her life. I make no promises, however."

"I shall do my best."

"Don't do your best, that will not suffice. Do *my* best," Zura straightened and pulled his white raiment about his shoulders. The scene flicked off.

Nacen grimaced and stood. He had to act quickly if all the pieces were to fit in place before the Unity's arrival.

"Get me through to Captain Tengrin," he ordered. "Make sure it is on a secure, direct channel if you can."

"No response still, Nacen," the pilot reported after a flurry of tapping.

Kaha. It appeared as though Nacen would have to go ahead with the plan without Florica. He was still up a worldship but did not know how dependable they would be when the going got perilous.

"Hold on, we are picking up something," Linasette said. "It is faint, but I can patch it through."

"Come in, come in! *Gaad mayn danda...*" A weak voice came in over the transmission.

"I hear you," Nacen bolted upright in his seat. "This is Nacen Buhari of the *Carmine Canotila*. To whom do I have the pleasure in assuming is still alive?"

"Florica Tengrin, no thanks to you," Florica said, levity faint but detectable in her voice. "Glad to see you're still buzzing around too, Nacen. We managed to repel the attack on the bridge. I have combat capability on the *Trishula* again, at least for now."

"What's going on with Manfri's forces? Have you defeated them? We must have killed a fair amount in that blast."

"That was you? I'm relieved. I thought for sure Manfri had destroyed your ship. He is still very much alive and wreaking havoc. Zura's boarding teams are currently moving toward my aft reactors. If they get there... Well, then so much for the final assault."

"Now I do have some good news on that front. Tosque and Belim are officially back on our side."

"Really? That is fantastic. Not that I doubted you. However, I'm operating without sensors right now... Don't ask. How much time do you think we'll have until the Unity reacts to what's been going on?"

"They'll be here in under five minutes."

Nacen heard a stifled yelp over the transmission. Nacen waited patiently for a response.

"That is... less than ideal," Florica said slowly. "Take up a defensive position at the stern of my ship. Captain Belim and Captain Tosque should form up with us along with Medios. Only Zura stands apart now. Maybe he will come to our side as well."

"I wouldn't count on it. He thinks we are all on his side right now, and that you are about to surrender to me."

There was another pause.

"What did you do?" anxiety strained Florica's voice.

"I had to promise a few things to open this channel of communication. You have nothing to worry about. Except for half of the Precept navy, of course."

Nacen waited for a reply that never came. Perhaps Manfri had taken the bridge after all, he thought with a pang of fear. Nacen's worry diminished some when he checked the display. The *Trishula* was still intact. On the screen to Linasette's left, he saw *Faith Immutable*, *Wayfarer*, and *Nivasi* moving into position behind Florica's worldship.

"I was a fool to think you would obey me, brother," Zura's voice sounded from all around. Nacen slammed back in his seat. How was Zura forcing communications? Had he hijacked Florica's encrypted channel? "When Manfri has overtaken the *Trishula*, I will see to it he turns its weapons against you. Being destroyed by your ally's weapons will be a suitable fate for a traitor such as yourself, though far too quick."

"It's not too late to join us, Zura." Nacen did not plead with his brother but merely stated the offer. "Help assist in the fleet's survival."

"Neither of our plans ends in survival. We have no place in this universe anymore. Do you not understand that yet?" Zura no longer sounded angry, nor even desperate. His voice was hollow with a tired resignation. "The more of quickspace we discover, the more trade we set up, the bigger the empires get and the more they push back. Did you know the Unity actually wishes for peace? When I first arrived at Fomalhaut, I negotiated with the governor of Dagon for our safe escape. But the admiral leading the Precept fleet won't listen. She wants us destroyed and is pulling rank. I will at least accomplish something before I bow out. But you wouldn't know anything of accomplishment, would y—"

"Hold on, I'm going to put you on line three," Linasette said. In a moment, the transmission from the *Burning Stag* was cut.

"Thank you," Nacen sighed.

"My pleasure."

"Alright. Take us up behind the stern of the *Trishula*, Lina," Nacen said. "Maintain that position until the breach is made in the enemy flagship."

"I never thought I would see the inside of a Precept battleship again," the pilot said somewhat longingly.

Before them, somewhere in the pervading darkness of space, the Union Precept fleet approached. Nacen was surprised he could not see the telltale signs of the ships as the Precept navy drew in, less than a minute to engagement now. Then he remembered that the trails of more than one hundred ships would not be visible from the front, as every single one was moving directly at him. At the head of this massive fleet lay his quarry, the ship that could hopefully do the most damage by propagating the Void Protocol.

"Alright, I need to get strapped in with the crew. Let me know if there are any urgent updates, Lina. Good work here." Nacen stood and turned to leave.

"Nacen, wait," Linasette said, rising from her chair in turn.

He turned, not knowing what to expect. Linasette walked toward him. He braced for... he knew not. But then she was walking past him, opening one of the large cabinets in the rear of the small bridge. There were various tools and replacement parts for items on the bridge, Nacen knew, but not much else.

"I really do need to—"

"I hope you don't mind, but I took a resonance scan of your sword earlier when you allowed me to hold it," Linasette said, still elbow deep in the compartment.

"That's what I get for showing off," Nacen said with a smile.

Linasette ignored him, continuing to rummage. At last she emerged, holding something... green. A deep, emerald green.

It was some sort of long object roughly a meter long. Was it some sort of case? It had a dull gray tip, and pale gold trim at the opposite end.

"It is the best I could do under the circumstances," Linasette said, not looking up from the object. "I had the ship's portable artificer print it out of pyrolytic timbrace. It's the closest thing we have to wood around here. It is wrapped in some emerald fabric I had lying around."

Nacen recognized the object now. This was a scabbard, a sheath for Talavaar Bhaganadi. The pilot had the ship manufacture a makeshift scabbard to the specifications of his sword. Linasette thrust the object forward. Nacen took it gently. She had done exquisite work with what little time and materials she had to work with. The emerald fabric... he knew he had seen that before. Yes, it was her dress. The one Lina had worn on the *Etrusca*.

"Lina, this is beautiful," Nacen muttered at last. He began affixing the scabbard to his combat belt. He held back a comment about the cloth looking better on her out of politeness. This was not the time.

"Yes, well... we cannot have you go stabbing yourself in the leg by accident."

Nacen gave the sheath a tug, and it remained in place. Carefully, he tilted the sword back and slid it home. It made no sound as the hilt came to rest at the mouth of the scabbard.

"Again, thank you Lina. For this gift, for your service, for everything." Nacen shifted to go.

"This is not the last time we will be seeing each other," Lina said.

Nacen smiled and nodded. He desperately wanted to believe that.

Chapter 22

As his restraints tightened around him, Nacen felt a compulsion to unleash them and go to the bridge, to be side by side with Linasette and watch the plan unfold. He wished dearly to be able to sit back and issue commands from his safe perch where he could be above the action, not lost within it.

But Talavaar Bhaganadi had chosen him. Or had his father chosen him? Nacen supposed the distinction didn't matter anymore. He possessed the phase sword, latent with the barely understood powers gifted from the Colonies of Xandra, if Zura was to be believed, and it was up to him to see it through. Nacen did not feel as though he was commanding a small fleet of worldships. It seemed to him that his crew had gotten just a bit bigger. He wasn't sure he could lead an entire fleet. But he might be able to see his crew to safety.

"Two minutes until we are inside Precept engagement range, Nacen," Linasette said through the captain's earpiece.

"Thank you, Lina," Nacen replied. "Keep in touch."

"I've got a communication here, Nace. Patching it through to you now."

Nacen girded himself to weather another round of insults.

"Greetings, Buhari the Younger," an uneasy voice began. Nacen recognized it belonging to Timbo Belim. "We're close enough for short-range transmissions now. Zura cannot hope to jam all of our communications if he wants to maintain position by the planet. I have been informed you survived the steya's attempts to subdue you. Congratulations."

Nacen smiled to himself. "Captain Belim, I am pleased to have you join us in what I hope to call our finest hour."

"You mean final hour," Timbo Belim corrected. "Danior Tosque informed me Zura would likely not be joining us. I reluctantly accept, seeing as though there are few options open to me."

"Inadvertently or not, know that you have made a wise choice. The *Trishula* and the *Faith Immutable* will lead the assault. *Nivasi*, you will flank to the left and *Wayfarer* to the right. All directions are relative to the *Trishula's* bow. The primary goal is to breach the target's hull and get as many troops in as possible. Save the transports and your strike craft until the last possible second to bypass the point defense systems."

"And our target?" Danior Tosque asked expectantly. Apparently he had hopped on at some point.

"The lead battleship: the flagship *Exemplar*."

"You could have led with that," Timbo noted gruffly.

"Think of it as another opportunity to prove yourself, Captain Belim. Just follow our lead and stick to the plan," Leander said.

Nacen hunched in his seat for a few moments, gathering his thoughts. It was too late to make any intricate changes. The plan was solid, and simple, and adaptable if need be. All that was necessary now was the courage to see it through. Not to mention this secret weapon functioning as intended, and a lot of luck. He took a calming breath, then transmitted to his crew on the *Carmine Canotila*.

"The forces that make up the Union Precept navy are fierce and deter-mined. They are descended from the ancient empires of old Earth who united under necessity to cease their eternal conflicts and instead turn their tireless efforts to the conquering of the great void. But in their innumerable victories, they have also known defeat and dishonor. Today we shall add another tally to that list. Unlike them, we do not fight for duty or honor. We fight to preserve our families, our very way of life. By their gods and ours, I swear that they shall break upon our bows, and we shall ride the waves of the great blue sun once more."

A second passed, and the cargo hold erupted in whooping and ap-plause. A new message came in over the *Canotila's* speakers.

"Fine words, Captain," Danior said jovially. "Fine words to go out on indeed. Rather took the wind out of my solar sails, actually."

"Seconded," Florica added.

"How did you..." Nacen began, confused as to why the captains were responding to his extemporized speech to the crew.

"Apologies, Captain," Linasette said. "When you started your speech, I took the liberty of expanding the transmission to the rest of the fleet."

"I could have you hanged for that, Lina." In his stifling embarrassment, he was unsure whether or not he was joking.

"My court martial will have to wait. We have entered engagement range. Enemy missiles inbound," Linasette said over the speakers in the cargo hold. "Most of them are targeting the vanguard of our attack: the *Faith Im-mutable* and the *Trishula*."

"Wanna put odds on whether we make it or not?" Brecca said. His shaky voice did not instill much confidence in the former outcome.

Shukernak peered around the plasma support gun he held vertically between his legs. "Forty to one says we make it."

"Forty to one?" Brecca exclaimed. "You're on."

Shukernak nodded contentedly, then patted the spherical drone locked into the storage rack above his seat. "Feel free to collect from the U.P. if I lose. You know, when we don't make it."

The cargo hold filled with nervous laughter as Brecca's face fell.

"First wave has impacted," Linasette reported over the cargo hold speakers. "Our vanguard ships repelled most of them, but the Union Precept is bringing a lot more firepower to bear."

Nacen fought the urge to go back and view bridge displays with Lina. He could confess his feelings toward her. Well, he didn't know exactly how he felt. But admitting there was something there was a start. Maybe she felt it too. Felt there was something worth exploring. There was no going back now, though, and no changing the plan. These fleeting impulses would have to wait.

"Third missile barrage is under way, and second barrage is imminent. We will be in range of projectiles soon. Everyone be sure pan-atmo masks are secure. The cargo hold will not have much oxygen after we breach it with twenty King Oxen transports."

The crew sat in silence, eyes fixed down to the floor or up at the ceiling. Like grim mannequins, their bodies were braced perfectly still. Nacen stared at the cargo bay ramp as though he could spot the first tear in the hull, the first weak spot in the repairs that would fail and suck them all into oblivion. Here they sat locked in anticipation. He heard a few light pelts of metal on metal. The enemy's flak was on them now, but the *Carmine Canotila* would be mostly shielded by the *Trishula*. They were close.

"Thirty seconds until contact," Linasette said. Nacen didn't care whether it was good news or bad news. Her voice was soothing to him. It gave him something to focus on other than the enemy fire, than his own ignorance of the dangers that awaited. He began to hum quietly to himself. The missiles sped onward toward them in the vacuum. Point defense fire fell on them like a rainstorm now. But nearly as soon as the barrage had started, it was over. The Armads glanced around as though expecting an answer to appear in the hold.

"We're in. Starboard hangar bay of the *Exemplar*," Linasette reported. "Sixty-five percent of the transports made it through."

Nacen's restraints flung themselves loose. He stood and unshouldered his plasma carbine.

"We only got two thirds through? What happened?" He couldn't help a twinge of panic seeping into his voice. Two thirds left the entire attack force with no more than four hundred souls, at best. Their sparse data on the *Exemplar* puts its crew between two and three thousand. Even with only a portion of that number capable of actual combat, the Stevari were monstrously outnumbered in addition to being on the offense in a hostile environment.

"We took minimal casualties from point defenses, but..." Linasette gave a long pause. "The *Nivasi* didn't make it. The third barrage redirected all of its firepower at the worldship when the U.P. realized we were going to close the distance."

"We lost the *Nivasi*?" Nacen was frozen in place. "There were over two-thousand Stevari onboard, most of them civilians."

"Still, at least we made it." A relieved Brecca strapped his shotgun to his hip and picked up his weapon from its rack above his seat.

"I'll take my winnings in money or drinks," Shukernak said, hefting his plasma support gun by himself. His utility drone, Betty, hovered below the barrel to provide the necessary lift to assist the trufalci.

"Okay, you all know the first step," Nacen said, shaking off his shock. The beginning was no time to panic. "Secure the landing zone. Lina will use the transmat to send pairs of us out to where we need to be. Beskin and I are up first. Shukernak, activate the assault drones and assign them to follow your position, ten meters behind and sticking to cover."

"Aw shucks, Captain, thanks. Betty always wanted some friends."

"Everyone else grab one nanite grenade." Nacen gestured to the crate in the corner. "There are enough for the druvani and Jeta to have two."

"Nace, I should go with you too," Camlo insisted.

"Sorry, Cam, we go in pairs. You're needed to give Shukernak cover so he can get in position with the plasma light support."

"Fine." Camlo lowered his eyes. "Err... yes, Captain."

Nacen turned and stepped onto the lighted pad in the aft end of the cargo hold. Beskin followed suit, looking straight ahead.

"Ready, Lina," Nacen said over their communications.

With a bright flash of light, Nacen found himself behind a King Oxen. The curved transport's stern contained many thrusters that the troop transport could use to accelerate at high speeds. The hull had been badly scorched in areas and chipped away in others where the matte black finish had been scraped away. Nacen peered around and saw that the object that had stopped the transport was a Union Precept bomber. The King Oxen's hull-breaching plasma cutters had deployed into the bomber's hull and burned through the side, and its momentum had flipped the bomber completely over. A motion caught Nacen's eye and he brought his carbine to bear. Thirty meters down the hangar, a lance trooper was making a run to a ship. Nacen took aim and brought the soldier down with two well-placed shots.

It was difficult to tell where the front of the firefight was in the crowded hangar bay, if there existed a discrete battle line at all. Across the bay, a ship went up in a roiling ball of plasma and smoke. The deluge was quickly snuffed out in the near vacuum of the hangar. Nacen continued to meander between the ships toward the opposite end of the breach, scouting for targets. Suddenly he found himself face to face with a pilot. The man was unarmed. Nacen shoved his carbine to the young man's chest.

"Down on the ground, hands behind your back," Nacen ordered. His eyes scanned behind the man for other potential enemies. When he looked back down, the man stared back with blue eyes. Nacen was about to bark the order again when he noticed a hole in the pilot's sage green vac suit that hadn't been there a moment ago. The pilot crumpled as two trufalci in crimson armor rushed past.

"For the *Nivasi!*" one shouted.

"Remember Carnizad!" someone echoed in the distance.

Nacen turned to Beskin and frowned. But there was no use in attempting to discipline these men, not now at least. These were Captain Leander Medios' devout troops, plain enough from both their fervor and heavily reinforced crimson armor. After all, these Unies were the enemy, unarmed or not, and that pilot could have been deadly in a cockpit. Still, Nacen felt his stomach drop as he stepped over the pilot's body.

Nacen and Beskin dashed from ship to ship as quickly as they dared, but the battle moved faster still. The Stevari were tearing a righteous path through the hangar bay. It was all Nacen could do to keep up. At last the labyrinthine rows of strike craft ended, and Nacen could make out a group of crimson-clad figures on a large gantry running the length of the far wall. There were perhaps two dozen in all. Behind them lay four large doors. Nacen hurried up the stairs. From the raised elevation, he could make out the occasional pocket of resistance by occasional flashes of plasma beams and the ricochet of flux rounds off of metal.

"All crew of the *Canotila*, make your way to my position. The hangar is secure." Nacen addressed his squad via their shared short-range comms.

"Maybe where you're at!" Shukernak belted.

"Very well. Secure your areas and converge on my location when you can. I want to move out at the first available opportunity."

The druvani addressing the others stopped as Nacen requested to join his encrypted channel.

"Sorry. Officers only," he said through a single target comm burst. Then the druvani glanced down to the sword hilt at Nacen's waist. "Apologies, sir. You must be the Little Captain."

"Yes, I... I'm sorry, the little what?" Nacen said incredulously.

"The... uh, I'm sorry, I thought you knew. Captain Tosque has been referring to you as the Little Captain to avoid confusion with the other Captain Buhari, your older br—"

"Of course he has. Fine, fine, but call me Nacen when I'm around."

"Yes... sir. I'm Druvani Patrin, of Captain Medios's third company."

"A pleasure," Nacen said with a brief flourish. "Listen, Patrin. We don't have long before the Unies retaliate. I recommend we split into our designated teams now. Medios's troops will assault the munitions storage as a diversion. Tosque's will stay here and clean up the landing zone and defend it until we can return. Florica's contingent will accompany me into the heart of the ship."

"Respectfully, sir," Patrin's voice dwindled. "All of Captain Tengrin's troops are fighting for their lives on the *Trishula*. From what I hear, the fight isn't going well."

"*Kaha*. Split Tosque's forces in two, then. Send his best with me."

"But sir, our mission won't be any good if there's not a secure landing zone to return to."

"Well, this is all for naught if I can't get to the control room," Nacen's tone deepened. "If you need reinforcements to defend the breach, ask Captain Medios if he can spare any more. But I need the main attack to appear to be grouping on the munitions, so as to keep our way as clear as possible."

"Very good," Patrin replied with a hard edge to his voice. The druvani still sounded displeased, but that couldn't be helped. "I will relay the orders to the officers. The munitions assault team will gather here. Those going into the ship interior led by the Little... yourself can gather at the entrance forty meters to port. I will have Tosque's lead druvani meet you there."

"And the worldships?" Nacen began. "Are they able to maintain their position?"

"Aye, sir," replied Patrin. "They are weaving between Precept formations to avoid direct combat, clearing point defense systems, and keeping enemy reinforcements out of the breach."

"Good. Thank you, druvani. Keep this channel open to me in the future."

Nacen gave the symbol of Drovina across his chest, then turned to go down the gantry. He saw that some semblance of order had started to form in the ravaged hangar bay. Small groups of trufalci began to drift through the wreckage of ships that were no longer able to burn, most of the oxygen having been sucked out of the breach. No more gunfire sounded in the hangar. Nacen walked against the tide of red impact armor and faceless helmets toward the port side of the bay. He brought up a display of the ship's schematics on the small screen of his digital pad. They had a long way to go to reach central control.

A blur of motion caught Nacen's eye and he whirled in place to meet it, bringing his plasma carbine to bear.

"Woah, hold on there!" Basaul thundered as he came to a dead halt. "You said to converge on your location. So, here we are."

Behind him stood his five remaining Armads. Each gripped in their hands the stout flux shotguns of the *Etrusca* but had slung on their backs an array of flux drivers and repeaters. Nacen was surprised to see them all covered in soot and scorch marks.

"Apologies. I was observing the ship layout." Nacen closed out of the schematics and placed the pad at his hip, protected by his cloak. "I didn't realize combat had been so heavy in the bay. I saw very little action," Nacen admitted, almost bashfully.

"We made sure we found it," Hortz said. His face and arms were covered in black ash, and he made no effort to wipe it off.

"Had an interesting little run-in with a Glom engineering crew," Brecca added with a wry grin.

"Well, they did most of the running. Didn't get very far though." Hortz added. This brought forth a short chorus of laughter from the Armads.

They made their way to the rendezvous point, and Nacen ignored their tasteless banter. The carnage of King Oxen strewn among overturned crates and smashed bombers soon made way to orderly rows of Precept fighter craft. The ships were thin, far too thin to contain a pilot. The spindle of a hull was packed around with racks of missiles. Three thrusters protruded from one end of the sleek craft. Nacen recognized these as Javelins, the dart-like ships that had pursued the *Lusterhawk* out of Daedalon Station.

As they approached the end of the bay, Nacen spotted the rest of his crew. Camlo, Jeta, and Shukernak were lounging on a Precept jetbike. Lash stood nearby surveying the damage in the hangar and waved as Nacen approached. Camlo quickly scrambled up to attention. Jeta and Shukernak continued whatever conversation they felt was more necessary than ranking up. As if to reinforce Nacen's displeasure at the scene, Shukernak whipped his head back and heaved his shoulders, apparently roaring in delight at some remark from Jeta. In contrast, Tosque's men and women had ordered themselves neatly into three rows. They bore light gray impact armor, an older and more rigid design, but still just as effective as the more contemporary design of Medios's troops. The front row consisted of druvani in brown robes, lacking any flamboyance since removing the brighter aspects of the Drovinian garb.

"All members of the central assault team, form up," Nacen commanded to all troops in the area through his short-ranged comms. Tosque's troops remained at attention as he strode toward them.

"We couldn't *all* form up," Shukernak said with feigned umbrage as he crossed his arms and leaned back on the jetbike. "If the Lunies regrouped, why, the entire team could've been cut down like cattle."

"How very strategic of you. Now fall in. I will take full responsibility for any disastrous consequences resulting from maintaining discipline." Nacen turned his attention to the ranks of his new team. "I know this mission could be far more dangerous than defending the breach. Thank you for joining me, Stevari of the *Wayfarer*."

"We are but the homefleet's humble servants," the druvani in the front row all transmitted simultaneously.

"Fifty-one trufalci and five druvani, serving the ready and ready to serve, my Lord. I am Motshan," a druvani in the front transmitted. He stepped forward and gave the sign of Drovina.

Fifty-six of Tosque's elite, plus Nacen himself and his motley crew of ten. Sixty-seven in all. It would have to do. Nacen brought out his digital pad containing the schematics of the ship again. He shared the files with everyone holding a similar device. "We're running off of incomplete schematics here. The gaps in the plans are projected from outdated designs. But it should get us in the right area."

"We can use resonance scans when we get closer, in order to pinpoint the control center," Camlo inserted. "It'll be a walk in the park."

"If you're blind and the park is on fire, maybe," Shukernak quipped.

"Hold your tongue, trufalci," Motshan took a short step forward.

"That is holding it back, for Shukernak anyway. You should see him when the captain isn't around," Camlo said.

Shukernak pointed an accusing finger at Camlo.

"He's about to see my foot up your—"

"Enough," Nacen said sharply. "Form up in teams of five, with at least one plasma carbine in each fire team. At any sign of combat, everyone gets behind something and covers the advancing vanguard teams. The back two teams form the rearguard and will watch for any other movement and reinforce the van if necessary. Any questions?"

"Just one..." Shukernak said, rising at last. Betty lifted his enormous plasma light support up to chest level. "Where are they at?"

Chapter 23

The wide, bright hallway had been mercifully clear so far, though Nacen expected that to change. Six gun drones flew in formation twenty meters ahead of the forward most fire team. Nacen kept his attention to the resonance scans while he jogged briskly alongside his crew. Every ten seconds they would flicker and update his digital pad's plans of the *Exemplar* as the Stevari plunged further within. So far, their schematics were a perfect match. A good sign.

"It's the waiting I can't stand." Shukernak threw a sidelong glance down one of the many side corridors in the long hall.

"Funny. It's the whining I can't stand," Jeta replied.

Shukernak snorted. "Oh, it has not yet even begun."

Motshan picked up his pace until he was just behind Nacen. The druvani leaned in and spoke in a voice so soft even Nacen could barely hear him.

"Patrin's assault team has made contact with the enemy. Last I heard was they were a quarter of the way to the destination. They just failed to check in."

"Let's keep that between us for now," Nacen whispered back, appreciating Motshan's discretion. He turned his attention back to the scans. A strange blip had appeared ahead. No, four of them, moving far too quickly...

"Take cover!" Nacen called out. He barely had time to dart into a side corridor before a drone no bigger than his fist flew into their midst and detonated. The corridor shook beneath him as he flung himself to the floor. Ears ringing, Nacen looked up. Where was the rest of his team? Nacen could barely see the next squad with all the smoke choking the hallway. In an eyeblink, the pristine corridor of the *Exemplar* had been transformed into something more akin to the tunnels on Carnizad. As he clambered up, a trufalci made their way over to Nacen in a clumsy, tumbling gait.

"Trufalci, report, where is your squad? Take defensive positions!"

The trufalci turned to him, and Nacen saw that his face was badly burned. In fact, half of the man's body was terribly scorched, with huge swathes of flesh torn apart under cracked armor. Nacen could tell that the trufalci's bloodborne nanites were doing all they could to stop the hemorrhaging and maintain organ function, but the biological enhancement suite could only do so much. He spun in place, lifting his rifle dutifully in a macabre waltz, and fell after taking another step.

"Regroup!" Nacen shouted, picking up his carbine and stumbling back into the corridor. "Take cover and repel attackers!"

Dusty red and brown cloaks lined the hallways, taking what defensive positions they could find in the desolate space. Nacen braced himself for another explosion, for the tread of armored boots. But the sounds of encroaching carnage never came. His crew all reported in via short-range comm bursts. They had all survived. He looked through the haze and found the red-clad figure with flowing brown locks he was looking for. Nacen sprinted to his chief engineer's position, keeping low. He counted five mangled bodies along the way, not five meters down the hallway. How many Stevari had they lost in that single blast?

"Jeta, program our assault drones to fly ahead, just behind our scout drones," Nacen ordered. "Four in the front, one on each side, and two in the rear. Have them set to intercept any incoming drones. I don't want any more nasty surprises coming through."

"Not a bad idea, Captain." Jeta's fingers tapped mercilessly at her own digital pad as she worked out the behavioral modification for the drones from tactical presets.

A figure clad in black strode through the haze, not bothering to take cover. It was Motshan. Apart from a layer of dust, the druvani appeared un-harmed. "Total of eleven dead from the blast, sir," he said.

"*Kaha*. We cannot afford to take these kind of losses this early on. I'm having my engineer program our assault drones to run interference."

Motshan nodded. "We will move out when this is done then?"

"Indeed. Gather up your troops and make sure everyone is prepared. Reassign trufalci who have fewer than three members in their team to other squads."

Motshan nodded silently again and walked back into the haze.

"Alright, Nacen, it's done. The drones are taking up positions," Jeta said as she cracked her knuckles.

"Good. Let's proceed." Nacen brought up the ship schematics as they moved back down the corridor. The next turn that led into the interior of the ship should be a right. As Nacen stepped out of the cloud of debris, he felt his heart jump in his chest. The next turn was a left.

Nacen slackened his pace until he was jogging alongside Camlo, Jeta, and Shukernak.

"We'll need to prioritize getting to some sort of terminal we can inter-face with. Our schematics are starting to encounter some discrepancies."

"Funny. I never took you for the kind to ask for directions," Jeta said.

"I hate to interrupt, but there's news from the frontline," Beskin said, keeping his gaze straight ahead. "Patrin did not make it far to munitions before his force got hit. A drone attack, similar to ours but with an order of magnitude more drones, with lance troopers following up."

Shukernak and Jeta muttered curses under their breath.

"What's their status now?" Nacen asked.

"No word on that."

"How do you know what happened then?" Nacen frowned.

"A trufalci fled the scene and reported back to our position at the han-gar bay."

"Well, ask them, then," Nacen replied quickly. This should be obvious.

"I can't, Captain, she's dead," Beskin said flatly, then sprinted back to his squad.

"What do you think Beskin was like as a kid?" Camlo mused as soon as Beskin was out of earshot. The squads resumed their job down the hallway, going straight.

"I don't think he ever was a kid," Nacen said.

"Wait, what? Like a clone? Or do you mean figuratively speaking?"

"Nope, he was born on a frontier world, flux driver in hand." Nacen paused to glance behind and saw the Armads still bringing up the rear. "Beskin popped out and immediately started firing on an entrenched enemy position."

"Okay, so..."

"Then he was ordered to take it, so he charged with a blood-curdling cry and got his first confirmed kill. Took a man's last breath as he took his first."

"Now you're just messing with me."

"What gave it away?" Nacen asked.

Suddenly, Nacen saw a bright flash of light in his left periphery and ducked down. A small explosion rang from far down a corridor.

"Drone interception. We're down to seven now. A vanguard drone is being rerouted to cover the flank."

Two more bangs echoed from the front corridor. Nacen winced.

"Down to five," Jeta amended nervously.

"Staying alive," Shukernak added.

Every twist and turn leading them deeper into the ship seemed wrong. He continued to scrutinize the resonance scans. With each update, his schematics drifted further and further from reality. With each flicker, he awaited the next blast that signaled the destruction of another precious assault drone. Every ten seconds Nacen felt a sudden dread as the schematics flashed. He began to feel trapped.

They approached a junction that was not on the plans at all. The teams fanned out, with a drone leading each group. Nacen stopped and considered their options. Straight ahead was clearly the most direct route to the interior of the ship. The left took them to the ventral side of the ship. No good. The right seemed promising, however, leading to a network of smaller rooms. Perhaps these contained something he could interface with.

"Motshan," Nacen said, keying his earpiece. "Hold position here with the group. I'm going to check out this side passage."

"Will do," Tosque's druvani replied.

Nacen took his crew down the hall. He found himself gripping the hilt of Talavaar Bhaganadi as they approached the first door. He nearly walked into the door as he checked his resonance scans again. The door had not opened automatically.

"Would you look at that, it's almost like they don't want us here," Nacen said.

"I can't imagine why," Camlo said.

"We could teach them a lot about being a good host," the captain knocked on the door three times. It remained perfectly still.

Shukernak leaned over his plasma light support gun and removed a conical attachment. He spun the gun around and fixed it to the end of the barrel.

"Let Betty give it a whirl, she can be very persuasive."

"Betty?" Lash asked.

"She's an old flame." Shukernak turned a small dial on the drone, and a bright blue flame flared up from the new tip of his gun's barrel. "Still has the hots for me, though."

Shukernak ignored the groans and set to work on the door, beginning in the lower left corner, and methodically cut his way up and over. At last he stood up and let out a loud groan as he stretched his legs.

"Would you like to do the honors, Captain?"

Nacen gestured to his cousin. "Camlo, after you."

"You know me too well, Nace." Camlo grinned. He stepped forward and delivered a solid kick to the door. It fell more slowly than Nacen would have expected, terminating with a deafening, metallic slam.

Camlo stormed into the room, plasma carbine at the ready. Basaul and the Armads followed with their stubby shotguns thrust forward. Nacen waited. Camlo broke the fragile silence.

"All clear, Nacen!"

Nacen stepped lightly over the smoldering edges of the door and into a small, rectangular room with a low ceiling. The walls were a dull gray and plain except for small, round apertures every few feet at waist and head level. Presumably, these were projectors for holographic screens and keyboards and the like. This must be some sort of ancillary control room. Weapons, controls, repairs, diagnostics... Nacen knew not for what they were used. As long as he could access the Counsel, that nefarious distributed artificial intelligence of the Unity, he didn't much care.

"If there was anyone in here, looks like they made themselves scarce a long time ago," Basaul said.

"It would appear so," Nacen said. "Check out the next few rooms. We're looking for any sort of terminal through which we can access the Union Precept network."

"Will do."

Nacen leaned forward until he could see his reflection in one of the midnight blue glass lenses. His murky likeness peered back.

"Got something, Captain!" Jeta shouted from an adjacent room. Nacen straightened and followed the trufalci's voice, taking the door to his left. He found himself in a room identical to the first, save for a small, cylindrical structure that rose to roughly his waist. Beskin and Camlo knelt beside it, while Jeta stood over. She stared blankly at the wall. Shukernak had packed himself into a corner.

"What is it?" Nacen asked.

Beskin shrugged. "Some interface linking the hardware of the room."

"Any idea why it's exposed?"

Jeta turned to Nacen and looked up from her digital pad. "It's filled with a solid core made of nanites. I believe it's some sort of repair mechanism for busted parts."

"Can we access the Counsel with it?" Nacen crossed his arms.

"We're about to find out," Jeta smirked. Her fingers were soon tapping out a little melody on her device.

"Remember, we're just here for updated schematics."

Nacen waited patiently for Jeta to do her work. After a few minutes, he started pacing between her room and the door that Camlo had kicked in. How long could they afford to remain stationary?

Nacen heard a crash and spun back to the room. Jeta's pad lay on the floor. It appeared to be unharmed.

"Jeta, you need to be more careful," Shukernak said, bending over to pick up the device.

"Are you okay?" Nacen frowned. "Any updates?"

"Jeta?" The big trufalci's voice was trembling.

After standing suddenly taller and widening her eyes, Jeta spoke.

"Your cunning serves you well, but you are a poor master," she sneered in a harsh voice, much lower than her usual pitch. It had a quality Nacen found hauntingly familiar. "The Counsel has guaranteed your defeat today. It is only a matter of time before things are set right."

Shukernak took another step forward, dropping his weapon and letting it float gently to the ground. "Jeta!" he shouted. "Something went wrong. Do we have a medi-drone? Someone call a medi-drone!"

Nacen stared in horror at Jeta's tense form. Then he recognized where he had heard that voice, speaking through his trufalci like some infernal puppet. It had been on the bridge of the *Etrusca*.

"There are things your artificial intelligence is not aware of, Admiral Sorkitani," Nacen stated, trying to sound bolder than he felt. "You do not know all the old ways of the Stevari, nor those of our allies."

"Spare me," Jeta scoffed. "Your baseless attachment to tradition is your greatest flaw."

"Your faith in the Counsel is yours."

"The Counsel does not require faith, it is based in pure reason alone. Its answers are beyond reproach, beyond questioning!" Jeta turned and stared directly at Nacen. Each of her pupils had dilated to completely eclipse her retinas.

"I'd rather have questions that I can't answer than answers that I can't question," Nacen said, staring back into Jeta's empty eyes.

"My, you Starkin are quite poetic aren't you? I can see why Eberwik wanted to keep you as his little pet," the Jeta that was not Jeta mused. Her face remained perfectly expressionless. "I am less tolerant of such pursuits, however. You have far outlived your usefulness. I intend to set that right."

"Just set my trufalci free from whatever this is."

"Where is that medi-drone?!" Shukernak roared.

"I have allowed you to come this far so you may trap yourselves. While you are lost within the *Exemplar*, I shall destroy your allies. First I shall expunge the transports from the bay. To clean out an infection, one must first treat the wound. Then we will wipe out your ships. You will be the last to die. This is not a mercy, nor is it to torment. This is efficiency, a calculated expenditure of resources."

Jeta's pupils suddenly shrank to the size of the head of a pin. She collapsed to the floor.

Nacen knelt beside her and placed a hand on her wrist to check her pulse. Fine metallic shavings came off of her fingertips. Suddenly he was shoved aside, having just enough time to catch himself with his elbow before his head hit the ground. Shukernak was over Jeta now. His wide shoulders heaved. Nacen shook himself and stood. He investigated Jeta's vitals and found her heart was not beating. Nacen felt a fear rising in him. Her enhancement suite should have automatically resuscitated her. What had her access to the Counsel done to her? Could the admiral condemn anyone who made contact to death?

At last the medi-drone sailed into the room. Its compact, white form hovered an arm's length above Jeta, and a lightshow in the visible spectrum played out across her face and torso. A long, thin needle protruded from the drone and jabbed into her arm. The lights snapped off. Jeta lay motionless on the floor.

Several seconds later, Jeta blinked hard and gasped for air. Nacen breathed in as well. He had not been aware he was holding it in. The breath was promptly knocked out of him as Shukernak threw his arms around Nacen. The medi-drone focused its attention on the Stevari captain now. It shined a red light in Nacen's eyes in an attempt to diagnose his condition as he sputtered and croaked in Shukernak's tight embrace.

Chapter 24

"Drone count is at three," Jeta noted anxiously as the crew made their way back to the main force.

"Doesn't bother me," Shukernak said cheerfully.

"It's always a rhyme with you Starkin, isn't it?" Basaul came up from behind the squad.

"How are your men dealing with navigating through the ship?" Nacen asked.

"They are handling it just fine. But it's hard to say." Basaul shrugged. "I thought Chalce was okay. A little rough around the edges, to be sure, but that was nothing out of the ordinary."

"Chalce bought us valuable time," Nacen said as he turned a corner. On the opposite end he saw one of the squads of trufalci gathered. "He may be the only reason we're alive right now."

"He was the only reason we were in that situation to begin with," Basaul rebuked.

"It's too bad he had to give his life to get us out, regardless."

"Whether Chalce set off those explosives or came back with us to the ship, he was never getting off of the *Trishula* alive. By turning on you, he betrayed me. Dying in the hangar merely saved me the trouble of painting your ship another shade of red with him."

Nacen grimaced. He knew the Armads weren't particularly emotional, but this cold disdain shocked him. Perhaps Basaul only meant to assure Nacen of his own loyalty. He took his mind off the matter by opening up the new schematics. Jeta had managed to download a partial layout of the ship. Though it was missing key details, Nacen knew where they had to go. Unfortunately, there would be little to no flexibility in their route.

"You ever thought about what you'd do on a frontier world, Captain?" Basaul asked. "If you didn't have a ship, or even command of an outpost?"

"Easy. I would take up playing my dulcinet again," Nacen said. "For whomever would listen. Maybe have a farm to keep myself busy. What about you? Are you going back to the mines after this?"

"After this..." Basaul snorted. "Yeah, I'll be back underground all right."

Jogging back to Motshan in the center of the Stevari perimeter, Nacen gave the sign of Drovina.

"We managed to get updated plans of the ship, after a few hiccups," Nacen said. "They're incomplete, though."

"So, what, that was a waste of time?" Motshan asked.

"Not exactly. But we don't have a complete layout of the ship, so I don't think we'll be able to find a control room that gives us direct access to the Counsel."

"So what's the plan, then? Back out?"

"No, no," Nacen sputtered. "It's just... the only place I can be reasonably sure of success in dispatching the Void Protocol is... the bridge of the *Exemplar*."

"What?!" Shukernak exclaimed. This outburst drew the attention of many of the nearby trufalci.

"I will not tell your trufalci to hold his tongue again, Captain," Motshan said. "If you think the best course of action is to the bridge, then take to the bridge we shall."

Nacen stepped between the two before Shukernak could articulate a suitably offensive retort.

"Yes. I believe it is our only option. We don't have to necessarily seize it either, just take control of some main control panel briefly. Even if we don't make it out, we can give our worldships a chance at escape."

"That's good enough for me, I suppose," Shukernak grumbled.

"Quite noble," Beskin added.

"I hear and obey," Motshan said.

"Good. Let's move out. Back to our standard formation. Two drones in front, one in the rear." Nacen set off down the hallway. He brought up the scans again. They were making good progress, but the bridge was still a long way off and Nacen didn't know what the intervening space held. Rather than alleviated at his force's unimpeded progress, Nacen felt a mounting dread at each turn into the interior of the ship they took. The admiral had exuded intimidation when speaking through Jeta, but had she been genuine in saying she was going to destroy them last? The threat could easily just have been intended to lure Nacen into complacency. He thought of Leander's forces headed to munitions at the bow, led by Patrin. How long could Patrin's assault force survive? Were they even still alive?

"Nacen, come in, can you hear me?" Linasette's voice came in loud and clear in Nacen's earpiece.

"Yes, Lina. Good to hear from you."

"Do you have an estimated time until your return?"

"Unfortunately no," Nacen admitted. "We need to go further in than we initially thought, though resistance has been surprisingly light so far."

"Not surprising. Patrin's team is going through the ringer, and… we are under attack as well. Nothing happened for a while, but then we got hit with a few hundred drones. They flew in between our transports and detonated."

Nacen stopped dead in his tracks. Trufalci streamed past. "Hundred?"

"Yes. We lost roughly a third of our force, as well as five King Oxens. We are currently under infantry assault. So far we have managed to keep the Unity from establishing a foothold in the bay, but it is costing us. I am not sure how much time we have left."

Nacen gulped. Sorkitani's dire promises were coming to fruition. "How are you—and the *Canotila*?"

"I'm good. The ship took some damage, but it has been in rougher shape." Linasette paused. "There's another thing, Nacen. Have you heard from Captain Tengrin recently?"

"Florica? No, I haven't." Nacen saw that he was being left behind. He took up a fast jog to catch back up to the group.

"The *Trishula* is in dire straits," Linasette reported. "Manfri has nearly seized the engines, and if that happens, she's at Zura's mercy."

"While they're doing evasive maneuvering around the Precept flagship…" Nacen trailed off. "Keep me updated. I cannot do anything about Manfri, but I will get to the bridge as fast as I can."

"Understood, Captain. Good luck."

"Listen, Lina…" Nacen added. "If we don't make it back, take as many people onto the *Canotila* as you can, and—"

Nacen stopped short as the corridor ahead lit up in a bright flash of azure light. The end of the hallway grew quickly more and more luminous. Somehow the light was moving closer. It grew ever brighter, and Nacen saw it was not a solid wall but an interlocking grid. Four beams cut across the hallway horizontally. They passed over one advancing squad who did not even have enough time to stop their forward momentum.

Nacen looked left and right, but there was nowhere to go without backtracking several dozen paces. The light overtook the next squad who had at least managed to turn in place and start running in the opposite direction. Their cries were quickly silenced by the blinding light. Nacen now saw the incoming grid was not mere light but thick beams of plasma.

Then, nearly as soon as the plasma appeared, it had gone. All that remained was smoke from the burned material of anything and anyone unfortunate enough to be caught in its path. The gray walls had been marred with black streaks from the path of the plasma. A motion to his left caught his eye. Four black nozzles had appeared in the hallway.

"Forward!" he shouted, and dove straight ahead. There was a clatter of boots and grunts. Dazzling light filled his periphery and a buzzing filled his ears. His back felt painfully hot.

"Did we all make it?" Nacen glanced around. Beskin, Camlo, Jeta, Shukernak, and Lash all stood before him.

"Yes," Camlo stood wide-eyed. His gaze was focused down. "Nacen, your cloak, it's…"

"On fire," Shukernak finished.

Camlo and Beskin dove on top of Nacen, patting down his crimson cloak. In the distance, the second plasma grid faded. A deafening klaxon sounded, an abrupt buzzing that sounded over distant speakers.

"*Kaha*, what was that?" Camlo asked of no one in particular.

"Some sort of automated trap. A sweeping plasma beam." Jeta ventured. "Somehow it just appeared out of the wall and traveled across it. No telling when it will show up again."

"Or if it even goes in the same direction."

"Right," Nacen said after he was convinced his cloak was no longer ablaze. The bottom third had completely singed away. "Let's move up and see who made it. Turning back is no longer an option."

They set off down the hallway. Except for the hastened tread of their boots, the silence was unbroken. Nacen did his best to ignore the burning stench. At last they reached Motshan, who was barking orders at a squad of trufalci. Nacen was relieved to see the Armads had made it past the plasma fields. Motshan turned, and his shoulders rose as though a heavy burden had been lifted when he spotted Nacen.

"I do not revel in battle, no Stevari should," the druvani said. "but what

I strive for is *in* the battle, the chance to prove oneself. The chance to rise up and put your whole worth against another's and see who prevails. This though, this isn't... this is just..." Motshan trailed off.

"Butchery," Nacen finished. He shoved the horror of the sliced bodies and the putrid stench down deep, covering it with the immediate peril of his homefleet's survival. There was no use dwelling on this, but he needed to re-assess the situation. "How many did we lose?"

"Four whole squads. No survivors. Plus the two forward assault drones and all of our gun drones."

"That leaves us with... thirty-six, including ourselves and the Armads?" Motshan paused, then nodded grimly.

"Alright," Nacen said. "It could have been worse. If we were any more clumped together, we could have all perished in a single stroke. But we'll need to change our pattern of attack again."

"What about the Unity's dive-bombing drones?" Jeta asked.

"We're down to our last assault drone for intercepting. We can't rely on it to protect us," Nacen said. "Our only hope now is splitting up and converging on the bridge separately. If one of us gets wiped out, the others can carry on the mission."

"Unless you're taken out," Beskin said, then nodded to Nacen's waist. "You carry the phase sword."

"Right." In his drive to get to the bridge, Nacen had completely forgotten about the reason they were headed there at all. If he were to be caught in any of these traps, the entire endeavor could be a failure.

"Okay. Motshan, you take three squads and take a left at the next junction. I'll highlight your path on the schematics and share them with your device. Basaul, you take the Armads and the remaining two squads of Tosque's trufalci straight ahead. I'm staying with my crew. We'll backtrack to the last junction and take that around. We should be able to reach the bridge that way as well."

"Splitting up?" Basaul asked, almost incredulously. "I don't like it one bit. This place is a death trap."

"That's precisely why we need to split up," Nacen countered. "You have your orders. I will see you all at the bridge. Without wood, the fire dies."

"Where the houses go, the wealth shall rise," Motshan returned. Basaul gave a silent nod. Nacen watched them go, wondering if he would see them again.

Chapter 25

Back they turned into the hallway, hurrying past walls still radiating heat from the scorching of plasma. The acrid scent of singed metal burned their nostrils, even through helmet rebreathers and pan-atmo masks. Nacen jerked his head back and forth, looking for the reappearing nozzles that would herald their doom. So far, none materialized. They might have a limited use, both in terms of location and time.

A figure appeared in the hallway. It appeared to be a trufalci. It occurred to Nacen that they could have left some stragglers behind in their haste. A plasma round whizzed past Nacen, the death knell to his hypothesis. He raised his carbine and returned fire, crouching lower as he continued his fast pace down the hall. His shots connected with the distant figure. A field flickered in defiance, projected by the distant target's prismotion shielding, but it did not protect the trooper from a direct shot at the center of mass. Nacen now saw the trooper was enclosed in dark green armor, not the reds and browns of his homefleet. How could he have missed that?

Darting around the corner, Nacen managed to avoid another volley of plasma rounds. The crew did the same. He simply kept running, not wanting to get bogged down in a fight. He hoped that with their own troops nearby, the Unity would not risk using the plasma beam grids. Or perhaps they were being corralled into another trap?

The crew ran past more doors, mostly officer barracks by the look of the signs plastered on the frame. That was a good sign they were getting closer to the command center. Plasma rounds scorched the wall behind them. The hallway ahead split off into two side corridors, neither of which interested Nacen. They needed to go straight ahead. Nacen grinned inwardly as the door whisked open for him. He could have had Shukernak cut open the door, but that would have cost valuable time they didn't have. Nacen stepped in, taking in his surroundings with a ping from the resonance scanner.

The room's function was as evident as it was terrifying for Nacen. Rows upon rows of weapon racks lined the walls of the large hall. Each rack was slightly taller than head height and was constructed with metal frames. This place was expansive and crude compared to his own armory, where compressor crates efficiently packed massive amounts of ammunition, and suspensor shelves could keep weapons in perfect condition in perpetuity. But whereas space on his ship was a valuable commodity, this part of the battleship appeared to be more concerned with outfitting a large force with expediency. The thought quickened his pace even more. As he walked past the first shelf, it drew out to meet him in a swift and clattering motion. Nacen jumped forward, but the weapons rack stopped an arm's length from him. He saw that the extended rack held dozens of stubbed flux drivers and sleek plasma carbines. As he continued farther into the room, more racks to the left and right clattered out to meet him as well. One held heavy flux drivers and cannons. Another, plasma weaponry. Another, rows upon rows on tightly packed grenades.

"Woah." Shukernak lagged behind to stare longingly at a particularly volatile and sizeable grenade. "Anyone need to stock up?"

"No one touch anything. The Armads can do what they wish, but we're not using Union Precept tech," Nacen insisted. "We need more time to get to the bridge. I hate to use them now, but let's deploy the nanite grenades. Everyone chip in one grenade and we'll blow them at the entrance to turn it into a slab of metal. That ought to keep them off our tail for a little while."

Each member of the squad passed one of the small, cylindrical devices to Jeta, who fastened them at her waist.

Nacen's next order was drowned out by the high-pitched whine of Shukernak's plasma light support gun. The trufalci had swung the weapon around in a wide arc and was now firing a withering hail of plasma fire at the door before the lance troopers could get through. Two were cut down instantly, and the rest of the squad scattered back to the corridor from where they had hastily emerged.

Jeta sprinted from rack to rack while Shukernak kept the entry inundated with plasma fire. As he continued to spray into the hallway, Jeta worked only an arm's length from the superheated stream of high-speed plasma. She activated and planted three of the grenades to the inner frame of the door. Shukernak ceased his suppressive fire for a moment as Jeta skipped across the gap, and began to activate the next nanite grenade.

A spherical object was lobbed into the room in the split second before Shukernak resumed his fire. Nacen looked away and squeezed his eyes shut before the room filled with blinding light.

"Good enough!" Nacen opened his eyes, but all he saw was bright lights playing across whatever he tried to focus on. "Bring it down now!"

The shape Nacen assumed was Jeta darted across the room. He squinted around the rack and found he could barely make out several figures running down the corridor where Shukernak was still firing. The front lance trooper was cut down by plasma light support fire thrown across the room wildly by Shukernak who was more blinded than Nacen, as far as he could tell.

The grenades detonated with a metallic clap. Nacen's vision had returned enough to where he could see lustrous, formless globules where the doorway once stood. The blobs coalesced into silver tentacles that writhed in a languid frenzy. After a moment, two tentacles met and fused together. Another second passed, and another joined their metallic bond. The lead lance trooper attempted to turn back but was caught in the contorting extremities. Soon the appendages and trooper had formed into one solid, undulating mass. The surface gave one last shimmer, the perturbations stopped, and the entrance appeared no different than the surrounding wall.

"I don't envy that trooper," Jeta said. She was blinking hard as she approached Nacen but seemed able to walk a straight line at least.

Nacen would feel worse if the festering memories of his smoldering allies didn't threaten to bubble up whenever he wasn't in immediate danger.

"We don't have long before the Unies cuts their way through," Nacen replied. "Let's keep moving."

The crew made their way down the hall. Elongated weapon racks stretched out to meet them briefly, then clattered back as the Stevari paid no heed. Eventually they reached the end of the long hall, where weapons lay strewn about in piles of spare parts and scrap. There were heaps of drone chasses, from small scouter and shield drones to hulking combat drones.

In one corner was a partially disassembled Javelin fighter of the same thin, dart-like variety that had pursued the *Carmine Canotila* after Daedalon Station. Nacen recalled a large number of the same craft were situated in the *Exemplar's* port hangar as well.

The crew filed out into the hallway and proceeded along Nacen's high-lighted route to the bridge. Nacen kept his eyes to the walls as Beskin led the way, ever wary of the threat of the plasma traps. Each time they passed a junction, they peered around the corners, aware of the potential for an onrush of enemy troops or the surprise fire of a hidden drone or turret. Camlo signaled to Nacen after the crew had checked their third junction in this way.

"Targets... left side of the far hallway," the druvani hissed. "They're big bastards."

Nacen leaned around his cousin to get his own eyes on the hostiles. He let out a short laugh and stepped into the hallway. His cousin leapt up to shield him, startled at Nacen's audacity.

"Don't worry, Camlo, we're perfectly safe. Well, relatively speaking." Nacen waved at the five figures down the hallway.

Camlo jumped up and brought Nacen's arm down. He raised his rifle but did not fire on the group.

"We might need to get your vision checked, Cam. That flash grenade might have caused some permanent damage." Nacen continued down the hall until the Armads waved and came to join him. The crew trailed idly behind, with Camlo bashfully bringing up the rear.

"It warms my heart to see you made it through." Nacen grinned, scanning the hallways beyond. "But you're down a man. What happened?"

"Kurt didn't make it," Basaul said grimly. "We ran into trouble about halfway to the bridge. Lance troopers."

"Are you being followed?"

"Not that we can tell. We made sure none of them were in condition to follow us after they took out Kurt."

Nacen nodded and made to mutter some affirmation when he noticed a black-clad figure turn the far corner. Unlike earlier, there was no mistaking this robed figure. Motshan strolled coolly down the hallway with three druvani in tow. A handful of trufalci followed him. Nacen waited for the rest of Motshan's team to round the junction. They never did.

"What happened to the rest of your men?" Nacen shifted uncomfortably in place, already knowing the answer.

"They didn't make it. More of those accursed plasma beam traps." Motshan slowed to a halt.

"*Kaha*. Were you followed by any Precept forces?"

Motshan gave a curt shake of the head in response.

"Good. We have some time to plan out our bridge attack then. By my count, we have twenty-six men and women all told."

"It appears so," Basaul grunted. "We passed fairly close to an entrance earlier, I'll lead the way."

Basaul and his Armads formed a wedge and forged a path back through the corridor behind them. Despite the wide hallway, only three of the big men could stand abreast at any given point. The group spread out, keeping their weapons trained on each corridor they passed. They were attentive to every shift in the light, every creak of the ship, every perceived movement that flickered in the shadows. The short way to the bridge was clear. Basaul held up a craggy hand as they approached the next corridor.

"We're here. I think."

Nacen unclipped a small device, roughly the size of his fingernail, from his pad and threw it into the open hallway. In the moment before it was disintegrated by enemy plasma fire, the one-shot resonance scanner got a detailed image of the space and transmitted it back to his digital pad. The door beyond led unequivocally to the bridge. Between Nacen and his goal stood at least a dozen slanted metal barricades, each of which could hide half of a squad of lance troopers. Twenty drones hovered in the air around the barricades. Most of them sported twin flux drivers, but some had shield generators. Turrets dotted the ceiling at regular intervals like light fixtures. Behind them lay a wide arc leading to a vast, open room. That had to be the bridge.

"Why don't they rush out and take us on?" Camlo asked, crouching a bit lower.

"They don't need to take the risk of losing bridge personnel," Nacen guessed. "They just need to stay put and wait for reinforcements. We're up against the clock, they're not."

"Fair point," Camlo admitted. "What's our plan then? They have us outnumbered, outgunned, and out...defensed."

"We're going to need some help," Nacen nodded pensively. "Hold on, I'll see what I can do."

The captain brought up his encrypted link with the *Carmine Canotila*. To his relief, the signal was still present.

"Lina, we've reached the bridge, but we're in trouble," he said.

"Nacen, I was just about to contact you." Linasette had a notable urgency in her voice, but he needed to press the seriousness of his own situation.

"Great. Listen, I need you to peel some of the munitions team off and send them our way."

"That's what I needed to talk to you about, Captain. All of Leander's men, Patrin... they're gone. The Union Precept overwhelmed their position. We just got confirmation."

Nacen couldn't bring himself to swear. He was frozen in place, his brain paralyzed in its natural state of jumping from problem to solution. This was simply too far a leap.

"Captain? Nacen, are you there?"

"Yes." Nacen blinked rapidly. "Yes, I'm here. How goes the defense of our landing zone?"

"The Unity have multiple breaches in the bay. But we are holding for now. Tosque's Stevari are making them pay for every step."

"Can you defend against the influx in Uni reinforcements from Patrin's position?"

"Right..." Linasette began. "They're not headed for us, not anymore at least. I'm reading over one thousand hostiles moving to the interior of the ship."

It finally hit Nacen. They were coming for him.

"*Kaha*," he swore at last. "Look, if we get overwhelmed... take the ship, load it up with as many people as you can, and get out of here. Get aboard the *Wayfarer* and get as far away from the Precept navy as possible. If we can unleash the Void Protocol, maybe Tosque and Medios can get out of here."

"Okay, Nacen," Linasette said solemnly. There was a long pause before her next transmission. "I can do that for you."

"Thank you."

"But I will be waiting here. Until this ship is a single stroke from destruction, I'll wait."

Nacen prepared to bid farewell but saw that Linasette had ended the transmission. Right. He had work to do. One thousand troops headed his way. There was no way his little team could stand up to that in a straight fight. They had to get into that bridge before it was too late. He may be short on manpower, but rarely was he short on ideas.

"Jeta, how easy was it reprogramming our assault drones to intercept the Precept explosives?"

"Easy enough," Jeta shrugged. "Most of it is just altering preset behaviors."

"Good. You did seem to make quick work of it. Would it be possible to reprogram some other device with a similar behavior?"

"In theory, sure, but I have no idea what you're talking about. I don't see what throwing away our last drone could do to get us into the bridge." Jeta contorted her lips in a thoughtful pout.

"I'm not talking about our drone," Nacen said. "Could we hook up our assault drone to a Javelin, that spindly Precept fighter back in the armory? To gain control of it?"

Jeta's foot began to tap.

"Didn't you say something about not using enemy tech?"

"Consider this a very special case."

"Well then, there's a number of concerns." Jeta stilled her foot and held up her hand, counting off on her fingers. "First, we might not be able to interface at all. Not likely, considering our success so far. Two, from what I recall, that fighter had seen better days. Three, it may take a prohibitively long time to get the Javelin up and running under our control, with the capabilities we need."

"Granted," Nacen said sullenly.

"But with our advanced programs, and especially with Linasette's experience in modifying Union Precept systems, I'd say it's at least worth a shot. It's just..."

"I know it isn't easy, especially after last time when you interfaced with the Counsel. I would understand if you didn't want..."

"No, I'll do it." Jeta brushed her thick, dark curls over her shoulder.

"I know you'll do us proud. Motshan, stay here and make sure we don't lose this position."

Nacen did not like the idea of turning back into the ship and risking unnecessary confrontation, but he couldn't press on out of sheer stubbornness and expect any modicum of success. Presented with an unassailable position to his front and an unstoppable hoard to the rear, he would search for a solution in what little space was afforded to him between. There was always a solution, he told himself. He found himself repeating the phrase to himself like a mantra, losing any remaining focus on his pad's ship schematics. Soon, the phrase itself lost all meaning. Familiar corridors and barracks flashed by, and still Nacen pressed on, eyes fixed ahead. There was always a solution.

Chapter 26

The Javelin fighter lay in the same cluttered corner Nacen had seen it in before the crew made their leave of the armory. More importantly, the entrance sealed by the nanite grenades and unfortunate lance trooper was still blocked. Either this meant the Unity was having difficulty getting through or were simply going around. Crouching down, Nacen cleared some of the rubble around the small fighter. The craft was in worse shape than he had remembered from his first hurried impression. Scorch marks covered much of the tarnished surface, and the whole fighter appeared to have been battered by the spray of some sort of projectile weapon. On top of all this, every missile rack surrounding the thin chassis was completely empty.

"Alright, Jeta, do what you can." Nacen exhaled sharply, his dejected tone more accurately reflecting his pessimism than the order.

"I work with 'Nak every day, I can handle a challenge," Jeta replied, crouching next to Nacen. She commanded their last assault drone to hover next to her. She glanced thoughtfully from drone to fighter, fighter to drone, and back to her handheld device.

Nacen and the crew waited patiently around her in a loose semicircle, occupying themselves by glancing at the brimming weapon racks. He tried to set an example and not crowd the trufalci engineer.

A bright flash drew Nacen's attention to the opposite end of the room. A small pinpoint of light emitted from the wall, swiftly growing into a flickering, sputtering spark.

"I hate to pressure you, Jeta, but..." Nacen began.

"Then don't." Jeta's fingers tapped away as though she was performing a particularly intricate piece on the piano.

"I can't, that's fair... but the Unity certainly can." Nacen glanced anxiously at the brightening flare at the end of the hall.

"Well, I'm in. Currently I'm trying to reconfigure the Javelin's programming to match our assault drone using Linasette's template from the *Etrusca*. Care to shed some light on what you had in mind with this fighter? I take it we're not going to deliver evening mess to the bridge with it."

"Depends on what you mean by *mess*. I was thinking more along the lines of crashing it into the defenses outside the bridge. Maybe after unleashing its entire payload?"

"Hmm... that will be difficult without missiles," Jeta pondered. "But hey, we're surrounded by ammunition. Try... rack seventeen. About halfway down the hall on your left. Sorry, no, your right. Javelin M4 Corsairs, maximum yield. Rounded tip with the yellow."

Nacen meandered down the hallway, inspecting the weapon racks more carefully this time as they clattered out to meet him. Here there was a rack of drone weapon attachments. There laid an array of prismotion armor, ranging from minimally protective straps to fully enclosed suits. Finally, he came to rack seventeen. Missiles lined the packed rack like cigars in a long, wooden box. He glanced at the opposite armory entrance. The light had moved up from waist to head high. Whatever the Unity was using to breach or cut through the newly formed thick wall, it was working now.

"Shukernak, help me with the missiles. Basaul, you and your men do the same. Carry one at a time, please. No need to show off," Nacen called from across the room. "Beskin, Camlo, take up defensive positions around the door. Be prepared to toss plasma grenades into the enemy breach or repel attackers."

Beskin and Camlo jogged up between two of the far-most weapon racks and kept their plasma carbines trained. The rest of the crew formed a sparse line up and down the hall. In short order, they had carried a full complement of missiles, twenty-four in all, and loaded them into the barren missiles racks of the Javelin fighter. The crew then busied themselves with other small tasks Jeta sent them on around the armory, including refueling the fighter and welding on a few pieces that Nacen hadn't realized had been missing. Soon the craft resembled its brethren that had chased them off Daedalon Station and the Tantalos system. All the while, Nacen kept a wary eye on the sputtering sparks slowly shifting around the outline of the old door. When they approached the floor of the opposite side from where they started, Nacen turned back to Jeta. She had not moved from her original position.

"Okay, it's do or die," Nacen said.

"Just five more minutes," Jeta demanded.

"We don't have it. I was being very literal when I said do or die."

Jeta exhaled and continued her work. Nacen waited for longer than he thought was prudent, then called the crew back to his position.

"Jeta, I mean it, we—"

Nacen stopped as the pile of scrap in front of him jostled. The Javelin rose, tip pointing to the ceiling. The rear then lifted itself and the craft leveled out at waist height. The fighter was nearly four meters long, but only the width of a large tree at its widest point, not that he had seen many of those. The Stevari assault drone had been tacked onto the rear near the engine exhaust ports. It hovered in place unsteadily, as though it could fall over or careen into a wall at any moment. Soon enough, though, its lurching stilled. In the span of a heartbeat, it rocketed down the hallway, leaving a booming pressure wave in its wake that nearly blew Nacen off his feet.

"If it crashes, it's because you rushed me." Jeta frowned at what must be a shocked expression branded on his face.

"Okay, fair enough. Let's follow the drone," Nacen gulped. "Do we have all of the Javelin's functions?"

"Not even close. We won't be able to travel outside the ship very well, or perform combat maneuvers," Jeta explained. "But we have basic movement and weapon systems."

"Perfect."

Shortly after the crew had left the armory, they heard a great blast behind them. Precept troopers must have stormed the room. But they could deal with these soldiers later. For now, Nacen and his crew had other concerns. Nacen sent a message to Motshan's channel and quickly apprised Tosque's druvani of their position and the status of the incoming Precept fighter. Nacen thought about the damage the Javelin could potentially cause in his own ranks. He was taking a risk by using this drone fighter. A necessary one given their desperation, but uncalculated and potentially immense. Nacen noted that Motshan did not send back his own message, or even acknowledge that he had received it. A worrisome sign.

Quicker than Nacen thought possible, he and he his crew returned to Motshan's position following Jeta's drone. As he turned the final corner, he saw why Motshan had been unresponsive. The druvani and his squad were not huddled around the drone. They were crouched at the junction, taking fire from both the corridor to the left and right. The corridor in the front was clear for now, only due to the unrelenting efforts by half of Motshan's trufalci, artfully synchronizing their suppressive fire.

One of the trufalci turned around as the *Carmine Canotila's* crew neared. Shock registered on his face and he brought his flux driver to bear.

"Do not fire on the fighter!" Nacen ordered to any and all nearby Stevari through their comm link. "It's on our side. Everyone fall back and stand down."

"What are you doing?" Motshan approached Nacen with his cloak flying behind him in a frenzy. "I thought you were going to get reinforcements from Patrin's force, and you come back with... *this*?"

"Patrin's company is gone," Nacen paused as the weight of the words fell on Motshan's squad. They whispered amongst themselves and glanced nervously at each other. The Unity fire had let up, but their footsteps were audible in the distance.

"Gone? What do you mean, gone?" Motshan tensed.

"I mean they have been wiped out, and now the hundreds of lance troopers they were holding up are on their way here."

"So, what? We're going to ride your new toy back to the ship?"

"Wrong direction," Nacen flattened himself against the wall, ahead of the Javelin and its rear thrusters. "I suggest you all follow my example. Jeta?"

Jeta stepped forward, cast down on her device's screen. Vents on the Javelin's thrusters opened up, and a dry heat emanated from them. The twenty-some men and women in his company followed his example and hugged the sides of the corridor just before the fighter bolted down the hallway with a clap like thunder. Nacen was jostled in his armor as he was slammed back against the wall. He dropped a hand to support himself and regained his posture. Looking around, Nacen saw that not all of his team had been able to remain standing.

"On your feet, everyone! Follow the Javelin. It will clear the path for us," Nacen shouted. He only partially believed his own words. "We need to get to the bridge before reinforcements arrive!"

Beskin and Camlo were already on their feet and leading the charge. Camlo waited for Nacen to catch up before taking a defensive position at Nacen's flank.

"Where the needle goes, the thread will follow," Camlo said.

Nacen's reply was muffled by an enormous blast in the corridor ahead. Bits of detritus chipped away from the ship's walls and broken barricades flew across the junction. Nacen dashed around the corner just in time to see the

Javelin dart around the next. Beskin, still leading the charge, put a round in a lance trooper as he fumbled with a broken flux driver. His blackened armor fell limp to the floor. A series of explosions followed, their concussive blasts drowning out all sensation. In the aftermath of the destruction, Nacen heard falling hunks of metal and panicked shouts. Rounding the final corner, he saw the destruction Jeta's creation had wrought.

The hallway he had seen captured in a single image before was barely recognizable. The immobile turrets and heavy combat drones were the most powerful defenses, and they appeared to have been targeted first, suddenly and systematically destroyed by the high-yield missiles of the Javelin. Their smoking carapaces littered the floor amongst jumbles of unrecognizable debris. As Nacen ran to cover, he noticed the barricades next. Their proud and jutting right angles had been warped and shattered by the impacts of the fighter's swift payload. He noticed they bent outward, rather than inward. Jeta must have set the missiles to detonate behind the barricades, or else they did so automatically. A glance behind the closest fortification confirmed this. He grimaced as he saw what remained of smoking, dismembered bodies.

Nacen walked through the room now, not bothering to take cover. The Union Precept here were not putting up much of a fight. They did not, or could not, offer much resistance as the Armads and the household troops of Drovina vaulted over the ruined barricades, howling and shooting as they went. They seemed to encourage each other with their mad antics.

"For the *Nivasi!*" he heard a trufalci shout across the hall, and a string of flux rounds followed his cry.

The Javelin had not survived its finest hour. It lay smoking on the right side of the room, its thin shaft of a hull bent in several places. It appeared to have taken a fatal shot from a plasma cannon before careening into the wall, its forward momentum alone enough to ensure its demise.

Further on Nacen walked, catching more distant glimpses of his troops as they reveled in the bloodshed. Rarely had they seen such a one-sided fight, but still it shocked Nacen to see the carnage they so eagerly wrought. A slight movement to the left caught Nacen's eye as he passed the third tier of defenses. With horror, he recognized the unarmored, bloody visage of a Unity lance trooper. The man's visor had been utterly shattered, and shrapnel riddled his torso. But still he moved defiantly with his last breaths, raising a plasma pistol as though it was made from lead. Nacen brought up his plasma carbine to defend himself, but even as he did so, he knew he was too late. The trooper's lidless eye had Nacen in his sights.

Suddenly the trooper's head slammed back as a beam of plasma seared into his broken helmet. Camlo strode up, putting two more shots into the trooper. Camlo, his cousin and druvani, who had stayed behind while the rest of the team had surged forward in macabre delight.

"Gotta pay more attention, Captain," Camlo said cheerlessly. "That guy had your rights to dead."

"That's not how that..." Nacen began but thought better of correcting him now. Actually, the improper phrasing kind of worked. "Thank you, Cam."

Camlo opened his mouth as if to respond, but something caught his eye. He walked on, nodding to himself and staying close to Nacen.

At last they reached the end of the hall. Nacen recalled seeing the arch leading to the bridge wide open before, but now the opening was sealed by a massive door. The crew gathered around the now dead-end in a semi-circle, and Jeta walked up and knelt to inspect the thick door.

"What are we waiting for, an invitation? Let's get some charges placed," Basaul said.

"I'm afraid we're all out," Beskin responded dutifully. "But we could try our remaining nanite grenades."

Nacen got closer to the door. It was not smooth and even like the rest of the ship's surfaces. It was coarse to the touch.

"That won't work either." Jeta rose from her investigation of the entrance. "This is reinforced disruption steel. See the fine, uneven grain on the surface? Well I guess you can't see it but it feels... off. Sort of rough, right? Nanite grenades, or really any nano-based weapon, won't work on disruption steel. It will simply shrug off any attempts to bind with it."

The ring of men and women around the door began to shuffle. Armads shrugged and turned their attention elsewhere. Trufalci glanced down and kicked their feet.

"So what do we do?" Basaul asked, his tone rising violently. "Just go home? After all this?"

"I don't know," Jeta said, "but we're not getting through with what we have on us. Not even a Javelin's missiles are getting through this, even if we could get another one."

Nacen became suddenly aware of his own heart pounding within his chest. He calmed his breathing, took a step back from the door, and looked it up and down. He gripped the hilt of his sword. It had remained within its scabbard the entire time he'd been on the Exemplar, but it had not been far from his thoughts.

"Maybe there's another way in?" Camlo suggested with a hint of uneasy optimism.

"There are at least two more, you can check Nacen's schematics. But they'll likely be sealed too, and heavily defended like this one was," Jeta answered impatiently.

Nacen slid Talavaar Bhaganadi silently from its sheath. The blade came free easily, as though it longed to breathe in the air and the bloody mist of combat. He pressed the point of the phase blade against the door.

"Yeah, well, aren't there a bunch more in a hangar bay somewhere?" Camlo insisted. His voice rose in defiance, but it seemed far off to Nacen.

"We have no way of getting to them, if Tosque's troops even still hold the breach," Basaul countered. His voice was muffled as well.

Nacen closed his eyes. Only he existed right now. He and this door. He gripped Talavaar Bhaganadi in both hands and raised the hilt above his shoulders. He thrust the blade forward toward the door and did not stop when the tip made contact with metal. The blade buried itself nearly to the hilt before Nacen stopped. Then he brought the hilt up and over his head, keeping the blade deep within the bulkhead. He swung it to his left, and the thick metal gave way as though it were no more than paper. Sparks flew from the incision and burned themselves out on his face, but Nacen paid them no heed. He swung Talavaar Bhaganadi down to the floor and over to its original breach, shifting his hands as he did so. He withdrew the blade at last and it came free with a sickening screech before it changed its composition yet again.

Nacen stepped back and the world rushed back into focus. He found Basaul and gave him a curt nod. Basaul looked taken aback for just a moment, as though Nacen had taken the blade and slapped him with the flat of it. Then he returned the nod and stepped toward the door in two mighty strides.

"You Starkin always want a dramatic entrance, don't you?" Basaul put a step between himself and the door, and he swung a heavy boot up at the section Nacen had carved. He hit it with a single, solid kick and the piece of door groaned as if in agony. It swung in and landed on the floor of the bridge with a deafening thud. The entire team, Stevari and Armads alike, stood frozen in place. They stared, awestruck, between the breach in the door and their captain.

Nacen did not return Talavaar Bhaganadi to its sheath. Instead, he pointed to the gaping hole in the door.

"Forward, men and women of the homefleet! I have given you the bridge. Now take it!"

Chapter 27

The colossal room dwarfed the command centers of the Stevari vessels Nacen had known all his life. The rows upon rows of tiered seating reminded him more of their amphitheaters, if anything. The walls of the bridge were a dark blue and stood nearly thirty meters high. His team had moved up and taken cover behind the first two rows of panels. Security guards fired back at them from several rows up, flux rounds piercing and shattering displays and ricocheting off panels. All around them, Unity officers and technicians ran, stricken with blind panic at the sudden assault. Sage green and pearl uniforms were cut down seemingly at random.

"*Kaha!* Focus fire on the security personnel!" Nacen shouted. He fired on the nearest hostile holding an actual weapon as he took note of his surroundings. There were only six guards in the immediate vicinity, but more were closing in fast from elevators and staircases built into the far walls.

Long aisles led up to the next tiers of stations. Soft flashes of light pulsed and spread across the aisles as Armads and Stevari fired into the room. Shield drones were apparently being utilized to cover the battleship personnel's retreat.

The battle around the *Exemplar* played out on a massive projection on the wall behind them. The three Stevari worldships were continuing their evasive loops around the Precept fleet. Bullet holes pockmarked the wall showing the frenetic fleet action, while gunfire both real and virtual played across the display. He was reminded that any spare time was being paid for in Stevari blood.

Nacen waited until two security guards knelt back behind cover as his own men returned fire. Then he leapt from his own stations and bolted down the aisle.

"Keep moving up the room! Get away from the entrance and keep moving toward the back!" Nacen ordered.

"But the show is just getting good!" Brecca protested. He fired off a fast volley with his shotgun and followed up behind Nacen.

As he reached the first guard, Nacen stepped behind a panel to shield himself from incoming fire and slashed out with Talavaar Bhaganadi. He cleaved the guard in two at the torso, his blade bypassing the armor completely.

Any son of a baroni was expected to learn the art of swordsmanship. As the son of the eccentric and proud steya, Yoska Buhari, Nacen had excelled at all forms of the craft from thin rapiers to long broadswords. He had always assumed that swordplay would be about as useful in combat as his proficiency with the dulcinet or baliano. Nacen was happy to be proven wrong, though wholesale slaughter hardly counted as proper swordplay.

He thrust the phase blade out and cut a second guard's gun in half. To his credit, the guard maintained his composure and went for his sidearm. Before the guard could even get his fingers on the grip, Nacen had run him through.

Screens shattered all around. Nacen ducked down and waited for his team to catch up. On the far end of the room, just under the high vaulted ceiling, stood a jutting platform with thin rails all around. Nacen peered around for a way into the place, judging it to be the command center. At last he found two elevators built into the back wall, thick black channels leading up to the platform. In addition, staircases built into the wall on either side appeared to wind up, forming an alternate route.

For the first time, he also noticed curiously faint lights along the wall twenty meters up, just below the ceiling. Had these lights been there the whole time?

Beskin and Camlo led the charge, stopping briefly where Nacen crouched.

"They're evacuating the bridge," Beskin said. "The guards are fleeing along with the non-coms."

"Easier than I thought it'd be," Camlo noted with a grin.

"That, or the strike force is close," Nacen glanced back at the breach, already long behind them. Light from the corridor spilled into the dim bridge. "It may be easier to let them deal with us than lose critical bridge personnel fighting for every inch." That reminded him. "Jeta, we still have one assault drone, correct?" he asked over the short-ranged comms.

"No, Captain, I used the last one to command the Javelin," Jeta shot back.

"Right. We're moving forward without drone cover then. Keep an eye to the sky."

Nacen leapt out of cover with his druvani fast on his flanks. They cleared each row as Nacen strode forward. Up ahead, Armads leapt or crashed through stations in their frenzy to reach the back wall. Shukernak wasn't much better, roaring as he swept his plasma support gun at anything even remotely conceivable as a threat. The group made quick progress up the long aisles in the wake of the Unity's retreat. As the elevator controls came into view, Nacen glanced up at the command center again. Some of the Unies had fled up the elevators, but most were running up the long, gradual ramps and stairs on either side. He was surprised that no enemy fire had come from the high vantage point. He supposed the commanders and their retinue were likely the first to have fled. He had to admit this was a shame. He would have liked the opportunity to see the smug look get blasted off that admiral's face.

Then the lights along the wall and ceiling caught Nacen's eye again. One of them moved, slowly out from the wall. No. *All* of them were moving. Every single one of the lights stringing along the ceiling was floating out into the room.

"What are those?" Camlo wondered aloud, vocalizing the entire team's thoughts.

"Looks like the Unity is rewarding us with a little light show," Basaul huffed, stepping back for a better view.

Then one of the lights drifted into view. Nacen realized it had turned to a white light. The white status light of a Uni gun drone.

"Yes, though reward may be the wrong word," Nacen replied. "Take cover!"

Nacen's order was followed immediately by a downpour of bright flashes of light. Tight beams of plasma fell on the crew like rain. Three Stevari were cut down immediately, while the remaining dashed under the commander platform or up against nearby control panels. Nacen sheathed Talavaar Bhaganadi and joined his own carbine to the chorus of his crew's. They returned fire in short order, knocking out light after light. But still the drones came, spreading out into the room. Once far enough in, they began firing at Motshan's team hiding under the shadow of the command platform as well. Motshan's troops scattered, but not before another two men were cut down by plasma fire.

Nacen took careful aim at a slower drone and sent three shots into it. The drone sparked and plummeted to the floor. He took aim at another and repeated the process, and another. But on and on they came. Shukernak howled insults at them, unintelligible in the din, as relentlessly as his heavy stream of fire. Drone chassis streaked to the ground like hail, exploding all around.

There was no telling when this would end, and there was already a legion of lance troopers en route to the bridge. As bad as this seemed, Nacen had to get everyone moving.

"Call the elevators!" he shouted over the comms.

The Armad called Phyl strode up to the elevator controls, being careful to hop over the smoldering remains of several drones.

"Express line from my foot to the Conglomerate's exposed ass, now boarding." Phyl jammed a stubby finger to the call button.

Nacen lowered his carbine and walked out into the hallway. With a chime, the onyx elevator doors opened wide, and Nacen's eyes with them. They were packed with something, and Nacen didn't stand around to guess. He flung himself back behind the nearest control panel. Phyl didn't have the time to put any meaningful distance between himself and the elevator before the current occupants of the elevator, a dozen flux grenades, went off and he was flung across the room, body punctured by hundreds of pieces of shrapnel and utterly broken by the pressure wave. Motshan's entire team was riddled with shrapnel. Most were hurled to the ground, but two were sent violently into control panels.

The pressure wave alone would have broken most of the bones in Nacen's body, had his recast armor not absorbed the brunt of it. As it was, Nacen lay in agonizing pain on the floor. Every muscle ached as though he had been struck by a hammer in every extremity. Every nerve ending he possessed was firing, telling him to stay put, to not move until help could arrive. But he knew that to remain meant certain death. He willed the nanites in his bloodstream to work harder, to pump up ever more adrenaline in his bloodstream and block out the pain. He grabbed his carbine and stood. His knees felt like they were on fire and nearly buckled.

He glanced about and was relieved to see several of Motshan's team stumbling to their feet.

"Everyone split into two teams and take the stairs! Armads and Motshan's squad to the right, my crew on me!" he barked into his comm link, hoping his crew would still be able to hear him.

"Motshan's fragged!" Nacen faintly heard a Stevari cry into the channel. Nacen glanced around but could find neither the person shouting nor Motshan.

"Just keep moving, and keep firing on those drones," Nacen ordered. "Shukernak, take your support gun and put suppressive fire on the breach, I don't want anyone getting through that door!"

"Not even if they knock first and say please?" Shukernak replied. Nacen was ready to reprimand the trufalci on the spot but saw the that the gunner was already settling into position beneath the overhead cover of a collapsed panel.

He made his way up the stairs, focusing on one step at a time. After he got the right cadence going, he directed his attention back to the room, where drones buzzed like an angry hive. He aimed, fired, shifted to another one, and most importantly kept moving. He felt a burning in his side, much more intense than the aches and pains from the explosion. But he trusted the repair functions of his body's nanites and kept moving. He wouldn't stop until he physically could no longer move.

"They're in!" Shukernak's voice boomed in Nacen's earpiece. "I'm piling that breach full of them, but they just keep coming. Repeat, we have lance troopers on the bridge!"

Nacen heard a whooping sound coming from ahead of him. It took him a few moments to realize he wasn't imagining it. His hearing was returning, at least partially. With each drone Camlo felled, he let out a great whoop and bounded farther up the staircase. He looked back and saw Beskin and Jeta bringing up the rear. Nacen continued his deadly rhythm of firing and advancing up the stairs. Was it just his imagination, or had the buzzing swarm grown smaller? Perhaps they had simply dispersed. Nacen felt a lurch in his left leg. His concentration broke and he looked down, expecting to see a bloody stump. Instead he saw a solid floor, as white as marble. The next step was down.

He stepped onto the flooring and the stone rippled, sending out little perturbations along the smooth marble finish. It must be some visual effect of the floor, or else Nacen supposed he was going mad from trauma. He supposed the two weren't mutually exclusive. Much of the command platform looked similar to the rest of the bridge. Control panels lined the perimeter, though they were larger and more elaborate than those in the galley below. A central dais was raised three steps above the rest of the command platform. Nacen made his way over, each step shooting jolts of pain up his back. His left side burned, and he gripped it. His prying fingers found not hardened recast armor, but wet flesh.

His team was doing their utmost to keep the drones at bay. Each time one crested the platform, a plasma beam or flux shotgun round sent it careening to the floor below. But for each they felled, another drone got a shot off. The floor below was littered with the little robots. Nacen heard the hum of Shukernak's plasma light support gun, a sure sign of his recovering hearing. But he knew Shukernak could not hold out indefinitely.

With a grunt, Nacen gripped the rail of the command platform and hauled himself up. He glanced about. There appeared to be ports in the floor where projections might appear, but none revealed themselves. Jeta was busy trying to gain access to the control panel nearest him. Nacen let his plasma carbine clatter to the ground, where it sent ripples across the ersatz marble. He drew Talavaar Bhaganadi and held the blade vertically before him. He let his gaze slide along the phase sword's fine edge. In the flickering illuminations of combat, he could just make out the inlaid pattern of the hawk swooping down on the snake. What was he supposed to do now?

"This place will work right?" Nacen asked Jeta.

"It should. This is one of the few places on the *Exemplar* we appear to have core access to controls and to the Counsel." Jeta did not look up from the control panel. "I can get us into the mainframe, but not any further. The Void Protocol will have to do the rest."

"Okay, do it."

"Trying," Jeta sighed and tapped nervously on the control panel.

"I don't need to remind you that we've got a thousand troopers pouring in down there and functionally unlimited drones right in front of us, right?" Basaul shouted in exasperation.

"You're not helping," Nacen called back.

"Yeah, well you're not helping just standing around with that sword and a dumb look on your face."

"Both of you shut up!" Jeta snapped. "I'm in. The Void Protocol should be a go."

Nacen swallowed and held the sword out farther in both hands. He waited.

"*Kaha*, nothing's happening," Jeta exclaimed. "Why is nothing happening?"

Nacen glanced over. "I think—"

"That was rhetorical." Jeta had forsaken her cracked handheld device and was now working directly at the bridge control panel. "I think you need to enter an activation code, and the Xandran virus should do the rest."

"Code? What do you mean?" Nacen stared at the sword, willing it to work.

"Some sort of activation code, I suppose so not just anybody can use it."

Then it hit Nacen. His brother's animosity toward him for wielding Talavaar Bhaganadi, his insistence on leading the fleet, it all made sense. Their father had left Zura in command and given him the secret code. One brother was given the sword, and the other the cipher.

He opened up his comm link to *Carmine Canotila* and was rewarded with the light click indicating a healthy signal.

"Nacen, I'm sorry. I've waited as long as I could, but the bay is getting overrun," Linasette said in Nacen's ear. Her voice was low and tired. "We've held out as long as we can, but we don't have the manpower. A few of us have made it back to the ships. We're…"

"It's okay, Lina," Nacen replied, trying to keep his voice steady. "We all took this on knowing what it could cost. Go. But I need you to do something for me first. I need you to open up a transmission to Zura."

"Okay, I can do that," Linasette said. "Look, Nacen. Thank you for all you've done. I will keep flying the *Carmine Canotila*… wherever it is asked."

"And that is why you need to go. Please put me in contact with my brother. Goodbye."

He left it at that, content that he had at least been able to bid her farewell. He found he was no longer numb from the adrenaline coursing through him. He felt empty. Exhausted. Finally the hopelessness of his situation had set in.

The next voice that crackled over the channel was his brother's.

"Here to brag about my defeat?" Zura spat over the transmission. "Well you'll get no satisfaction from me, and no apology. Know that you consigned us all to this meager fate. We could have achieved a glorious death, had it not been for—"

"Zura, shove it," Nacen said impatiently. "Your defeat is my defeat. We need to work together. I need the code for the Void Protocol."

"I was wondering how long it would take you to find out," Zura sneered.

"I'll give you whatever you want. You want the stupid sword? It's yours. You want to be steya if we live? You're steya for life. Just help me. For once, *help me.*"

"Even if you kept your barren promises, they mean nothing. Even now my *Burning Stag* is strained to the point of breaking against the Precept navy." Zura sounded enraged. There was no hint of sadness, no hint of regret in his words. "I suspect your allies' worldships are in a similar position. Well you've had your fun now, your moment in the spotlight. Enjoy what time you have left in it."

"Zura, please," Nacen pleaded. "Don't do it for me then. Don't do it for all Stevari in the homefleet. Do it for our father. What would he have wanted? What would he have called on you to do?"

There was no response. The channel was dead.

Chapter 28

The railing that encircled the platform split in two as Nacen sent the phase sword crashing through it. His torso burned under the strain of the exaggerated swing and his fresh wounds. Warm blood ran in rivulets along the cracked recast armor at his side and dropped to the marble floor.

"No!" he cried, lashing out at the rail behind him next. It separated and twisted to the ground. "This will work! This has to work!"

Nacen glared around the command platform. The control panels, with their rounded edges, now just resembled tombstones. How had he not seen that before? Around him, the crew did their best to hold the platform. Beskin leaned out over the edge, giving covering fire to Shukernak by trying to keep drones off of him. Only five trufalci remained of Danior Tosque's contingent, but they kept up their fire despite their dwindling numbers. Basaul and the three remaining Armads sent drone after drone crashing down with their pilfered shotguns.

Nacen lashed out again, this time making a deep impression in the floor. Again and again he hacked at nearby consoles, and each time the phase sword cut through the silichrome as if it were a twig. At last he caught Camlo's eye and, seeing the horror and fear in the young druvani, stood still. He panted, growing more aware of the terrible wound on his side and the pointless devastation he had wrought in his careless anger.

"Keep holding, everyone!" Nacen shouted. He drew his plasma pistol and stepped off the raised central platform. He wasn't doing any good there anymore. He saw Jeta still plugging away at the console. "Trufalci, grab a weapon and help."

"I'm plotting the fastest way out of here back to the hangar bay," Jeta said.

"Don't bother. They're already evacuating, and we have no way of getting past that strike force."

"The *Trishula* is hailing our encrypted channel," Jeta cracked a thin smile. "I'm guessing you haven't checked it. Manfri is standing down."

"Has Florica overpowered him?"

"Word across the fleet is that he seized control of the engine block but didn't have the stomach to do what Zura had ordered," Jeta explained. "He surrendered shortly after. Florica has ten King Oxen inbound to the breach on *Exemplar.*"

"Well, at least some might make it out," Nacen said. Indeed, this turn of events was fantastic news. His heart should be soaring. But in the midst of calamity, this small respite had come far too late.

Shukernak's plasma support gun had long been silent. The tide of drones had ebbed, but scores of lance troopers now spread out in the gallery below. Return fire, even with their superior position, was now impossible. Shukernak now bounded up the left set of stairs. Errant plasma rounds struck the wall just behind the trufalci as he arrived. He threw down his plasma light support and placed his hands on his knees, panting heavily.

"It's really... really starting to get crowded down there, despite..." the trufalci began to catch his breath. "...my efforts... to the contrary."

"Yeah, so far they don't seem to want to bomb their own bridge either. Let's see how many we can take out," Basaul said.

Nacen did not console himself with such trivialities. He had failed, and they all knew it. They could not buy time for their comrades in the hangar, because the worldships to which they would flee were doomed as well. His final wave of rage fled, replaced utterly by numb acceptance. He had made it further than anyone could have hoped for, but it had all been in vain.

Nacen was yanked from his reverie by a booming voice. The cold, chilling peel of Admiral Sorkitani's voice spilled over the bridge, propagated by hidden speakers.

"I commend you on making it this far, Starkin. But we can pilot the ship remotely," she chided. "Your little attack on my bridge has given you no advantage."

"Yeah, well... it made me feel all warm and fuzzy to mess up your workspace!" Nacen cried back, unsure if she could hear him. He was tempted to go to the edge of the platform, had a legion of lance troopers not made camp below. He would prefer a face to face confrontation with the admiral, where he could actually put Talavaar Bhaganadi to use.

"Give up now, and I will guarantee you and your friends in the bay a swift death. Continue to fight, and I may resort to keeping hostages. Surrender your lives now, and surrender the sword."

"You will have to come up here and take both from me!" Nacen shouted.

There was a hushed silence in the massive command room for a moment.

"You'd better keep that sword, then, to return to your father. You will be going that way soon enough," Admiral Sorkitani said with finality.

A bright light flashed in front of the platform and the entire bridge shook. Unity troopers had set up heavy weapons, a plasma cannon at the very least, and had resumed their attack. Stevari and Armads ducked behind cover. They could not hope to match the troopers' firepower, or even put a dent in the forces marshaling below them. But they kept the drones off for the time being. They came in waves, keeping the Stevari occupied with destroying them while the lance troopers filled out the room below and prepared for their final assault.

Basaul cursed and toppled to the ground. At first, Nacen thought the Armad had simply tripped. Then he noticed a dark pool of blood start to grow. Nacen was not familiar with the Armad's suite of nanites. Maybe with their built-in genetic hardiness, they didn't even use them. It wouldn't surprise him. Either way, the man needed help.

"Get the medi-drone!" Nacen roared.

"It's gone! We lost it when the Unies rigged their elevator to blow!" Beskin shouted, not missing a beat in his defensive fire on the current wave of drones.

"Nacen, you could use it too." Camlo shouted, looking wide-eyed down at his captain's left side.

The Sword and the Cipher

"I'll be fine! Just keep those drones off of us and avoid those heavy weapons platforms!" Nacen crouched by Basaul. He had been hit by a plasma shot, like Nacen. But Basaul's wound went straight through his chest cavity, and the entry was not small. Plasma had cauterized the wound, but shrapnel from his own armor had gouged deeper wounds still.

"Well, we gave as good as we got." Basaul gritted his teeth, his chest rising as he suppressed a cough.

"It's not over yet," Nacen insisted, for his own benefit more so than his wounded friend. Basaul smirked. His rough hand played along the gaping wound in his chest for a moment before jerking away. "Earlier you asked me what I'd do after we got done here. Or maybe if there wasn't a war, hell, I don't remember. You never gave me your answer."

Basaul coughed violently, now unable to stop the deep convulsions in his chest. "I would have built my own hauler. Not the prefab one like we used in the tunnels. A real speeder, to see how fast I could go out on the flats. We always talked about making our own racing circuit on Carnizad. Just never seemed to have the time."

Nacen didn't know what to say. The final lines of a few epics and poems came to mind, but he stayed silent. This didn't feel like the right time. This didn't feel real.

"I'll make sure—"

"Shut up," Basaul snapped. His tone was playful but harsh. "If you start singing, I will throw you off this platform. We both knew how this would end. From the beginning we knew. But we... we had to..." Basaul gritted his teeth and closed his eyes. He did not reopen them.

Nacen whirled about and found his plasma carbine. He marched out to the edge, heedless of the exposure to the lance troopers below. He felt something sting his shoulder but fired on, felling two lance troopers near the breach. A blaze of light filled his vision, and the platform around him shook. He blinked, struggling to make out what had happened. The ringing in his ears was back. As his vision returned, the blob in front of him sharpened. It was Camlo. He was shouting something, but Nacen was once again nearly deaf to the world.

"Nacen, Nacen! Are you alright?" the druvani shouted in a familiar, feminine voice.

Nacen furrowed his brow in confusion. Camlo sounded exactly like Linasette.

"Nacen, can you hear me?" Camlo's mouth was not syncing up right anymore. What had happened?

"No, I can't hear you!" Nacen shouted. Then he realized—the voice was coming from his comm link. He gave Camlo a thankful pat on the shoulder and dashed behind a nearby control panel, keying his earpiece and grimacing through the pain.

"Hello? Come in, this is Nacen," he said desperately. Could Linasette still be here?

"Nacen, you're alive," the female voice stated with uncertainty.

"Yeah, I'm just realizing that now," Nacen said, growing aware of his numerous wounds again. But the pain did not distract him from Linasette's voice. That voice he never thought he would hear again.

"I just received something strange," Linasette said.

"You're alive, too, and still here," he stated flatly, ignoring her comment.

"Yes, for the time being. Florica's troops just got here and are trying to push the Unity back."

"Great," Nacen said breathlessly. "Fantastic. How are you?"

"I'm fine," Linasette said, a little impatiently now. "But I can't say the same about your brother."

"No love lost there. What's up?"

"The *Burning Stag* has been destroyed. A few lifeboats made it out, but they're all being wiped out or captured."

"A tragedy," Nacen sighed mournfully. "One that's about to befall us all I'm afraid."

"Your brother sent me something on an encrypted channel. He said he couldn't reach you directly. All he said was… do father proud. I'm not sure what I'm looking at here… it's some sort of program, but it wouldn't possibly work with anything I've got. Beyond some preliminary tests, I haven't touched it. Do you suppose that this is a trap?"

Nacen's heart felt like it had skipped a beat. He didn't allow himself to hope. Not yet, while the Unity pushed for their final attack on the battered command platform.

"Quite possibly. I wouldn't put it past him. Send it my way anyway," Nacen turned and climbed back onto the central dais, through a gap he'd slashed earlier. He drew Talavaar Bhaganadi from its scabbard. "Jeta, quit whatever you're doing and get back to your Counsel connection. Get on our local connection and upload whatever Lina sends us to the U.P. mainframe."

She waited for a few seconds, distracted by some other task on the panel. Nacen centered himself on the platform and gripped the hilt of the sword in both hands. Closing his eyes and exhaling, he held the blade still. He felt nothing. Not a flash of light, nor a hum of the blade. He opened his eyes and looked the sword up and down, disappointed. Nothing but the etchings of the hawk and the serpent in their endless duel.

"Okay done, but I…" Jeta stopped and stared at the panel, wide-eyed. "All security has dropped. I have access to the Counsel, but I can't change anything. Like it just pulled up the curtain but there's nothing there."

"Did it work?" Nacen opened his eyes.

"Did what work?" Jeta asked.

A drone landed in the command center with a thud against the marble surface, screeching over to the panel where Shukernak crouched. The drone lay there, motionless. With growing courage, Shukernak slid over and kicked it. The chassis skittered along the floor, leaving behind a rippling pattern on the marble floor hologram as though it had been a stone skipped across a pond.

"Did anybody shoot that one?" Shukernak asked. When no one replied, he shrugged. "I guess it's nap time. I call next."

The drones clattered to the gallery below simultaneously. None remained to fly over the platform to fire on the crew. Brecca, Hortz, and Perido emerged from one side of the bridge. Motshan's two surviving trufalci joined them. Lash, Camlo, Beskin, and Shukernak followed. They all wore a look of shock on their faces, relieved to be free from holding off the seemingly endless stream of drones.

"Camlo... your arm," Nacen said, suddenly awash with guilt. "Did that happen when you tackled me?"

The young druvani raised his right elbow, where just a stump of his mechanical arm remained below the shoulder.

"It's okay, I've lost that one before. It hurt a lot less this time around." Camlo waved the remaining metal limb up and down energetically.

"Unless you want to lose a whole lot more, I suggest we get out of here," Jeta said, inserting herself between them. "I've unjammed the doors behind us."

"How? No one could get through them before." Nacen stepped up to the wide blast doors, and sure enough, they began to peel open with a rumble.

"The *Exemplar* is dead in the water, Captain. The Void Protocol is subverting the Counsel and all local command. No news on whether or not the effect is spreading, though."

The crew gathered up near the door, fully aware of the legion of lance troopers on their way to end them, whether their ship's systems were functioning or not.

"I don't know what you have done, Starkin!" Admiral Sorkitani shouted in a small voice from below. "But I will get up there, and I will reverse it!"

Nacen tried to open communications with the bridge on his pad as he waited for his crew to form up on the door. To his surprise, he was able to connect to the bridge's sound system. He gave a grim smile, which broadened at another update from Linasette. Jeta and she had been sharing secrets. Maybe the crew had a chance to get out after all. Now cognizant of this new information, Nacen heard a quiet but high-pitched whine deep within the ship.

"You are the ones who burned the olive branch to ash, I am merely returning the flames." Nacen's voice boomed in the hall, barely recognizable even to himself.

"We are already regaining control of our ship. You failed!" Admiral Sorkitani cried in protest. "Do you hear me? You—"

The whine grew to a deafening vibrato that drowned out all other sound. Nacen peeked over the edge of the platform and saw that panic had begun to spread through the admiral's ranks. He spotted Admiral Sorkitani toward the rear, protected by a glimmering mob of shield drones. She lost every shred of her careful composure as she raked her hands through her immaculate hair.

"You impudent, little...!" she shrieked, her voice rising and cracking. Her shout blended with the whine of dozens of Javelin jet fighter engines, then was drowned out as they darted into the bridge, one on top of the other in rapid succession.

Each fighter released its payload into the crowd before flinging itself onto the scattering ranks. Again and again the fighters came, until the room was filled with little more than smoke and ash. Yet still they thundered on. Every object on the gallery level was shredded beyond any trace of recognition. Nacen did not stay to survey the remains as the dust settled. He and the crew were already racing back to the hangar bay. Linasette had sent the most expedient path back to his digital pad and was now humming a pleasant ditty over the comm link. If they had passed any of the plasma traps, they were inactive now. The crew had donned their pan-atmo masks as they neared the hangar bay, not wanting to be caught unaware by the vacuum around the breach. Nacen let himself be lulled into complacency by his pilot's aimless tune, rounding each corner in the knowledge that he drew ever closer to the source of the melody and sweet escape from this carnage.

Chapter 29

As the Counsel had effectively gone silent, as near as anyone on either side could tell, many systems on the *Exemplar* seemed to malfunction. Others ceased functioning entirely. Much of the ship had lost its artificial gravity, case in point being the initial breach of the hangar deck. This was not readily apparent to Nacen until he dashed out onto its clear expanse. At first he did not notice, too surprised at the pristine space and the direct route to the *Carmine Canotila* in the distance. Then he saw it. With the artificial gravity gone, the graveyard of fighters, bombers, transports, and maintenance craft had piled up in a monstrous heap on the right side of the deck from the acceleration of the battleship's maneuvering.

Nacen's right foot found no purchase as he brought it down. His stomach turned as he realized he was floating a foot above the deck. He reached back, hoping to grasp the frame of the door he ran past. His hand swept by, empty, but found purchase on an armored gauntlet. Beskin had anchored himself on the door that Nacen had blown through and pulled him back. Nacen caught himself on the frame and straightened.

"Thanks. It appears I'm getting ahead of myself."

"Keep your grip on things, now," Beskin scolded. Nacen could imagine the druvani's mirthless glare behind the pan-atmo mask.

The small red craft in the distance quickly grew bigger, and soon the *Carmine Canotila* had touched down mere meters from the crew's hallway, but it could come no further due to the constraints of the bay's dimensions. Its rear cargo ramp opened invitingly.

"There's no gravity in the deck," Nacen explained. "We'll have to push off from here."

"What if we miss?" Camlo asked.

"It's close, but I'm not known for my grace." Brecca swallowed hard.

"Easy," Nacen grinned. "Just don't miss. But if you do, we should be able to get to you well before you exit the hangar."

Motshan's remaining men hung back.

"We've hailed one of Tosque's King Oxen. We'll push off from here and they'll come get us."

"Are you sure? We could drop you off later. We're headed back to the *Trishula*, but..."

"We insist. We have family aboard the *Wayfarer*. If we don't make it out of Fomalhaut, we'd like to see them one last time."

After returning his plasma carbine to his rear harness, Nacen swung himself around on the door frame with one arm. He bent his knees and pushed off against the wall. He soared through the vacuum, grinning wildly as he flew, as unable to stop his elation from being so close to home as he was from stopping his forward momentum. He whooped in delight, and the others followed in kind. Then he was inside the cargo bay, looking around for a place to stop.

Gravity suddenly decided for him, and Nacen's crashed unceremoniously onto the floor and slid into a compressor crate.

"Nice of you to turn the gravity back on for us," Brecca said as he saun-tered up the ramp with Hortz and Perido.

Nacen stumbled to his feet and straightened his cape.

"I assure you I... wait you got pulled down before you hit the grav plates on the *Canotila*? Gravity must be back on in the ship. The Unies must have more control than we expected. Is everyone here? Sound off."

The crew sounded off one by one. All were present who had survived past the battle of the bridge. Motshan's men had taken off at a run to meet their transport farther up in the hangar.

"Linasette, the Unity is getting some semblance of control back. Get us out of here," Nacen commanded through their communications.

"You don't have to tell me twice," Linasette replied. Nacen felt the ship shudder and the cargo ramp hissed closed. Curious to get a better perspec-tive on the overall tactical situation, Nacen made his way to his own bridge. He pushed past Jeta and waved away the ship's backup medical drone as it hovered over to him.

As usual, Linasette had multiple displays projected on the front of the small bridge. Nacen's attention was drawn to the fleet disposition. The screen indicated they were in the midst of a massive swarm of Union Precept ships. But something was off. They were not arranged into their customary rank and file. Their Catalyst-class battleships drifted at the heads of scattering columns of frigates and carriers. Not a single ship had corrected course in the last few minutes. They were dead in the vac. Nacen's heart pounded in his chest. It had worked. He felt lighter than air as he stepped to get a clearer view of the other screens, despite his grievous wounds.

As the *Carmine Canotila* lifted off, movement on another display caught his eye. It was the view to the starboard side of the *Canotila*. Had he imagined it, or... no, there it was again. One of the larger bombers at the top of the pile shifted. But that would mean...

"Oh, *kaha*. That movement has to be caused from acceleration. It's a course correction on the flagship. The Precept are regaining control! The rest of the fleet can't be far behind." Nacen trembled. "We wasted all that time get-ting back when we should have just told Florica to leave us!"

One by one, ships at the top of the pile began to tumble down as grav-ity reasserted itself on the jumbled pile of shifting wreckage. The *Exemplar* was turning. Nacen looked on in horror as a fighter toppled down onto one of Motshan's men. The remaining men made it to the King Oxen, but the bulky transport was an even bigger target for the avalanche of strike craft. It lost control when a bomber skidded across the top. Another King Oxen, wrecked from the initial assault, struck next. Motshan's men scattered, looking for a way out of the rumble.

"Quick, Lina, we have to help them!" Nacen shouted, realizing the im-possibility of the words as soon as they left his mouth.

"We don't have time!" Linasette countered. She was focused on getting the *Canotila* out of the hangar now. They had picked up considerable speed, but the exit of the expansive hangar was still a long way off. Linasette skimmed the trade ship just below the ceiling to avoid the worst of the falling craft. Nacen tore his gaze away from the screen as dismantled craft became even more mangled as they crashed to the ground. Motshan's last surviving troops had disappeared from sight.

The *Carmine Canotila* flew out of the hangar, swiftly catching up to a formation of King Oxen transports. Nacen had never been so close to such a large fleet of hostile ships before. Even in their catatonic state, the mere sight of them sent a shiver up his spine. His ship arched low beneath a huge strike craft carrier. The carrier continued to drift in its long-obsolete path.

Eyeing the bridge screens Lina had arrayed, Nacen found them. The three surviving Stevari worldships were making a pass over the *Exemplar*. If the flagship's firepower had ever wavered or ceased due to the Void Protocol, Nacen did not know it, for the missile racks, rail guns, and laser defense system were all firing on his people's ships. The surviving transports, now with Nacen's trade ship at their rear, gave the battleship as wide a berth as they could afford.

"Nacen, you did it!" Florica's voice was high and triumphant on the channel. "The sword... you released it!"

"Yes, but it seems the flagship has already recovered," Nacen said, unable to share in his fellow captain's enthusiasm.

"But most of the ships haven't. We'd all be dead right now if you hadn't managed," Florica shot back.

"We'd be done for if your troops hadn't come to relieve the bay."

"Will you stop patting yourselves on the back and focus?" Linasette grumbled. "We are nearing your position, but we cannot afford to get close to the *Exemplar*. It's putting out way too much firepower, and the firepower from its prow isn't even on us yet."

"Of course," Florica sounded taken aback. "We are already on our way."

The King Oxen spread out in their formation as the *Exemplar* continued its ponderous turn. Every second it was able to bring more weapons to bear. This became evident as thick beams of plasma began stabbing out at the cluster, and clouds of flak mottled their formation. Two ships ahead, a King Oxen was sliced clean in half by a plasma beam.

The carrier that Linasette had dodged a few moments prior now crashed into the surface of the *Exemplar*. Thick plates of metal were shorn away and sent spinning into the vacuum of space, but the sheer mass and speed of the *Exemplar* swatted the carrier out of its path. Still, there was a short relief from many of its guns.

The curved hull of *Trishula* loomed ahead, transports from the *Burning Stag* still clinging like barnacles to its surface, flanked by the *Wayfarer* and *Faith Immutable*. Linasette swept the ship to the starboard side of the *Trishula* and away from the fire of the enemy battleship. The crew of the *Trishula* had designated bays for them, and with no hesitation, Linasette brought the *Canotila* down hard into the friendly hangar. The starboard engine attempted to compensate for its damaged port thruster and wings, but the result was an uncontrollable skid across the floor. Sparks shot up from mangled landing gear, but eventually the craft came to a halt. Linasette remained upright and staring straight ahead, hands motionless but still at the controls.

"Come on, smile." Nacen patted the back of the pilot's chair. "We made it."

For the first time since he had entered the bridge of his ship, Linasette's eyes met his own. They appeared softer now, her face less firm and tense. But the moment evaporated as a terrible rending crash made its way through the *Trishula*, audible even in the tiny trade ship it housed. Then Linasette's attention was back on the controls, and in seconds they were linked to the *Trishula's* network. The captain and pilot scanned the damage report in silence.

A round from a rail gun had fired a solid slug of steel fifty times the diameter of a flux driver round clean through the *Trishula*. Contents of the ship spilled into space as bulkheads sealed and repair drones went to work.

"That was the first hit from a heavy rail gun. At this range, they won't miss," Linasette said.

Nacen nodded grimly.

"And shields won't do much against a projectile of that size and speed. Can we make it out of the system?" Nacen asked, sweaty hands gripped his seat. "Assuming the rest of the fleet stays unresponsive?"

Linasette shook her head once. Her short blonde hair waved and then stilled.

"The *Exemplar* has three more rail guns equal to that caliber, and they'll be in line to fire soon. Realistically, Nace, each worldship can withstand three or four more shots like that. Assuming they do not hit anything critical. They can fire once every twenty seconds. Sixteen, if they are fine with saturating the coils and overheating the rails."

"I forgot… you know your ships. Next time you know the situation is hopeless, feel free to lie to me," Nacen said.

"What about the whole honesty thing we talked about?"

Nacen had no reply to that. If these were his last moments, what would he tell her?

"Nacen, you're getting careless," a familiar, rumbling voice echoed faintly over the comm link. "You left your remaining nanite grenades on the bridge of the *Exemplar*. Well, I took them from Shukernak. Same result."

Nacen knew that gruff voice. It was the same one whom he had negotiated with several weeks ago on Carnizad. The same that fought alongside in many encounters since then, and who he thought he had said goodbye to on the bridge of the *Exemplar*.

"Basaul! You're alive?!" Nacen blurted out.

"Sure seems that way. Not sure how much longer I have," he said. His voice was noticeably weaker. "Look, the Gloms have regained control of the bridge. They patched it up some, but they haven't noticed me pretending to be dead in this corner. Can't blame them, it's pretty convincing…"

"I am so terribly, unforgivably sorry we left you behind. If I had thought for a moment—"

"Don't sweat it, I'd have only slowed you down," Basaul said.

"Would you like to speak with your men? One last time?"

"Naw, they already made their peace with it. Just… take care of them, Nacen."

"I'll treat them right, if we can get out of here."

"I know you will. On both accounts. I've got one last surprise in me.

The Sword and the Cipher

Whaddya think a few nanite grenades will do to this bridge?"

"Only one way to find out. Thank you, Basaul. For everything." Nacen's grin faded. "Basaul?"

The *Exemplar* kept its pace, but its weapons ceased firing. After a few seconds, its forward momentum visibly slowed. The battleship had stopped accelerating to catch up to the Stevari worldships, who already had the advantage on speed. Other Precept ships had appeared to regain some semblance of control now but were only just beginning to move and, facing the wrong direction, in no position to pursue.

"So long, Fomalhaut," Linasette said. "I already left once. Here's to never returning."

"So long Basaul," Nacen whispered to himself.

"Pardon?" Linasette asked.

"I said… I'll drink to that." Nacen slumped back in his seat.

"I don't keep alcohol on the bridge."

"Well it's never too late to start."

Chapter 30

Torchlight flickered over the packed crowds in the gathering hall of the *Trishula*. Very little time had been taken to tidy the room, but this was of little concern to its occupants, who were too engaged in conversation and praise to pay the scorched tapestries and bullet holes in the wall much heed. Many of the surviving Stevari were present, yet the gathering hall was only at a fraction of its capacity. Many of the captains Nacen knew could not be there, but had projected their images through designated lenses in the floor and stands. Leander Medios had not and would not leave the helm of the *Faith Immutable*, yet here he stood by Florica Tengrin's side. Nacen recognized many faces in the crowd. These were the baroni of the homefleet, rich merchants, former captains and governors, famous artists and artisans. Zura had been his only sibling to stay with this fleet. His other brothers and sisters were spread out on the great blue sun somewhere. He had no doubt he would get to see them again.

Nacen stretched in his formal fleet attire, enjoying the freedom of movement that the crisp, fitted robes provided. He suppressed a groan as he overextended the motion and felt a burning in his side. A medical drone had finally attended to the burned flesh on his torso and the minor fractures in both shins, but it had only partially addressed these and others in the long list of diagnosed wounds before Nacen had been summoned before the baroni of this portion of the homefleet.

He felt a hard pat on his back and winced. Turning, he saw the grinning, bearded face of Danior Tosque. Nacen raised his brow in surprise. The captain had made it here in person, despite his duties on the *Wayfarer*. He held out his hand, which Nacen shook. Tosque shook with vigor, and pain shot up through Nacen's right arm. This time, he anticipated the discomfort and forced a smile.

"I'm surprised you made it to the celebration, Captain. Are you not preoccupied with responsibilities on your own ship?" Nacen asked.

"Nonsense. As the most senior captain now that the steya has perished, it is my duty to run the ceremonies," Captain Tosque stated brusquely. "I apologize for the state of the gathering hall. Florica has had neither the time nor the personnel to begin repairing less critical portions of the ship. Zura's man, um..."

"Manfri," Nacen rubbed at his right arm.

"Yes, Manfri! The druvani made a real mess of the place. Fortunately, he had the good sense to stand down when he did. I hear you played a part in getting your brother to have him surrender, even at the height of his victory over Captain Tengrin."

"I didn't know that, actually," Nacen said. Indeed, it was quite surprising. It made the memories that Nacen had forced down of Zura bubble back to the surface, this time slightly more bittersweet.

"Well, don't let it get to your head." Captain Tosque looked out into the crowd and waved at someone. Nacen did not check to see who.

"You said ceremony? What is the ceremony for? I thought Florica was just going to make a speech commemorating our escape."

"Well, it's a bit early to stay we escaped yet," Danior returned his attention to Nacen. "We have a long way to go until we are safely out of Union Precept space. But please, forget my pedantry, you are right of course. We have survived the brunt of the threat. I'll play that up for the crowd."

Tosque had not answered his question, merely danced around it. Had it been intentional? Nacen opened his mouth to reply, but Tosque raised a hand to silence him.

"Now, now, I won't have any of your humility or self-deprecation. The people are eager to get started." Tosque strode to the center of the round hall and held up both hands in supplication to the crowd. The din soon abated.

"Baroni of House Drovina, esteemed governors, captains courageous, and honored guests, I can now safely say in no uncertain terms that we have survived!" Danior Tosque lowered his hands as the weight of his words slammed into the crowd. They erupted in applause and cheer. Tosque looked immensely pleased, wearing his smug smile proudly. He raised his right hand again, and though it took longer, the crowd fell silent. "Although the cost was great, far too great indeed, we have triumphed. One day, we will flourish again. In the aftermath of this crisis, we have voted. Indeed, though our ranks have been thoroughly diminished, all voices were heard and given ample time to voice their due sentiments. We have heard you. We stand here, downtrodden but determined, without a steya to lead us."

There were a few light cheers and polite applause, but most of the Stevari in the room remained silent. Now the word *ceremony* made sense. The baroni of the homefleet had gathered to announce their selection of a new steya. Nacen was a little hurt that he had not been at least consulted in the decision, but he understood that he was still merely the captain of a relatively unimportant trade ship.

"The discussion continued for a long time. Too long, perhaps, had this decision not carried so much weight," Danior Tosque explained. His loud, assertive voice filled the hall with ease. "Leander Medios was an ideal candidate, with an impeccable service record and the undisputed loyalty of his men. Florica Tengrin came out even stronger still, having taken such an active role in our survival. But they are not destined to be steya!"

Now Nacen realized why the captain was so pleased with himself. Danior Tosque was here to announce his own promotion to steya. Though Nacen felt the captain could be a bit long-winded, even a blowhard at times, he was the most logical choice. He was many years senior to Florica Tengrin and Leander Medios both, and had been Yoska's right-hand man to boot. But still, Nacen felt the honor belonged to Florica Tengrin. She had been the initiator of the plan that saved the fleet, even if Nacen had been the one to ultimately carry out the crucial step. It was she who defeated Zura's forces and kept the homefleet alive in the middle of a Unity armada.

"Please welcome our new steya to the center," Tosque wheeled about, urging the crowd on. "Welcome... Nacen Buhari!"

Nacen's feet were rooted firmly in place. He was paralyzed, in shock by the announcement. He was sure Beskin and Camlo would have to come to his side, to carry him to the center by Tosque's side, or else out of the hall to avoid the embarrassment of his inaction. The baroni of Drovina had chosen him to represent the homefleet. Nacen remained there, taking in the roar of the crowd while staring directly ahead. He gulped. His mouth was dry. This had been his dream, hadn't it? He must have passed out in the medical bay. His old ambitions had not even come close to this, at least not so fast.

Danior Tosque glanced back and gave Nacen a quizzical look. He ruffled his goatee and strode over.

"Come now, Nacen. You must say the words. Then you will need to get the helm of a worldship, of course. The *Trishula* will do until we can get a new ship commissioned to replace the loss of the *Asura*. Then you'll need a new crew. No outsiders are permitted in command areas on the worldships, so we'll need to find new postings for those Armads and that ex-Uni pilot of yours."

This was all going too fast for him. He took a step back as the room began to spin.

"I can't keep my pilot? My crew?" Nacen eventually stammered.

"You know we don't allow outsiders on homefleet worldships. Your druvani will stay with you, though we will have to expand your contingent considerably of course."

Nacen considered this. He knew he wouldn't be working with his crew forever. But he no longer feared the thought of plying the old trade routes with them. He had shouldered part of the responsibility of leading the fleet, and it had proved a great burden. Even then, he had only led a small force. Chance had placed him in the position to lead and, though he had succeeded, he felt unprepared and uncertain. Power was no longer something he craved. He had received a taste of it, and the consequences had consumed many of his friends and family in the process. Perhaps someday he would be ready. But not today. He swallowed and stepped forward to the center of the room, brushing past Captain Tosque.

"My responsibilities have been to my crew, the brave men and women of the *Carmine Canotila* and the *Lusterhawk*," Nacen announced to the room. He was met with frowns and confused glances. Whispers and muttered conversations began to fill the hall. "I realize now I am not ready to take on the mantle of steya, just as my brother Zura was not. That time may come. But now it is time for another to lead us, while I continue my current charge. Florica Tengrin was the one who led the assault on the Precept fleet, and she was at the helm of the lead ship. It was she who stood up to Zura first and convinced me to join forces with her. It was she who resisted Zura's attacks on her vessel while keeping our last remaining ships alive in the fell clutches of the *Exemplar*."

Danior put a hand on Nacen's shoulder.

"Nacen, please. Take time to consider what you are doing. It is highly unusual to question a decision of the baroni."

"If I hold the office of the steya, then surely I may pass the mantle to one equally qualified, if not more so, than myself?" Nacen brushed the captain's hand aside.

"I, uh... I do suppose it is within your power, with the support of the baroni." Tosque looked past Nacen now. His cheeks were flushed, but he continued on. "Florica Tengrin, please step forward."

Florica had been as silent as Nacen had been during the entire ceremony. Now she moved forward with short, tentative steps. Her own ceremonial robes with their flared sleeves fluttered behind her. She looked up at Nacen with her bright green eyes, her lips pinched together.

"You have proven yourself time and time again now. Do you think I would have enlisted you to lead the attack had I not thought you worthy of leading? On top of all that, you are Yoska's son," Florica pleaded. "Do not give up your rightful place."

"It is mine to give." Nacen lifted his shoulders.

"You mask your true intentions," Florica shot back, her temper flaring briefly. The room was abuzz with activity now. The crowd had broken out into loud conversations, and many Stevari milled about.

"I wear many masks," Nacen admitted. "But they make my intentions no less true. I have worn the mask of a poet: a silver visage of bright reflection, where I looked upon the world and saw what was and what could be. I wear the stone-faced mask of the warrior, dark and grim. I look upon the world, and see what is and what I must do. Someday I may wear the mask of the steya, and see with blinding sight the many paths we may take. But I must play the part of the warrior a little longer, for my family has played their part long enough upon the stage."

"I suspect you wear other masks as well," Florica's surprised indignation had faded, and she now gave a sly grin. "I would be a fool to refuse the honor, as big a fool as you. I accept, and am humbled. I will do the homefleet proud. I will do the memory of your father proud."

"Of that, I am certain." Nacen bowed his head. He hesitated for a moment, then gripped the scabbard at his waist. "Though the raiment of the steya has now been lost, I present to you Talavaar Bhaganadi. All remnants of the Void Protocol appear to have vanished. I believe the Colonies of Xandra only ever intended it to be of a single use. It is unlikely that the exact virus would ever work against the Counsel again now that it has been exposed to it once, anyway. But the sword belongs to you now." Nacen extended his arms, offering both sword and scabbard.

"I prefer to stay out of close quarters," Florica stated flatly. "If I get to the point where I need a sword, I have already likely lost."

Nacen frowned. He had not expected to be refused. Then again, today was a day of surprises. "It's more of a symbol of office."

Florica placed a gloved hand gingerly on the scabbard. She pushed it back against Nacen's chest.

"Keep it then, as a reminder of what you and your family have done for House Drovina."

"You would give up such a valuable artifact?" Nacen frowned deeper still.

Florica shrugged knowingly. "It is mine to give."

Nacen drew the sword to his chest and gripped the scabbard tightly.

"Thank you, Steya Tengrin."

"Thank you, Nacen Buhari."

Eventually, Danior Tosque calmed the room. The baroni argued for hours more, citing ancient texts and obscure events. Nacen and Florica split apart and joined in the debates from time to time, but just as often reconvened and spoke excitedly of recent transpirings or to where the fleet would go next. There were many ships of House Drovina scattered among the stars, and they must be told they could once again light their beacons and travel unimpeded across the great blue sun. Florica regaled Nacen with the tale of defending her own bridge against Manfri's men, and about their daring attacks on the *Exemplar*. Nacen told Florica of their assault within the *Exemplar*, of the traps and foes they had faced, and their manipulations of the Unity ship against itself.

"Doubtless, the next time these tales are shared, they will be immortalized in the annals of the house," the new steya noted.

"Perhaps in song, as well," Nacen added.

After a while longer, after many more uncomfortable conversations, reflection, and explanation, the room stilled. Danior Tosque held up his hands one last time, addressing the mob of men and women around him.

"The decision to elect Nacen Buhari as steya is no longer in effect. The majority are in agreement: the honor and burden now pass to Florica Tengrin. Now, we shall take the oaths and return to our stations. We have a long way to go before we can rest and celebrate in proper fashion," Tosque stated.

"As well as mourn the honored dead," Nacen replied. "We have lost countless good Stevari in the last few weeks, and I have lost a father and a brother."

Florica clasped Nacen's arm gently. "You will have all the time you need. Am I right in assuming you wish to remain in command of your trade ship, the *Carmine Canotila*?"

Nacen nodded. "I would like that very much."

"Then there you shall remain," Florica said. "For the time being, at least. I suppose you will need some new routes. We will be working on expanding our current routes with the Xandra Colonies and the Globular Palatinate, both of which could be quite promising. If you are interested, there are several missions that may require a great deal of diplomacy and finesse."

***

"Couldn't hack it as steya, eh?" Brecca voiced the question loudly in the cargo hold of the *Carmine Canotila*. The entire crew had gathered in the hold, leaning or sitting on the massive new delivery of compressor crates intended for the Globular Palatinate.

Nacen set down the crate he was carrying. Not a compressor crate, just a simple silichrome chest containing a few items the ship and crew might need.

"My family has done enough for the homefleet, for better or worse. It was time to let someone else take the reins for now," Nacen explained with a soft smile.

Brecca turned to Perido and Hortz. "Yep, couldn't hack it."

"How about yourselves then? Are you going to join up with one of our frigates until we pass by another Armad guild?"

Brecca grinned and made as if to unleash another snide comment when Hortz stepped forward.

"We lost a lot of good people on Carnizad. Then more after we joined with you: Trute, Diat, Phyl, Chalce…" Hortz trailed off, appearing to lose the will to enumerate all his fallen comrades.

"The boss," Perido added.

"Yeah. Basaul sure gave it to those Gloms good and proper in the end." Despite his hearty boast, Brecca's smile faded and his shoulders sank.

Nacen nodded. "He was the last in a great many sacrifices to save the homefleet. You have given much to stand here today, more than most. And that really is saying something. If you feel you've earned something beyond your monetary reward and free passage within our homefleet, speak it and I will make it yours."

"Well, not really… I mean…" Hortz started.

"I think what Hortz means," Perido said, "is that it's really more about the journey."

"And the foes we shot along the way," Brecca added.

"We were actually hoping to stick around with you, uh… Captain," Hortz said. "You seem to know what you're doing, and if your logs are accurate, then there's good money in this Stevari trading of yours."

"High praise indeed," Nacen snapped open the lid of the chest and began rummaging through its contents. "I would be honored to have you aboard. We won't be leaving for quite some time, so make yourselves comfortable on the *Trishula*. You've earned the vacation."

The Armads shared a few grins and nods.

"We can comply with that, alright," Hortz said. He craned his head to see what Nacen was searching for in the box.

"I do have one condition, though." Nacen stopped digging and grasped three bundles of fabric. "To continue working on my ship you must take on the garb of the homefleet and become *prestari*."

Nacen threw a bundle from the chest at each Armad at the top of ramp. Hortz and Brecca looked at the crimson and brown fabrics wearily, whereas Perido immediately unfolded it and began trying it on.

"What's that? Can we not simply be Armads?" Hortz protested.

"I'm not going through any surgery to become this… this… prestari," Brecca stammered.

"Of course not." Nacen laughed. "We do not expect you to give up your culture or your customs, and certainly not go through any modification. Linasette took on the title years ago, you can talk to her about it. It is simply a designation for those who have proven themselves to the Stevari and decide to journey with us, for however long that may be. It means *friends who were once strangers*."

"Oh." Brecca looked at the crimson folds in his grip. "What must we do?"

"Well you've donned the robes, in a fashion, so next we must feast and drink," Nacen said, flinging his hands up.

"That doesn't sound so bad. I forget how much we have in common."

Perido finished wrapping his robes inelegantly about his large, craggy form.

"See Jeta or Shukernak before you go out onto the *Trishula*. They will show you how to adorn the robes to reflect your new status, and to prevent you from tripping over yourselves."

"Excellent. Thank you, Captain." Perido continued to fiddle with his sash as Brecca and Hortz unfolded their own robes. "Don't be so quick to rule out surgical modification, though. Brecca could really use some work on that mug of his."

Nacen simply laughed and shook his head as the Armads proceeded to grapple and scrap. He made the sign of Drovina and went around them into the cargo hold, giving them a wide berth. His druvani stood inspecting a new cache of weapons to the ship. When Camlo spotted him, he set down the plasma carbine he and Beskin were inspecting. Camlo wore his druvani robes over his incomplete right arm, having not found a replacement yet.

"Glad to hear you're sticking around, Nacen," Camlo said. "It would have been lonely here without you."

"Lonely?" Nacen cocked his head to the side. "You would have joined me on the bridge of the *Trishula*, until we got our own worldship eventually, and had a whole squad of druvani under you."

"A whole squ—" Camlo's jaw dropped.

Beskin grinned and gave Camlo a congenial pat on his mechanical stub.

"No matter what you decide, Captain, I'm here with you. That was my last promise to your father, and my first to you," Beskin said.

"I know, Beskin. Thank you."

Nacen turned to the familiar, narrow corridor leading to the interior. Linasette was standing to one side, immaculately dressed in her formal flight suit of soft velvet. It was rare to see the pilot outside the bridge. It was good to see her talking with the crew.

"Again with the formal wear?" Nacen exclaimed. "What's the occasion this time?"

"Ha," Linasette offered dryly. "I see all this attention hasn't gone to your head. Well, since I couldn't attend the ceremony, being prestari and all, I figured I would dress up to commemorate our big escape."

"You didn't miss much, anyway," Nacen replied. "You saved us back there, you know. Jeta and you reprogramming those fighters."

"Yes, you owe us... big time. You know, we're starting to detect Drovina beacons again, now that this part of the homefleet activated their own. There's one showing up around Chosan."

"The *Lusterhawk*?" Nacen asked, eyes widening.

"Could be."

They locked eyes for another moment but said nothing else. Nacen wasn't sure the pilot knew how much of an influence she had on his decision to return, though he suspected she knew she had played at least a small part. But he was her captain, and Stevari. No, there was no place for a life there, no love or romance, but perhaps their bond could grow in some other small way. He contented himself in the fact they would keep flying together, for a while at least. Nacen allowed a genuine smile to spread across his face, which Linasette returned with a polite nod before walking over to speak with Jeta and Shukernak in a remote corner of the cargo hold. Nacen strode down the hall to the meditation room.

"A whole squad? A worldship? Is it too late to reconsider this whole kingmaker decision, Nace?!" Camlo called out behind him, his right stub flailing.

Nacen grinned and continued back into the ship. He entered the meditation room and dimmed the lights. He doffed his belt and scabbard, his fingers lingering on the emerald fabric of the sheath. A bout of curiosity nipped at him, and Nacen slowly drew the sword. He held the blade against the warm light and squinted to see the raised etchings on the blade. Were any there at all? His eyes adjusted, and soon he made out the form of the hawk, its wings spread in flight, perhaps a quarter of the way up the blade from the hilt. He searched for the serpent, for any other symbol on *Talavaar Bhaganadi*. Had his connection been severed, or perhaps weakened, at its use to escape the fleet? In frustration, he picked up the scabbard to return the blade, but something on the reverse edge caught his eye. Yes... the snake lay coiled there, hissing up in the direction of the central ridge. He wondered idly at the nature of his connection to the sword. What ancient technology brought these shapes to life, and where was the line drawn between this relic and his own mind? Could it be drawn at all?

Nacen slammed the sword home in its sheath and set it against the wall with his digital pad. He flicked another switch, and a field of stars materialized above. A new file appeared on his digital pad with a chime. There would be countless details of the chosen world, people, culture, and customs for his new mission. He would know them intimately in time, but not yet.

For now, he concerned himself only with the dizzying mass of stars and distant galaxies above. They were only an illusion within the meditation room, a mere projection of the unknowable vastness of space outside his tiny ship. But it was accurate enough to fool him if he let his mind wander. Indeed, he was not familiar at all with this particular sky. He knew it would change as soon as the Stevari passed through quickspace again, not terribly concerned with the logistics of how they would leave the Unity with the main threats behind them.

He retrieved a familiar pack from the wall and collapsed on a nearby bed, now empty of the Armads' belongings. He withdrew his dulcinet from the bag and hummed as he put the strings in tune. He plucked a simple melody. His attention was not on the tension of the waxen strings, nor the sweet resounding of the wooden body of the instrument, but instead drifted to places he had been amongst the stars above him. He let his fingers glide and plant themselves on the fretless board where he felt they should be.

They started with a faint air of the melody Linasette had hummed as he had raced back on the flagship. From that pale imitation of her voice more complex notes evolved. He transitioned to a fast, headlong melody full of slides and low chords. The Armads had shared no songs, but Nacen found himself easily imagining a tune to go with the sight of a cobbled-together dragster with a heavy engine roaring across the barren flats of Carnizad. It was a simple transition to a hardy chant, full of bass and bravado, gleaned from a group of mercenaries as they crossed an icy strand on a nameless moon of Trondheim. Then there was a bright ditty he had learned from his father, sung by farmers in the scorching hot fields of equatorial Gliese.

Even had he given the songs his full attention, he could not remember them well enough to replicate the native sounds perfectly. But he gave his own take on them, letting each piece express itself to his contentment before fading back and allowing another to take the fore.

The fleet would not rest until they came to the fringes of the Unity where swathes of planets lay as buffer states between the vast empires of quickspace, their size only comprehensible in numbers too absurdly large to appreciate the endless spectrum of people and cultures spread across them. Nacen satisfied himself in the knowledge that he was still free to explore these planets, and more, for there was comfort in the intimate familiarity of even a remote fraction of this boundless space. There was violence out there, that was plain enough. He would certainly encounter more people out to do him harm, intentionally or not. But for now among these silent stars, there glinted a promise of peace.

Glossary of Terms

Alpha One: the Union Precept term for the enigmatic blue star that links the countless worlds of human-colonized space. Systems with habitable planets are mapped onto this star with passages that travel through its upper layers. Travel requires entry through a rift in space-time, which emerges within the mysterious blue star. Travelers must then navigate to the entry point corresponding to their destination and emerging through the second passage into the destination system after a journey of a few days or weeks, rather than the many years of a traditional voyage.

Armad: a variant of humanity who have improved their physique to the point of withstanding the vacuum of space for several minutes, and the hot interior of terrestrial mantles almost indefinitely. They are characterized by a rough, radiation-resistant exterior not unlike rock.

Armads typically organize into guilds for joint ventures in mining, manufacture, trade, research, or even mercenary outfits. It is believed that the process of becoming an Armad removes all biology associated with gender.

Chodra: a Stevari expletive indicating a contemptable or unreasonable person, originating from the Stevari term for one who has had their genome altered in an unfavorable fashion.

Counsel, The: the distributed artificial intelligence governing much of the society and actions of the Union Precept. Their consultations and orders guide military action, individual opportunity, interstellar trade, and most other aspects of life within the Unity.

Drovina: a House of Stevari active in the Prominar Rim. They traditionally dress in warm autumnal colors of red, orange, brown, and yellow. Their homefleets tend to be more isolationist compared to other Stevari houses, but still maintain trade with most factions across the great blue sun.

Druvani: a warrior profession unique to the Stevari. They are highly-trained, elite foot soldiers comparable to special forces in other factions. They fulfill the role of personal bodyguard to a Stevari individual of particular import: usually a ranking member of the military or political structure, or family member.

Ex-cal: a Stevari variant of the standard flux driver firearm, short for Explosive Microcaliber Railgun. This firearm is characterized by utilizing small slugs, but with a high rate of fire and explosive projectiles. Typically wielded by a pair of trufalci as a squad heavy support weapon.

Flux Driver: a small, portable rail gun fielded by many human soldiers across the galaxy. A solid metallic projectile is propelled along a rail at high speeds via magnetic induction, albeit smaller and slower than a typical ship-mounted rail gun. The weapon can be fired in nearly any conditions, even the vacuum of space, so long as the inner mechanisms are intact.

Globular Palatinate: a faction of humans controlling several dozen worlds near the Prominar Rim. They are not actively hostile toward other humans, but will defend themselves staunchly against invaders. They are known for their military prowess, stubbornness on and off the battlefield, and propensity for drink. Rumored to contain the lost passageway to old Earth.

Great Blue Sun: the Stevari term for the blue star that links the human-settled worlds of the galaxy together, also known as Alpha One by the Union Precept. See 'Alpha One' for more details on the known mechanisms behind the enigmatic blue star.

Kaha: a Stevari expletive indicating intense surprise or displeasure, believed to translate roughly as 'excrement.'

Prestari: members of Stevari homefleets that have been inducted as citizens from other civilizations after meeting minimum requirements of military service and patronage to the arts.

Prismotion Shielding: deflection technology integrated into the armor of many Union Precept foot soldiers. The armor creates a reactive magnetic field in response to incoming metallic projectiles. More effective against flux driver rounds and traditional ballistics at a distance, less effective against larger caliber rounds up close and plasma technology.

Quickspace Lane/Tunnel: the passage that link the rifts in space-time across the blue star know as Alpha One, allowing for the travel of spaceborne vessels across unimaginable distances in mere days. For more about the known mechanisms behind the Quickspace Lanes, see 'Alpha One.'

Recast Armor: armor typically worn by Stevari, the nanite weave can harden in specific areas to deflect incoming projectiles, and soften to absorb pressure waves from explosions or heat from plasma rounds.

Stevari: a nomadic group of humans that inhabits large mercantile ships, rather than relying on permanent settlement of a planet for long-term survival. One of the oldest civilizations laying claim to space around the great blue sun. They are divided into many separate houses, though are generally willing to work together for the common good. They are characterized by their affinity for music, art, oral storytelling traditions, and capacity for interstellar trade. They maintain a unique global ban on alterations to the human genome.

Steya: the elected or inherited leader of a Stevari house. Typically elected on a regular cycle by the wealthy class of merchants, politicians, and soldiers known as the baroni.

Starkin: an informal term for the Stevari people. Generally not considered offensive.

Trufalci: a worker class onboard Stevari vessels, encompassing many professions such as deckhands, mechanics, pilots, and engineers. All trufalci have military training and may be called on to serve in defense of their vessel.

Union Precept: the largest unified faction of humanity operating in Alpha One. Their citizens enjoy the highest levels of wealth and prosperity compared to any other civilization. Their distributed artificial intelligence, known as the Counsel, presides over many aspects of society.

Vulakaat: a meeting of Stevari baroni or military personnel, called in times of crisis. No set time limit is set for the duration of the ceremony, but it must always end in decisive action. The leader of the group has the final say on the desired action, see 'steya.' Originating from the Stevari term for a *touching of heads*.

Worldship: the designation of the largest known Stevari spacefaring vessel. Designs and functions vary greatly depending on the house, but are believed to hold up to many thousands of individual Stevari. Typical features include agricultural areas capable of greater than traditional yields, amphitheaters, parks, and even bodies of water.

Xandra, Colonies of: a group of former Union Precept colonies that were exiled after violating standard procedure for the governance of worlds and interstellar trade. Specifics are unknown but believed to be predominately caused by unsanctioned changes to distributed artificial intelligence. A successful series of wars ensured they maintained their independence from the Union Precept.

The Sword and the Cipher

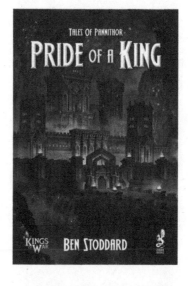

About the Author

Ever since he could clutch a d6 and a pencil, Riley O'Connor has been writing fiction for games. His early works for Mage Knight and Dungeons & Dragons have mercifully been lost to time. He took his first foray into the mainstream aboard the Carmine Canotila for Beyond the Gates of Antares, which he continues to explore with Nacen and friends. When not writing military science fiction, Riley works as an electrical engineer to help feed his tabletop gaming addictions. Riley currently lives among the rolling hills of Iowa with his wife and gaming companion, Maggie